THE AGE OF IMPROV
A Political Novel of the Future

THE AGE OF IMPROV
A Political Novel of the Future

BY RICK SALUTIN

HarperCollins*PublishersLtd*

First edition

Canadian Cataloguing in Publication Data

Salutin, Rick, 1942–
The age of improv

ISBN 0-00-223747-4 (bound)
ISBN 0-00-648092-6 (pbk.)

I. Title.

PS8587.A355A64 1995   C813'.54   C94-932381-0
PR9199.3.S35A64 1995

95 96 97 98 99 ❖ HC 10 9 8 7 6 5 4 3 2 1

Printed and bound in the United States

for Judy MacDonald
there are no words, but there oughta be

ACKNOWLEDGEMENTS

Many thanks to the Colberts: David, Nancy, and Stan. David, for his immediate belief in this project; Nancy, for her support during a difficult phase; and Stan, for his help not just with this book but in various ways since he first came to Canada long ago. Thanks to Eric Peterson and Saul Rubinek for the suggestions that began this work — far different in form and subject than the outcome. Thanks to Eric, Saul, Robert Thomson, George Luscombe, Paul Thompson, as well as virtually all the actors and directors I've worked with in theatre and elsewhere over many years; I'm sorry it's taken me this long to begin to fully comprehend the enormous courage and craft they possess. Thanks to editor and publisher Iris Tupholme, for her respect and encouragement, without which this book would not have been completed. Finally, thanks again to Bernice Eisenstein, who makes copyediting a full-service function.

CHAPTER ONE

After all these years acting, what I really want now is — to act. Be a true actor, one who acts, who does. Normally you have your script first, then you go up onstage and act it. This is different. First get onstage, then create the part. Hell, my best acting times were back in the improv. God I loved it. This is politics for the year 2000. Acting at the Improv. Now is the time to mount the stage.

Here's the setup.

The G.G. was perfect casting. He looked like a hockey player. He was perfect casting for a hockey player too, which he'd also been. He hailed, as they say of folk heroes, from the Ottawa Valley. He was French-speaking, but from the English part of Canada. He led his Canadiens teams to several Stanley Cups with the same quiet dignity his legendary predecessor, Jean Beliveau, always showed on the ice and even after retirement — whether hawking coffeemakers on TV or visiting sick kids. His memoir of a life in hockey, *The Straight Shooter*, even outsold Dryden's phenomenal *The Game* of the early 1980's. Appointing him Governor General a year and a half before, had been less an inspiration on the part of the Canadian government, in the early years of the twenty-first century, than an inevitability.

"I hope none of you will describe what I am here to do as dropping the puck in the great national face-off," he began. The press relaxed, you could see them loosen, as usual, in his presence. The way the team always did when he skated on for a critical face-off in

1

their own end, down a man maybe and trying to hold a lead against a club basically more talented than themselves. Like a grown-up among kids. You just felt better when the guy was there.

"The prime minister has requested I dissolve Parliament and call an election for forty-two days from now. Believe it or not, I agreed." The crow's-feet agitated a little round the eyes, his twinkle equivalent. This was the conventional style now among public figures, including semi-monuments like the G.G. You didn't pretend to be an inhuman vessel of official procedure. You reacted, you leavened rite with personality. Even the new king of England showed his human side, grew ironic or self-deprecating, as his mom never had.

The G.G. rose to go, duty done. There was an odd pause, as though a hundred questions stuck on their way up a communal throat. "Sir," a voice quavered. The G.G. paused, looked this way, then that, as if the last thing he expected at a press conference was a question. It was one beauty of a take. Almost as if he was used to performing in tense situations before millions of people. His jaded audience basked in it. "Are you worried?" was the question — not from one of those authoritative resonators on network TV, or even a metropolitan supper hour. This was maybe the *Arnprior Weekly Chronicle*. Somebody scared who just cared.

The G.G. had the knack — unlearnable — of *not* pausing a moment while he pondered what his questioner might want to hear, what'd sound best or do him the least harm. Even those rare occasions he hesitated, it would be a true pause, for genuine thought, not calculation. That's how it read anyway. "Why?" he said thoughtfully, as the anxiety in the question suffused the room. "Why . . . *worried?*"

"It's so . . . so . . . I dunno." This felt tasteless. Who wanted to recall what you spend most of your waking life suppressing? Dreams are bad, but at least you can smack them under when you wake up. This was like a bad dream but you were still in it, eyes wide. Cork it, Arnprior. "Yeah," said the G.G. "Yeah" — sort of moving the problem around in his mouth.

"So what do you think'll happen?" It wasn't the quaver any longer, now it was one of the mellowtones that sign off each night on national TV. Its owner looked around. As if she didn't know whose plummy voice just spoke.

"You think *this* constitution will *work*?" asked Canadian Cable News. "Why now? None of the others did. You get your hopes up — then THWACK!" It had become group therapy. It made you wonder if other countries go through these jags. Doubtful. You can't picture France wondering if it would cease to be just because it didn't have a government or a constitution for a while. Or Poland. Someone said Poland wasn't even on a map for 125 years but the Poles always knew it was there. Not us. We need *stuff*. A government, a constitution, "the system." Or we start to worry we don't exist.

The G.G. craned around in a craggy manner, stuck his hands in his hip pockets like he was doing a braincheck back there. The guy's suits hung off him like they were part of his body, just as his hockey gear used to. He leaned in again to the podium, as though he was noodling around centre ice before heading for goal on a penalty shot. He looked like he had so much *time*.

Time is good, especially when people are anxious. "Of course it is not my role to discuss politics in a specific way," he mused. "But the future of Canada may be a general enough subject for me to make a comment." A sigh rose from the press and the country beyond. It was an endless trauma they had been put through. Crises and their afterbirths. Commissions, surveys, polls, followed by yet another national election — complete with the disappearance and resurrection of parties that had once seemed normal as winter; now no one even knew what a party meant any more. Then maybe a provincial election in Quebec that the rest of the country held their breath for, or an indeterminate and frustrating referendum there, followed by more consultations with citizens and subsequent secret and/or public conferences at many levels. From which emerged, each time . . . *another* desperate scheme: Meech Lake, the Citizens' Forum, Son of Meech, Meech Plus, the constitutional convention of the late nineties. More breakdowns, rescue operations, experiments in elections, further demands and rejections. This last run, consuming another two years, and out of it had come, again . . . something. Called Canada still, but still, only on paper. Quebec was part but separate. It was bilingual and multicultural. It was regionally oriented *and* had a strong central government. It was proportional *and* representative — with special provisions for women, natives, the disabled, and the West. It had a trunk, a tail, a thick hide, big floppy ears — depending on who was describing it. But once the magic word was spoken, it would materialize out there, perhaps as all the others had, horrific and unworkable. After that, it could never be put away again as something you can tinker with and hold on to in hope. It would no longer be a mere object of faith and fantasy; it would be something you had to live with. The magic word was election.

That's the setup and it's just as Matthew would have written it. If it came to him in a script sent over by Elinor, he'd tell her to say yes to it in a minute. She could negotiate for him, but to be honest he wanted it so bad that in the end he'd pay them to get in. So why does he hesitate?

He hauls the two-man trapper's canoe down from pseudo-concealment behind the pump house and drops it off the dock. Damn. A little water seeps in through that screwhole in the bow he hasn't polyurethaned. Either that or remember to lower it stern-first next time. He slips in. Some water laps at his sandals. He shifts slightly, at least gets his knees off the edge of the ribbing, the canoe dips left, he shifts again, and of course tips.

But he's wearing old clothes: jeans, sweatshirt, the broad-brimmed Ranger hat is waterproof. Stuff he'd have slung into the outdoor bin at St. Vincent de Paul's in the city if he hadn't bought this place outright shortly after he quit the series. He drags himself and his waterlogged gear onto the dock, hauls the canoe after, upside down, draining it. Laughs — for the benefit of the chickadees or ducks over on the shaded rock or the osprey in the marsh he'd meant to paddle through in order to contemplate his role as citizen, now that it beckons persuasively in the form of a coming election. How to say no? Why say no? He usually finds a way. He's been finding reasons for no steadily over the years since he left the show.

Matthew's plain, appealing Canadian face said no a mere six months later when the national public network asked him to host their most earnest documentary series, "The Human Condition." He was made for that job, he knew it. At the time the money mattered; Dal was still in school, TV and film work were growing irregular — mostly because he'd gone up to Ottawa for hearings into the

4

network's licence renewal and told the regulators that his former employer's contribution to Canadian drama was a disgrace.

Not a smart career move. Elinor hadn't bothered to say so, she just cast an eye across her desk and shuffled the files of other clients she represented, ones who hadn't troubled to attack — no, make that humiliate — the major source of work for actors in Canada. Maybe she could still get him some parts in the U.S., but as he knew, they'd cracked down at the border due to friction about renewal of the free trade agreements, and anyway, as he often reminded her, he didn't really yearn to work down there.

So when "The Human Condition" beckoned, he didn't even tell Elinor. He dropped by the Bluer though, where as he'd hoped, Morris sat at the counter in the window, nursing a *latte*, scowling his way through the *Globe*, or maybe *Workers' Vanguard*, if it still existed at that point in the post-Cold War. Morris said there should be a sign that read The Mayor Is In whenever he sat there looking out on Bloor Street.

Matthew took a stool. He angled his back toward the window since he didn't like it when passersby pointed at him and asked each other, was that really the actor they'd seen in . . . (or maybe he was the populist candidate for city council, or the suspect in the Mississauga rape case . . .), and told Morris his problem with the offer. If you go to work in public affairs, they make you sign this pledge saying you won't speak out on public issues because it would compromise your impartiality as a broadcaster. Morris, drawing on his ancestral heritage, stroked his chin rabbinically and gave Matthew permission to take the job. "You'll do more good just putting that honest puss God gave you in front of millions of viewers every week and showing them what a real human being looks like. And what do you give up? Signing some pointless petitions or newspaper ads? Going to Ottawa to sacrifice yourself because others with much less to lose don't have the guts?"

Morris was surprised, as usual, when Matthew said no, he'd already decided to turn the job down. He couldn't stomach being unable to sign those dinky ineffective petitions and ads, he just wouldn't buy it. Morris, the professor of political science, looked back at this rare sight, unknown, perhaps, since Periclean Athens:

5

an authentic citizen. Being part of public debate, no matter how marginally, was in the nature of his friend the actor. Forgoing pointless petitions or masochistic appearances before public inquiries was the equivalent for Matthew that ostracism and exile from the city — a punishment far crueller than death — had been in ancient Greece.

So why does Matthew now hesitate, looking down at the over-turned canoe, dripping dry already on the dock? From here, he thinks, you get a different view: *it has no real keel*, that's why it's so tippy. Just a wide flat bottom, made that way so the trapper can lay his pelts out in it and a puny ineffective strip running its length that dares call itself keel. The problem is, he thinks, the setup is fine, the script looks good. But he doesn't know where he comes in. He is hesitating because he can't find his entrance.

"I got a good feeling about this constitution," said the G.G. Christ, thought the members of the press. The guy puts in words what everybody thinks. Stuff you'd say yourself if you had the confidence and weren't afraid to look like a sap before your fellow sophisticates of the media. Maybe this thing'll work, maybe we'll have a country despite everything. After they've told us so often a country like this doesn't fit in the world any more. It's too big, too troubled, too dis-united, too uncompetitive. Or maybe countries altogether don't fit the world any more. Stuff that made your head hurt.

"I read it, our new constitution. Right through. I talked about it with my wife, with some of my old teammates. We were a good cross-section of this country, you know. Not perfect. No women. No disabled." Twinkle, twinkle, pause. "We think it's not perfect either. But it's not bad, as Canadians say when they're feeling very wildly hopeful. So. It's time for me to stop. Thank you." He was followed immediately by the prime minister.

"Does that guy ever miss?" said the P.M. to the front row. A laugh rippled to the exit doors. "What, zis thing on?" She tapped the mike. "And to think I chose politics over hockey so I'd never have to compete against someone with real skills . . ." She was followed by the leader of the official Opposition, the leaders of all the unofficial oppositions, some in Parliament, others restless to get there, and the radical populists, whose distinguishing policy was refusal to enter Parliament even if they were elected. In the old days they'd have been anarchists. It filled a long lazy Ottawa afternoon.

By then the print journalists were filing and TV reporters were wrapping up outside. There was lots of talk about "the national mood" the way only pundits can — as though you could sniff it once you were in the open air. Their tone was upbeat, thanks mainly to the G.G. The country did still exist, you hadda admit it, after so many years on the operating table. Hanging around in the waiting room, you kept faith with hope. Maybe the G.G. was onto something. Still, during the last exhausting years that this new national . . . thing was being designed, tested, rejigged, a kind of comforting stasis had set in; you'd almost started to think it wouldn't one day really have to happen. The mere exercise had a calming effect, it became a kind of end in itself. If only it could have gone on a little longer, just a little, that is, because we were all getting so comfortable with the process . . .

So of course you'd be crazy not to want to prolong the process, if it's anything like the rehearsal process for a new play, one you've had lots of time to work on. First you drag out the workshop phase long as you can, when there's no pressure for performance, no opening-night deadline rushing at you. When it's no longer avoidable, you schedule a production. You arrive on the first day of rehearsal. You introduce yourselves. You gossip. Sit around the table. You turn lazily to the script, you read through, drinking coffee, everyone underlines their parts. You have little conferences and debates about character and plot. Everyone's very patient with everyone else, so long as their turn comes too. It's comfortable because there's no deadline, no judgements. Opening night is far away, you don't yet feel terror about the reviews that will come the day after you open, there are no costumes to try on along with tantrums over what I have to wear and I won't go on stage in that thing! Even the days following, and sometimes the weeks, are still an extended workshop. Doesn't matter how long you've got, you're still okay until a week or so to go, when you know you're truly going to take this leaden thing and put it in front of people and try to keep them paying attention to you and it for two hours and fifty-five minutes! The sweating starts. You — not the writer or the director or anyone else. They aren't going to be out there with nothing but potential humiliation between them and the bums in the seats. You are! Of course you wish you could prolong the rehearsal process forever. You'd be psycho if you didn't.

Tilley Poon hits play on the VCR, and the thin-line screen on her bedroom wall projects last night's cross-country interactive focus group.

"So why you bother voting at all?" says a day-care worker in Moncton.

"That's how it is, I guess," says a former maintenance engineer in a B.C. pulp mill. The crawler at the bottom of the screen says he hasn't worked since the mid-nineties.

Tilley thinks, That's how it is? How what is? Is how?

She likes going straight from dream life to real life. Loosens the imagination. Sometimes she makes the best connections of the day lying here, in transit.

"It's all just part of it, I guess."

Tilley hits freeze. She knows there's something in this exchange. Don't push, maybe it'll come while she fights traffic on her way into the office. She calls up the overnights on the rolling polls; there's something in those undulations. God knows what, she doesn't. She tosses the remote into the rumples of the duvet.

On her way past reception, she asks Justine if she watched TV last night. Yeah, Justine saw the election call, that G.G. really has it. Maybe we'd all start watching hockey again if they were still like him.

She calls a meeting of Research, then Analysis, and walks out while they're talking. Below, in the Sweetheart Café, that used to be Sweetheart Lunch back when this building housed a dozen garment outfits, back when there was a Canadian garment industry, before SkyDome and Communications City and free trade changed a part of town that produced things people wore to one which turns out concepts. The menu says nothing to her, it just looks back. Don't lose patience. Eavesdrops on waiters and customers through the sound booster in her pocket while pretending the earplug is connected to

8

the hand-held thing she's got which is flashing figures and transcripts. *Wonder if all this stuff is cooking my head.* Back upstairs by now the graphs, analyses, and projections will look neat and shiny for tonight.

She's where she is because she knows everything about polling and statistical analysis and has zero respect for any of it. Gregg was the last genius in this field, could do no wrong for over a decade of Tory party rule till the election of '93 when his prowess was useless and the party evaporated. He had a perfectly good excuse for the failure of his advice: it didn't work. Sometimes the advice works and sometimes it doesn't. If you win, you get to be a genius and tell everyone why your strategy succeeded. If you lose, someone else does. It was kind of him not to tell the truth, because all the pols and pundits assumed he'd simply fucked up, forgot to get it right this once, so they went looking for someone who'd put it in place next time. So Tilley became the next genius, leapfrogging past her competitors, mostly men twice her age. Maybe it's the leather she wears. Maybe it's because she's Chinese. Maybe they think she uses ancient Oriental wisdom.

But she knows the one true secret known by all the few geniuses of advertising and PR: what counts is the creative part. The bounce you make between reams of demographics and an image that actually sells the stupid beer or government or whatever. For that, you refer directly to the fact you're human — which can be dodgy if your humanity is what you ditched while acquiring your credentials as an expert. There are no substitutes. You're bathing, you're driving — you get this idea, it moves you — maybe you yelp out loud: true sign of a winner. *Then* you test. Either it checks out, or you go ahead anyway. Whenever she had a huge contract like this one on the election, she did what she'd just been doing: ingested the data, then ignored it. Suddenly you'll know what it means. It always worked. It was working now.

There was one problem. It didn't mean anything.

Leaving here is like moving from space to time.

He tops up the fuel tank and puts the gas can back inside the pump house, then snaps the tiny rusty padlock shut on it. The only thing ever stolen from here while he was away shooting — or shooting off his mouth — was a near-empty gas can.

That's because what truly exists up here is space. You see it and feel it, it encloses you. But up here time . . . merely passes — passes through space. The sun hits the roof in the morning, it moves across the sky all day — its movement is the day. I watch it slip behind the marsh as I sit on the dock or the porch in the evening. There goes Time. There he goes. Comes and goes. But space never slips from view, it's always there. The lake is space, smooth or choppy. The trees, the marsh, the sky. They change a little but when they do, they change back to what they were. In the city it's time that's always there, surrounding you, it doesn't move, it's anchored, like the hands of a clock — the way lake and trees and sky are up here. In the city everything except time seems insubstantial. The sky? You rarely notice it. All things in space there move and shift, as people move, as I move. They alter and alter some more. They never change back. There's no basic state for them to change back to.

Politics is about change, as is time.

He pulls into the slip. Perfect landing of course, since no one's watching. He ties onto the rings, tugs the key off the motor handle and takes the life jacket it's clipped to with him. Foolish city habit, no one's ever had a boat stolen on the lake. But it adds to the stupid-cottager lore collected by people like Len. He believes in supporting local production. He heads for the car. He has the essentials: laptop, day calendar, *The Complete Works*. He locked the cottage, that's all, didn't close it up. That would be a tip-off, eliminate all the suspense. Gotta leave something in doubt.

The PMO is where they do the vile work.

Tilley lowers her head indicating the binder on the table between the two them. "What's it mean?" says the P.M. Somebody always asks. Everything always gets asked.

"It's in there," says Tilley, tapping the binder.

This is the point at which the P.M. seems to lose interest. As if she senses nothing in the file or the hours of campaign strategy ahead will count dick compared to the unease at the back of her mind. Tilley and the P.M. understand this in each other. That's why they work well together. The binder data, the bullshit analysis built on it, is for the benefit of others in the room.

About eleven, they reach the spoilers, those "independents" who get elected these days and then muck up the clear lines of party discipline and parliamentary manoeuvring. There's a rumour about Matthew Deans. The P.M.'s chief of staff, who's from Quebec, says, "Anchorman? Some kinda scientist? Guy who does phone-ins about handling your kids? Give us a hint."

No, says Tilley. Deans is the actor. Used to play the Healer in a series by that name maybe ten years back. Still in reruns. Good-guy pediatrician, uses all kinds of nature treatments and kinky mental tricks plus very hi-tech medicine when he needs it — a dab of environmentalism, dose of the old New Age mystical hoopla, the usual idealizations or demonizations of science and technology. Stir to taste. Tilley used to like the show; even when it started to slip, she still liked it. He also dabbles in left-wing stuff like attacking free trade and screaming about Americanization. Capable of making a certain amount of trouble. "Sexy, though," says the P.M.

Then she smiles a smile that says: "No problem, that kinda politics went out with Reagan. Shows like 'Entertainment Tonight,' 'Lifestyles of the Rich and Famous.' Then the shit about Woody Allen, Michael Jackson, O.J. — they took the glamour out of Glamour." Her media coach grins too. "Like that writer who was president of Czechoslovakia," he says. "Looked good at the start. After a few years in government? He was back writing poetry. Or something."

Driving down 11 in a late-summer rainstorm. It slashes in just where the road adds a passing lane for two kliks, so you can whiz by the poky minivans and the trailers hauling their lugubrious outboards. But passing would take too much concentration, with what's on your mind.

Fernie, B.C., back in the early 1970s. Friendly Fernie, City with a Future. Nobody ever knows how bad it can get till they've washed up in Fernie on a weeknight. The show had been rained out. The rain whipped across the mountains and dumped on the wagons, the big tent was swamped. You made sure the horses were safe. The rest of the company huddled round a fire, made hot chocolate, smoked dope, laughed uncontrollably. It was the first time, Maurice the hosteler said, that he'd ever toked up. "It's not having any effect," he objected. "Except . . . everything . . . seems . . . veryveryveryfunnyallofassudden. Is that part of it? Am I getting stoned?" No one else wanted to join Matthew for the movie in town. You're kidding. Redford? So he went alone.

Redford was superb. He played a California lawyer, a guy who really cared, and had a radical critique of U.S. society too. If he'd been Canadian he'd have founded the Canadian Law Union, the way Morris founded Radical Academics of Canada. He decided to enter the race for a Senate nomination just to raise the issues. That was his only reason to jump in, not because he believed you could really do anything inside the stupid system. He despised the whole shallow electoral process, he knew how it gutted content wherever it touched. Yet despite his disdain, or because of it (the boss is always most intimidated by the employee who doesn't give a shit whether he gets fired), his campaign started to roll. Oh, how he resisted committing to it at every point, sabotaging each rosy opportunity to the fury of his campaign manager, who'd have torn out his hair if he hadn't been totally bald. (Peter Boyle? Was that him in the part?) Redford as the candidate fought the process and his own success through till the end, when he'd won, and he and baldy fled through the corridors of their hotel just ahead of a howling press posse, up another floor and into an empty suite, collapsed on bed and couch — reporters baying just beyond the door. "Whadda we do now?" gasped the winner. His manager, fount of his triumph, looked back blank as the cosmos and shook his head. He had no idea. Politics had no connection to what you actually *do* with power.

Matthew sloshed back to camp in the rain, surer than ever that elections, parties, voting — all the apparatus known as "politics" on the newscasts — weren't about politics at all; they were about annihilating real politics, which is about taking genuine action to change the world. Organize locally, get out in the street, raise consciousness as you tour the boonies in a wagon train, a literal wagon train, with a politically challenging collective creation, seeding

12

social awareness among the real people of your society. And never, ever, get sucked into that election crap.

The rain is over, just like that, and the road widens to four lanes plus a divider, but hell, Canadian drivers always ride in the passing lane. They don't acknowledge any difference. They settle there, you can see from the back of their heads how complacent they are. "I'm going five or ten kilometres over the limit now, why would anyone want to pass? That would be illegal. Anyway, what's the rush?" You could honk, but no one honks on the highway. Matthew honks.

Ever since the free-trade election defeat of 1988, Matthew has hated how Canadians dawdle in the passing lane. They don't understand the concept. Possibly they don't know it exists. There's something sweet and uncompetitive in how they drive, but it makes him crazy. It's like an invitation to the Americans. Come on up and overtake us, pass us by in our own country, we don't care, we don't even know there's a contest on. If we did, maybe we'd at least put up a fight. The way he and Roland did, that time.

Take on the megamusicals on our own turf, was the idea. They bring their Broadway and London products here and hoover up all the entertainment dollars we need to create our own culture. Well, we're not afraid of the fucking marketplace either. We may not like it, but we can do it. Roland and I were both awash in series money at the time. I'd just quit and was looking for a way to spend it out of my system: like a bad money purge. We fitted up one of our favourite collective creations — The Fur Trade in Canada, *based on the economic tome by Harold Innis — with a huge production, like we'd always dreamed of doing, and a musical score by Roland's buddy, Darren, then we rented the Pantages in Toronto. The social democrats were in power and tried to give us money to prove something. No way, we said; we're doing this by their rules. Maybe it wasn't aerospace or the information highway, but it was culture, and that's business too. Of course the show got creamed and closed. We hadn't set it up with a two-year lead-in of centrefold ads every weekend in the dailies, plus cover stories in* Time *and* Newsweek *years before about the orginal, pre-Canadian productions of the show. In other words, ticket buyers hadn't been guaranteed a perfect night out which, if they didn't have it, proved something was wrong with* them, *not the show.*

So, having failed to win when I took them on in my own back-yard, now I'm going after them right where I'm completely not at home? That makes a lot of sense. I gotta see Morris.

Morris sits at his kitchen table preparing his lectures on "Marx and Theatre," or Marx and something. He is the last practising Marxist within miles — including the downtown university at which he defends his shrinking territory. He is thinking about the country. Can we attribute this mess to capitalism? he thinks. Or just human nature.

A Marxist still. Thirty-five years ago Morris discovered Marxism as if he'd come on a new plant species or the Loch Ness monster. He dedicated the rest of his life to understanding the world through its prism, plus helping others acquire the same tool. He never received genuine academic credentials; his advisors at Berkeley, where he launched his study of post-colonial reform movements, were displeased when he ditched the carefully framed topic he'd gone to research in the communist state of Kerala, in India; and equally distressed by the Niagara of scholarly articles, books, and platform appearances which began to pour forth from their student. (By the year in which the Soviet Empire crumbled, according to standard bibliographies, he'd become the third-most cited Canadian of his time — after only Frye and McLuhan.) His mentors were troubled most of all by his adherence to those few scrawny national liberation movements that still remained, many in Africa, others in Central America and Asia — long after most such movements had won their victories and moved on to become responsible, compromised, studiable governments themselves. The leaders he sought out still tied the language of social revolution to that of national independence, as Morris faithfully documented. Hence no doctorate. But as each underfunded movement in whose cause he'd enlisted, and which held their meetings in some kitchen, occasionally his, went on to win its war, Morris was invited to their Independence celebrations as Canada's official representative. External affairs was not amused. Those were high points for him, being called on to present his credentials as his country's entirely unofficial representative in newborn state after state. "So, we did it," said one charismatic revolutionary Morris first met darting around the Accra campus on a motor scooter. "Now we must continue." Everyone in those movements transmuted into governments agreed the hard part was only about to begin, but none of them truly believed the future could be anywhere near as draining as what they'd already passed through.

His kitchen is unusable. Many years ago, as his dream of Third World socialism crumbled — while the Soviet Empire did the same — he and Marta decided to renovate. It took forever. It took longer than the breakup of the whole socialist world. They never got it right; eventually they just left it, an unfinished work, like his socialist vision. When reno hell first began, he'd sit in the rubble — live connections, drywall dust — thinking of the former young men (and a few women) who'd kicked the asses of various imperial armies all the way back to Lisbon or Johannesburg or Washington. With the collapse, those aging idealists had suddenly to begin thinking about getting jobs and supporting their families. Their movements would no longer look after them as had been the case since they were teenagers. There were no movements. What were they supposed to do: look in the want ads? Did they know what want ads were? Were there want ads in the party papers?

Since Morris still had his job — he even had tenure — he became their critic, sadly scolding those who'd formed and moulded him in the name of ideals he'd learned from them. He didn't blame them, nor they him. He could afford to maintain their ideals when they no longer were able, and it was nice that someone could. It was as though Marx took refuge in the bourgeois world of Western academics, as he'd once holed up in the British Museum library. Here in the imperialist racialist patriarchal capitalist — and above all triumphalist — West, it would continue. "I am the Old Mole," he mutters amid the debris. He clings to the long view.

At the sound in the driveway, he picks his way out of the kitchen, steps through the sunroom and opens the door to the fire escape. Matthew is mounting the stairs.

15

"Why was it," says Matthew, coming through the door, "that it meant so much to us to know we were on the winning side."

"History would absolve us," says Morris. "That was it."

"Eventually," says Matthew. "No matter how long it took?"

"Those motherfuckers would be up against the wall one day," says Morris.

"Sooner or later," says Matthew.

Morris drops onto the fold-out couch. "I think it had to be sooner," he says, "rather than later. It was the picture of them getting theirs while we could still watch it. That's what kept us going."

"Which motherfuckers? All of them?"

"Mainly the guys in the hotel. Those are the ones I think about." He describes the first convention of RAC, Radical Academics of Canada, in Ottawa over thirty years ago, just after he came home from India. On the final night of the convention, he and some radical psychologists were strolling the corridors feeling revolution was at hand, maybe just around . . . this corner. Instead they found the hospitality suite for a big-business convention also booked at the hotel; he didn't know which business, he didn't make distinctions in those days. They strode into the raucous suite and "confronted" the businessmen. That's what you did at the time: confront. Most of the execs and bean-counters in the room looked unsettled; this was probably the New Left they'd read about in the newsmagazines. But one brown suit unpacked himself from a chair and poked Morris in the chest. Hard, no ceremony. Morris gasped. No one had poked him that way, invading his body's territory, since he was a kid during recess. "So tell us, what're you gonna do, not just talk, do," said the man — a man, Morris recalls thinking as he gawked back, herding them out into the hall. Morris collapsed right there. Not physically, it was his politics that collapsed, though only for a moment. He had no comeback for someone who didn't argue, who just poked. Ever since, when he's been at a left-wing meeting or even a conversation, he's often asked himself: Would the man in the brown suit feel threatened if he walked by and looked in on what we're planning?

"Yeah," says Matthew. "It was about revenge. They got to have it all their way. Even when we were riding a crest for a while there during the sixties. Once when we shut the universities down to protest Canadian complicity in Vietnam, I had to go downtown for an audition. I rode my bike by the stock exchange and the TD towers. I was stunned: they were just going about their business, walking through the revolving doors in their suits with their briefcases. It didn't matter to them what we were doing. They didn't care. Probably they didn't know. That really hurt. You just wanted to believe they'd get what they deserved. Sometime, some way."

"We didn't have hell or purgatory to fantasize them into," says Morris. "But we had history. Same thing. Them or their kids or their class, they'd get it and we knew they would and we wanted them to know we knew."

"But why did it really matter?" says Matthew. "I mean, what if we knew for sure we weren't ever going to win. Would that have meant we shouldn't have been fighting them anyway?"

"That's a *tremendous* question," murmurs Morris. "I don't know if I've ever actually asked it."

"It seemed to matter so much," says Matthew, "to be certain we'd win."

Morris has made his way back into the kitchen. He searches for the coffee. He plugs in the kettle. "I wish I'd thought about that question," he says.

"Now it doesn't seem to matter at all — whether we're bound to win."

"Should I assume," says Morris, "that you're about to do something you think is right and you don't have a chance of succeeding?"

"I don't even know if it's right," says Matthew.

"The only unquestionably good thing is a good will," mutters Morris. "Or words to that effect."

"Who says?"

"Kant."

"Immanuel Kant?" blurts Matthew. Morris does an eye roll. How many Kants are there?

"We're all the way back to Kant?" says Matthew.

"Sometimes I slide as far as the pre-Socratics. I may even reread the Bible."

"What happened to Marx?"

"He is . . . indisposed."

"I was wondering if, ah, I could count on your support if I, ah . . . that is your support at the, ah . . . "

"Oh fuck. I knew it."

"Chill out, Morris. I'm not talking about becoming a stock-broker."

"An honest profession. Comparatively."

"Cut me some slack."

"You don't know what you're talking about. You haven't thought this through. You're making it up as you go."

"How do you know? I mean, what makes you think that?"

"Because you're reverting to cliché. 'Chill out.' 'Cut me slack.' You told me that's what actors always do when they start improvising."

"I won't run if I can't count on your vote. It means that much to me. Don't ask me why. It just does. It's like I need your . . . blessing in this."

"What if I promise not to vote against you? I'll abstain."

"I won't run."

"Shit."

"Think of it as the road to radical structural reform."

"Radical structural reform is a crock."

"I thought you invented it."

"I did."

"You wrote a book about it. You said in the post-Cold War milieu, activities like elections could lead to radical structural reform. You said even Marx thought so. You thanked me in the acknowledgements. It wasn't easy reading that sucker right through."

"It didn't work. It was a dumb idea."

"You gave up on radical structural reform?"

"*Years* ago."

"I didn't know that."

"A few months ago anyway. Don't expect me to issue bulletins on the health of my latest attempt to keep the revolutionary tradition alive."

"I'm sorry. But maybe you were right about structural reform —"

"It didn't work. It was a noble effort on my part, I concede that. But look at Mandela. Look at the ANC. You cannot reform this fucking system, you'll just end up shattering all hope including your own that things can ever be different. It's better to hole up in the caves above Yenan the way Mao did after the 'Long March' and wait for the chance to make a real revolution. At least that way you keep hope for a truly different future alive."

"On a respirator."

"Better hope on life support than false hope at the ballot box."

Morris always wins. The miracle is that Matthew can sometimes sustain the argument for a few minutes. Years ago, when they first became friends, their relationship consisted of Matthew phoning Morris and asking questions about politics. "What do we think about . . . ?" he'd say, and Morris would supply the answer. Matthew has also developed a fallback strategy. Once he concedes defeat, he pouts. It often works. It plays to the egalitarian element in Morris's Marxist soul. It works now.

"You'd run in this riding?"

"Yeah."

"Shit."

"I know it's ridiculous. I know I'm an actor. But look at it this way: there's no chance I'll win."

"Stop whipping yourself. I think it makes sense."

"You just said the system is hopeless."

"The system *is* hopeless. Given the system, you make sense in it."

"Because I'm some dumb artist — "

"Why not? Everything else has been marketized out of existence. Nobody thinks government does anything any more. Everything is business. The schools are business. Collecting the garbage is a business opportunity. Even the prisons. At least with art, it's harder to reduce it to an item in your VISA bill. Harder. Not impossible. It's the only thing left with a little life of its own. Who knows, maybe you can put some life back into politics. Unlike the rest of us." Morris looks depleted by this admission. But he's drained himself to give something to a friend.

19

"That's brilliant," says Matthew. "I could use it on my first campaign householder." Morris smiles a grim smile. "Except as usual," Matthew goes on, "nobody would understand what the hell you're talking about."

These are my halls, thinks Lars. I traverse them, a hand-held camera with legs. I have projected this environment and in so doing I re-create myself in its image.

He swivels by the alcoves and corners designed for stand-ups, the covered outlets for cable plug-ins, some of which have yet to be used. Twenty-five years ago he imagined it. Five years later the station moved in. But even today it continues to feel like a home for an extended family of video equipment who made it uptown but haven't learned to live there. His station staff still huddle in their main-floor studios, like an immigrant family in the basement kitchen of a big new suburban house they bought but can't figure out how to live in. Yet that first floor works, even on its own, it always has. Vast, vaguely divided, essence of TV — they come from Denmark, Malaysia, everywhere in the world, to rip off Lars's bright idea.

He enters his inner sanctum. Like stepping inside a TV set and looking out. All black and griddy, screens surround you, they hover on the walls, leer down from the ceiling, there's even one beneath you that can shoot its images up your anus. You are bombarded by electrons here. He seats himself behind his black desk — more a horizontal TV screen than a desk — black too, blackandgreyandgriddy, just like the medium into which he's projected himself for thirty years.

"I'm ready for you, Matthew," he says.

He built this quirky empire against the wisdom of the experts, then forced their acknowledgement. When it succeeded *he* became the expert. Now others approach him to bless *their* premonitions. On a Sunday afternoon, decades ago, sitting by himself in the old hat factory that was the station's first home, some tattered movie running, no one else around, not even the community college grads who would have worked for nothing and usually did — in that pathetic closet he called an office — he realized what he was in it for, and it wasn't money. He was there for the heroism. To be the hero of a story — his own. He made his moves because he liked how he thought they made him look to the world: innovative, fearless, creative. Omnipotent. Money-driven too, if that's what it took to impress them. If what he felt he needed was going to cost too much, he'd rather not know. It was like the first house he ever bought; he'd been twenty-two. I'll pay for an inspection, said his old man, you never know what shit and rot is happening in the walls or under the roof. Lars declined, he wanted that house, he liked how it made him feel. If there were problems, he'd find out later and with luck, never. He built the station that way. It lead to profits most years, about five of seven — until the last six in a row.

"I want a regular slot for seven weeks, daily," says Matthew. "It has to be the next seven because it's on the election."

Lars is disappointed. "I've tried non-journalist journalists," he says. "And it doesn't matter. They aren't watching us any more, Matthew."

"Lars — *they* don't exist any more."

Lars knows. He also knows that no one has come to take "their" place. For years, generations really, he had their number. He knew what it was to be born with TV, though he hadn't been so himself. He felt his way into it, then played their own sense of reality back to them, moving generationally as they moved. It was heady: once you caught the flow, you didn't just reflect their world, you shaped it. But a few years back, his sure feel went hazy; he couldn't follow the generational flow; or maybe there weren't generations any more to follow; the speedup had broken down distinctions. This is a truth also felt by his peer (one of the few, in his opinion), Tilley Poon, but it bothers Lars more. He has a deep sense of generational continuity, as Finns tend to. Perhaps it's what gave him that exquisite sense of "flow," key to the medium. His granddad was a Red Finn. He got off the train in Toronto and went to work in "The Big Shop," where the Finnish workers paid one of their own to read aloud from the socialist classics as they laboured. Sometimes in Swedish or Finnish, sometimes in English — so they could acquire the language in order to contribute to the revolution in their new land. Lars's dad thought his old man was full of shit; he went so far to the right he didn't just call himself a White Finn; he said he was albino, but he was proud of those origins too. Flow need not be smooth; it can jar. Lars feels he combines both generations. He's made plenty of money; and he did it by communicating in revolutionary ways. Now though, there's something out there and no one knows what to call it. Therefore you cannot market to it. Hence it might as well not exist — yet it does.

"I'm not a journalist. I'm a candidate."

This Lars likes. He gets a feeling. He wants it. Like that first house when he refused his dad's offer for the inspection.

"You give me a crew. You get the video diary of a candidate. Like the ones on 'Dying of AIDS.' Those were good. There hasn't been anything that good since then."

The feeling is gone, something just wiped it. As if the inspectors got in anyway and tried to destroy his dream by overvaluing the house. Lars says, "I can't do that because they'll hate it if I do. They won't watch. They don't exist much when it comes to watching any more, but they still exist when it comes to not watching. I am going down the drain because of it. Do you know what I'm saying?"

"Why would they hate me?"

"It's not you they'd hate. Nobody can *not* like you. It's your secret weapon, I've seen you do things, on screen, on the stage, on the street. If anyone else did them, they'd be obnoxious. Not when you do them. Your likability is your secret ingredient. Like Gardol, the old secret ingredient in toothpaste from the first days of TV. "The Colgate Comedy Hour." I know you don't recall that. It is my fate alone to know both the birth and death of my medium. They hate us now. They hate media. They hate media the way the peasants of Mexico and Spain came to hate the church in their revolutionary hour. Do you understand what I'm saying. They hold us responsible the way those others held the church responsible. I'm doing you a favour."

"What if I do it without you? What if you're not involved?"

Ah now. This has possibilities. Lars has toyed with video

22

populism but he's never pushed it all the way. "You'd have to seem not just like you weren't doing it for me," says Lars, "but as if you don't give a shit whether you're on TV at all." Matthew snorts. Of course that's no problem. If he gave a shit about being on TV, he wouldn't have quit the series. "But that's not all," Lars goes on. "You'd have to seem as if you don't care whether you're the candidate; it could just as well be one of them." Matthew cocks his head, it's the curiosity tic he used sometimes in the series when a symptom didn't merely baffle him, but also appealed. He asks Lars what that means. Lars says he's not sure, it just came out of his mouth.

But this is the line along which Lars has been urging his imagination to drift. Whenever he hears or reads a good idea, it strikes him instantly as his own: either something he must already have thought or is about to think. His area of genius is TV, and his media muse visits roughly once per decade, to rescue him from extinction, that is, from becoming unknown again. He has been feeling that edgy feeling lately, like the distant early tickle of an erection, it tells him he is about to reinvent his medium one more time and survive a few years longer. Matthew is part of the visitation. Tonight perhaps he will light a candle to McLuhan.

The deal they make involves purchase, at a nominal price, of one video kit. Matthew will run for office and record his run. The key is: there will be no media-tion involved. He will shoot himself and the people he finds along his campaign's path. He will phone it in. Not unheard of, but it has the stripped-down conceptual simplicity Lars has sought throughout his innovative career. Each day of these last twenty-seven years Lars has turned out a daylong show. He thinks of it as Lars's movie of the day, starring the station, the population, the galaxy, wherever he chose to point the lens. There is something in the notion brought in by Matthew which advances the impulse a step. Perhaps it will become one piece of a breakthrough he has yearned for since the definitions began to fail: the loss of the separation between the makers and the program. He affirmed long ago the convergence between art and life, politics and culture, television and reality. After Matthew departs with his kit, Lars fiddles with the concept. Everyone his own videographer. No separate class of recorders, no more the separation which has defined life in his time: us and them, we on the inside, they on the outs. The information industries versus the information. He has toyed with blurring the border. He pictures the quest mystically: to merge realms. It drives him nuts to think there is anything out there that escapes his grasp. If it exists, broadcast it. That includes existence itself, the final reduction. Or is the final reduction — elimination of the medium? What does a medium do but — mediate? That is, separate. Is this video narcissism? Or is it democracy?

"Will they say it's favouritism," Matthew asked as he left. "Will they complain about equal time? Will every candidate in the country demand a video kit?"

"The hell with them," said Lars. "I program here. I program what I like."

"You could give the other candidates in my riding an equal shot. It would be okay with me."

"Let them complain to the Video Fairness Board. That'll get them heard by the year 3000," said Lars with a wave of dismissal. But he was thinking at the time: no one will see you as a real candidate anyway. You aren't politics. You are culture.

"Hello?"

"It's, um, it's me."

Pause. Then, not quite flat, "Hi."

I've always felt our bad period, still ongoing, began one night in '88. It was late, around midnight — because the Olympics were held in Seoul that year. Ben Johnson and Carl Lewis were running to settle who was the fastest man in the world and she was curled in a corner of the couch. She was big enough to centre her school basketball team by then, but she could still squeeze herself into tiny corners. I had just come in from picking up the early Globe. *It had a rosy review of that season's first episode. Incandescent in fact. I'd been anticipating a slaughter, which we certainly deserved by then, if not sooner.*

When Ben flew across the finish line, fist overhead, she squealed as though nothing she'd ever meet in the future could bring her down. A few days later, I heard the news on the radio while I was studying a script — well, less studying it than trying to figure out how to emerge from it with dignity. I went upstairs to the deck we'd just added onto the third floor. She did her homework there in good weather. She did it anywhere except her desk. She never did anything at that desk. "There's a report," I said. "Ben tested positive for steroids, if it's true, they'll take the medal away." "Asshole," she said. First I thought she meant me. "Everybody does it," she said. "Everyone knows everybody does it. He was stupid. If he was gonna do it, he shouldn't of got caught." If you glanced over the fence around the deck, you could practically see the whole country cursing the same way. I'd have given a limb, gladly, to stop her from hurting like that — though I'd have soon run out of limbs.

Later I called Morris. I said, "Can we attribute this to capitalism or just human nature?"

"I'm, uh, going to need some help for a few months. Maybe longer. It pays."

"Fine thanks, Dad. And how're you?"

"Fine. I'm all right. You know I want to know. It's . . . clumsy. Me. I'm clumsy."

"That's okay. Anyway, I don't wanta work in movies. Did I tell you I decided that?"

"It isn't movies. It's political. Like . . . the election. I'm, ah, going to be a candidate."

"Jesus. What happened to you?"

"It's politics. You know me."

"It can't be politics. You always said running in elections wasn't politics. It was a diversion from politics. You both always said that, even if you didn't agree about anything else." She can feel he's sweating. She relents. "You have to tell me why you want to do this, maybe then — "

"I think you could really help me — "

"No. Listen to me. Why *you* want to do this. Not why you want *me* to do it."

Pick a motive, any motive.

I'd flown to Ottawa for the hearing. I went there to chew on the hand that fed us. Why me? "You're an institution," said the head of the

Public Broadcasting Front. "Only you can get away with it." The show was in its fourth season. That made me a national institution. I don't think people really liked it, what I think is they felt so battered from the loss of everything they'd thought was Canadian (the railroad, the health care, hockey) that if they dared not like our show, they were afraid they'd probably lose it too.

I was nervous, as I'd be not just for an opening or a premiere, but the first night of a collective, where the words I spoke were my very own, it was on me, and I couldn't count on the reviewers to pin this mess on some playwright while feeling pity for the poor actor. Those collectives were agony; every time we opened one I'd wonder why I was doing this to myself again. I guess I always forgot.

I took my dreary notes and sat in an anonymous restaurant near the Hill, looking for a way to pump some life into them for the regulators and any viewers who might accidentally flip by on cable. If there was room at the counter, I'd have done breathing exercises to calm myself. Everyone looked like a civil servant, eating toasted sandwiches or soup. Thumbing sheaves that must have been policy papers — the way people in a real place leaf through newspapers or novels at lunch. I ordered a burg I couldn't down and across the counter this guy is reading Take Our Country Back, in which I had three and a half feeble pages on how I learned what acting's really about by coming home from my apprenticeship years in England and acting in plays on mining in Goose Bay or the prairie heritage of Poundmaker. I didn't even know that book was out, I don't think I believed it would ever really happen — an actual book with something by me in it, my drivel alongside pieces from real writers. He caught me looking.

"Whaddya think?" I said. He looked back, no recognition, which was a relief. The series was a success in places like Toronto, I got noticed too much by then, on the street, in the store. There were ads in the bus shelters. I'd started to wear hats. It would have been different if they recognized me for work I was proud of. It had finally happened, every actor's dream, for the worst work of my life. Up in Ottawa though, it appeared they hadn't been ravished by my embarrassing triumph. "Pretty good, Matthew," he said. "It moves me."

He worked at External, as it used to be called. International trade division, special section on communications — in other words, he was paid, like many others, to peddle a set of murderous economic policies leading off with free trade to the rest of us. He was reading "our" book (he had an advance copy) as part of his job, for which we of course were paying. They wanted him to find out what the "other side" (us) were saying, try to anticipate our obstructive moves, make sure there were no slipups during the next big sell of the next hideous trade deal, no overlooked manoeuvres that might almost gum the works. He said it started after the free-trade election of late '88. They nearly lost that one because they hadn't anticipated the opposition. Ever since they'd made sure they kept up with "us." He laid it all out, very frank.

And I thought: Jesus, I slip away from shooting when I can steal the chance where I try to read a few things Morris gives me about what's happening in the country or the world so I can write little endorsements or make speeches and presentations the way I'm here to do now. It's hectic, I worry what I read'll get mixed up with my lines for the show, as sometimes they do. Then I think of your mom, who even when we were in theatre together long ago, made me think about the ways of a world I found easier to deal with on a stage, and who at the time was working for the Servers and Cleaners' Union in Toronto. We were all still together but the strains were heavy. She typed her own letters and emptied the wastebaskets at the end of the day; went to bed most nights around two and got up again at five to bang out some report on the latest attempt to destroy the health-care system or unemployment insurance; by six-thirty she was outside an office tower or fast-food franchise to leaflet the few remaining members of her union about what they could do to try and save their crummy jobs — and this guy's work is to read what we're cobbling together in our unpaid spare time so they can figure out how to derail us before we even get going! Is this any way to run a political opposition?

At the hearing I found myself strangely inarticulate. Normally I figure if I get myself onstage, the rest will follow. I'll pull it off. Not that time. I horrified everybody, including me. I attacked my own show. My own character! "Why are we obsessed with formulas developed everywhere else in the world? Who needs another series about

27

*caring, helping heroes? What does it have to do with the disintegra-
tion we're all complicit in? You go on licensing this torrent of self-
delusion and reassurance — you should be subject to recall and
retraining just like the politicians who appointed you should!" I
guess my mind was elsewhere. Having my day in court lacked the
kick I'd been counting on. Maybe I was preoccupied, wondering
whether your mom and I might have made a dumb, though noble,
choice about what really was politics.*

"So years ago you had a peak experience in a restaurant in Ottawa
and it just now hit you that you should've run for city council
instead of being a famous actor with a TV show and no family like
you once had?"

He's sure he deserves it. He's not sure why, but the possibilities
are many. He can always find cause for feeling guilty. On the other
hand, he wants her with him. The idea just came to him before he
picked up the phone to call; now he feels the whole thing won't
make sense without her.

"And you want me to give up what I'm doing. Which I grant you
isn't much. The world is not crying out for Ph.D.s in economic history."

He tries silence. Silence can be immensely effective onstage. It
is the neutron bomb of acting technique. On her it doesn't work.

"Exactly what would I do to help you?"

"I don't know. That's the first thing I need help with."

He hears a sigh on the line. She's always been a great sigher.

"Maybe," he says, "I'm just tired of playing myself."

"You some kinda radical left-wing actor?"

"Yeah. You some kind of big-shot banker?"

*Playing yourself, in the end, is like any role you've played too
often, hundreds or thousands of times. You can always add a twist to
the performance, a touch that will revive your own interest and keep
it fresh for those who haven't seen it or who've come to see it again.
Basically though, it will grow boring.*

*But what's the alternative? Not playing yourself? Playing some-
body else? No, the alternative is playing a different part of yourself,*

one you haven't played before in your life. That's scary though. You thought you'd been yourself all along. It turns out that was just one possible role among many you could just as well have been. "And I thought it was the real me!"

The day after their brusque introductions ("You some kind of . . ."), Matthew and Waring found themselves trudging up a dry creek-bed. They were on scheduled downtime during a "retreat" held by the Interchurch Alliance at the Banff Centre. The idea was to save Canada by defining it. Again. Matthew wondered if other countries did this. Unlikely. These events proved to him there was a unique Canadian culture. The others who'd signed up for the walk in the foothills had pushed far ahead. Waring had on his Bay Street shoes and looked winded. Matthew decided to slow up and pick a fight with capitalism. "The trouble with all of them," he said, meaning those they'd just lost sight of, "is they're too competitive."

"They probably have type-A personalities," puffed Waring.

For two and a half hours they plodded toward a waterfall which, it turned out, wasn't there. By the time they returned to the rental car, the sun low, they'd touched on most of what mattered in each other's lives. They were mellow. Driving back to the centre, they revisited the issues that divided them sharply at last night's session. Labour rights, social spending, deficits. Neither of them had moved an inch.

"And yet," Matthew told Morris when he got back, "I felt better with Waring than the people there I should've been more comfortable with. The left profs like you, the church people, the artists. I didn't exactly find them boring. I bored *myself* — I knew exactly how I'd react to everything that got said. The left scripts. The right scripts. Waring felt the same. He said he felt locked into his role. He sounded like an actor in a bad hit series. So he quit as head of the bank. He's going to run in the next election. He'll lose, of course. The guy is made to be more of a mystic than a politician. At least that's how I'd cast him . . ."

Matthew quit the series around then. He too wanted to get *un*locked in. It didn't really work for him either. In the years since, he felt he'd still played himself. So maybe this wasn't about politics at all. Maybe it was about the effort to shake an old role and find a different one, something that doesn't happen just because you leave a TV show . . .

"Sorry," he says. "I'm afraid that's about the best I can come up with. It doesn't sound like much of a reason for getting into an election. For either of us." He'd have liked to explain it was connected to Ben Johnson, but he didn't know how.

"It'll do, Dad. Take my name and thank the others."

Jesus. This may already have been worth it.

What else do I need for an election campaign? Like going on tour, but without leaving home. Something to pull from the shelf to read each night as I drift off, last thing into my head, as you deposit a line or a cross you don't know what to do with and hope it sorts itself out by rehearsal next day.

The Complete Works, *published by T. Eaton Co. in 1946, right after the war, when the true necessities — electric trains, the CNE, Shakespeare — which had been discontinued for the sake of weapons production came back on stream in Canada. Its leather covers droop back gracefully and I submerge into its pages, like a U-boat commander ("Dive, dive"). Or in this case, maybe just the histories — the Henrys, the Richards — in a little volume I have which says, to my shame, "Yukon Library System." Was it when we did the* Spell of the Yukon *show in the mid-seventies, based on Robert Service poems, or the raid we made a few years later to document the theft of native rights by big-game hunters from the U.S.? Did I stop by a local branch and walk out with this book?*

At bedtimes during tours, in motels or billets, I felt like a kid in class hiding his Playboy *inside the math text. I knew I should have been dipping into Marx or at least Sartre as I slid toward sleep. Some writer of the now, with a theory or worldview. Not Shakespeare, whose worldview, if he had one, was mostly world while the views kept shifting from character to character and play to play. One world, many views.*

Like, ah here, Prince Hal. Your need to transform yourself in order to surprise and delight the old man. The compulsion to outshine

Hotspur, your brother emblem and alter ego. You did it to show them. So irrelevant from an objective historical standpoint. But we know it's why you acted; you confess it when no one else is around, we over-hear you say it to yourself. Thus we learn, despite what we were taught in history class, that the "Causes of the War" did not cause the war. It was about Dad.

Back when there was a left or we believed there was, we said his-tory wasn't made by individuals like Hal driven by feelings for par-ents and rivals. Maybe, we conceded, individuals make history, but "not within circumstances of their own choosing." Get those circum-stances right — the class conflicts, the stage of development, the tech-nology; then "factor in" messy personal elements like Hal's hurt and need if you must.

These days at least I can pull Hal out from under the covers, stop reading him by flashlight. Is it just my desperation for understand-ing, or do his justifications seem to light up the murk now as once only Marx seemed to do? Have I merely switched, as her mother claims, from a class-based theory of why things happen to what she calls my "that's life" analysis?

Once more unto the . . . sleep — I ride through London, come straight from my coronation, my chief justice at my side, the crowds hail their new king. Suddenly before me steps Falstaff, my old fat Jack, tutor of my venal youth; he is ebullient, his ship has docked at last. Hal, my boy, he cries, my prince, my light, my sun —

But I'm not Hal at all, I am Fat Jack himself, and Hal is speak-ing to me the most wrenching lines I ever heard (or learned for a part). "I know thee not, old man. Fall to thy prayers." The king passes me by, a corpulent bag of failed hopes.

Was that it? The king passed me by. Not just once. So I left the fringe for the mainstream. Then I left the theatre for the screen (big and small) and then the series. With other leavings in between, including wife and daughter. Wanting always to pass by rather than be passed, leave before being left. Left by the left . . . And now Fat Jack remounts the horse and becomes his own prince again? Remounts the stage? To finally act and not just act . . . ? Once more unto . . . 'night then, g'night . . .

Elinor is on the line. She's heard. He's expecting a blast: "So you finally found a part you want to do. Hope you can find another agent too" Etcetera. That's not quite right. She asks if he's set up a campaign staff. "Dal," he says, "that's all so far." "Dal?" she says. "Yes," he says, "should I give her your best?" "Don't bother," says Elinor. "The two of us talk all the time." Something else he didn't know about his daughter. "For a while she wanted to go into film but I think I talked her out of it," says Elinor. "So I'm wondering if I can apply to be your finance chairman," she goes on. Yes, he says, you could apply. The lineup isn't overwhelming. "Good," she says. "You know I hate auditioning. I refuse to audition. But I can send a résumé with references. I'm known to be fiercely loyal." He'd like to reply in a witty vein but he's feeling moved. He tells her that. "Don't worry about it," she says. "I'm furious about what they've done to this country." He says he didn't think she thought about politics. "Are you kidding?" she says. "I couldn't even name the parties. Of course they change so often now most people couldn't. But I couldn't name them back when they were the old standards. Tories and whoever. You're not going to run for some party, are you?"

For what is politics except the attempt to bring out by collective and conscious acting *some of the possibilities inherent in human life besides those which happen to have been realized in the course of individual and social existence already? Which is just what the artist does in his art, and the actor does in his playing . . .*

CHAPTER TWO

Democracy is the worst political system except for all the others.
— *Winston Churchill*

Including democracy.
— *Morris Mott*

Morris canvasses at every election he can find: federal, provincial, municipal; if there's a dry election spell, he'll even canvass for school board. Voters are shocked when someone arrives on their door to talk school board. He doesn't even believe in elections, he's always been certain they're a trick to fool people into thinking they have a say in their destiny; elections, he's long said, are what they give us instead of real democracy. But he does it anyway, he does it for the contact. He knows scarred sectarians and former members of the Weather Underground in the U.S. — most have adopted respectable identities the way Abby Hoffman did — and even they surface to cover a poll or two when an election's called. They don't believe in the candidates, nor in the process, no more than Morris does. They all do it for the contact. On what other occasion in this society do citizens have an excuse to talk with one another about politics, even in its degraded electoral form? How else does someone like Morris ever meet the people?

In winter of '73, we did The Immigrant Odyssey. *I don't know if it was before we did* History on My Back *or after we did* Giving

33

Business the Business. *You could say we weren't modest in choosing our subjects. Homework, as usual on those collective creations, meant rushing out after rehearsal to dig up material for a scene to improvise next day. I went off with Michele. We were living together by then. She'd given up on acting and started work as a volunteer for a union that was trying to organize workers at a dinky appliance factory owned by an alliance of pro-apartheid Dutch Afrikaners and hysterical anti-communists from Eastern Europe. (That union really knew how to pick 'em. Michele kept wondering why no one else had tried to organize the place.) For hours we drove across the top of Toronto among the high rises and subdivisions, visiting workers. Blacks, Greeks, Macedonians (ferocious about not being taken for Greek), Chinese, Portuguese, Italians. "It's a regular United Nations in there," they'd all say about the plant. They said it with pride. Then they'd go on to bad-mouth all the other groups in the place. When we got back downtown, I said to her, "There are a lot of those people up there; why don't I see them much around here?" She just parked the car and we went inside. Next day I climbed on a streetcar to go to rehearsal and glanced around. They were there! The whole mélange. What happened? Was this a special streetcar for immigrant workers — or did I normally screen them out, and register only the riders who looked more or less like me, people I might know and vice versa, who I'd easily fall into conversation with? Had they been there — that is, here — every day of my life?*

We eventually performed The Immigrant Odyssey *on a streetcar. It was Kristof's idea. The immigrants weren't coming to the theatre. Big surprise. But as I pointed out cleverly, they ride the streetcar. We rented an old red rocket complete with driver from the transit commission for an evening and advertised the stops we'd be making to pick up audience. People could book seats by phone or take their chances. We figured immigrants and workers would be more comfortable that way, as farmers were readier to come to plays in the local auction barn than at the little theatre or opera house in town. So when we got to those designated streetcar stops, who got on? Our regular crowd: university profs, media people, culturally adventurous dentists. I'm still looking for that audience. I know they're out there. I've seen them.*

There was something peculiar about the campaign data Tilley Poon was collecting from across the country. For three days, she made herself not think about it. Then one night, stepping over the bodies and up to the automated teller, she got it. Nothing staggering, not an insight you could restructure a campaign around. It's just — there were more candidates than campaign offices, by far. In the past, candidates equalled headquarters. You had your fax list, your mailing addresses — almost all on main streets and in malls. This time campaigns were being run out of people's homes, cars, vans, and computers. It was a desktop election.

Matthew positions the camera. It obstructs no one's view in the school auditorium, but even if it did, there are lots of empty seats — also rows. People could relocate. He flips the remote. The camera is nearly silent; a modest light says it's functioning.

"Let me start by saying I have no writer for this part and no script. This isn't the first time. Before I worked in film and in series TV, I used to do improvisational theatre. That was in the 1960s and 1970s. I worked mostly in what we called collective creations. It meant we made up plays that had no scripts when we started, though they usually did by the end of the process. We created the scripts ourselves, together, over the rehearsal period. Some of them were good enough to be reproduced by other companies around the country, sometimes even elsewhere in the world, just as if a writer had sat in a garret and gone through the usual creative agony. We had our reasons. There were few playwrights in the country back then who could sit down, even in a garret, and turn out a producible script. We could have waited for the playwrights, I guess, but we were impatient. It wasn't just that though. We felt a hatred for the individualism and greed we saw around us as we grew up — in our own families or on TV. Along with greed went smugness and complacency. We wanted to live differently, helping each other and cooperating.

"The first collective creation I worked on was a play about the Cuban Revolution as it swept through a peasant village in the mountains of the Sierra Maestre. The actors were the peasants, the stage was the village. It was based on a book called *Cauldron!* that had a line which said the lesson of the twentieth century was that collective action was the only way to fix the world; individuals couldn't do it by themselves. That's what we were trying to do in theatre. I gave a talk to some theatre profs around then. I called it 'The Collective Creation Is the Wave of the Future: The Individual Playwright Will Be Consigned to the Dustbin of History.' They asked me to their convention alone, but I brought along the whole company. We gave a collective lecture.

"The wave of the future didn't quite happen. Before long I was doing mostly one-man shows, as we called them then. If that sounds like a contradiction, I'm sure it is. There was a lot of friction and competitiveness that happened in the collective process — though that's not what I want to talk about right now. So after a string of plays — during which I got to be known as the 'King of One-man Theatre' — I moved to film, then to series TV, which is why some of you call me Max, or Dr. Max, even though the last time I shot an episode of that show was years ago. Reruns can be a blessing or a curse, or both. I guess that goes for TV and politics.

"But I never lost my love for improv, which is why I have the nerve to stand here now. Because all the scripts, and I mean the political ones, are down the toilet. Marx is down the toilet in the same flush with Ayn Rand and Milton Friedman. Liberals, conservatives, neoconservatives, neoliberals. Remember when we had a party called the Progressive Conservatives? Remember when we had the socialists and social democrats who called themselves the NDP? There are no scripts any more! There's nothing left except improv. That means taking our experience, our wit, our common sense — our collective common sense along with our individual common sense — bringing it all into rehearsal, lugging it up onstage, on the public stage you could say, and doing the best we can with our limited means — including, I should have said, our imaginations. So, would anyone like to call out a political . . . situation, issue, problem? I'll do what I can with it. But I'm warning you. It won't be a one-man show."

As they begin calling ideas, he casually lifts the camera and turns it on them. In all Canada only he could do this in a way that causes no break in the flow or contact. Because he is not self-conscious with it, neither are they. Everyone is comfortable when he's onstage. They always have been. You feel safe in his presence. It is his gift. The first proposal from the audience is to improvise a political system. From scratch.

"From zero. Ooohhboy."

They chuckle.

"Well, I said I'd improvise an answer. I didn't say I'd act it out."

There is a groan of disappointment.

"But if I *were* going to act this one, I think I'd take the hackneyed old role of an alien from another planetary system, sent with others of the species to begin life anew on Earth. If that sounds like an ambitious improv for one person, don't worry. I personally have improvised the Battle of Montgomery's Tavern from our show, *Rebels Ride by Night*, about the Rebellion of 1837 in Toronto. Four full days of hysteria, misinformation, skirmishing, a few deaths by gunfire. I've also done, on my own, the invasion of Normandy, the Industrial Revolution, and the theory of relativity. I once created the inside of a quasar in the Goderich auction barn on a sunny Sunday afternoon, and what I'm doing now, as you've guessed, is stalling to let the improv take shape in my mind. Okay. A race of intelligent beings arrive on earth; they need a political system. Where do they start?"

"Voting," says someone.

"Probably," he says. "You can see the argument for it. Not everybody will agree on everything no matter how long you discuss some issues. In cases where you can't get agreement, you're going to have to decide — unless you're Quakers. That usually comes down to taking a vote."

"Elections," says a voice.

"Possibly," he answers, weighing it as if no one ever proposed such a thing before. "Each citizen can't participate in every zoning decision or choice of contractor to build roads and airports. Some people aren't interested. Some are better than others at it. It could make sense to choose representatives who'll make choices, as long as they're responsive to the people who choose them."

Someone yells, "Political parties."

"No fucking way."

Whoops, something happened. A new level of animation and passion from the candidate/performer, and he wasn't exactly on cruise control up to here. The audience slips into another gear as well. Nothing grips spectators like an actor who's lost interest in them and become absorbed in what he's doing onstage. He feels it, as he ploughs forward. His voice is crisper, more the candidate now, less the performer.

"I challenge you to give me a single, normal, logical, common-sense reason that would lead any human or extraterrestrial to invent political parties. You can imagine an entire system of government and politics without the idea of parties ever occurring to you. They're about as inevitable as lawyers. Does anyone have trouble imagining a society without lawyers? They're not like doctors, they're not like teachers. So where did they come from if they're so illogical? That's a different improv."

There's a ripple in the crowd, they'd like to see it: the improv on the first person who got the dumb idea to create political parties — or lawyers. He stills it with a move of his hand.

"I warned you this would be no one-person show. So now I want you to join me in another improv. Relax. No one has to come up here with me. I'm just going to ask you to think about something unusual and risk the consequences. It's a thought which generations of our ancestors found unthinkable. I want you to consider — just consider, merely in your heads, as a mental experiment — voting for somebody in this election who has no connection with a political party and doesn't want one. Does that make anyone tense? Light-headed? Try and stick with it a moment longer. Hold the thought, hold it, no permanent damage? Okay. Bravely done. Thank you. Next situation?"

A sea of hands rises.

"Jesus. I forgot how you get after a performance. You still do."
"Yeah."
"You're so hard on yourself."
"Did you think it was perfect?"
"More or less. Maybe some room to improve."

Fiercely: "Like what?"

"Nothing I can put my finger on."

"A little arrogant? A little pat? Condescending in that bit about the thought experiment?"

"Not so most people would notice."

"They always notice. Even when they don't notice, they notice."

"How did I forget? So what do you do next time?"

"I'm not sure."

"Isn't the director supposed to tell you?"

"Directors tell you what to change. They could say anything. Usually you feel so vulnerable you do it. But there's no way they can know the way you know. It's better without one."

"So what do you do when you don't know what to do?"

"Work on anything you can. A word. A phrase. A . . . pause. It improves by dribs."

"Christ. What a way to live."

For the first time during a Canadian election, none of the candidates were in the same studio for the national TV debate. Few were in studios at all. Their heads along with those of their questioners were superimposed on a map of the country locating each of them; at other moments they were laid over visuals of "real life" in that part of the country or of the subject under discussion: the remnants of the Atlantic fishery, say, or nuclear power. This was done through a new technique called Simule-Presence (with a significant Canadian component in its development), by which electronically assembled figures were positioned on-screen to respond to one another as though they were all present in a room.

It looked like a zodiac. They were drawn into place from nowhere, then pinned in temporary position while others zoomed in and out of view. They appeared to look around and nod as though they were at a cocktail party of the torsoless: the P.M., the leader of the Opposition, the other party leaders, national correspondents — they greeted each other by first names, nodding, chatting, spinning their heads on their necks full circle, glancing suddenly around or craning offscreen. Occasionally someone registered an unfamiliar face.

Till a curly, bearded young head with rimless glasses detached itself from the zodiac and floated toward centre-screen. Other heads glanced at it, then disregarded it and carried on with heads they knew. This face eyeballed the rest and appeared, by a deft flick of his gaze, to rearrange them around him as their centre, as if he were the sun and they the planets. He said nothing. "Excuse me," said the moderator of the segment on "Economic Growth or Planetary Deterioration." "Will you identify your party or the organization of questioners you represent?" There was no response, but the other heads began to revolve gracefully about his youthful face.

"By now," he said, "those of you in the control booth should realize you can't eliminate me from the screen or blank out my signal. My name is Hartley. I'm here to see certain concerns are addressed. I won't interfere unless there's a problem." His head slid to the circumference. The moderator's head floated back to centre and enlarged to the dominant size it previously was. Debate continued, heads drifted in and back, sometimes slipping from view, though Hartley never quite did. When another head scowled toward him, he nodded courteously. When several suddenly vanished with a pop, Hartley drawled, "It won't work so stop trying." He intervened twice during the segment, saying, "Would you go over that, please?" and, "I don't understand." During the next segment — on "Gender, Culture, and the Marketplace" — he seemed emboldened. "Just a moment please," he said, and a woman's face in dark glasses and a hat appeared beside his. She looked like the restaurant critics for large newspapers who allow photographs of themselves, but only in disguise, so they won't be recognized by restaurateurs and given special treatment when they're out on patrol. She made a short statement in a muffled voice, then vanished. One of the journalists tried to bring discussion back to where it had been. Hartley shook his head and said, "Sorry." The screen went soundless and the heads seemed to lose contact though they remained visible. When they addressed the issue the woman in the hat had raised, their contact was restored.

On the late news that night, the networks unleashed a new category of experts — airwave piracy and sabotage. The experts explained that technology behind the intrusion had long been available in general form, and examples of the takeover of local cable channels, for example, were more widespread than was generally known. "The authorities" had considered it wise to keep the information quiet in order not to encourage copycats, just as they did, say, regarding jumpers on the subway. But the experts agreed that nothing this daring had been attempted before. It would be like building a continental antimissile jamming umbrella in your basement shop. It had now been done and the real question was: why hadn't it happened before this? Hartley remained unidentified despite a search through international police connections. He was doubtless heavily made up. Possibly he didn't exist at all, he could be a hundred per cent electronic construct, like the recent experimental movie starring Humphrey Bogart and Julia Roberts. High-tech nationalists said they weren't surprised that the first prominent use of the technique happened here; Canada's genius has always been in communications — its size and underpopulation made that inevitable. The CPR, the CBC, the space arm, Innis and McLuhan — and now Hartley, whoever he was, whatever he was.

The best minds in communications technology began work on a blocking device. But no one believed they'd succeed until sometime after the election. In the meantime all future national TV debates and debate-substitutes were cancelled. Most parties, anticipating more incursions by Hartley, scrubbed some of their national media ads and altered others with his sensitivities in mind. Many local stations moved in with debates and coverage of their own to fill the void created on the national level. This added to a sense of chaos and giddy unfamiliarity which already suffused the election.

"What are you up to these days, Randy?"

"I edit a magazine."

"What's it about?"

"Local thing, it's called *Atlantic Canada Computes*. Myself, I still work on an old Kaypro, no one can believe it. But I know everything about the latest models. I hear you're running. Not looking for someone to voice ads, are you?"

Randy had his limits as an actor back when Matthew worked with him in the collective theatre, but he was always great in the bar after the show. That's because Randy did voices. Not just John Wayne, Jimmy Stewart, and Walter Brennan, where he'd started; Randy acquired Trudeau, Nixon, and Stanfield in the seventies; later he added Joe Clark and Mulroney, then he moved into media heavies. Walter Cronkite plus assorted Canadians. As the night grew long, his repertoire expanded. If you needed voices, get Randy. If you had Randy, find a way to use voices, because it was really all he could do.

The call to Randy was the fruit of something like a memory fragment. You pulled a memory fragment when a role called for a state of mind that didn't come easily. Actors varied in what came easily. Some had access to anger, others didn't. Matthew, for instance, had no problem with anger, not onstage anyway. What made him angriest was how he could get really angry only in character, instead of in his life, or his society. He had trouble, on the other hand, portraying states like joy and need. So to get to them, he'd pull a memory fragment. You learned to do it at theatre school. In this case he didn't need a state of mind; he needed a campaign gimmick.

Shaunavon, 1973. Working together on *Prairie Fire*, a show that eulogized the rise of co-ops among Saskatchewan wheat farmers in the 1920s. A drama of pure heroes and pure villains, complex or ambiguous figures need not apply: farmers versus bankers (railroads may be substituted). Each morning I pick up a *Leader Post* from the box in front of the Dominion Hotel, then join Angie, Dave, and Harold at the Kosy Korner Kafé. They eat the (enormous) wheat cake special and talk about their agents, I read the latest on Watergate and explain to them what it means. Hell, I lived in Berkeley for three weeks during the 1960s, I know the codes, I know who rules America, the hollow rhetoric of freedom behind which the ugly motives of U.S. imperialism hide.

"You mean it's not really the press uncovering this dirt on Nixon?" says Harold. "It's the corporate millionaires who decided to dump him so they can get out of Vietnam because they're losing the war and it's shaking their hold on American society?" Shaking their "hegemony," I mutter, but he's not really listening. Try eating with an actor. "So they leak it to reporters like Woodward and Bernstein to make it look like the free press in action?" he says. "Jesus, you're brilliant, Matty." He looks at me as if I'm still playing Bertrand Russell in *The Relativity Show* where he was Einstein and got the best line! "I don't care what they prove, Bertie, it's a hell of a good theory!" "You oughta have your own radio show," Harold goes on. "You should be there every morning with Gzowski to read the *Globe* and decipher it for the rest of us." The rest of us look at each other over the wheat cakes. What a great idea!

We jam with it through the rest of breakfast and all day on rehearsal breaks, then improvise it into what happens after supper. We drink some beer and walk upstairs to the Shaunavon radio station, where we know the night man, Jeff. He often joins us at the Dominion bar after sign-off. We tell him what we want. Just before eleven, he tells his listeners to tune in "The National" on CBC-TV but turn the sound down and keep their radios going. *We'll provide the sound.* We lip-synch to the politicians and journalists while their jowly faces mouth off soundlessly on the screen. We throw in sound effects where we can: a train wreck, a stock market crash — all of it laced with interpretation based on the analysis I developed in our breakfast sessions. Each new item, they look to me in a panic, deer in the headlights. If only we'd had Lloyd Robertson's script about two hours ahead. Too late we realize we could have phoned anywhere east of Manitoba and got the lineup because "The National" hits Ontario an hour earlier and the Maritimes two before that, two and a half in Newfoundland. There was another problem as well: those familiar faces and familiar voices. Leaders declaiming, reporters with their punchlines. "But is it too little and too late? This is me, CBC News, reporting." None of us do voices, not even a passable Trudeau. So we only tried it once. The station got no complaints, which made them edgy; they wondered if anyone even heard us, or followed instructions.

The campaign team — father and daughter — make their first strategic decision. They buy a slot on a university radio station. It's easier to do than arguing for their right to free time on a larger outlet even if they don't represent a party — and it's cheap. They take twenty-two minutes, the length of the nightly national news. Randy does the voices, men and women. In another strategic decision, they decide Matthew won't participate. It would be confusing. Matthew isn't running as an actor, he's running as the candidate who *was* an actor. That's confusing enough. They're comfortable with the choice. They start to feel like players.

The first show works, everyone agrees, so they book more, they ask people who liked what they heard to send money if they want it done again. They add music. The P.M. has just made a deal with business groups who've been fighting her over kids' dental care for the last two years. The press conference where they reconciled was like a sixties love-in. So Matthew unearths an album called *The Travelling Wilburys*, made by the war-horses of the 1960s: Bob Dylan, George Harrison, Roy Orbison — something you'd find on a pop culture dig. Their voices whinge with sour musical congratulations under the celebratory visuals that night which lead the national news. Next day Matthew's campaign organization gets its first query from the broadcast regulators, the ones he immolated himself before, that time in Ottawa. There's been a complaint.

They make another decision. They cancel further broadcasts. They won't bother defending the form they just created, its point has been made. Strangely, it doesn't die. Instead it becomes an instant tradition. It happens somewhere in Canada every night for the rest of the election. People drop by their nearest radio station to see if they can go on air simultaneously with the national news. Or they try to call it in: a voice, a jingle, a sound effect. Large numbers of Canadians are watching the news now with the sound muted and the radio going, or getting on the phone to improvise. If the station's line is busy, they call a friend and improvise together as they watch. Others gather at bars for the news or paid campaign broadcasts, they kill the sound and feed in the true meaning — as they see it — of what they're being told. It's like a party game, mutated charades. An election campaign in the video age without audio but radios and phones running while everyone joins in.

Lars watches, fascinated: it's the revenge of the audience, he thinks. He's seen public skepticism about the media rise, more or less in tandem with his own career as broadcasting genius. He's

44

been perplexed by the growing cult of Chomsky, the U.S. media critic who says the whole apparatus is an arm of thought control serving business interests. There are sharp, educated kids out there today who pay no attention to the news any more, they just wait for Chomsky's analysis. That endless documentary on the guy made by some Canadians years ago has been playing at Saturday midnight movies the way *Rocky Horror Picture Show* used to. Now these heretics have carried it farther; they've split one limb of media off from another and used each to cancel the other out. He loves it. He must have anticipated it, anything that clever has to be something he already thought of. This is the future, it's gotta be.

He watches everything about this peculiar campaign. As he does, it seems to him the event unfolds more and more around one figure: his friend the actor. This makes no sense: Matthew is just an unelectable independent running in a single riding, an interesting sidebar, there's no way he's the focus. Each day Lars gets his Matthew feed from the previous day's campaign meetings and tape. They start to feel like episodes in a series. They're built around an event — the election. But they're full of subplot and subtext — with the election, you could say, as pretext. They're not about it as much as they're around it. The viewers (who are also the voters) seem as intrigued by the secondary incident as by the main event. Does this *mean* something about the current phase? If Morris were naming the series, its title would be "Politics, Yes, Theatre, No." If Matthew did so, it would be called "Act! Don't act." Lars doesn't know what he'd call it. Maybe "An Actor's Story."

"When I was a beginner in theatre I spent three years in a company called The Revellers, based in Leeds, in the north of England. I was almost always the young man in the plays they did. You'd be amazed how many scripts have a young man. They're plays we don't hear about over here. They're not classics, they're stock, and they keep companies like The Revellers a normal part of life in Britain, where theatre isn't something special, the way it is here. At least it didn't used to be. People went to theatre there the way they watch TV or go shopping here. It was a generic activity, you just took in

45

whatever was on. Sometimes if there wasn't a young man in the script, I'd be the old coot. They're similar types.

"After my third season I went to visit Canadian friends in London. I was trying to decide whether to sign on for another tour, or move down there and try my luck. Those were the only options in my mind. My friends took me to a play by a company with an odd name, "7-84." I was told they chose it because 7 per cent of the world's population consumes 84 per cent of its resources. Wow. That's what it did to me: Wow.

"I felt like Erwin Piscator, a German director — I'd read his book — he was an actor before he went off to World War I. During his first battle, he was so terrified he couldn't climb out of the trench. His sergeant was furious. He asked what the hell Piscator did before the war to be so pathetic. Piscator said he was an actor — and saw a look of contempt spread across the sergeant's face. At that moment, Piscator said, he felt utter shame at the stupid thing he had been doing with his life. He swore if he survived and the war ever ended, he wouldn't be the same kind of actor again.

"All through that show in London I kept looking around at the audience and thinking, If people just knew that 7 per cent use up 84 per cent of the wealth, everything in the world would change. It would have to! How could it not? It would just be so . . . embarrassing. Life couldn't go on in the same old ways. I decided in that instant to stop doing the kind of theatre I'd been doing and come back to Canada.

"I flew home via New York on a cheap airline called Icelandic. They scarcely had seats. It took off from a meadow in Luxembourg. Halfway across they'd swoop over the Reykjavik airport and decide whether enough people were waiting to merit a stop. In New York I stayed with friends. One of them was in a production of a Greek tragedy called *Iphigenia in Aulis* at a theatre in Greenwich Village. She left me a ticket at the box office. The theatre was called Circle in the Square because the audience surrounded the stage and there was no real separation between them and the actors.

"I was almost late, the lights were going down, so I cut across the playing area to my seat in the first row. I just had time to apologize to a nice-looking older woman in the seat beside me as the lights went out. By older, I mean in her thirties. Sometime in the early scenes our fingers grazed each other, then I guess they sought each other again and laid side by side a while, gradually pressing slightly and responding to the pressure till we actually linked pinkies, then held hands. It was exciting as hell. We even gathered enough courage to whisper comments about the play in front of us.

"The show ran without an intermission or we'd have had to face each other in the bright light of the lobby. The climax — of the play — came when Iphigenia, played by my friend Marina, got laid down on an altar by her father, Agamemnon, king of Greece. He was going to sacrifice her for the sake of a victory over the Trojans. It was a horrible moment, truly horrible. But he was convinced her death at his hands was the only sure way for him and his people and, as you find in theatre, if the actors believe it, the audience will too, no matter what it is.

"As he raised his knife over her, I suddenly found myself standing and walking toward them. I must have let go the hand of the woman beside me or I'd have dragged her out there too. Maybe by then our hands were roaming over the rest of our bodies. Perhaps I was so full of excitement, it just propelled me out of my seat. I heard myself say, 'Excuse me, my lord, you don't have to do this. I know you think it's your fate and you have no choice. But fate doesn't exist. Neither do the gods. I can feel that you're desperate for a reason to avoid murdering your daughter — we all can — and because I come from a different time than your own, I can give it to you: it won't make any difference!' You could see the face of Agamemnon fade from his features and a New York actor take its place. Suddenly we were standing there, actor to actor. 'Of course this makes terrific theatre,' I said, 'but it's basically false and today we know it. I don't believe we can afford any more to do or say things just for the sake of powerful theatre.'

"Marina, still in character, swung her legs around on the altar to a sitting position, the way you do at the doctor's. She stepped down and moved gracefully to where I stood, still Iphigenia, but also to some degree my friend Marina. She put her hands out, took me by my upper arms, and guided me back to my seat. She seemed to have all day. I felt completely secure in her grasp and so did the rest of the audience. I smiled to the woman beside me as I sat back down.

"Then Marina turned to the audience and said very simply, 'We will now do the traditional version of the play's ending.'

"You could say I was ripe for some non-traditional acting."

Lars gave Tilley her first job. She was twenty, in the last year of an incoherent three-year course called Radio and Television Arts at Ryerson Polytechnic. RTA wasn't for serious reporters. They went into the journalism program, they were going to change the world, they modelled themselves on Woodward and Bernstein, their mission was to level judgement on power. Tilley's classmates had other dreams. They'd become, in their fondest fantasies, weathergirls and sportscasters for channel three up in Barrie. Close enough to catch the rock concerts in T.O., but cross-country skiing right out your door. Tilley liked them, the journalism program never occurred to her.

When she was at Lars's station for a week-long internship at Christmas, Lars sent her an E-mail. She'd never met him, but these things happened when you looked like she did. He told her to come to his office. Like all who entered there, she felt as if she was standing inside a TV set. He said he had two things to suggest. "What's the second?" she said. "You become an on-air entertainment reporter," he said. She said yes, she'd start tomorrow, there was no reason to complete her course. He said there was a condition. She rolled her eyes. "We're still on number two," he said. The condition was she had to change her first name to sound as Chinese as her last. Poon was good, Tilley was Newmarket. He proposed Ti. Ti Poon. He had no idea if it was a real Chinese name. She said she thought so, probably. Everybody would call her Ti, he said, on camera. Off camera she could be anyone; if her family thought of her as Tilley, it was okay with him. But on air she was part of Lars's downtown, urban, ethnic, multicultural and proud of it . . . concept. Then he told her his first idea. "You like hotel rooms?" he said. She said nothing. He slipped to his knees. "I'm begging you," he said.

A year later she was chief entertainment reporter and bored. Lars said her problem was she was too smart, he'd seen it happen.

"Too smart for what?" she said. "Maybe I should do politics, maybe I should anchor. Maybe I should have my own interview show. Or executive produce." Lars said he wouldn't offer her those. She wasn't too smart for her job. She was too smart for television. Three years later, the polling and consulting firm she created that evening after leaving her job at the station went public. She was the cover girl on two of the country's three business magazines. No one had hit that mark since Stronach and his auto parts empire in the 1980s. Four years later she was named chief adviser on trends and public opinion to the Liberals when they swept out the Reform-Bloc coalition of the late nineties. *Newsweek* (Canadian edition) called her "The Most Influential Private Citizen in Canada." Once a month she and Lars met for lunch in the power corner of the King Eddie. People who saw them there asked how they'd met. Lars described that first meeting. He included everything. "What did she say?" they'd ask. "I think," he'd answer, "she's weakening."

The clue Lars and Tilley seize on is this: the only topic about which they both grow animated when they discuss the election is Matthew. Toward everything else they feel distant, they test and discard hypotheses like old pinochle players dropping cards. But on Matthew and his video missives from the campaign trail, they burble, they generate theories, they don't want to stop. He talks so much about his experience as an actor in the country, so little about government and policies. It engages everyone they know. They're fascinated by the fascination of others, and they're hooked themselves. Yet what kind of candidate is he? One who seems to have only a loose, optional relationship to politics. Will anyone vote for him or are they just enjoying the show?

Tilley says it's a sign of exhaustion with politics, people like anyone who diverts them from a futile, discredited process. Usually they look outside politics for diversion, but here's someone who happened to slip inside the frame. Like watching basketball on the inset, while you watch the news on the large screen.

Lars says exhaustion has played itself out. People are tired of being exhausted. It's fatiguing. That's why societies always regenerate enthusiasm. It's less demanding than despair. True despair takes a discipline and commitment he's always admired but avoids. He thinks "people" have reached a shrewd conclusion: political action is fruitless, it never leads to serious change along the lines they yearn for. The yearning remains, but leads nowhere. Therefore you turn to someone running for office who actually talks about interesting things, like his life. We all have a life, we can all get interested in that. He says he thinks her theory converges with his, but his is broader, it includes both.

Tilley says Matthew is revealing the course of no ordinary life. He's a second- or third-order celebrity. What attracts others is their passion for information on the famous, people unlike themselves.

Lars doesn't buy it, he's working on his democratic impulse. What people respond to in Matthew, he says, isn't celebrity, but that he's at ease with them. They're at ease with him. If he showed up at your house one night, he wouldn't put on airs, including the pose of being no different from you — which he clearly is. But he'd be himself with you and you could be yourself with him. So he's both a real democrat and a real Canadian. To tell the truth, in the sweep of his enthusiasm for democracy, Lars can't see any difference between being democratic and being Canadian. In Matthew you get two for one. A celebrity who's a real person. Matthew after all is the Canadian anti-hero, it's a part he's been creating throughout his career. "That's very insightful," says Tilley. "Did he tell you that?" To Lars, personal jibes from others are as flies to the gods; he doesn't answer. He expands his point. An anti-hero is a real person. There are no more heroes. The heroes are us. Matthew is the famous person whose historic mission is to renounce Warhol's famous fifteen minutes of fame.

It's one of those conversations which McLuhan licensed back in the 1960s. If you call the ideas "probes," they don't have to be consistent or add up to a real viewpoint. As long as each thought is a morsel with some taste, you're happy and move on to the next. Tilley knows they've reached the point at which her presence, or anyone's, is nugatory. Lars is on his own, out there generating. He needs no partners for this part of the exercise. She can leave, which he might not notice. Or she can fight to recapture his attention. "Maybe," she says, "it's just that the man is so fucking smart."

"You really know how to hurt a guy," says Lars. He's back.

"Why is it," she says, "that on your station the women all look like models and the men all look like human beings?"

"Your problem," he says, "is you think every intelligent man has to be sexy."

"And your problem," she says, "is you think because you're smarter than anyone in your field, you're the smartest person in the world. Whereas you're merely the smartest person in television." She waves for the bill.

"We don't have a clue, do we?" he says, out in the hollow cold of King Street.

"It might clarify," she says, "if we keep watching. Who knows? Something might happen."

"Something always happens," he says. "Do you think we'll notice?"

Something happened.

Anka was known as the president's Canadian. That made him sound like a drink but, anyway, it was true. They'd met at a White House gala just after the inauguration. Anka had been introduced as the biggest Canadian steal next to the free-trade agreement of 1988. He sang "My Way" and then at the president's personal request, delivered by the Secret Service in advance, he sang "Canadian Sunset," which the president said he considered Anka's masterwork. Anka had to get the sheet music out of an archive, but he sang it like he'd written it himself. The two bonded. The only thing he and the president talked about, in their many chats, in person and by phone, was Canada. The president was obsessed with the place and nobody else in Washington was even curious. Sometimes he called Anka from foreign trips to talk about how great Canada would be if only it had decent management. Being in Moscow or Jakarta made him yearn for a foreign country that didn't feel peculiar even if it wasn't quite American. He didn't understand why the country still existed. Anka called it the 54/40 syndrome, showing more historical knowledge than most Canadians had, or would have credited Anka with. He considered it a potential presidential dysfunction, liable to erupt in embarrassing moments, like a version of Tourrette's.

Pattullo ran into Anka that weekend in the lounge at Atlantic City. Anka always came to the lounge after a show, officially to relax — really needing a fix of adulation. Management made sure a small crowd, usually retirees, were herded in from the casino to provide it. Pattullo was finishing off a boozy gambling weekend — or was it week? — with some mates from the D.C. press corps. He'd met Anka once before, when he was a callow TV interviewer co-hosting a Canada Day special for which they'd rounded up every fading American who'd once been Canadian, to coax the country to stay together. That was before Pattullo turned the career corner and practically invented the category of scathing video wit. The transformation in his career was instantaneous. People didn't just quote him, the way they quoted print pundits, they recognized him. Within months he was syndicated and everyone wanted to carry him. He had become, in a deft if familiar move, his own subject. The camera had swivelled to focus on him. It went on like that for years; there was no growth, there was too much success. Then he moved down to the U.S. to inflict his acerbic style on a global, i.e., American viewership. But despite the early enthusiasms of his New York agent, only Canadian stations continued to run his punny (his quip) commentaries. Four months after he arrived the agent's assistant began taking Pattullo's calls. Rumours began circulating in Canada about why he'd left, or didn't come back. Some people said he was there to dry out. Others said he was trying to recover his self-respect as a journalist. When he noticed Anka on the marquee, something in him wanted to connect. Pattullo felt he knew from Anka.

Anka sat on a big banquette near the rear of the lounge, beaming brainlessly. Only forty years ago, he'd come here to Atlantic City and the Steel Pier. That was decades before the gambling and casinos. Anka had pulled in the biggest one-week gross Freedomland ever reported. These retirees had probably been part of his original audience, their parents would have driven them over from Englewood and Tenafly. They asked how his career was going and told how besotted they'd been with him all their lives. Then they drifted back to the tables. Pattullo played his own game carefully.

You could call it "Hangback." He'd learned it when he was

young, when he was still a journalist, not a personality. Say nothing. Speak only if you have something impressive to contribute, and drop that so casually you barely notice it yourself. Then hang back some more. When he became a celebrity, he still hung back, but he was always surrounded, and he never stopped talking. When he started approaching people at parties instead of waiting to be approached, he knew he was in trouble. That's when he left.

Anka was already on his way over. "Canada," he said cheerily, pointing a finger like a gun.

"Actually, I introduced you one Canada Day in Ottawa."

That's how Pattullo learned, four and a half hours later, with Anka nearly hidden behind a tower of dinner and dessert dishes, what he needed to know in order to go home. First though, he'd had to relive Anka's sorrowful Canadian and American passage — the story of one life. He'd almost forgotten the experience: you sit for hours, sometimes all night, even for weeks if required, appearing to genuinely care about the tale the subject has to tell, getting them ready for the on-air. Maybe that's why he gave up interviewing and became a pundit: those unrecoverable hours of existence. Time you spent unpacking someone else's baggage instead of your own. You could say only one irrefutable thing about it: you got their story that way, and often there was no other. It worked with corrupt subcontractors, disillusioned agents of international spy agencies, and heads of state. So he heard how Anka by the early 1990s had grown to resent the sudden and surprising Canada fad in American culture. The flood of stories and snipes in the New York magazines about a Canadian conspiracy to take over American entertainment. Lorne Michaels and "Saturday Night Live," Martin Short, John Candy, back in history to Lorne Greene, Monty Hall, and Alex Trebek. Yet in all those litanies of Canadian invaders, Anka — he who preceded all others — never made the list! By then his fame was fading; he'd have gladly joined their entourage, though it meant being one among many. Something Canadian in him had stirred. It could have become his ticket to re-entry as a public figure. But the bastards always passed him by. Then came this new president and the White House invitation. He'd been told all the "real" Canadian invaders had refused, just because the incoming leader was seen as *outré* in Hollywood and New York as sub-Reagan, sub-Nixon, even sub-Quayle. Finally, when he'd spilled so much of the past, Anka unblocked the present. "I sometimes play a little game when I'm with him," Anka said. "No one knows I'm doing it but me. I try to get him to blurt out the word, before protocol can turn the conversation somewhere else." "What word?" asked Pattullo, working to not sound overanxious. "Annexation," said Anka, "Do you know Eric Lindros?"

Pattullo drove to Washington immediately, no time to sleep over or touch base in New York, the sun rising with a gritty glow. He read notes into his microcassette recorder, which he'd never used. He couldn't remember making preparatory notes for an assignment since J-school. Though he couldn't remember a lot since then, besides his speedy ascent. Somewhere he gave up research for the pickings from cocktail conversation.

When he got to Washington, he walked. He walked in the dawn and looked up at the Lincoln Memorial and the Washington Monument. He crossed the river and gazed at Jefferson. He felt as if he was in a movie he'd seen. *Mister Something Goes to Washington.* This was *Mister Pattullo Bids Farewell.* At last. He had a plan. It was no plan really, that was why they couldn't defence it. His secret was — he had no strategy. It works or it doesn't. You go in, you keep your head up, and you hope for luck. As . . .

The doors burst open and the worst seat at the farthest table in the enormous banquet hall turned out perfect. True, once the official party reached the head table they'd be obscured by a platform of cameras, soundboards, and reporters. But right now there they stood together, two leaders: one of whom Pattullo admired more than any person in the world and the other among those he most despised. Janya Jirapalin, the Thai strike leader who now wore the mantle of Mandela. Walesa with humility. Beside her, arm in arm, President Stutts, who made Reagan look contemplative. They strode by the table, right by him; they'd likely use this as their return route too.

He'd acquired this seat along with his press pass. You take the measure of a leader by sitting among the followers — not just meandering around as a privileged observer, in the manner of most journalists. So he sat through dinner, view obstructed, rather than in the press section down front, with its excellent view, free wine, and phone jacks. Now, dinner and speeches done, they left by these same doors. There'd be a press flurry in the lobby right after; no American leader would permit a foreign woman with democratic pretensions to dominate the Washington agenda for a whole evening. Anyway, they'd been testing these on-the-run press conferences recently — easily controlled but don't look as gutless as claiming not to hear questions while you scamper across the White House lawn and duck into a copter. Soon as something sticky hits, you head for cover, hustled along by aides. In other words, they'd discovered the Canadian-style scrum, Canada's unimpressive contribution to international political culture.

So while Janya Jirapalin signed autographs in the foyer just beyond the banquet hall for tickled Thai teenagers — probably kids of officials who'd kept her on the run and nearly assassinated her just eighteen months ago — the president chose to field what he chose to hear. Yet even in this manipulated setting, might the president also hear what he wanted to? Pattullo had planted the seeds. He'd cajoled every drinking buddy he had in the Capitol press corps; and called in all the favours he'd done American reporters who'd been assigned, always briefly, to a Canadian story. "Just ask about an *annex* to the trade agreement. Just use the word! Make sure he hears it, I don't care how. I'll owe you, it'll be worth it, I swear." It would happen fast, if at all. Then you'd have to react or the moment would be gone.

". . . an annex to the trade agreement, something directly bearing on human rights, Mr. President?" He didn't even know the reporter who said that. Was it sheer chance? Fate? Had he somehow insinuated this term into the air? Was it wish fulfilment? Is there a God?

No, said the president with aplomb. Economic relations with Asia are too important and delicate to throw in a rider on access. Absolutely not. No most-favoured nation. No annex on human rights. But was there a hesitation? The man liked that word. Something in him wanted to yes it. Now they'd passed to other issues. The chance had blown by, it was whistling out the revolving doors — and the president was breaking away . . .

"You won't *annex* Thailand. Why not, eh?" — barked Pattullo, in a tone so aggressive and aggrieved it quieted the others for a moment. What a hopeless transparent ploy. Is his desperation this deep? And where the hell did that "eh" come from?

"Annex Thailand?" said the president, picking it up in the strange momentary silence. "Ha! Thailand isn't Canada!"

OH MY GOD, HE SAID IT! But did I get it? Yes, the micro-recorder is running. And the cameras, they're on him. They must have it too. The president has been hustled off now, a perplexed aide casting a backward glance.

What did it? A grunt, not even a word really, a little term that's made everybody who ever travelled up there immediately associate it with our big little country. Why not . . . *eh*? Now, finally, he could go home because he had something to declare when they asked as he passed through customs: Yeah, I got something to declare, I was the one got it outa that bastard, his real intentions for us . . .

Since the campaign started Matthew had said things unlike any other candidate, usually in answer to questions. He felt serene, he wasn't planning to be elected anyway. He just wanted in. When his statements were replayed on television, he sometimes sounded like he'd been drugged — even to himself. He said that the current U.S. administration probably had a plan to absorb Canada, for instance. It made sense really, but when you said it aloud, it sat out there alone, unaccompanied by any backup. The press played it in the early weeks because they needed off-centre material and the guy had a recognition factor plus surface credibility — based on kids whose lives he'd saved (on TV, okay, but how many people know the difference any more?); he might help draw attention to their reports in that somnolent opening phase of an election before the public tunes in. In their fashion, once they'd given him a platform, they attacked: wasn't this a nostalgic replay of the free-trade election of 1988? Matthew stayed serene: a new situation had arisen under the new president, he said. It was worse than the days when we had that sycophant Mulroney as prime minister of Canada. Now it was like having Mulroney as president of the U.S. In order to tease out the theme and fill space, assignment editors told their Canadian correspondents to raise the issue in Washington, where the president's press secretary dismissed the charge. *Dismiss* may give too much weight to his response.

Then Pattullo sprang his story, backed by tape. He did it in three separate commentaries for three separate outlets: his weekly vitriol for the national TV news, his Friday wrap-up for the business channel and a virtual replay of that on the Sunday morning newsmags. Then he did it revised for one of the twenty-four-hour TV news services and a shortened version for the headline channel. He also put it in print, for good measure. In snide asides, he referred to Matthew's predictions early in the campaign: he said it proved even an ex-actor, like a stopped clock, is occasionally right. Other reporters, in coverage of his coverage, played up the Matthew connection, in order to underplay their rival, Pattullo. As a result, the president couldn't just weasel in his denials, as he would have had Pattullo's tape appeared without the groundwork laid by Matthew's doleful prophecies. Of course the president weaseled — but with difficulty. The story dominated coverage for a day and a half; after that it was contained; then it faded; then it vanished. But Matthew had become a voice with something to say, from outside the party framework. He was no longer just that actor running for office. He had anticipated political reality. An uneasiness seeped back into the national mood which had only begun to disperse following the G.G.'s gracious and reassuring election call.

Morris found the fervour about annexation peculiar. "Even my students are upset," he said. "And they can't spell Canadian nationalism."

"Maybe," said Matthew, "when you have almost nothing left, you cling desperately to every shred that remains. Or what's gone looks better than it did when it was still there."

"That makes sense," said Morris. "But after a country has given away so much, why not go the whole way? Get rid of what little remains: the separate government and the border crossings. Have it all done from the U.S. Why pay extra?"

"That makes sense too," said Matthew. "Maybe we just aren't there yet."

The discreet click of the remote, the low whir, the red light. Only there's a difference now. Other cameras are present, and crews, something is happening though no one knows what. Attention is being paid . . .

"Eventually I found myself back in a world where you had scripts. In a way I'd never left. Even when we improvised, in my mind the goal was to create something solid as a script. The point was to have strong drama: scripted, improvised, live, filmed. Then I started the series. That's when something changed. So long as you move from one show or medium to the next, you can keep telling yourself you just haven't got it right. But when you do *eight years* on the same premise, you start wondering if the problem is the whole idea of drama itself. Strange how it happened. You spend day after day on the set — it's incredibly routine. The set gets more familiar to you than your home. Now what I was there for was supposedly the show we were filming: it was all about my character, my through line, my arc, the other characters I interacted with, the plot, the subplot, the social issues we hammered. All that was the centre of what we did, the dramatic centre or, as I started to think of it, the fictive centre. We were there — this huge mass of people — to get that fictive centre on film. But the funny thing about the fictive centre is that it actually takes up very little of your time when you're on set. Mostly a central character like me just sits — a vast amount of waiting — while other things swirl around you — lights are hung and rehung, they retouch your makeup, the continuity person makes sure the coffee mug you're drinking from is showing the same face in the same direction with the handle to or away from you as it was in the last shot, the director and story editor are fidgeting with line changes and a flunkey hoping for her own big break is running out to get them copied for a scene later that day. You feel like a piece of furniture while all this goes on around you — yet it's also *fascinating*, this sidebar stuff. It's intricate and technical, and at the same time human and tense and emotional. Especially compared to the puny little chunk of mediocre drama they're all putting this incredible energy into getting in the can each day. I honestly believe there's more drama in the preparation, the rejigging, the workup — the undramatic framework I got to think of as the 'factual surround' — as opposed to me and the dreary little fictive centre I was part of. You start watching the pressures the crew is under, it's so compelling, how they interact, the power struggles between the director or cameraman or A.D.; even the tension happening between the cute kid who sets out the sandwiches and the guys eyeing her. And she knows it, too, so she plays with it, because like so many others on the set she too has her dreams. I suppose it's what happens in every office or workplace every day and on the subway for that matter, even if it's just a matter of the people on the car trying to avoid looking at each other. I mean the drama is out there in the world. What gets presented in any play or film or book is immeasurably thinner and less gripping than the least event happening just beyond it. The gardener turning on the sprinklers on the lawn just outside as I arrived here at the school for this meeting — he's infinitely more complicated than Hamlet. I see doubt in your faces but I've been there and I can tell you it's true. Hamlet is confined to a mere three or four hours, which is far more than most fictional characters get to unfold their complexity in. It's a miserly little structure, and there's not much you can explore about a human life within it. Shakespeare does more than most with those limited means, and he far outshines the competition. But even he is thin gruel — compared, as I say, to any of you out there. So I guess what happened as I sat all those seasons on the set growing less and less absorbed by the fictive centre of which I was, in fact, the centre; and more and more mesmerized by the factual surround — I guess I decided to stand up and step out of the centre into the surround, where so much more is going on and which I find so full. I have nothing against people who continue to work in theatre or film. But I've decided where I think the real drama is and I'm trying to get there. Here I am and here we all are together, and I'm asking for your vote to help me make that step."

Later, at Bluer, Matthew tells Dal what he'd thought of going on to say.

It was with his cousin Bram. He was six and Bram was seven. They were playing cowboys and Indians and their cousin Charlie, only four, took an arrow in the shoulder. It was a rough ride in the back of a wagon to get him to help but the wound was bad, so they brought him to the nearest hospital. "What's the name of the hospital we're going to?" Matthew asked Bram, as they loped through the sagebrush. "The Western Hospital," said Bram. Matthew erupted. "Just 'cause we're playing cowboys, you can't call it the Western Hospital," he screamed. He gushed tears. It was gone. Bram had wrecked everything they'd built with their collective imaginations through a long afternoon. It crashed in one idiotic literal choice. What a stupid, brutal end to their play.

"Do you understand why it was so horrible, why it's never left me?" Matthew asked Dal, six-year-old sadness spread across his face.

"I know how you felt," she says. "But why are you thinking about it now?"

"Bram and I were born at different hospitals," he says. "I was born at Toronto General. He was born at the General Hospital of Western Toronto — it doesn't exist any more — but everybody called it the Western Hospital. It was a perfectly okay name for him to choose, it had nothing to do with cowboys and Indians."

She creases her forehead and stirs her almond milk. "I think people play too much now," she says. "Too much movies in their lives. TV, music. What happened to the real world? Friends. Jobs that matter. They want to get it back. Like you do. That's why they're responding . . ."

He looks at her. He appears stricken. "You're very smart," he says. The thought seems to intimidate him.

"Relax," she says. "You can take some credit for it, you know. Anyway, you're still going to be an actor. There's no way you can shut that off. Even after you're elected." It's the first time either of them has uttered the thought. The vote is four days away.

That night Matthew dreams one of those dreams in which you know you're dreaming.

He's rehearsing a one-man show called *The Audience*. When the lights go up, what the audience see onstage will be Matthew in the role of the audience. They'll watch him watch a play taking place somewhere between them. Kristof, or someone Kristofesque, is directing from the distant reaches of an empty theatre. He's trying to infuriate Matthew into a decent performance. Matthew opens his mouth to release a stream of petulance but before he can speak Kristof is gone. Matthew knows this by a sense of absence in the seats. He relaxes and begins to enjoy rehearsal. He flexes all his abilities, he tumbles and sword fights and sings, his work is just fine and to his surprise he is also enjoying it, like a sculptor or painter or playwright who can step back from their work. In the dream he is aware that in waking life he often envies artists who are not themselves the art, as actors are. They get to stand back and be their own audience. That way no one else need ever come and judge them. He continues to innovate: each change he tries works brilliantly. He feels a fullness he has never felt in rehearsal; he wishes it went on endlessly. "Fruitful," he says each time he alters what he's been doing and finds a new and satisfying way.

Into the theatre (in the dream) walks a critic in a long cloak and a wide-brimmed hat that conceals his face. Matthew freezes in fear. The critic does not register Matthew. He looks crankily about the empty house and says, "I must be early." He sits and falls asleep.

The audience enter slowly but inevitably, as if emerging from Plato's cave. They inexorably fill the theatre. It feels like a painting of the final judgement. Matthew tries to find a seat in the theatre from which he can watch both stage and audience equally. This is something he does in waking life when he attends a performance; it's another part of the dream in which he is aware of himself as dreamer.

Before the play has even begun the members of the audience rise, pick their coats off their seats and stride from the auditorium. Matthew is horrified, he realizes he should have been onstage. Then they wouldn't have left. But at least the suspense is over, judgement has been rendered. He lingers in this feeling as in a bath. Just then the audience file back in, coats still over their arms. They only stepped out for a pre-show intermission, they've been in the lobby. Now they return. It's not over.

With them back in their places he feels he must mount the

stage and perform. But he can't make the move from his seat. If he could draw their attention to him, he suspects it would release him from this lethargy and propel him onstage, but he can't attract their notice. Instead they rise again, deliberately, and move onstage, where *they* perform.

As he wakes, he is thinking, Why is acting in a play like running in an election? He lies in bed drawing blanks, rolls over, falls asleep again, and knows the answer: because neither is real until the audience takes its turn. "The audience," he says aloud, "is the factual surround."

Things nobody knows:
  Why some things work in drama and others don't.
  How people make up their minds when they vote.

After the start of the recession of 1990 (which for many Canadians never ended), celebrity sports matches took over from Disease Dinners as the main form of charity fund-raising. Each cause voluntarily limited itself to one event per year. The hockey game for research into incurable illnesses, which had been sponsored by the G.G. for several years before his appointment, became the leading event in the genre. It was covered on a specialty channel in its first years, then graduated to coast-to-coast coverage on all networks. It became a national ritual, cathartic in its way. Maybe the country felt it was incurable. The G.G. insisted the game continue to be played in local community arenas as a reminder of the golden age of hockey, whenever that was. The year Matthew ran for office, it was scheduled for the very day before the country went to the polls, when campaigning was prohibited anyway. It seemed like a good omen.

The G.G. faced off with the popular minister of health who before that had headed a national women's campaign to save social programs. She had a following comparable in quality though not quantity to his own, but everyone knew she wasn't as shifty in the corners. National personalities vied to take part. The chairman of the Bank of Canada served as "equipment manager," since his previous athletic experience with the Bangladesh national rugger squad had taught him little about ice skating. By the middle of the third period, both sides were locked in a high-scoring tie, an outcome which would have satisfied every player except one. Was it an atavistic urge in the G.G. to be young again, or never old, or was it altruism, a desire to impart confidence and a sense we can still overcome, a selfless will to victory, to do more than survive in a perpetual tie, that surged in him as he snatched a loose puck outside his blue line, reversing the direction of motion, playing the transition game the Russians first taught us back in the 1970s when they shook Canada's sense of self by showing us our own game anew.

Quick as always — not on his skates but in some psychic ability to redirect attention and thus action — he shovelled the puck to the director of the National Arts Centre and headed up the wing. The Director took a few strides diagonally toward centre ice, then slid the puck back. The Ottawa correspondent of the *Washington Post* (who planned to become Canadian) slapped a pass back across ice to the G.G., just as he hit the blue line. No offside, signalled the independent member for the Eastern Arctic. The G.G. swerved — what memories in that sudden lateral redirection! — moving parallel to the blue line and just inside it, cradling the puck on his stick, his skate, then pivoting again down toward the end boards and eyeing the net. Just as he made this move, the former head of the campaign for a permanent constituent assembly brushed a hip under that cantilevered body, slightest of touches but it sufficed, given the exquisite cornering in which the G.G. was engaged, to upset him. In the old days — no way. He'd been like one of those plastic birds on the lip of drinking glasses you saw in novelty stores, they dipped and tipped but never slipped from their perch. This time, less a playmaker and more a statesman to his own surprise, his skates slid out from under his body; yet more a heart and less a body, while actually in the air, so it seemed to those who watched, even in replay, he shot as he fell, the puck lifted off the ice, sliding just inside the kicking skate of Canada's most controversial phone-in host. The noise was overwhelming even before the red light glowed, so that no one heard the soft hiss as the G.G. slid on his side toward the end boards, his own attention too absorbed by the trajectory of one of the most perfect goals of an immortal career; nor the crunch as his underleg met the boards and collapsed on impact.

By the time the cheering subsided from ecstatic to a low appreciation waiting for him to rise, while the sportscasters on national TV filled the moment with metaphors of Canadian self-sufficiency which may have been somewhere in his mind as he made those moves — by then he'd stopped shuddering. Gradually the shouting died. He was gone, not of the impact, but of cardiac arrest which resulted. Or perhaps, as the doctors explained for days afterward, it could have happened had he been sitting at the opening of parliament or investing new members in the Order of Canada. With this kind of thing, with a man of his age, as the old guys say in the sauna when talk turns to mortality, "Yuh never know."

The country went to the polls next day with dread. The results were chaotic.

So after a lifetime of saying politics has to be more than voting, of saying politics is exactly not *what happens on election night — here I am watching TV ("With .001 per cent of the riding reported so far . . .") as if it's the only thing public life is about. The hardest line in the part to say is . . . Just say the line, Matthew — Yes, I care. Okay. I said it . . .*

When we got The Last Messiah *to preview state, Kristof cancelled. "This one isn't ready for an audience, people," he said. "We'll keep rehearsing till opening night, don't worry, we'll get there." I was sitting in the back of the hall, waiting for my cue. I entered down through the audience. Actually it was the foyer of an ex-church that we'd converted into a theatre. Which was appropriate for the characters in that play because, though the world press dismissed us as a cult, we knew we possessed the only true religion, and I was the saviour himself. In a gorgeous silk robe with purple sash — found somewhere on Queen Street and smartened up. It was grim. The show wasn't working. I couldn't have felt less messianic. I slumped in a puffy chair that the Ladies' Auxiliary must have donated — oh God, that's why I'm thinking of this now: it's exactly the way I'm slumped here in front of the TV watching the results. Up the stairs to the glass front doors of the church came a couple of theatregoers.*

They must've missed the announcement about the previews; it was
too late to get it in the papers, it had only been on radio. They
looked at the notice on the door, gazed over at me, shrivelled within
my glorious gown — despondency in a wing chair. They shook their
heads sadly and marched away. I shuffled to the door and watched
them go. I glanced down at the sign. "The Last Messiah," it said,
"has been cancelled" . . .

It's simple human nature, that's all. You get caught by plot. It's
not that you believe it's important or meaningful, it's just the drama
of it. It's instinctive — we make dramas of whatever we live, then get
trapped inside them. Like Chomsky says about language, whatever
he says. Structural linguistics/structual. . . theatrics. Now it looks
good, now it looks dire. Now I can't even bear to look. Hooked on vot-
ing, at my age . . .

So it's like the election of '93, two old parties obliterated, others
born. Except no one will be strong enough to govern.

I know it doesn't matter, it's not how change comes about. It's the
drama that's impossible to detach from. Now I'm closing the gap. I
was afraid of this. Concentrate on that incoherent national picture.
More bad news. I win. I'm a winner. Winner of what . . .

They're on the phone. They ask how I'll vote. Will you support
the prime minister? Or will you support Mr. Potatohead? Who gives
a fuck? You find yourself trying to answer. You've auditioned for the
part, fought for it, got it, now you have to play it. You hear the sound
of your voice. It's the voice of a liar, you can tell, even though you're
not lying. "You're a politician, son," said Redford's dad in that film.

"Did you ever think you got so deep into politics to make up for not
having much of a family?" says Dal, next morning. They're at Bluer.
They're going to prove this doesn't have to change everything in
their life, starting with breakfast. "Either when you were a kid yourself or after you left us?" She tries to take it back. "I mean, after we
weren't all together any more."

"If that was true, it would make a mockery of everything I've
done."

"Sorry about that. But answer the question."

"I think about it all the time."

"Me too."

"About whether I try to replace family by politics?"

"No. About whether I do. Even if it's a different kind of politics. Whether everyone does. Whether that's what politics is."

"Sometimes it seems so blatant," he says. "Nobody could miss it. I substitute the working class, or the country, or the human race — "

"Try the whole planet," she says.

"Just to feel part of something, in the absence of a family to go home to. Or call in to." He says this across the pages of confusing election results. "And what about all the collectives I worked in. You don't really need Sigmund fucking Freud to theorize about what I was looking for. It's embarrassing. If I had a family, somewhere I connected to, maybe I'd never have gotten so angry at the way things are. Maybe I wouldn't have wanted to change them. Maybe none of it."

She nods. "Me too, maybe."

"It would be a bottomless embarrassment if it was true. What else can you say?"

"You could say two things," she says. This he wants to hear. "You could say it's lucky for the country you're fucked up that way, because we'd all be poorer without what it's led you to do. And if you ever find a family, you better not lose that stuff completely." She of course is the family he's found.

"What's the other thing?" he says.

"Even if it's true," she says, "take it easy. You never *looked* like you were doing it because you were fucked up. You put on a good show." He adopts the hurt look. She doesn't buy it. "You trying to tell me that for you appearances don't matter?" she says.

What if the best part is past? What if elections, which I've always despised as shallow and at most minimally democratic, are as good as it gets? At least they pay attention to people out there while a campaign is on. They have to. For a few weeks, they can't ignore them, even if they're treated as mere voters and far less than citizens. But once the people have voted? Politics retreats and resumes its course. The pros take over. Do I want to be part of that?

Redford asked, "Now what?" His campaign manager said, "Don't ask me." What they both left out is: "And the fun is over!"

CHAPTER THREE

The actor must come on the stage not in order to feel or experience emotions, but in order to act . . . An actor must not simply stand upon the stage, but act.
— *Eugene Vakhtangov*

"You know, Matthew, this could be the beginning of a beautiful friendship," says the P.M. Still P.M. after the bizarre results of the oddest national election in Canadian history.

Does she know she's quoting Bogart? Is that why she pronounced his name *à la français*, *Mathieu*? They are strolling by the canal, it's dark enough that no one from any distance will recognize them. Or if they were spotted, people might say, "Probably shooting a public service ad: the politician and the actor, pretending to have a conversation about the importance of literacy, or wilderness preservation, or children with AIDS in Africa. Must be a camera around somewhere."

"What I don't understand," she says, "is if you're a good enough actor, why you couldn't become anything, just by playing the part."

"A hockey player?"

"Of course not. That takes genuine skill. But politics? Why couldn't you play the part, say, of a great leader?"

"You'd still need a script."

"There are speechwriters. You find them stacked up in the closets when you're in power. Also advisers. Experts from the universities. Civil servants. They write you more scripts than you'll ever

67

need. You choose the ones you're going to do anyway, don't you. You sit around the pool and toss away scripts until one comes along and it feels right."

"In Canada?"

"Anyway you don't need the actual words, do you? Just some general advice, some ideas to react to?"

"Like improv," he says.

"Pardon?" she says.

"You could improvise it, I suppose," he says. "But then you'd need the given circumstances. Did you ever go to Second City back in the eighties?"

"They used to have the Improvisational Olympics. In Montreal they had Le Coupe Stanley d'Improvisation. Is that the same? The audience throws out ideas or situations and the actors make up something based on it."

"That's it," he says. "But what happens when you have to solve a real situation? Whether to send out peacekeepers. Or call them back. Whether to sign a treaty."

"Your job is to stall," she says.

"What?"

"I'm giving you circumstances. The circumstances given any political leader most of the time in office is you try to do as little as possible. So whatever decision you're faced with, your task is to stall. Could you do that? Could you do it creatively, and not look like you were stalling?"

"Probably," he says. "But then what?"

She shrugs. "You go into your office and talk about what to do, with whoever you trust. That's when you get your next set of lines. Or circumstances."

"So when I'm back in the office, the prime minister's office, I can drop out of character? I don't have to be a convincing leader then? So I'm just a kind of sham leader. I'm an actor pretending to be a leader. Like in one of those movies where they substitute an actor for Churchill or the crown prince or somebody? So really, my role would be playing an actor who's acting the part of a leader."

"I'm not sure that would work," she says. "Everyone wants to believe. Could you continue playing the leader when you're back out of the public eye, so you're playing the part for your staff as well?"

"And where do I stop? In the limo? What about the chauffeur? What about when I get home to my family? If I still had one. What if I live alone? When I get in the house and shut the door, do I drop out of character then? Or do I keep it up in case I'm being bugged by the CIA or somebody but when I pass the mirror am I allowed to wink?"

"I don't know," she says. "Does anybody? I mean, when you're alone, don't you keep playing your part?"

"What part?"

"Whatever part you are. The person you play all the time. Isn't that what everyone does? Play themselves all the time. I feel I've been playing myself all my life."

Coming toward them a jogger goes by. "On your left," says a cyclist, and passes from behind. Her helmet looks like a bobsled. Someone some day will design a bicycle helmet that doesn't humiliate its wearers. Matthew's head hurts. He knows exactly what she means. He once loved these conversations about acting. They went on endlessly, circling round themselves, snaking through some little hole and shooting off again in another direction. Discussions on acting didn't exhaust all possible creative thought, but he never found another focus that drew together so many meaty ideas. When he was in grade ten and worked on the stage crew, he went to a cast party after the opening night of Arthur Miller's *The Crucible*. Lorne Holden sat on a sectional in somebody's parents' living room, radiating his success as John Proctor. Matthew asked Lorne why he'd want to work so hard at being somebody else; Matthew said he was finding it hard just being himself. He couldn't recall Lorne's answer, maybe Lorne didn't even try, but the question stuck with Matthew for years, even as he submerged deeper in the profession, neglected his courses in university, dropped out and went to theatre school instead. It was like the scratching pole your cat returns to, it was what your life had been about for such a long time.

"My nightmare," he tells her, "has always been taking a part I can't stop playing."

"You mean the most awful thing you can picture happening to you?"

"I mean my nightmare when I'm asleep in bed. My lifelong recurring dream. Like people who try to run away from something and their legs won't work. Or you go to the corner to mail a letter and your hand gets eaten in the mailbox. I haven't had it in a long time."

She looks at him. His face is blank, as if for a moment he's not playing a role. Not even himself. As if he's suddenly wearing a mask which corresponds more to his self than any role he could ever take on. The self as substratum and that's all, on which roles are mere overlay. Very peculiar, then it's gone. "I'm sorry," she says. "I should listen better. Maybe it's because I'm thinking about changing roles myself now. The normal rule for a politician is: when you're out of government you listen to people because you need them to vote you in. When you're in, you stop listening, and then they vote you out and put the people who are listening, in."

He laughs. "Once in Dublin," he says, "during the festival, I was in a bar near the theatre after our show. I was flavour of the week there. Dublin adored me in that part. I caught the eye of a red-head — it was a horseshoe bar, the kind people go to when they're looking for someone to connect with across the way instead of staring into a mirror behind the bottles searching for themselves. She looked back across the bar at me and I felt like I'd just been given the circumstances of a stud at le Coupe Stanley d'Improvisation. I slipped into the part as if I was born a stallion."

She laughs.

"I really *did*," he says, sounding hurt. "I really was."

"I believe it," she says. "That's why I laughed."

"I can't believe how cool I was. I played it perfectly. She wanted me desperately. I think she loved me."

"And in the morning?"

"There was no morning. This was all in the bar. I went to the bathroom before we made our exit for her apartment or my hotel. I looked in the mirror and I thought, So when does this part end? What happens when I undress? What happens when I get an erection? What happens inside her? It's not that I didn't think I could pull it off. Maybe I could've. But there was a lot of stress."

"You didn't want to act a part, you wanted to be yourself."

70

He shrugs. He doesn't know. These are the questions that always get asked. Everything always gets asked when you talk about acting.

"There's another problem," he says. "Acting is acting. It doesn't make sense if you don't know that's what it is."

She doesn't see the problem. "If it's good acting," she says, "who knows the difference? Who cares? Better a good actor leading your country than a bad politician."

He shakes his head. He's stubborn on this point. "It's like the difference between wrestling and boxing," he says. "Wrestling is acting. Very good acting often, in my opinion. The pain is acted, even though it sometimes hurts. It can hurt to pretend to have your head slammed straight down into a mat. But boxing really hurts, even if it often doesn't look like it does."

"How does anyone know the difference," she says, "when they're just looking on?"

"I don't know," he says. "It's just because it's acting. There's a difference between acted and real."

"What if people can't tell the difference?"

"I don't think it's acting if they can't tell the difference. When you see an actor acting a boxer, it's different from a boxer. If the actor went into the ring to play a boxer, at a real boxing match, he'd just be a boxer, a bad one, who would have made a better actor." Now his head really aches. He's back in it, round and through, under and back, the questions, the questions.

"Did you ever see *The Candidate*?" she says. He's grateful she's willing to shift ground. You can always use help getting out of it. "With Redford and Peter Boyle?" she adds. Something in his manner says he has. Or she just knows. You pick up clues about a person. You spend most of your life honing your knowledge of what the clues mean. Then it's a matter of learning to trust them. It can save a lot of conversation. "It really is like that," she says. "Where they say, after they win: 'What do we do now?' And they have no idea."

He wasn't expecting this conversation. When her office called to say she wanted to talk to him, he assumed she wanted to talk about *something*. He didn't think she just wanted to *talk*.

"How did you get into this?" he asks.

"Ronald Reagan," she says, with a warm glow. "He meant a lot to me."

Whoops.

It wasn't the parts that got me down — each dumber than the last — as I moved into higher, or higher-paying, regions. Not the endless repetition of roles either, as I achieved success, in the terms everyone else recognized. Even though it was like coming down a wide highway that keeps merging lanes, till you're not an actor any more, merely a star. People don't come to see the characters you play. They come to see you play those characters, you're like a model going up and down the runway with a change of clothes for each trip. It wasn't really the series either, finally compacting it all into one earnest hunk so lovable he got renewed each year like the seasons. Hugged and thanked by people I didn't know for doing the worst work of my life.

"Love your show."

"Thanks. (Wish I did.)"

I could justify that. I was fighting to say something before a mass audience, to have an impact, really influence my society. The stakes were higher, so of course the fight would be harder than it was in theatre. There would be compromises. I could live with them, not a problem. It was just . . . really . . . Reagan. Making me ashamed of what I did. The way Piscator was shamed by his sergeant for admitting he was an actor. Not merely embarrassed. Embarrassment goes with acting. What a thing to do with a life. Dress up and pretend to be somebody you aren't, yearning desperately for people you don't know to smack their hands together like seals and adore you. Acting equals embarrassment. We must like the humiliation or we wouldn't do it.

But he tarnished it. Even after he was gone, it never returned.

So I quit my series, Roland quit his. Together we'd retrieve the honour of the craft. We'd revive the Canadian Voyageurs, the legendary troupe Roland's dad launched when he came out here in the 1950s from Ireland, obsessed with painting the colours of theatre on a cultural canvas whose blankness thrilled him. I listened to his stories of those days. Acting Richard III to the trappers of Moose Factory. It never sounded to me like he was wrong to try; it just hadn't worked. If something had been different, maybe it would've. And if something else, maybe Reagan wouldn't have been president and Canada wouldn't have got free trade and gone down the road it did — if something. But it did and they didn't, and Roland and me — we never got the company untracked again. Maybe we were like those guys who quit the priesthood. They all said they left to preserve their faith, not because they lost it. They needed to get out because it was the church that was unfaithful. Then once they were out, the faith went too, usually fast.

Maybe I was just sick of acting and didn't have the guts to know it. The more I did and the better I did — the worse it felt. Maybe I wanted to do — not just make images of doing. Tugging back the curtain that conceals reality, year after year, holding up that mirror to it got so heavy. Then you pictured Reagan, not acting — acting! Was that it?

She asks if he minds talking about these things. He says he likes it. She asks why. He says he likes it because it's sheer speculation, it's in the arena of imagination, it involves no responsibility. He won't ever have to be a leader. Or act the part. It's like an improv you'll never perform, one you only do in your mind. As he speaks, she says nothing. Maybe she doesn't understand, maybe she understands but doesn't agree; it doesn't matter, she listens. A problem solver all her life, she seems to know the function of friends is not to solve problems. He might take her hand, or arm, or pat her shoulder or rub her back, she might do it too, if it wasn't so damn cold. If this wasn't Canada. And it isn't even winter yet. Some time they'll talk about her and Reagan.

"So what do we do now?" says Lars.

"Now," says Tilley Poon, flexing her fingers like a bookie or a *shmatte* manufacturer, "now we massage the numbers."

It's a phrase Tilley learned from the accountant she hired the first year she made enough money to need one. He poured her figures into his computer and told her how much "it looks like" she owed the government. She gasped. "What do we do

73

now?" she said. "Now," he said, cracking his knuckles, "we massage the numbers."

Due to the new system of quasi-proportional representation under Canada's revived constitution, Matthew held the potential balance of power in the Parliament of Canada. He didn't hold it by his own vote as the representative for his riding, but because of the surprising number of votes he received across the country from people who followed his campaign over Lars's station and its satellites and who wrote his name in. (Write-ins weren't just legal under the new system; they were encouraged.) Each riding in Canada continued to elect a representative; but besides that the total number of votes received nationally by each party now entitled it to an additional batch of seats which together totalled half the votes in the new Parliament. By this reckoning Matthew's party held seven seats.

"Except I'm not a party," says Matthew. "I don't even believe in parties. I hate them. I think they're idiotic. I said to people that if you were going to start from scratch to make a political system, you might have a Parliament, you might have elections and even representatives. But it would never occur to you to have parties! You left that in, didn't you?"

"Practically every show. It was one of the best points you made. People thought: that's just what *I* always thought about parties, only I never realized it till he said it. You empowered them! That's why they voted for you."

"They were expressing their revulsion at the party system by writing my name in. There is no party to accept those seats."

"Wrong," says Lars. "I gave you one."

"Again please?"

"I registered you as a party."

Matthew is speechless. He sputters.

"I had to give it a name," says Lars, sounding abashed for the first time in Matthew's experience. It would be the first time in anyone else's experience too, if anyone beside the two of them were there. "The name I gave it is the ACT party. ACT as in active, action, actor."

"Does it stand for something?" says Matthew, stunned but curious. "I mean the letters."

Lars shrugs. "It could be Association of Canadians to . . . something."

"You told me you didn't believe I'd get elected," says Matthew. "You agreed it was an exercise in consciousness-raising, mine and theirs. The whole purpose was to use the campaign to discuss issues." Lars fiddles with a dial on his desktop. The lighting in the room changes in some way Matthew couldn't define even if he was paying attention. "But it doesn't have any members, does it? It doesn't have a list!" Lars looks at one of his wall screens as if he's never seen it before. "So we'll just have to tell them it was a mistake," continues Matthew. "They can distribute the seats among the other parties. I mean among the parties."

"That's not how it works," says Lars. "I checked into this. For your sake. I talked to . . . people. They're people who have constitutional savvy along with an innovative mentality. Grounded groundbreakers, you could call them." He's regaining confidence. You can tell by the volume and pace. But it's still a hollow confidence.

"Who?" says Matthew. "I want to know who now thinks they're pulling my strings."

"There is a loophole. Nobody ever thought this might happen, so it wasn't covered. It's possible to submit your list after the election. Maybe it seemed democratic to somebody on the drafting commission. So long as you've declared you have a party beforehand."

"I can't give back my seats?" seethes Matthew.

"No, damn it, you can seize them as a democratic gift that comes to you from fucking democratic heaven. You don't have a choice! Or maybe you wanta drop out of the whole process and go back to whatever you used to do which you left because you wanted to be a player in this game — excuse me for somehow getting the idea!"

Not fair. Suddenly Matthew is in the backspace at Four Walls. Imagination is a sadist. It could have dropped him anywhere, on any experimental stage of any alternate theatre. But none can match the grimness in Matthew's memory of 4WT. The backspace experience at 4WT is Dantean for actors and audience. Nobody is comfortable, no one can hear, the wind in winter whips through the cracks in the mortar and stings the faithful as they huddle inside. He hasn't played that space for over twenty years, close to thirty, but when he pictures a serious return to theatre — or should that be a return to serious theatre? — he's always there, hapless and irredeemable. Nowhere else.

He is playing Man in the Coven Company's production of its show on sex stereotyping, funded by the provincial women's directorate in its high militant phase, and sponsored by public sector unions with mainly female memberships. Every other character in the show has a name, sometimes a first name, sometimes a full one. But everyone else in the show is a woman. Only Matthew plays a man, therefore he is Man. Man as boss, man as fore*man*, man the harasser and exploiter. Offensive by virtue of stupidity or malevolent genius. It's not the largest number of parts he's done in a single show, but altogether it's the most relentless. There's no hint in any of the figures he hauls onstage, scene after scene, to relieve the villainy. The audiences in the dingy backspace, usually papered by unions or feminist groups or the local NDP (R.I.P.), have been egged on, like the spectators at talk shows. Maybe that was the condition of their comps. They hiss and shudder but most of all laugh. At him. Matthew has built the part to that end. It seemed less soul-destroying to be laughed at than hated and reviled. It gives the women in the audience confidence, he told Agatha, Coven Company founder and director. It's more empowering than anger and gall. Still, for him (Him), it's been devastating.

Occasionally he'll glance out at the audience while he cowers beneath their ridicule. Squinting against the lights, he'll think he sees an expression, on no more than a single face, of sympathy. No, not sympathy, that would be too consoling. But perplexity. Joining in the laughter, yet something else too. Doubt, or just a question: Might I, a woman sitting among sisters, have something in common with that oaf on stage, and if so what is it, and why am I laughing so hard if that's true? Maybe he just imagines the look, an illusion forged from need and humiliation. The production has been on national tour, to great success in booking terms, and acclaim from the (mostly "political") people who came to it. But whenever he finds his thoughts coerced back to that show, it's playing in the backspace at Four Walls Theatre.

Lars must have hit a control during Matthew's gruesome flashback. Maybe the whole room is wired into Lars's central nervous system. Maybe the global information superhighway is. "Do me a favour and look," Lars says. "That's all I ask." On a wall screen positioned within both their views flashes a sequence of names, descriptions, clips, profiles, and audiovisual issue packages of the type Lars's underlings pioneered during the elections of the early nineties. The flypast includes video-bios of prominent figures from the women's movement, environmentalism, labour, anti-poverty groups, the arts, and the participatory democracy movement.

"Every one of them is available," says Lars.

"Are you on it?" says Matthew.

"No," says Lars proudly.

"No thanks," says Matthew.

"You'll make your own list? That's fine. But you know you'll end up with the same look."

"It's an elite."

"You're kidding. These are the faces, the voices, of every popular, populist, anti-elite force in this society."

"It's the non-elite elite."

"So where will you get your members?"

"I'll pull their names out of a box. You can televise the draw if you want but they won't be revealed till those chosen have accepted."

Lars starts to worry. This has the sound of something horrible but possible. "Where will you get them?" he says anxiously.

Matthew shrugs. "The phone book? I dunno. You just stuck me with this set of givens. Where the hell do they get those people's panels for election night on the networks?"

"They do heavy research. The polling and survey teams do it. It's not easy coming up with genuine ordinary. You can't pull responsible decision makers out of a hat full of nobodies who just

77

happen to be citizens. It's never been done. It won't work. They won't buy it. And all right, yes, it would be great TV! But you cannot justify it."

The wall screen fades to a grid. Matthew looks oddly at ease. He props his chin on his hand and rubs his lower lip. He is in improv mode. This is the pose he struck when an audience or director threw out the circumstances for a scene. In this mode he is the intellectual equal of others when they are in court, in the lab, or in the showroom trying to close a sale. Everyone gets smart when they're doing what they do, or talking about it. "Ever hear of the jury system?" he says.

"Hello, Matthew?"

"Matthew? Matthew! I mean — Alex! You're back!"

This is what always happens when Alex calls. It's the damnedest thing, Matthew always calls Alex "Matthew" when he hears his voice after a long absence. He's asked clinical psychologists and literary historians about it. They say they've never heard such a thing. It could become a syndrome with its own name, if they could find another case.

Alex assumes he'll be invited to move in with Matthew for . . . the duration. Yes, he knows Matthew is now here in Ottawa much of the time as a member of Parliament and even the head of a little party ("I think of it as a parliamentary collective," says Matthew tightly). The apartment he's rented has two bedrooms and since Matthew also has the office on the Hill he only needs one of them. Alex says that sounds fine, he too has things to do in the capital. He's back in Canada to recuperate and spread the word about whatever hellish Third World bloodletting he's just returned from. This time it's Indonesia, or part of what used to be Indonesia. He'll be debriefed by the condominium of NGOs that sent him there. He'll explain what basics — sewage, drinking water, shelter, a little schooling — he managed to restore in the midst of the butchery. He's the world's top and only "battlefield civil engineer," his coinage. He doesn't go in afterward to see what can be salvaged; he says you have to save the "signs of humanity" from obliteration *during* war, or you lose them for generations, possibly forever. Those

78

who've watched him operate in civil wars and battle zones call it miraculous. They use the word so routinely for Alex that it sounds like they're talking about the weather. Matthew pictures it as the way experienced trippers can canoe onto a campsite during a thunderstorm, set up a tent with a big fire and dry woodpile nearby, cook a gourmet dinner and sleep comfortably till next day. He knows it can be done, in fact he's done it. "I wish I could get you on my list," he sighs. "Why the hell can't you?" barks Alex into the phone. "And what the hell is your list?"

Their routine resumes, as it has every few years since the mid-1980s, when Alex returned from the siege of Kabul looking like a wraith. He came to see Matthew — who was playing Alex in the show a British playwright crafted from Alex's letters to his older sister and her children in Montreal. It had already succeeded modestly, first in London, then off-Broadway; finally it came to Canada. When the show ended, Alex swept backstage and after a cursory introduction drew Matthew into intense discussion, pretty technical, of the choices he'd made as an actor. Then Alex switched to his own critique of the script, which he found "very insightful — at moments, not at all at others — but what the hell." It was the verve! That may be why Matthew always cries out his own name when he hears Alex's voice after years apart. It is a call to an enthusiasm for engagement which he wishes he could perpetually summon in himself.

Alex stays in bed each morning till almost noon. Then he goes into the kitchen, drinks very black coffee and smokes the strongest French cigarettes Matthew has ever smelled. There he also reads the papers or the stack of magazines Matthew himself never gets through. (Matthew's main role as subscriber is to trim the pile when new issues of the magazines still perched there unread, arrive.) Alex can do it all — coffee, smokes, papers, magazines — till late in the day, sometimes early evening.

Eventually he'll go out, with or without a reason, and by late that night he'll find himself at a jazz club, where he'll drink Johnny Walker Black (for nostalgia's sake — it was the drink of choice of the old PLO, among whom he also worked: what a disaster, they wound up with nothing, shut right out of the arrangement that briefly settled over the Mideast five years ago. He'll befriend the waiters and bartenders. He'll occasionally meet a woman, or a lonely travelling businessman who recognizes Alex from some newsmag or TV item, and who'll become a lifelong friend for the next few hours.

Mostly what Alex and Matthew do is talk, just as they did that night when he came backstage. Alex can talk about anything: baseball, mystery novels, jazz — but his specialty is international affairs. If you leave him alone, he'll just keep going. Yet it's all astute and informative. If you throw in a comment or argument, he's easy. He'll grasp your point and respond. If you continue to argue, he's happy. If you lapse back into silence, he'll carry on brilliantly, as before. He is the most congenial conversationalist Matthew ever knew. There should be a special channel devoted to him on the in-flight audio programs, alongside light classics and comedy. Strangely, he's never met up with Matthew's friend, Morris. They're the two people Matthew knows who are most devoted to building a better world yet he senses something incompatible in how they view the process. He wonders if he's deliberately kept them apart.

"I ran because I wanted to get involved in politics, not government."

Monday will be six weeks since the election, four since Alex arrived in Ottawa. The situation has changed again. There is still no government. The prime minister has failed to create a coalition. She announced three weeks ago that she'd continue in office only until a new government was formed. She wished all contenders luck. The many leaders of the Opposition pulled back warily. They knew her, they were certain she'd baited a trap. Then she'd resurface in the afterwash of their inevitable failure. When one of them could bear caution no longer, he lunged for the prize but missed. Then another. Then all. Several combinations have come close but stalled. Matthew has been approached to ally with one bunch or another, or give support in return for something he wants: a piece of legislation, a minor cabinet post, culture perhaps. He's said he won't do it and has been supported by his . . . the members of his . . . party. But the pressure grows. The longer he lingers, the more they offer.

"Then let this cup pass from you."

Alex is the most inherently dramatic conversation partner Matthew has ever known, excluding actual actors. When he and Alex are out together with other actors over, say, a meal, it's hard to tell the difference between Alex and the actors. Everybody performs.

"I don't know enough to be part of a government. Not yet."

"Nobody knows enough," says Alex. "Not ever."

"That can't be true."

"To tell you what's true," says Alex, "nobody knows anything."

"About what?"

"About anything."

"*You* know things!"

"Like what?"

"Wartime social reconstruction. You told me you know more than anybody in the world."

"And I'm a walking catalogue of ignorance on the subject. Imagine the rest of them. I approximate. I improvise. I do what I can but I know what I don't know. Who do I think I am — Socrates?"

Can it be? The intimidating feature of Alex's pronouncements is that they sound like what Matthew would say, if he had the nerve to trust his gut.

Consider an actor's research.

Consider Matthew's celebrated performance as Frederick the Great during his series' final year, when he decided to spend his time off working in theatre again and wound up, to his surprise, at Stratford.

For that show, he refused to set a foot on stage, not even in the rehearsal hall, till his "research" was done. He thinks of it now as "research," in quotes. By the time he finished — a robust five weeks — he'd learned about as much as a competent undergraduate would know in order to write a term essay along with four hundred others in modern European history. Definitely more than a high school kid, even in an enriched class at a good school like Dal attended. Every few days he went to the reference library and signed out a few more books. Gradually his net widened beyond biography, to related biographies, general histories of the time, then treatments of contemporary themes: science in the mid-eighteenth century, the rise of Bach at the Prussian court, the influence of Voltaire. Morris gave him titles on nascent industrialization and the birth of the working class. *Then* Matthew stepped into the role, bright with confidence. He knew his man. Did that little payload of information help him play the role to the acclaim he received? For sure. *How* did it help? There's no way to know.

When the key moment in the play came each night — Frederick decides to carve up Poland in collusion with Russia and Austria — Matthew called to mind only one association: his decision to leave Dal and her mother. He played that decision and it alone in his "transcendent" moment on the festival stage (as the critic who came all the way from the *Independent* in Britain wrote). He relived that wrenching, entirely autobiographical experience each time the script arrived at its climax. Would he have played it differently if he hadn't spent five weeks tunnelling through a small mountain range of historical and sociological background? Would it have emerged exactly the same had he not even known in which century Frederick wrought his mighty works? Who the hell knew? Who knows anything?

Or take the case of Kelly in the cannery. Matthew directed that show. He also played the anarcho-syndicalist ringleader. The revolutionary fugitives, in the aftermath of the Haymarket riot, gather in secrecy by night, at a cannery owned by a sympathetic capitalist. The night shift stand watch while the radicals on the run analyse their situation. The dialogue is fierce and dialectical. Their rhetoric soars above the mundane tasks of the plant. In the background, the workers toil. That was the point of the scene — and the play too. The workers, always background, even in their own political movement, while their "leaders" natter. Their stolid, disciplined behaviour, which has underwritten and outlasted every left-wing leadership or philosophy — as it must, for only the steadfastness of the working class assures victory among the vicissitudes of movements inevitably commandeered by well-meaning but unreliable left-wing petit bourgeois intellectuals — blahblahblahblah.

The whole scene depended on Kelly since she played the work force in toto. But she had a problem, you couldn't miss it. She was immobile and unexpressive. "What the hell are you doing?" yelled Matthew. "You look like you're on strike. Do some canning."

She blurted that she knew nothing about canning and needed guidance. Nobody in the cast had ever been in a cannery, much less worked in one, or even a factory for that matter, though Ernie Hartt once had a summer job at a dry-cleaning plant till he fainted, and later was a bicycle courier. "Okay," said Kelly, "I'll take the rest of the day and research canning at the library." Matthew said no way, opening night was coming, they'd just got the basis of the scene worked out that morning. There was no research time; she'd have to find it in herself. She could play steadfastness, she could play hope for the future. Do *something* with conviction and the audience will buy it. Their argument escalated. Kelly was not a fiery person but she was obstinate. He said she was gutless, she was just stalling because she was afraid. "Afraid of what?" she asked. "That you'll look like an idiot," he said. "It's about fear. Do you think you can avoid fear — fear of the audience, fear of yourself — in the stacks at the library." Whenever he recalled those words in his later life, he shuddered. That's what all his own "research" into Frederick the Great had been. A way to get yourself onstage opening night for the absurd task of impersonating an eighteenth-century European auto-crat in front of a bourgeois North American audience.

Kelly, sensing weakness, had stood firm. Finally he simply called for the top of the scene. She went to the rear of the set and began, as they unfurled their passions and theories downstage, to enact, without props, something. It was riveting. It kidnapped the scene and annihilated the other actors. Whatever she was doing, she was absorbed, and it didn't look like *not* canning. When it ended, Matthew asked what she'd mimed.

"I was putting the lawn chairs and patio furniture from around our cottage in the utility shed for the winter," she said. "Then I locked it up."

Nobody knows anything. And it doesn't matter. This can be empowering. "Shit," you think. "Then I wouldn't be worse than any-body else." All right, he'd play the game. Within limits.

The process of forming a government over the next month was like casting in public, except there was no script to read the hopefuls from, and no director to make the choices. *The aspirants were auditioning each other.* Imagine a casting call like that. It happened more or less in view. This was demanded by the democratizing mood which took hold years earlier, during the referendum on the Charlottetown Accord.

Each morning the potential members of a coalition came to the National Arts Centre. The cameras covered them as they arrived. They spread out for interviews, then reconstituted as a bloc and went inside, like kids on a bus tour of the capital. All day they bargained. No one was clear which part in the new government they were testing for or what that government would look like.

Matthew once felt he'd escaped this process forever by becoming the star of the longest running TV series in his country's history. No need to ever again expose himself while they lolled in their seats judging you, striving to persuade them you were right for a part that, if you got it, you'd then spend weeks or months trying to comprehend — in other words, for which you were clueless even though you'd convinced others you were perfect. It was so *Platonic*. (According to Morris, Plato thought people already knew everything, but had forgotten, so nobody ever had new ideas, they just recalled old ones.) There was one comfort for Matthew: even if he was cast at the end of the process, it would be minor, supporting, maybe a character role. He wasn't up for the leads.

They took lunch and coffee breaks, during which they were swarmed by reporters and cameras. It lasted a week, then two, then three. At first Matthew practised avoidance. He no-commented, or drifted through with disdainful generalities. "My hostility is showing," he said to Alex over some murky coffee. "Why don't you say so?" asked Alex. Next morning, day one of week eight since the election, a reporter asked why he was reluctant to do interviews. "I feel I have an unfair advantage," he said. "I've spent so much time before cameras in my life."

"Maybe you're just bored," said the reporter.

"Maybe you are too," said Matthew. "You're on camera as much as I used to be." It led the news. Maybe everybody was bored. From that moment, people began to mention him for prime minister. It was absurd, he said to Alex. Alex shrugged. "Everything is absurd." He didn't look up.

It would have been different, everyone knew, if the G.G. were alive. His steadying presence, captain of the national team — it would have led to something definitive by now. His temporary replacement, the chief justice of the Supreme Court, was a good choice, people agreed, since no one would think of comparing her to him. She was a model suburban matron, with a lightning career trajectory. Canadians liked suburban matrons in public posts: think of our tradition of radio and TV interviewers. Yet it was hard not to yearn for something else — the return of a national father figure. If not as Governor General this time, then how about as P.M. And who had been the whole country's family doctor?

This is a political actor's fantasy. You gather a select, rambunctious group of the most informed people you know, then point them at a crisis. The crisis is the national impasse and Matthew's role in it. The players are Morris the Marxist, Alex the global handyman, Canada's almost immediate past prime minister, and Matthew, member of Parliament, centre of the storm.

She's there first. "It's bizarre," he says. She asks what. "We had that long rambly totally theoretical chat along the canal about what it would be like to play the role of the country's leader. Now we're actually taking it seriously." She looks back in mild surprise — or is it disenchantment? "You mean," he says, "you thought it might happen?"

"It's a long way," he says to Morris who arrives next. "From what?" says Morris. "From 'the cultural part of our evening,'" says Matthew, "which is where you people usually slotted me." He'd always felt honoured to do a scene or set piece at rallies and teach-ins. Provide a little relief from the genuine politics. "Condescending shits that we were," says Morris. Alex bursts from the kitchen. The discussion starts with no intro, nothing to ease them in. The way Jerry says to a total stranger on a park bench, "I've been to the zoo," in Albee's first play. It's like a meeting of the four winds at maximum gale. If we get nothing else, thinks Matthew, we'll have a first draft in the theatre of ideas.

The almost-former P.M. sees no problem. She is firm and contemptuous. We *are* discussing politics, aren't we? she sneers. We aren't talking about revolution, ideal societies, or personal salvation. We have an elected Parliament. One leads, all the rest sit on their hands which they raise when they're told to. If any of you ever sat around doing what you're told by some mediocrity in control of your party, you might not feel so stressed by this tough decision. So what is it? Do you feel like you can't touch anything that involves real power? Is that unmanly if you're a sensitive guy? She stops as if she's decided not to add something: *You're pathetic*, maybe.

Morris has rarely faced, person to person, a true wielder of power in the bourgeois mould. Not since the suit in the hotel, probably. In person is different from in theory. You find action easy, he counters, since your acts have few consequences. That's because you're just a politician. He talks quickly, lest she spew her contempt on his phrases before they're out of his mouth. Whether it's you in office or someone else, he goes on, the effects on people's lives are minimal. The forces that affect us are beyond politics altogether these days: secretive corporate headquarters, money markets, international banks. The only serious impacts your decisions have are on your own career. There was a time when I thought it might be possible to work inside conventional politics for some kind of structural reform that would make deeper transformations possible. But I watched those like Mandela who went that route and I saw them fail. Better to stay outside and hold up the banner of a truly different future, sometime, whenever. Who knows — capitalism might crumble as quickly as socialism did. Then we'll be ready. But stepping across the line into the world of ordinary power is fateful and I don't know any way to make the move and control it rather than be controlled by it.

"Perhaps you haven't noticed," says the P.M. — her voice is essence of disdain — "but our friend has stepped. He *is* an M.P."

Alex has been flicking his gaze back and forth between them. There's something frenetic in the look, as though he's on a loop without enough time to make transitions. It's rare for him to go this long without speaking. In fact, it's rare for him not to dominate a conversation. Perhaps he's stuck equidistant from the standpoints of Morris and the P.M. and doesn't know which to attack first, like the donkey who starved midway between haystacks. The withering quality of the P.M.'s last line opens a space.

He tells her to can the lectures on the real world when what she means is cobbling together enough sycophants to shoehorn herself into the leadership of a party composed by her own definition of dolts; or navigate a piece of legislation through Parliament that will be so compromised by loopholes it's unlikely to accomplish any of its purposes even if the motive remains visible at the end. "Flog me with your contempt after you've tried to restore garbage disposal in the middle of ethnic cleansing," he tells her. "Better still, figure out where the real 'real world' is."

"Exactly!" interjects Morris. "But equally, practice without a guiding theory inevitably degenerates into mindless eclecticism." There is a dull pause. What the hell is he talking about? Then:

"I might be willing to die for your fucking revolution," screams Alex at Morris, "but don't expect me to sit around listening to your fucking rhetoric." He has leapt onto Matthew's coffee table, his hand is raised above his head. Everyone looks up at his clenched fist, symbol of a bygone (and, think both Morris and Matthew, never to come again) time. Alex looks too. "Maybe it's time to retire that line," he says, hopping down. The battle shifts to him and Morris. They flay each other with accusations over the failure of the national liberation movements, once so full of promise in both their eyes. Was it absence of theory — or surplus? The P.M. now withdraws; she looks on. She's never heard such nonsense. Matthew too lays back. He likes his two friends so much, he's learned from them and tried to emulate them. He never thought they'd agree on all the basics — but this . . . polarity? He feels like that donkey himself. Does going ahead mean he's on his own?

"It wouldn't be the first time," says Morris on his way out, clearly winded. "The parliamentary system sometimes gets balanced on a knife edge. Whoever has the weight — no matter how little — to tip it one way or the other acquires power. It's kind of inevitable. It happened on one of the Caribbean islands, Dominica, I think. A hotel owner was prime minister two or three times — just because he didn't belong to either of the parties that sawed off in seats. They had no choice really."

"Are you telling me now I should do it?"

"If I wanted you to do it, I'd say, 'Don't do it.' You know how these things work. I don't know what you should do. I haven't exactly been right about everything in politics for the last thirty years."

"I don't want to be prime minister. I realized it while you were screaming at each other."

"End of discussion then. We could have turned on the hockey game."

"I just can't see myself leading the country, so forget it."

"I already did."

"I simply don't believe I could do it."

"I'm convinced. But what," says Morris stepping out the door, "about *The Last Messiah*?"

The Last Messiah was a bloated fake from San Francisco who led his many followers off the end of a theological cliff, then off a real one. Hundreds plunged onto the rocks of the Pacific shore, serene. The play based on him was about charisma, leadership, and fraud. It was heavy political theatre in the late twentieth century. Kristof asked Matthew to read for the part, he looked, the script was juicy. "Could I play the messiah's chief organizer instead of the saviour?" Matthew asked. "The guy they called his prophet. I don't think I could really believe I was a messiah, but I can see myself proclaiming him, bolstering him when he gets low, explaining his moods to his disciples." Kristof said forget it, he already had the henchman; he needed a messiah. Matthew said okay, he'd read, for the hell of it. He thought there would be just the two of them.

Instead Kristof had a full entourage of followers. There was an investment banker who folded his business to go and serve at his master's feet; there was a Vegas gambler who came full of doubt and even fuller of need. A skeptical journalist who demanded proof, and the only proofs that counted were miracles. A dazed hooker. An architect, a diplomat . . .

"What the hell are they here for?" asked Matthew. "I thought *I* was auditioning."

"They are here to believe in you," said Kristof with his usual cunning. Matthew stepped onstage in what he pictured doubtfully as messianic mode, script in his left hand like a sceptre, but before he'd said a line they were crying out, "Lord, we adore you . . . Lord, we need you . . . Lord, grant our prayer." When he spoke they gazed back as if he was the archangel Gabriel. He heard himself sound authoritative, serenely confident, he felt his presence swell. God damn, when everyone onstage treats you as their saviour — if you don't start feeling it. At that moment he caught Kristof's eye, surely this would break the spell. Kristof leapt into the scene, put his arm round Matthew's neck and drew him upstage, as he did when he wanted to make you feel special. "All right," Matthew said "so if they treat me as the messiah, maybe I start to feel like I am. But what about the audience?"

"I'm not concerned about how *you* feel," said Kristof, copping an advantage with a confusing answer. "I know once I get you there, you will get yourself to the part." Matthew never knew if these statements, delivered with such fervour, were the distillation of deep self-knowledge or just whatever occurred to Kristof on the spot, delivered like the wisdom of ages. "How many people at a hockey game do you think can see the puck?" Kristof shouted this so even the actors loitering on the apron could hear it; Matthew had no idea what he was talking about. "How many people watching television can see the puck?" Kristof bellowed again. "Maybe none. They know where it is only by the actions and movements of the players on the ice. They *divine* the existence of a puck, they know it's there because everyone behaves as if it is. They *believe* in the puck. I have seen experiments conducted, never mind where, it was behind the Iron Curtain but I can't tell you more than that, in which carefully coached teams performed an entire period of hockey *with no puck*! And the spectators never knew!"

"But what about the puck?" yelled Matthew. "Did the puck believe it existed?"

"Ha!" answered Kristof, clapping him hard on the back and redirecting their stroll to centre stage. "A game of hockey is not a work of art. Places! From the messianic entrance — everyone, let's see what we can discover here . . ."

"I believed you were the Last Messiah," says Morris, stepping back inside the door and removing his strange winter hat: false fur yet real leather. Radical politics has gone completely to hell. "Everyone in the audience the night I was there believed it. The critics believed. It was one of your greatest triumphs."

"Hi."
    "Hi, Dad."
    "You in the middle of working on a study or something?"
    "A post-doc application to LSE. I'm okay to talk."
    "There's this suggestion about — hem, haw, sigh — prime minister. Me being."
    "I saw it on TV."
    "It would be everything I've ever said I don't believe in about politics. Going right back to the collective theatre."
    She pauses, then, "Tell me about the collective theatre."

Nothing *in theatre brought out egomania like the collective process. Those collective creations were sheer artistic Darwinism. Survival of the fittest lines and most aggressive actors. A fight to the finish inside the collective, tempered once in a while not by socialist comradeship but by the thrill of discovering our country.*

It drew on the most competitive feelings I ever had. I hated anyone who might outshine me — even in rehearsal. Unless you felt that way, you'd have vanished by the time the piece made it to the stage. The rest of them would have disappeared you underneath their own improvs. You'd have moved somewhere pastoral like the film business. Fierce isn't even the word. No one had lines as you do with a script. You couldn't wait for your cue, then make the most of it. You had to cue yourself. If you didn't pry open a moment and jump in, the play would be over and you'd have had less focus than the backdrop, the rare times there was one. My first show, days before opening, I had no scenes of my own. I was hauling lines like the water boy for everybody else in their *scenes. I threw up, I didn't sleep; in a panic, I*

90

manufactured a desperate little moment — and made them support me! I clung to it like proof I existed, then as the show ran, I began to build it like I was a ragpicker, gathering and inserting details. I saw hatred in their eyes. I'd become a player. Collective my ass.

Before the next show, André, who'd been in more collectives than anyone, took me to a bar and gave me advice. "Monologues!" he whispered, like the family friend who said "Plastics!" to Dustin Hoffman in The Graduate. *Monologues keep you onstage, he said, with total focus; they're theft-proof and hard (though not impossible) to upstage. Monologues — I realized as I brooded later — could practically destroy the competition, which was fine, because I didn't like head-to-head combat. André never did them himself. He'd come from the States as a deserter during the Vietnam years and had competition in his veins. He came up here to lose it, maybe that's why he gave the tip to me, to unload it. It worked. Monologues in theatre were like monopoly in the economy. It was like skipping the frenzy phase of* laissez-faire *and going straight from paternalistic feudalism to the cool control of monopoly capital. I loved it.*

We were doing a show about economics. I went to rehearsal next day after my chat with André and spun a monologue in which I was money. Money as a character. Did it work? Does it rain in Vancouver? I could be anything to anyone. I was historical and contemporary. I started life modestly. Helping folks exchange potatoes for grass skirts or something. But like all great tales of success, I went from strength to strength without noticing the decay of my soul. I became a sinister force that fed war and catastrophe. Things happened too quickly, it filled my head, I became overbearing. I fell like Satan, who once was beautiful. But I recalled my origins and was plagued by regret. And no matter what else you called me, I was creative. I felt I'd ascended to improv heaven.

That monologue kept expanding. I lifted lines from Marx's Grundrisse *and* The Merchant of Venice. *The next step was inevitable. Everyone was miffed and I didn't really need them anyway and neither did the play. In its next incarnation, for a university tour,* The Ec Show *become a one-man piece called* Money. *After that came the other one-man shows, which were really all just long monologues. They took me to Broadway, the West End, the Kennedy Center, the*

Edinburgh Festival, on to TV in highly gimmicked-up versions of the same basic me-centred scripts. Those improvised collective creations where I began wound up as complete, detailed scripts, nothing improvised and nothing collective.

"Do you regret," she says, "doing any of those shows even though they amounted to a repudiation of the ideals you thought you had in the theatre?"

"No," he says. "They were the best work of my life."

"Hmh," she says over the phone.

"Whadda you mean, 'Hmh'?" he says. "And would you consider staying here instead of going to LSE, wherever it is, if I take the part?"

First you go to the acting G.G. She greets you like a Jewish mother, which she is. Before you can say "Dorie," she gets you in a body hug, the one she attacks everybody with, even in official situations. It's a grip that draws her so close she can see right around the huggee and scan the room for others she has reason to accost, er, embrace. "Eat something, sweetie," she tells you, "then we'll get formal."

She's been the model of a Jewish mother since she was a teenager, working at a summer camp for the arts on the shore of Georgian Bay where you first met her. She seems to have met everyone in Canada who could be of value to her as she clambered up the ladder of her ambition. First as a lawyer, ripe with feminist concern apt to that first phase of the movement, though never too militant. A Tory yet a Liberal too, or just liberal, lowercase, being so Jewish, so concerned about the unloved and minorities. Onward to family court, where many able women languished in those years, then a surprising sideways step to the commission on rail transport, demonstrating an unfeminine sense of the harsh world of costs and layoffs. More judging appointments, plus kids and grandkids, faithful wife to shrink husband, you lost track, but you were always hugged when you met, as she craned to see who and what was beyond. Finally the Supreme Court, and then, chief justice. Surely the climb would end there.

Yes and no. She accepted the call to replace the late G.G., but only on a temporary leave from the court. She'd learned how to have it all. Besides, who else could have replaced him, even for the moment. Nobody, that's who.

You have an impulse to decline the hug, as a way to define your new persona: the nation's leader. But hell, rule one of serious political struggle: no bullshit confrontations. Remember Nelson, the retired smelter worker in Kitimat. He taught you how to play these scenes. "So sweetie," she burbles, "what's doing!"

You pause before answering. Like Gretzky holding the puck. Holding and holding. He taught you how to play them too. It won't rattle her, but it registers. She takes the point. It's not a matter of winning something, just establishing your game. "I'm at your service," he says, "your Excellency."

"Please sit," she says, abiding by the rules he introduced. "Have you succeeded in the task I invited you to perform?"

"I believe I have," you say.

Next, the press.

Step onstage at the auditorium in the national press club. Unpreceded. No entourage, no media adviser, no need for protection here, playing the loner card as only Trudeau did in the past. Don't go straight across to the podium. Stop instead as you appear at the edge, grab focus though it looks like you're just orienting, a man gathering himself who's about to begin a mission. It's a matter of stillness, that's all, make them come, it usually works, it does now. They're fascinated, no one has ever started a press conference, or a government, this way. It won't be reported, that's not the point. Just establishing something again. Presence. Intensity. Walk slowly to the podium, then step *around it*, as if avoiding a hazard. By not using it, you draw attention to it: that which would have blocked and hampered your relationship with them, though they hadn't noticed it was there. Hiding in plain sight. Lean on it with an elbow, transforming it from symbolic pomp to casual personal prop — all the more symbolic. "Yes?" you say.

They wait. You nod, acknowledging the courtesy. "I have just informed the acting Governor General that I've succeeded in forming a government as she invited me to do." Totally unnecessary. They know. The country knows. But it's nice, after these tortuous years in Canadian politics, to tell people something they already knew and which triggers no release of tension. You're at ease. Not a surprise, you always figured this wouldn't be the hard part: playing the role. Your next trick will be to relieve them of feeling too impressed. At the first question — "Can you tell us how your meeting with the Governor General went?" — you move in front of the podium (a cheaper trick, but not every move can dazzle) and tell them more of what they already know.

Finally, Stan. You came down here to Toronto to pack up the house. It was against their advice. National leaders have others to collect the dry cleaning and fold their underwear. Others could deal with the house. They insisted on sending staff, who are staying at a hotel. Since you haven't been sworn in yet, you made the case for staying at home alone. Security are . . . nearby. You promised to keep them informed as you did what you came for: see old friends, buy some books. As if Ottawa was a hazardous Third World posting you're about to depart for. Mostly because of Stan though.

You're only down for one night. You slip out about nine-thirty. Stroll over to the light and cross Bathurst. Stan's bright store beckons, a small lineup at the cash as usual. You walk past, don't want to disrupt or play a special part. You've lived here so long, they've all seen you before. They're discreet, Canadian, if they treated you with polite distance when you were a TV star, why change when you're about to be prime minister? Down along the shelves, always stocked with something new. Videos, fresh pasta, talking books. Stan pays attention to his customers. To the fridges at the back, rummage around among the yogurts. Then, over the shelves, coming from the cash at the front, floats his voice, low and hoarse but audible: "Gonna miss ya, Matt."

It's a gusher of emotion, for Stan. The longest exchange the two of you ever had was maybe three minutes when the Leafs became respectable again in the early nineties. He does good, that's all, he doesn't talk it. Gives the neighbours credit, put in a pay phone so people won't have to use the one outside in the winter cold, tells single mums and dads not to bother buying milk if their kid was already in and got some that day. You line up, pay, praise the new stock, though no banter about the book he makes in the back room: the only sign between you that things have changed. This is why you came. The contact. The great danger in the current phase is: you'll lose contact.

It works. Or as Kristof used to say before an opening, if he deigned to bless you: "Ladies and gentlemen, it flies. It creaks and moans but the thing rises off the ground and lumbers through the air. One can make out what it was meant to be."

Only one thing about this part irks him: it's not the role he has spent his life developing. Which role is that? The Canadian anti-hero. Others have called Matthew the Canadian Henry Fonda, the Canadian Alan Bates, even the Canadian Montand. A wide range of incongruous comparisons, none of which ring true, because there is no comparison. The Canadian anti-hero expresses a unique experience. He was born from the diffidence and deference of life under three successive empires, each with a mighty cultural component: France, Britain, and America. Especially the last, which came with maximum proximity: Matthew and his *concitoyens* live a national life abutting, as the real estate agents say — not just neighbouring but abutting — the mightiest cultural force in history. Abutting as in: actually an independent structure but without separation. No other modern people has lived in this state. When he moved from theatre to film, Matthew realized the Canadian anti-hero was the character he'd been striving for, one version after another. Nobody else in theatre had been aware this figure existed, but they came to know it: as the Canadian colonel who furiously, futilely sent his soldiers to die at Dieppe because Churchill and Mountbatten ordained it; as McLaughlin who built a Canadian car in Oshawa one hundred years ago, then sold it to General Motors, so that no one now even recalls its existence; as Naismith from Canada, who invented basketball and then the Americans took it over. Surely that is the character he ought to draw on at this moment in which he has finally mounted the (other) stage. Instead, he feels he's accepted a different role. Did he find something else in himself to play, or has he mistaken the part?

95

They're walking again beside the canal. "You did it," she says.

"I've been here in lots of scripts," he says. "It feels like it's ending where it ought to begin. Just at the point everyone else feels is a conclusion, as the curtain falls, credits roll, whatever, is where I often get really curious about what happens next. How will the characters behave once they've reached the place they were aiming at? Will they be able to get along, now that they have something to do together?"

CHAPTER FOUR

The struggle between the stage and dentistry still raged in the breast of young Talma.

— From a biography of Talma, the French actor (1763–1826)

The first meeting of the new government discussed the paintings on the wall. The members of cabinet didn't know each other well, if at all. None had been ministers though many had served in Parliament. They were the flotsam of the old Canadian party system, they'd never fitted comfortably into its disciplinary folds, voting as they were told; in the past, people like them would have soured and left electoral politics after a term or two; instead, as the traditional parties disintegrated or transformed into unrecognizable, often contradictory states, they surfaced in one configuration, then another, or as independents. Not one had been in the cabinet room till now.

First they discussed their trouble finding it and congratulated themselves on getting there; they marvelled that it was here, just off the P.M.'s office where you wouldn't have thought there was space for anything; it was like a secret chamber, like the wall hanging you can lean against in Toronto's Casa Loma, and suddenly it gives way to a hidden staircase. A number had been in Casa Loma, they thought it was ridiculous, just the kind of stupid thing you find in Toronto. This brought them together. Then they turned to the paintings — turned literally — in their chairs.

Muttonchops mostly. The founders of Canada and its subsequent leaders glowered down. Was it inspiring to have them watch

97

as you governed? Did it hurt? Would it affect debate? That was
something you could discuss. Were they avoiding the issue? What
was the issue? The future? Saving the country? Efficiency?
Democracy?

"We could take 'em down," said their new leader.

Really? Yeah really. This was like the first day of rehearsal. You
can read through the script if you want but the main thing is for the
cast to get comfortable with each other. There'll be lots of time later
for animosity. Besides, there is no script. It's another God damn collective creation. But who will actually act? The Japanese Canadian
from B.C. who used to run a community re-insulation project and
then, when all the asbestos had been replaced, a wife-battering hot-
line. She stood deliberately, a little self-consciously, and walked
around the table, back to her colleagues. She was trying to decide
which painting she liked least. "They're all related, I swear," she
muttered. "But this one — he looks mean, not just stupid." She
reached up, it started to tip, four colleagues lunged to her aid, it
teetered, but they had it. They backed off, leaving her in possession.
It was about the size she was. She propped it against the wall; by
then others were on their feet. They were doing something: acting.
Like trust games on that first day. Falling backward and counting on
the person behind to catch you. Or the beach-ball game, Matthew
couldn't even recall how it went, he did it for some fading Brit director over here to show the Canadians how "theatah" is really done,
the way the English used to pension off the war-horses of the
Napoleonic era and retire them to the colonies. He was making
mental notes: who will act, who doesn't fear looking foolish. He had
to work with these folks.

Now the walls were bare. But many of them had their own
favourite Canadian painter. That guy on the Prairies who does cows.
The Lady of the Rock in Newfoundland who paints her kitchen and
whatever's in it. The provocateur in Toronto who puts streetcars in
everything he makes. Nora the ex-prospector from Yellowknife
loves a painting she once saw of Hamilton harbour, though she's
never been to Hamilton and the scene in the painting, she's been
told, doesn't exist any more: steel mills, belching furnaces, lake
freighters, a sense of bustle and end of the line, a country that once

was filled with factories. A moment of melancholy settles around the table, then lifts. This is verging on becoming a group, maybe a government. Are we ready? Not quite. Do they all have to be Canadian? All what? All the paintings. Does it all have to be covered? All what? All that bare space on the walls. Or could we just leave it clean and white? "Kinda helps ya think," said an organic wheat farmer from near Davidson, Saskatchewan, "having it blank like that." It's true, thought Matthew, it does help ya think.

Like the great Talma, I make "fugitive" observations in the midst of apparently overwhelming experiences, storing them for use in future roles. This is how government will be in the age of improv. People in power will react with spontaneity and not according to formula. Why? Because they have no choice. The scripts are down the toilet. Yet I also wonder: Can this be how it always was in the cabinet room? Beneath a veneer of assurance, people acting on need and impulse? Little confidence, much bluster. No road map once you unfold it, just a blank sheet. Who can say since none of us was here. But has it been our illusion all this time — those of us far from power — that "they," huddled in the cabinet room and cabinet equivalents like corporate HQ or the military, knew what they were doing? Did it comfort us to think so? Because then the world was knowable, so they could control it, and some day, when we gained power, so could we . . .

The clerk of the Privy Council, held over from previous governments, reminded them they were bound by oath to reveal nothing discussed in cabinet. But it was too late, the pictures were off the wall; other features of the place were doomed as well. "What have we said that we can't talk about?" "Why should it be secret?" "We never had secrecy on city council." "We never had it on the board of ed." He brought them together, as the redecoration had. "That could be our new policy — no secrecy." It would be nice to have a policy come out of their first meeting.

Did this mean press would be invited to cabinet. Not necessarily. What about installing surveillance cameras to record the meetings? said the maverick police chief from Manitoba. Surveillance is a shit term, said the ex-union steward. It sounds like you're trying to catch people swiping steaks from the meat section at the super-market ("Put that back!") or employees who sneak equipment home from the factory (those still left in the country, ha ha — it had become their bonding in-joke). Call them video cameras, then, everybody has one at home. They'd be less intrusive than a TV crew or reporters with tape recorders (or the dinosaurs who still take notes). Then you release the tapes. Not always. Certain things might stay secret; the point is, everything wouldn't be, not automatically.

In weeks to come, the new openness seemed less momentous than expected — like the disappearance of the Progressive Conservatives and New Democrats after the election of 1993. Before, their absence seemed unthinkable; after, it was hardly noticed. Partly this was due to the infrequency of cabinet meetings. Business was done over the phone, on walks, at meals — then a consensus was built through a call-around or via E-mail. The clerk of the Privy Council said it was impossible to govern this way and the press complained it was cosmetic; they called it "the new secrecy." So ministers began handing out tapes or minutes of their conversations and meetings. It became competitive. One minister would reveal a disagreement with another. Then they'd talk about it in public together. Next day, somebody would announce he'd not only disagreed, but lost a battle, or changed his mind. The point was to be there, not to win. "Dare to struggle, dare to lose," said Alex, resuscitating a slogan.

The party at the opening of the new German Embassy was a good place to be blindsided. On the way to his first diplomatic reception, Matthew told Dal about the old Bohemian Embassy Club in Toronto. "Are you trying to prove you know how to behave in an embassy?" she said. It was long ago, he told her, even before the sixties. Toronto's avant-garde read its poetry there. He listened to the blank verse of Raymond Souster, which people called "bank verse," since Souster worked in a bank. He hungered for the black-stockinged body of Erika Kaibach, who was in the music program at Northern Collegiate by day and rented herself out to Rosedale parties as an authentic beatnik on weekends. Through Erika he met her younger brother Hans. The two of them sang together — songs you didn't hear on the radio, like "Railroad Bill" ("You never worked and you never will . . ."). They were exotic, though only mildly compared to their mother, who treated Matthew as family. She told him about a European playwright named Brecht, whose works she was translating, and begged him to help her kids acquire a modicum of bourgeois respectability, as she put it, to help them survive the economic catastrophe she knew would engulf the West once the artificial postwar boom expired. Hans was the first person who told Matthew about dialectical materialism. "Dialectical — as in action and response; materialism, because conditions create consciousness rather than the reverse." Hans owned a five-string banjo and took Matthew to see Pete Seeger play one at a concert. Hans gave him that banjo as a going-away gift when Matthew quit university to study at the National Theatre School in Montreal.

Truscott blindsided him first. Truscott had been a national culture hero since the documentaries he made during the 1960s for the NFB. Each was like a personal assault by Truscott on a major public figure. Kissinger filed a diplomatic protest over his interview. During the FLQ crisis of 1970, Truscott became obsessed. He interviewed all the officials involved and, it was rumoured, the kidnappers of Laporte. Then he spoke at a rally in the shade of the Peace Tower, denouncing the imposition of martial law. "It's the most important event of my lifetime," he told those not afraid to be there with him. He was fired by the NFB, his film on the crisis was confiscated (it disappeared permanently); his appointment as youngest head ever of the film board was derailed. He went to ground in the Okanagan for the rest of the decade, surfacing occasionally to host a safe TV series or special. People still thought of him as a troublemaker but when he did his confrontational interviews, they were with typecast Third World villains like Baby Doc Duvalier in Haiti or Arafat at a safe house in Tripoli while the Palestinian militia were being evacuated under fire. "So, Chairman Arafat," he snarled, "how's it feel to be caught like a rat in a trap?" In the old days he'd have flung that in the face of Trudeau. Still, something in him yearned to erase the ignominy of that early defeat; he lobbied for an ambassadorship, then a Senate seat. He was appointed chair of the mid-1990s commission on Canadian culture in the age of globalization. The commission recommended a permanent role for itself, with Truscott as the obvious candidate to head it. The government dithered so long that Truscott resigned. He acquired the look of a hustler, which he wore now. He was hustling Bethune. He drew Matthew to an alcove.

No one, he hissed, ever got that story right. Not the flop film with Donald Sutherland. Nor the earlier CBC mini-series with Sutherland. Nor the impersonation on Patrick Watson's "Witness to Yesterday" series with, sigh, Sutherland yet again as Bethune. The goal of Truscott's hustle was obscure. Was he offering the new prime minister a part? *The* part? Did Truscott know Matthew had already played Bethune — in a one-man show that actually toured China? They'd done it in commune cafeterias, shop floors, lecture halls. Not once had the audiences paid attention. They talked through every moment of every show. On the tour's last day, in a recital hall at the Peking Opera, attended by the company's administrative staff and props department (the company itself was on tour in France), Matthew cracked. He leapt off the stage and screamed at the audience, "Shut up — I'm preserving your fucking history!"

"Ahem, Prime Minister." Trying to rescue him from Truscott. But he was hooked.

"Uh, Dad?"

"I heard you. It's okay."

"The point is," Truscott said, "none of the Bethune projects addressed the great question, the enigma of Bethune at the point of his death, a riddle pleading for a solution: here was a world-famous battlefield surgeon, a man who'd improvised what became the standard treatments for bullet wounds, along with the first mobile transfusion unit. He's operating in a tent, he neglects to put on surgical gloves, nicks his finger, it gets infected, he fails to treat it, and he dies." Truscott paused. Matthew sensed this was the climactic moment in Truscott's discourse, as well as Bethune's biography and possibly Western history. Yet he hadn't grasped the mystery. "It is," muttered Truscott, "Utterly . . . totally . . . *impossibly* . . . preposterous!"

Matthew waited. Truscott knew how to nurse puzzlement in an audience. "All his life," Truscott enunciated, "Bethune was a nonconformist. He stood against the crowd. In his bourgeois family. In the stuffy medical society of Montreal during the 1920s. Among artists and academics in the 1930s. As a communist he spat in the face of Canadian politics. When he went to Spain he pursued women while he should have been reading Marx and Lenin; he battled with the party commissars. Then he goes to China. It's the culmination of his journey. He's surrounded by 800 million people and every one is a revolutionary. He no longer stands out. He is not now what he always has been — the loner, rebel, contrarian. They threaten to swallow him, to nullify him. He has an identity crisis and commits suicide. *He cut his finger on purpose! It's the only explanation!*" They were far enough from the rest of the reception that no one else could hear. But with tact, the whole room was following their conversation. It was like a silent movie.

"Truscott, you are so full of shit I can't even think of anything to say," breathed Matthew. He heard Morris use that line once. It was at a meeting of the anti-free-trade coalition during the 1980s. Some sectarian zealot was about to shatter their fragile unity by alienating every group in turn. Matthew and Morris looked at each other, knowing his effect had to be killed instantly. Neither could think of anything to say. But Morris acted. He improvised, Matthew told him later, and it worked. Ever since, Matthew had wanted to say those words. You carried lines like that around, sometimes for years. They took up space in your memory. Once in a while you got to use them up, like putting down a burden or taking a good dump. "I hope you aren't thinking I can send some public money your way," he went on. "I'm so far up the pipeline now I'm the last person who could help fund this." He didn't know if that was true, but it might be.

"I don't expect you to peel it off the wad in your hip pocket," said Truscott, in a crasser tone than Matthew ever heard him use for a documentary. "We're not standing on some used car lot." They each glanced toward the uniformed waiters and diplomats. "Maybe though," Truscott went on, "someone farther down the pipeline will see us chatting. Or the word will go out. They'll draw conclusions. That's all I want. It's a matter of . . . ambience." Having achieved what he came for, Truscott was gone. Fast fade.

Maybe Matthew got cocky after his good line with Truscott. And so, much later, about to make his getaway, he was blindsided again. The first time is rough but you're ready; then you relax, you think you've met your quota for the night. The smart ones wait. Like the ambassador. As if he had nothing to prove.

He was tall and broad like John Wayne. He talked like Gary Cooper. He was a type: the type that knew how to get what he wanted. No bluster, much action. Besides, Matthew knew, he was a real ambassador, not just a campaign donor collecting his reward or an ad agency director responsible for concocting the character demolition of the president's opponent in the last election. He'd been at State all his career, some said by way of the CIA and NSC. His routing had run through Indochina in the last stages of American military presence there, then southern Africa as white rule and apartheid teetered, then the obligatory Central America stint and Eastern Europe to watch the fall of the Wall, with significant interludes in Washington itself. He was chief of mission for his country at the U.N. during the Gulf war. Posting him to Ottawa was a surprise: like transferring the Pope to Vancouver Island. For Matthew, it was a role he could imagine playing. He'd like to get inside that head.

But this meeting in the foyer of the new German Embassy was unscripted and uncued. No protocol, no briefing. Clearly it wasn't supposed to happen here and now, you don't think. So improvise. Hello, hello. Shake, shake. Self-effacing embarrassments exchanged.

"I hardly know what to do," said the ambassador. "We'd better not start meeting like this."

"You could present your credentials," said Matthew.

"I'd have to have some new ones made," said the ambassador. "I already gave the real ones to the acting Governor General." Whoops. Right. Ambassadors formally deal with the G.G., who is our head of state; in the U.S., the president does it.

"I guess I've been watching too much American TV," said Matthew. A decent recovery.

The ambassador's grin covered his face like a well-used map of

Texas. "Speaking of television —" then instead of rehearsing some of the U.S.'s renowned demands for yet more access to Canadian airwaves, he launched a sentimental journey through Matthew's greatest hits. Not just the Healer stuff, but the older, mostly forgotten and almost always better material, some of it never replayed since. The mock interview in which Matthew played José Marti, Cuba's nineteenth-century poet-revolutionary. The half-hour "first directors" series that ran one summer when Matthew was still touring B.C. with the Wagon Train, his first real shot at TV: he played a star-struck Canadian hayseed with a lifelong Annette Funicello obsession, who goes to find the Mouseketeer of his dreams, searches the California beaches and malls, looking for her filming her peanut butter commercials, and finally runs into her by pure chance and enthrals her with memories of the Canadian children's shows of his youth: "Maggie Muggins," "Razzle-Dazzle" —

Didn't really work, said Matthew, right back there, regretting the way he handled his first time ever in front of a camera. The ambassador, immensely empathetic, nodded in thoughtful agreement but added speedily, "Yeah sure, but *hell*, it was more interesting than most of the stuff that *does* work!" Which was true. Besides, the ambassador went on, that show more or less conformed to Atwood's thesis in her classic 1972 thematic study of Canadian literature: the protagonist as victim trying to move from position two (failure as inevitably etched in the cosmos) to position three (rational understanding of failure's cause). Where the hell did he get this stuff? Had he been camping in the national archives? You don't pick it up at a briefing. He must take the briefing, then work it out on his own. Does he sit there with the old tapes? Does he have a Canadian culture coach? Or was he winging it? The whole point of a two-handed improv is to use one another to propel the performance higher; if your partner isn't pushing, you don't get there.

"I didn't think this was the kind of talk about telecommunications you and I would be having," said Matthew.

"What can I say?" said the ambassador, arms spreading wide in surrender. "I'm your fan." Was this now a reference to an old Canadian album of tributes to Leonard Cohen's songs? Matthew shook his head; he couldn't disguise his admiration even if he'd wanted to. "I feel I should turn to camera," he said, "and repeat what Carol Channing did during her interview with Brian Linehan." The ambassador merely waited, as if he knew a reaction shot would suffice. "This boy knows *everything*!" concluded the prime minister, with a modest attempt at the Channing voice. The ambassador narrowed his eyes and dipped his head, à la Cooper; then stepped away, as if he was headed for the hitching post outside, where he'd saddle up and ride for the border.

The ambassador, thought the prime minister, is a player. In the car going home, he told Dal about it. "Those imperialists didn't get to have an empire," she said, "by being assholes."

The hardest thing to do onstage is nothing. The most distracting drivel you ever see on a stage or a screen is actors in the background pretending to chat aimlessly at a ball, or eat. Eating is the worst. When *Cultural Revolution for the Hell of It*, the collective play on China in the seventies, was in rehearsal, the whole company knew Kristof would eventually have to put them all onstage at once: he had to, the community was the context for every scene. Community was what that show was about. But he rehearsed for weeks with everybody in the wings except the characters with lines. Then, two days before dress, he told them to get onstage and "spread yourselves out." "I knew you'd do it!" groaned Matthew. "Why didn't you get us out here before this?" The company moved into position with their stylized rice bowls, Kristof's only concession to props. "I didn't want to see it, I couldn't bear it," said Kristof, more articulate than normal about his reasons. He was right, within seconds they were miming chopsticks, miming rice (or millet, for those who'd done heavy research) between their fingers, miming munching and mastication. It was a frenzy of background activity, all pointless, sheer distraction, while the centre of the play vaporized. It was inane. Maybe it's because no one ever consciously does nothing, you're never in the background of your own experience. Most of the time we're self-absorbed; the only time we aren't is when we're rapt, caught up by someone or something else. You can't concentrate on doing nothing, you can't put your mind to it. The sole way to do nothing onstage is to be still — a terrible challenge. Yet stillness onstage is riveting.

Matthew was a master of stillness. You don't really need it in film. The camera comes in close and blows you up so big everyone has to pay attention. So he'd let the skill lapse. Now he was back onstage. He had their attention. But you gain it in order to do something, not for itself. Deliver a soliloquy, report tragic news, make the choice that will determine the rest of your life, or your country's. The strangest part of his current role though: it wasn't clear there was anything to do. Government wasn't about *doing* any more. Since Reagan and Mulroney it had been about acting to get government out of the way — off the backs of the American people, as Reagan always said. It was about approaching the point of zero public activity, political entropy. It took a long time to get there and required lots of government activity to wind government down — but the goal was in sight. Now you could hardly remember what governments once did. He had their attention, they were rapt. The script however indicated no move out of stillness. You had to improvise or lose them. It's best not to do what they expect. Audiences resent the predictable. They may buy it but you feel sullenness in the acceptance. Yet he felt he'd been cued: the Americans wanted concessions in culture — telecommunications, entertainment, and the information industries. They'd demanded it publicly and through normal diplomacy. The ambassador had merely heightened the tension by not mentioning it at their chance, ahem, encounter, then moving off camera. Matthew was in the shot now, extreme close up. He was Mister Canadian Culture. Everyone knew where he stood on these matters. He'd spent his career being blunt about them. He'd run and won as who he'd always been. Now he could deliver the speech they all expected and let the plot unfold. Or he could do something else.

He woke at five the morning after the embassy reception with Money's song in his head. "First ya create me/Then ya hate me . . ." Reik — or was it Reich — anyway some Freudian — wrote a book he'd read once, he bought it at a garage sale in the Annex. It was called *That Haunting Melody*. Reik, or Reich, said everyone always has a song running in their heads. Identify it and you'll know what counts at that juncture in your life; it's a message from the unconscious. Anyway it's better than checking your horoscope or the

Magic 8-Ball. It was still there when the news came on at seven. "World Report" — *beeng beeng boing beeng*. "First ya create me/Then ya hate me . . ."

The ambassador expected him to act on telecommunications and culture. Everyone did. It was his strength. Acting on money, on the dollar, would run against type. It would mean dealing from his weakness, but it would catch them off guard and anyway, who can resist a plot twist. Then let *them* react. They deserved it. They deserved it for what he found when he got to cabinet that morning. Rocky was there. It was a sign.

These weren't meetings any more, they were drop-ins. People in the government came before they started their day and exchanged ideas. It was part of the new openness.

So it was agreeable enough to arrive late that morning, last among equals, and find the room dark. At the front, where the prime minister would have presided back in the dark ages, just below the faded rectangle over which the Fathers of Confederation had posed, was a huge VCR screen. The former finance ministers of New Zealand, France, and Mexico were explaining, synchronically, why intervention in a modern economy has to fail. A touch on his arm. "It's Rocky," said Dal, "he showed up and said he wanted to show it." Rocky's slim, fit frame leaned against the wall near the screen. He winked at Matthew. Even in the dark it was a wink. Something about the posture, the head and neck relationship where so much can be read. Ugh. Men who wink.

It was a horror film, a genre Matthew always wanted to work in. The other was westerns. As an actor there are a few things you'd like to do, just once, then get back to your mission creating the Canadian anti-hero. Not a lot of horror films have been done in Canada, and when Cronenberg was making them, Matthew had the series. Then he left the series, and Cronenberg entered his religious phase.

It was restrained horror, well gauged for this audience. There were no right-wingers or neocons in the film. These were socialists, social democrats, populists, and greens. They'd come to power on the premise there was another way than the marketplace chaos of the 1980s. They'd believed government was not outmoded and it got them elected. Now they repented, each in turn. The aged Dupras, frail and passionate. His first term in France, no one could have tried more earnestly. We took on the banks, we were wrong. Each had hit the debt wall, their credit was downgraded, their spirits drooped. It was a cry from credible voices: we tried and failed; at least learn from our failure. It had a liturgical quality, like the recitation of sins for the Day of Atonement Matthew once learned when he played *The Jazz Singer* at a Muskoka summer theatre: "For the sin we have sinned by overspending . . . for the sin we have sinned by regulation . . . for the sin we have sinned by obstacles to trade and transitional nonconforming measures . . . For all these, pardon us, forgive us, make us whole again!" Last came the Canadians: the Rae ministers, saying they entered government as Keynesians, their first budget was their witness, but it was not to be. Others, who'd been trade unionists, had choked over breaking contracts with their own public workers, literally puked in the members' bathroom when the bill was introduced. Now — we did what we must, to save what we could. The NDPers from out west were less penitent, because they'd promised less all along.

Rocky signalled for the lights, making you wonder why he'd had them turned off. This was just a video, not Cannes. But the move was stark, almost violent. The people in the room looked stunned, terrorized, it was impressive. As if an A.D. told his extras: "I want horror, stark horror, on every face as you pour up onto the street from the haunted subway stop. Action . . ."

Rocky took their pain, as it were, into consideration. He assured them the video was solely for them. This was the only copy, which he'd leave with them to review or show others, like spouses and constituents, as they chose. It was not — he felt embarrassed mentioning this even if only to deny it — part of a communications campaign targeting the new government. After all, they'd done nothing (so far) to offend his fellow employers.

They looked to Matthew. Could he make them his again? What the hell do you do? Matthew put on the mask. Maybe it was that head and neck structure silhouetted in the dark room; that's what masks were about, as Keith Johnstone told Matthew one summer at Banff before they turned the Centre for the Arts there into the

Centre for Business and Related Forms of Creativity. Matthew loved watching Johnstone do mask work with the students but Matthew himself never managed to "find his mask." He tested different ones, even tried making his own. Then one day at Bluer, while Morris raised an obscure point about surplus value, Matthew found it. He let his face drop. That's the only way he could describe it. The mask of his personality as expressed by his physiognomy — the set of features and repertoire of expressions he'd built up all his life. He let it drop. His face fell into something . . . neutral, inexpressive. Exactly as if he'd put on a mask. He said nothing, kept listening to Morris. But Morris looked like a wind from hell had blown through him. He didn't know this person sitting in Matthew's place! That other persona, the familiar personality, was gone, replaced by a substratum for personality instead of an actual personality. As if the skin had slid off the face revealing a skull, except it was all still there: skin, hair, eyes, openings.

They didn't discuss it. Before that could happen, Matthew repealed the mask (which was *no* mask, which had *replaced* the actual mask he donned every day) and the face of his personality returned. Sometimes the mask happened by itself, as it had by the canal with the former prime minister; sometimes he forgot it was available; sometimes he drew on it because he needed it. Like now.

It worked. Rocky had never been confronted with the truth of the mask. You could almost pity him. He simply ceded control of the room. Since the mask was directed fully only at him, others didn't feel its impact. The mask works best when directed straight at you: that impassive blank confronting and nullifying you at once. But by Rocky's release, they were freed, for the moment. It won some time, is all.

"What was that?" said Rocky. They were alone now, in the elevator. Matthew did the mask again. Rocky jerked, like someone hit him flat in the chest with a palm. He shook it off — one of Rocky's strengths was lack of introspection — and asked, "Don't you think I mean it? You think I'm tryna make a sale here for my own benefit?"

Rocky had botched everything he'd done in his careeer; as a result he rose like a rocket. He began selling encyclopedias out of his car. He'd cruise around till he found streets with names like Shakespeare Avenue or Euclid, then start working them. The home owners adored him but he never made gas money. Somehow he snagged a PR job with the Trudeau Liberals in Ottawa. He began by vetting press releases but soon made it to head of communications. Then he bailed and ran for the Tories. Maybe he sniffed the Reaganism drifting up from the U.S., well before Mulroney came to power. Everything always arrived in Canada five years later. The Tories rewarded him for his conversion by making him a junior minister in the brief Joe Clark government. Luckily he was defeated in the next election. He was named VP for PR at CanCom Inc., an internationally competitive Canadian firm, the model, everyone said, for Canada in the new global economy. Like Volvo. Like Sony. When its CEO balked at transferring most of the company to the Carolinas, he was parachuted out and Rocky took over. In his brief tenure, CanCom's headquarters moved to the U.S., followed by the bulk of production and research. There it was picked apart and absorbed piecemeal by the big players in the field. But Rocky had moved again, to Synergo, Canada's largest food and beverage empire. He'd learned the game. He sold its major assets to foreign buyers, then reinvested in entertainment, chiefly co-productions. He now spent much of his time telling Canadians about the hard realities they'd have to accustom themselves to — a message they didn't like much, but which they didn't seem to mind hearing from him. Or he was on the yacht with his second wife.

Through it all, the constant in his career was that name. Others underestimated the value of a name. Actors knew. Matthew failed three times to register his name with Equity in New York. We have a Matthew with your last name, they said. He tried Matt and Matty but they had those too. They said he could use his initials. The hell with it, he said, and stuck to his name. He was the first Canadian actor to defy the convention. No one he met had ever heard of the American Matthew with the same last name; he once researched it and learned his homonym's career peaked at a summer theatre in the Berkshires, then he died in a crash coming back to Manhattan on the Sawmill River Parkway. Once in a while, after Matthew became famous, interviewers or profile writers would bring it up. Was it eerie? Did he feel implicated in the death of the other Matthew Deans? It was tricky to answer without sounding callous. Rocky though was a formidable name. Especially in sports. Athletes named Rocky often stuck around even if they weren't very skilled. Something about Rocky got people on your side.

"I believe you mean it, Rocky," he said.

"I'll take a lie detector test. A polygraph. Do I really believe what I'm saying or is this just so my shareholders can clean out the pockets of their customers faster than they're already doing?"

"I believe you'd pass," said Matthew.

"Y'know what really frosts my balls? Your contempt for my motives!" said Rocky. Pause. "If you believe I mean it, why the contempt?"

The answer was "bad faith." It was "false consciousness." Terms from the Hegelian legacy that Morris sometimes used to explain the world. When Matthew's star rose, he started meeting captains of finance and industry, sometimes at fall launches of the series or awards ceremonies — as he'd first met Rocky. He'd talk with them about what they did and thought. That's when he realized they weren't all lying merely to befuddle the masses. They *believed their bullshit*. He understood false consciousness and bad faith: believing your own bullshit. The elevator stopped. The door opened.

"I know you believe your own bullshit," he said.

"Thank you," Rocky said. "But it's not bullshit."

"It is bullshit."

"Would *you* take a lie detector test to prove whether you believe it's really bullshit?" said Rocky. He'd hit a note outside of his normal range. But overachieving is what Rockys are all about. Not just in sports. Rocky grinned. He knew he'd pulled one off. Matthew wouldn't reach for that face thing now, whatever it was. What the guy needed was a comeback. Matthew could only open his mouth and hope it was there. "Even if it isn't bullshit," he said, "it's bullshit." Rocky pulled back warily, an overachiever in mild quandary. Stalemate, for now.

Not the greatest line I ever came up with, thought Matthew.

This will take chutzpah. *Where do you get* chutzpah? *Acting needs* chutzpah.

The first time he tried it he was alone, his parents were out. He'd spent years on the stage crew watching other kids act in the school drama festival. He used the stage crew the way Castro used the Sierra Maestre: to nurse his wounds and *prepare*. He'd made it an intellectual commando unit. He wrote articles for the school paper and invented revolutionary meetings backstage, where Trotskyites battled anarchists and hammers flew. When the school board ran a conference on "The Changing Role of the School in Modern Society," he announced one on "The Changing Role of the Stage Crew." He even sent out invitations. Guys drenched in Brylcreem showed up from the downtown schools in their Chevies. He wrote a stage crew anthem to the tune of the school song. It kept him sane and feisty in suburban purgatory.

But in its other identity, as Clark Kent, the stage crew built sets and moved flats for the kids who acted in plays. His final year, he watched Chip Morrison skulk in the wings "getting into" his role as the noble loser in O'Neill's *The Hairy Ape*. He saw Chip do it three nights in a row. Something about it moved Matthew. I could do that, he thought.

So later that week, when Mum and Dad went for their cha-cha-cha lessons at the South of the Border Dance Studio (or maybe it was bowling night), with no one around to see, he pulled a play script from the pile of textbooks in his room. *Julius Caesar*, in a red cover. He'd studied it three years ago. It was underlined, there were notes in the margin, and lots of checks. All in pencil, as if he intended to erase it some day and sell it back to the bookstore. He threw the play down the half-flight of stairs into the living room, hard. That's how teachers marked final exams he'd been told: top of the pile gets A+. He followed it down, stopped with it at his feet, felt something happen inside, lifted it, open to the place he'd decided to try. He took his time, there was no rush. He liked the sense of waiting. He wanted to . . . get there, however long it took. Be there, wherever that was. Get there, be there. It started, you could feel it;

amazing, it wasn't so tough, he'd seen Chip do it, just take the whole dumb thing seriously: and he was gazing at Caesar's stabbed, gashed corpse on the floor — of the Senate. "O pardon me thou bleeding piece of earth," he said, "that I am meek and gentle with these butchers." No one around to wince or snicker. Just Matthew and Caesar's corpse, but Matthew was Marc Antony; he was Matthew being Marc Antony. It made sense. "Thou art the ruins of the noblest man that ever lived." His voice rose like it came from a deep, anchored place. He was impressed, he looked around to check he was still alone, and laughed a little laugh of triumph. It worked. Back in grade two, Miss Scott, his busty singing teacher, tapped him on the head during music class. She said the people she tapped should whisper while others sang. Years later, his camp counsellor, Sean, who taught them union songs on a canoe trip ("Which Side Are You On"; "Solidarity Forever"; "There Once Was a Union Maid"), said he should sing out. Matthew told him about Miss Scott and the tap. "She committed a grave crime," said Sean. "Anyone can sing. Not to sing out is politically unacceptable." He put one hand on Matthew's throat and the other on his stomach. "Sing from down there," he said. It had worked.

Matthew strode through the living/dining room, the kitchen, speaking Antony's grim words. He'd got there. In the bathroom he glanced in the mirror and smiled at the face he saw. Had he just lost it? He glowered back, he was there again. Like stepping through a door right beside you, you only had to turn and find it. He walked onto the driveway. It was dusk. Mr. Fitz was lowering the garage door across the street. Matthew lowered the volume to almost a whisper, but it came from the same deep place. "Cry havoc and let slip the dogs of war." That was *better*. Making it harder to hear worked if you spoke deep and low rather than shouting. It compressed the power in a smaller space. The trick of acting, he'd learned, was getting there. The trick of the trick, he learned later, was how to get to getting there, and get *back* there night after night, or whenever you wanted to. It wasn't complicated, but it took *chutzpah*.

When he went on television several weeks after the reception at the German Embassy, he said the government's new program for the

Canadian dollar would be announced next day in the House. That was the appropriate place, where the people had sent their representatives to deal with national business. He planned to speak to them instead, in this, his first address in his new role, as fellow citizens. Everyone brings their own experience to the public space, he said, and he supposed many of them expected the first main policy of a government he led would be about culture. But instead it would deal with money — and he'd like to say why.

Since he was young, he went on, probably when he first got an allowance and started planning how to spend it, money amazed him. You took these papers and coins and turned them into things you could eat or drink, read and wear . . .

(Lars and Tilley watched from the rooftop bar of the Park Plaza in Toronto. They sat on the couch in front of the big fireplace with a palm-size TV and two earpieces. The rooftop had never been penetrated by television or music. Lars looked at her with an expression that meant: he knows how to connect. Tilley pictured a country nodding its head from sea to sea.)

So he used to ask business and economics students, when he was at university, how this trick worked: turning symbolic stuff into usable things. He got bits of answers, then as a young actor he lucked into a role where he played a character called Money. After all even Shakespeare wrote about the power money held over people, although human beings had invented money to start with. It's like the old Frankenstein story, he said. It's as if there's always been a struggle over whether people will control money, or money will control people. That's what the policies coming tomorrow are about.

(As good as Reagan, thought the former prime minister, as she watched. Better, thought Lars.)

For many years, he went on, people have been told by experts and leaders that only one approach to the economy existed, and any effort to do differently would be like defying the law of gravity. None of them said any more that the economic policies of the last twenty years were good for us; there was just no alternative. You can't defy gravity. So money speaks the truth, and human beings take the consequences, mostly unpleasant. He said he had nothing against experts but you don't go to the same people who got you into a mess, to get you out of it. And sadly there were no alternate experts on the sidelines with another playbook to try — as the socialists used to have. So in his opinion and based on his life's experience — he hoped they weren't put off by the word he was about to use — you had to be creative. Now, quick as a bunny, he wanted to explain what that meant.

"Creativity isn't something you can buy or acquire from others," he said. "But it *is* available to us all. Artists aren't creative because they have a special thing called creativity. Artists are the people who draw on the creativity everyone has. What's surprising," he said, "is that there aren't more artists, considering how normal creativity is." He was thinking about Kristof.

Kristof couldn't explain why he did things. When he tried, it was embarrassing. He was just creative. His plays looked like ballets; actors he directed moved like gazelles. People who hadn't worked with him would say, "Well, he must spend all the time in rehearsal just blocking." But Kristof never blocked a scene. Never told anyone where to stand or when to move. Occasionally, if he was staging something really complicated, like the "Long March" in the Chinese Revolution or the War of 1812, he'd move down toward the stage and say vaguely, "Spread yourselves out." That was it. Spread yourselves out. So we would. And people called it ballet. I don't know how it worked, and he sure didn't. Maybe it's that he trusted us, maybe we felt sorry for him. We could feel what he wanted to see, even though he couldn't describe it. For the China play, he went off to the record library one day at lunch and came back with electronic music. He went into the sound booth and started playing it as we worked. Why are you doing that? we said. "I've always wanted to use it in a play," he said, and went over to the lighting booth where some kid from a youth employment program was puzzling about how to light the show. Kristof said to throw some lights on the rehearsal and they'd discuss it later. Other directors often spent the last days before opening just setting lights. As for the music, it sounded contemporary, revolutionary, and Oriental all at the same time. In other words, it was perfect. He had it in him and he was no intellectual genius, so might not we have it in ourselves too?

Tilley and Lars agreed with Norman the waiter: coming from him, it was plausible. *He* had solved problems creatively. Most Canadians saw him do it: a select few, in a theatre; the teeming masses, on TV. He wasn't talking abstractly. Creativity wasn't a gimmick he invented for a late-night infomercial. If we *all* pitched in and looked for solutions, who knew what might happen. "He makes you feel like the G.G. did," said Norman, picking up their glasses and wiping the table. He spoke it first, though Tilley and Lars would later claim they'd each thought it. People across the country knew those two men. They'd met each as part of their Canadian experience: one playing hockey, the other playing roles. For both, teamwork mattered, not just individual brilliance. Everything they did had happened in public view: the games and the shows. It was as though the G.G. was reborn, as if his spirit migrated when he crashed the end boards and, with a little skip, entered the hospitable body of the ex-TV star. The guy could get away with anything as long as *that* magic was working.

Matthew finished by talking about one of his roles: Galileo in Brecht's play on the seventeenth-century scientist, ordered by the Church to deny that the earth moved around the sun. "They told him it didn't move, when he wouldn't buy it they just told him to believe it. I feel like I'm playing that part again when they say there's no other way, we have to give in to economic forces because they're like gravity. At the end of the scene they show Galileo the torture tools of the Inquisition and he gives in. Okay, he says, The earth stands still. Then he steps outside the chamber, looks up at the starry sky and says, '*Eppur si muove.*' And yet it moves." It was the only line of the night which Matthew spoke as an actor rather than as prime minister. He said it with the compression of "Cry havoc and let slip the dogs of war."

"You reminded me of FDR," said Dal after. "What are you accusing me of?" he said. "FDR saved capitalism by forcing it to change. The business class hated FDR but they wouldn't have survived the Depression without what he did. Do you really think that's what I'm doing now — when there's no threat to their power?" She leaned back and her hair fell down behind the chair she was sitting

117

in. "I guess that's what Morris says about FDR," she said. He raised his hands, caught in an act of appropriation. "But that's not what you reminded me of," she went on. "FDR also said, We have nothing to fear but fear itself."

The policies announced next day in the House were presented by a team, not just the minister of finance. It was a parliamentary collective creation. They weren't what you'd expect from the government of an ex-actor. They dealt solely with the debt and deficit. Call it governing against type. It was like saying, okay, you want debt obsession? We'll give you debt obsession. The goal, said the ministers, was to break Canadian dependence on bondholders and raters, especially those outside the country. To snap their hold, the government would create a parallel banking system and issue special bonds, like the old war bonds, available to the public. As for the big Canadian bondholders, there would be a wealth tax immediately, to recapture some of the interest those folks had amassed. The government would announce further measures. You could take the program as a response to the sense of crisis imprinted on the national psyche for twenty years. Or as a way to redistribute wealth and restore equity. You could even see it as a declaration of independence. Many interpretations were available, and various speakers proposed them.

The prime minister spoke last. He said he lacked the kind of majority which would guarantee automatic passage. He said he liked it that way and looked forward to a debate. He got it in the days to come, and then he got his bills. No one in the political system was ready to unglue the government yet. The former prime minister said she was dubious. She stayed away during the final vote. Others did the same. "They're planning to head you off at the pass," said Morris. He meant the bond-rating agencies.

Sometimes I think the only thing that separates me from other actors is a fixation on ideas, as opposed to people. I was as happy playing the Theory of Relativity as being Willy Loman. I mean, life's not just emotions. You also try to make sense of it. Everybody does. I saw it from the stage sometimes, in the faces of an audience looking back gratefully, as you try to help them sort out unemployment or Africa or their own heartache. Besides, people like to learn. Learning can be as entertaining as love or murder, depending on how you tell the tale.

I do worry that this . . . fetish for ideas means I have less emotional stuff — antennae, curiosity, raw materials — than other actors. But theatre will always deal in passion; it's nice to offer a little understanding too. I once did a play called How Things Work *for a school tour. I was the host, a character who'd been a magician but decided it would be more fun to give tricks away than fool people. I started with card tricks and levitations, then moved on. It was based on a book I had that made great bathroom reading. It explained one "thing" per page — a toaster or camera or battery — with a diagram on the facing page. Then I went farther — not just fountain pens and computer chips, but political systems, neuroses — and for the climax, theatre itself: I drew back the curtain and flew the set, trying my best to reveal* everything *— crew, lights, makeup, even the acting process. Part of the fun, I found, is you can never reveal everything, no matter how hard you try, because how much do you really ever know . . .*

It moved. It moved because of the young man sent to Ottawa by the national bond-rating agencies to review the government's classification on its new offerings. They always sent a callow youth — as the money managers put it among themselves — to remind governments of the low esteem in which they were held by those with true power: the power to grant and withhold credit. As the callow youth walked the corridors of Ottawa or the provincial capitals, ministers and deputies cowered. "Sir," they said as he passed. "Good morning, sir, would you like something, sir?"

The youth sent to Ottawa had been on Canada's national track team. His name was Larry Lambeth. After an economics degree in British Columbia, he did an M.B.A. at Cornell, then joined an eastern consulting firm, specializing in problems of the Canadian cultural marketplace under free trade. He had just transferred to bond rating. Probably, that's why he was sent: callowest of the callow. "Sir," he said to Matthew, "I saw you play Tom Longboat when I was in junior high."

119

"*Going The Distance*," said Matthew.

"I think it made me want to be a runner," said Larry. This could be interesting. "It may have been the hardest role I ever did," said Matthew. "Although they all feel like that when you're doing them. I just didn't know what it was like to be a marathoner. I was middle-distance."

"So was I," said Larry. "I still am. There's this little layer of fat that's just started to appear all over my body." He began opening his shirt to show the prime minister, but he stopped. The others around the table wouldn't understand.

Then Matthew described how he'd found Longboat's old pacesetter, Hawkins, one morning as he opened a musty hardware store he owned in Dundas, near the Caledonia reserve on which both native runners were born. Hawkins must have been eighty. The store was a masterwork of chaos but Hawkins could walk directly to every washer and door sweep in it. They stood across the counter from each other. Hawkins pulled out an album: clippings, photos, programs. He said he'd had the same trouble as Matthew (and Larry). He was middle-distance, his job was to set a pace, often he just dropped out after he'd done the job, then cut across to the finish line to catch the outcome, which meant seeing how far Longboat left the pack behind; so, you see, he couldn't really advise an actor who wanted to know how Longboat felt. Matthew started for the door, he still had no idea how to play it. Hawkins came with him. When you're doing research, everything important happens at the door. "Sorry I couldn't help," said Hawkins. "It was a mystery to me why Longboat cared so much. Like a need or an itch. I could see the tension drain out of him every time he crossed the finish line a half mile ahead of the others."

"Did he have to be way ahead?" asked Matthew.

"Oh yeah," said Hawkins. "He didn't really enjoy it unless he humiliated them."

That was it, Matthew told Larry. It was about pride. It was about recapturing all the ground native peoples had lost since the Europeans arrived. He had a lot of ground to make up. Longboat had to run for distance.

"Did you ever get criticized for playing an aboriginal?" asked Larry.

"I was on the cusp of that," said Matthew. "It didn't really come up. A few years later I'd have taken a shitstorm of criticism. But by then I wouldn't have done it."

"Do you regret it now?"

Matthew didn't say anything, as if he'd rather not be on the record. But he shook his head almost without moving it and his eyes gleamed.

Matthew asked where the kid had seen the Longboat play. In Stratford, said Larry, where Longboat had won one of his biggest races. Matthew remembered that performance, because it's where Longboat's granddaughter came to see it. Larry looked with new interest, like a second wind. Matthew said he hadn't known a Longboat descendant would be there that afternoon. He learned from the stage manager just as he went on for the big monologue about what running meant to Longboat. Christ, he told the S.M. — how can I? I made this speech up — but it was the biggest thing in her granddad's life. It's what he lived for and it finally killed him, he kept going when he should have quit. The prospect terrified Matthew; he'd be revealed for the fraud, the mere actor, he was. Then he was on, into the scene, and out of it. The crowd cheered, they always cheered that speech. He couldn't think of anything else to do so he slowly paced, in that slo-mo style he'd learned from Kristof, over to Longboat's grandchild in the front row. She was middle-aged. She could've been Longboat's grandmother. Or anyone's. "Did we use slo-mo or rear projection to create the run in the show you saw?" he asked Larry. Larry was stymied by the question; in his memory Matthew had simply run twenty-six miles on the stage. "What did she say?" he asked.

"Her jaw kind of fell open. She said every word was right. She said that was exactly how her granddad felt."

"Shit," said Larry.

"I lucked out," said the P.M. "It doesn't always happen that way when they come to see you, the ones you've based your part on. Those other times, when they hate it, I don't talk about. So. I'll leave you with these people." He gestured at the suits with the files.

"They can get you any information you need." Larry asked Matthew if he'd like a chance to discuss the report when it was finished. The P.M. shook his head. "Do your job," he said. "We'll talk another time."

The report Larry submitted recommended no change in the status of federal government offerings. It was the first time in years that a Canadian public body had preserved its rating. The New York agencies took their cue from it. Canadians had always been more savage to their own governments than foreign firms were. The young man sent from the big New York agency to confer with Larry had a familiar name. He'd run on the Cornell track team while Larry was doing his M.B.A. there.

"Does this kind of thing count as history?" said Matthew to Morris. He'd just described the meeting and its result.

"Strictly speaking," said Morris, "it would be difficult to find a place for it in a class-based analysis."

"I'm glad to hear that," said Matthew. "I'd hate to think this is the way the turning points of world history happened."

"Don't worry about it," said Morris. "They may not get you going, but they'll get you coming back. That's why it's such a great system. It doesn't have to work all the time. Eventually it does, and you're toast."

The steady rating provided a small space for action. Grab it, those moments don't come often. When was the last time a government in Canada felt it had financial room to do anything but cut? It wouldn't last, everyone knew. The miracle was, it happened at all.

"I never heard that Longboat story," said Dal.

"You saw the show. You told me you loved it. You decided to be a runner for a week when you were four."

"I mean his granddaughter saying every word was right." Silent for a while, then, "You wanta talk politics or you wanta talk theatre?"

There is a moment onstage that only other actors know. It doesn't happen at every performance of a show nor does it happen at the same point each time. It's the moment when an actor gathers his or her resources to plunge. Instead of diligently reconstructing the scene as it's been worked out in rehearsal and in previous shows — re-creating the circumstances and mood which brought it to fruition in the past — the actor drives into the moment as if for the first time, uncertain of the result. It takes energy and recklessness; you could ruin the rest of the show. It can't be done every night; that would be too draining, which is why technique comes into play. But if it succeeds, the actor will be transported into another self, one which he or she possessed potentially, but which never before detonated, or only in anticipatory bursts. At such a moment the other actors in the company stand by and bear witness. They know something is going to be attempted; perhaps even achieved. Hush. So-and-so is going for it.

The new policies in telecommunications, announced after the economic plan, were tough and far-reaching. "So why does it feel anti-climactic? Where's the reaction?" said Matthew. Re-Canadianization of the broadcast system; higher standards of national content; for the first time, enforcement. Tax credits and grants to encourage production; fines for failure to reach the goals. Clear criteria for licence cancellations. Fraudulent forms of Canadian content would be disallowed. On what basis, he was asked. "On whatever basis it takes," he said. "If I have to watch TV and make the judgement myself."

"It's about me," said Lars, next time they spoke. "It all leads up to me."

"They have to obey," said Matthew. "Or we'll land on them."

"They'll do it," said Lars. "It doesn't seem to bother them. Maybe it would've twenty years ago. Ten even."

"That's how it feels with the investment policies too. The investors grumble but they say they'll abide. It seems to be working. There's more investment. But . . . but there's a lack of genuine response. Like being in a play that got great reviews. The audiences react the way they know they're expected to. They have a good time — dutifully. They laugh — but the laughs come too fast. It's not right. It's not real."

"The moment has passed," said Lars. "The Canadian moment."

Matthew shrugged. What does it mean for a moment to be past? Can it come again? "I liked those guys that believed in creating Canadian business heroes back in the seventies," he said. "I never played one, but it would have been fun. There was a series about an oilman. They wouldn't even let me audition. Somebody else got it. Remember the business magazines with Canadians on the cover? I'd have liked to play Walter Gordon. He was a true believer in Canadian business and he was trashed by his own class for it. It was a business tragedy — in the Shakespearean sense. Now they have a chance to do what Gordon only dreamed about. But they won't go for it —"

"Maybe you need a national hockey policy," said Lars. It was a joke.

"We're working on it," said Matthew. "It'll be announced next week."

"You could say it was the class struggle," said Angeline, "that caused his death." Her husband, Trevor, who died twenty years ago, was being inducted into the Canadian Labour Hall of Fame. Maybe she meant the blow on the head he got from a police club on a picket line during the wave of strikes they led after World War II. Or the chronic cough he picked up leafletting many early mornings during the 1950s, after they were expelled from mainstream labour for being too left-wing or too independently Canadian — as if those were the same thing then. "You know they passed a resolution barring him personally from ever coming in here," she said thoughtfully. Matthew asked if Trev would find it strange to see his plaque on the wall now. "I doubt it," she said. "We never chose to be outside. We just stuck to our principles. We didn't believe American unions should order Canadian workers around. He'd have been happy to come back. On his own terms."

She said it in the precise voice she must have used with company negotiators after all-night deadline bargaining. They'd break for an hour and by daybreak she'd be back, smile pasted on, every hair in place, single string of pearls, smart shoes. (She had opposed free trade in everything except Italian shoes.) The management lawyers loathed that routine of hers; how do you demonize Miss Prim? Meanwhile Trev would be outside assigning picket captains and devising the strategy for blocking trucks or scabs. They were a team, even then in the seventies when Matthew met them, through Michele, while he was doing research for the play about immigrants. Michele was their complete union staff; she got paid a pittance through a government youth program. They had few members compared to the great days before they were blacklisted during the Cold War but numbers were all they lacked. After they saw that show, they asked if he wanted to help organize some small plants, as a volunteer. Sure, he said. It was like acquiring another life. Rehearse all day; at night go to workers' homes and sign them up. Strikes. They even let him come to bargaining. One day after a play he loved got shit reviews and closed, he asked if he could work for them full time. He said he'd lost faith in theatre as a tool for change. Trev was blunt; he thought all that show needed was some humour, not that he knew anything about theatre, but there weren't enough laughs. "Does that mean no?" Matthew asked. Angeline, unlike Trev, shared the curses Matthew bore: a middle-class background, university. She told Matthew he could do more good where he was. Organizers they could find, but actors and writers were rarer — he continued as a volunteer. Once, after a day on the picket line at Delta Fabrics, fighting off the cops and scabs, he and the strikers jammed into his van and drove to the union hall for a meeting. They got blocked in rush hour; he looked around at the harried commuters and thought there were no people in the world he'd rather be stuck in traffic with than these guys. He was glowing like an isotope when he walked into the office. Angeline was working on a press release. "I can see how you got hooked," he said. She looked up and recognized something. "You mean the contact," she said.

He made a few comments about Trev's induction into the Hall of Fame. Then she made a gracious speech thanking the labour movement on her late husband's behalf. Afterward Matthew said he wished she'd added, "Oh, and by the way, you were wrong and we were right." She smiled. Each hair still in place, though she'd let it go white. In the old days it was black. "I thought about it long and hard," she said. "I decided it was implied."

He asked what she thought of their proposed changes to the labour code. She approved, of course. She liked the parts on sectoral bargaining. At last temps, contracted-out workers, and franchise employees would have a shot at organizing. She'd slowed down since retiring, but she spent a lot of time with those people — as a volunteer. What he couldn't understand, he said, was the muted response from business and the press. She nodded. "I've noticed they don't react as predictably as they used to," she said. "I used to know just what they'd do well before they did it. It was invaluable." He asked what she thought it meant. She thought some more. "It's the class struggle," she said. "It always was."

"Did you know Walter Gordon?" he asked. She said they'd met once, Gordon had been "gallant." She pronounced it as in French. He'd treated her, she said, with respect, though they differed on labour issues; he told her he'd always admired the costly stand she and Trev took on Canadian unions for Canadian workers. "He fought his own battles, of course," she added. "Did you ever meet him?" Once, said Matthew. At an anti-free-trade rally. All the speakers were told to take two minutes, max. The stage manager put a light on the podium to blink anyone who went over. Gordon spoke first. When he hit three and a half, Matthew freaked. He tore across backstage and told the S.M. to blink Gordon. The S.M. stared ahead. "Blink him," I said. "Blink him, damn it, blink him." The S.M. swung her gaze coolly around and levelled him. "Blink Walter Gordon?" she said. "No fucking way."

Something in the country doesn't like heroes. They try to do too much. When we taped On to Ottawa, *about the march of the unemployed during the Depression, I was Slim Evans, leader of the trek. I spent the whole rehearsal trying to scale down my part. This is about workers, I said, it's about the people, not the leaders. Kristof wanted the climactic moment of the Mounties' brutal attack to show me, Slim, atop a freight car, waving my fist. Fade to fiery silhouette ("To let 'em know you're still there!" he said), then to commercial. No way, I said. Too much leader, too little the led. It got fierce, the other actors joined in. We stopped working and argued for hours. You don't get much rehearsal in TV to start with. For the first and only time, a*

*network had agreed to try a collective approach in TV drama — the
whole crew was there: switcher, camera operators, even makeup and
costume. The idea was, when we got to studio, everybody would
improvise, not just the actors. They couldn't believe it. They kept
checking their schedules and saying there was no time for chaos. Of
course for us chaos was the essence of the process. Next day we went
back to the scene and Kristof skipped the shot. We don't need it, he
said. Uh-uh, I said, leave it in, it makes sense. What happened? said
the TV people. They switched positions, said the actors. It happens all
the time, it's the dialectic. But I think I just couldn't make up my
mind about getting out there in front and doing something. Taking
the lead. "Pity the people that has no heroes," said Brecht. "On the
other hand," he added, "pity the people that needs a hero."*

The policy that resonated, strangely, that finally got a big, hostile
reaction, was an echo of Lester Pearson. Talk about a Canadian
non-hero. He may have been a foreign affairs superstar, he got the
Nobel Peace Prize — but that bow tie? The squirrelly voice? He
loved *baseball* — not hockey. He alternated in his time with
Diefenbaker, his opposite: rash, self-absorbed, and who dared to
take on the Americans. No one ever did a show on Pearson when he
was alive or just a song, like the one on Diefenbaker: "Dief is the
chief/Dief was the chief/Dief'll be the chief again." Yet now Matthew
felt like Pearson reborn: the Canadian leader so unheroic that even
Matthew, master of the anti-hero, had never suspected he was rele-
vant, never imagined a link. It was the juncture in time that forged
it. ("Casting is everything," Kristof said. "Casting is destiny.")

The policy that echoed Pearson was foreign aid. As though its
moment had come again. The new government committed .07 per
cent of its revenues to international programs. This was the nominal
goal of all Western governments, few of which had ever fulfilled it,
or even remembered it. Till now. The reaction came first from
Canadian correspondents of U.S. papers and from business leaders
who'd been reserved about the economic policies that should have
ignited them. Was it displacement?

Matthew asked Alex. Alex came to Ottawa often though he
now lived in Montreal with a woman who used to phone and leave

messages cursing the "phoney little revolutionary shit" because he never called. She was transcribing some tapes for a book Alex planned to write called *The Death of Solidarity*. It would describe the loss of ideals in many parts of the world where he'd helped and advised.

"They should have gone nuts about our domestic policies. Banking, investment, telecommunications," said Matthew. "I thought they'd worry about the demonstration effect, about the menace of a good example. That's why they came down so hard on Vietnam and Nicaragua."

"And Cuba and Grenada," Alex added.

"I read it in Chomsky," said Matthew. "In about a hundred different books he wrote."

"They don't worry about examples any more," said Alex. "Because they've got counterexamples that show what happens after you set a good example."

"Like what?"

"Vietnam. Nicaragua. Cuba. And Grenada."

"You owe me for a perfect setup," said Matthew. "So why do they care about our piddling foreign aid?"

"Connections," said Alex, who never ducked a question. "They aren't bothered by examples. They're worried about people connecting. Solidarity, you know? But look. Are you really worried? Or are you exhilarated?"

Matthew blushed. He felt like he'd been discovered. "It's like that stage direction," he said, "with which Chekhov changed the history of theatre: *'She smiles through her tears.'*"

"Don't gimme that ambivalence crap," said Alex. "You nailed them! You're giving them fits! I congratulate you!"

Matthew warmed in Alex's enthusiasm. He lit up, the way he did at rehearsals when he had an idea he knew would infuriate everyone else. "They want connections, we'll give them connections," he said. "What if we send humanitarian aid to the U.S. and the U.K.? Teachers, medical supplies, shelter experts."

"You could do worse," said Alex.

"There's nothing like a reaction," said Matthew, "when you know they're out there."

Sometimes it amazes him that anything ever gets done. That the gap between what is and is not can be bridged. Like the first step you take onto the stage in rehearsal. It doesn't bother everyone. To him, he never believes it's possible, even after he just took it. Here you are, how did that happen? You just . . . jump. Leap of faith? He used to stand on the dining-room table with Dal when she was small, on New Year's Eve, and leap with her into the new year. It was the only sense New Year's Eve ever made to him. He wonders if she still remembers. (Yes, of course she does. She wonders if *he* still remembers.)

During those months he spent in England long ago, which stretched into years, a few actors he knew wanted to start a company, something working class and Marxist. They had a burned-out carriage factory and fine motives but no energy. They turned to him. Why? It was the lumberjack shirt, they said. They saw North American vigour in him. He accepted the role. ("Casting is destiny.") He rolled up those sleeves, let his beard grow bushy, and talked like they expected people from Canada to talk. Can-do talk. "Big Joe Mufferaw paddled into Mattawa/all the way from Ottawa in just one day." Yes we can, he'd say when they slumped. Six months later they opened a show, the reviewers came, the timing was right, they seemed to fit a fashion, the arts council got behind them. He'd pulled it off. When he came home he realized he could reverse the script. Lose the beard, style the hair, wear a cravat. Okay, lose the cravat. Hey, the Canadians would probably say, this guy is special, let's give him a shot. He never tried it, but he knows it would have worked.

How does anything happen? One day there's a Cold War. You were born into it. The Kremlin versus the Free World, an entire culture reflecting their conflict: spy films, Le Carré novels. You've never known anything else. You can imagine a different world, but you can't imagine getting there. Then it's gone. No Red Menace. Nelson Mandela is the president of South Africa. Change happens, but do you see it happen? Or do you just notice it afterward? What does it look like *as it occurs*? Do you just decide, and then you act? It feels like that's what he did. But he's not even sure he was there when it happened.

"From a Marxist point of view," says Morris over the phone, "that's the voluntaristic fallacy."

"What's the fallacy?" asks Matthew. "It seems to work."

"The fallacy is that it works. Men make history, but not under circumstances of their own choosing."

"*Eppur si muove*," says Matthew.

"Do you ever wonder if the CIA is on the line, and what they make of these citations?"

"Why the CIA? Why not CSIS? I'm a nationalist."

"I said the CIA, because if I was them — you know, *them* — that's how I'd do it."

"I know that line," says Matthew. "How do I know that line?"

"It's from 'A Very British Coup,'" says Morris. "A TV classic from Britain, home of awful left politics and great left culture. When the socialist becomes prime minister, he says if he was the other side, meaning Britain's ruling class, he'd get the CIA to bug his phone. It's easier to distance themselves from if it's discovered."

"I don't think we're doing 'A Very British Coup' here," says Matthew. "It doesn't feel like that."

"What does it feel like?"

"It feels like . . . like it's not so much about politics. It feels more like a show. You know how audiences are? They don't demand anything specific when they come. In that way they're different from critics. They don't have preconceptions; they'd just like to go out with something they didn't have when they walked in. That's how they seem with us. We haven't done that much. But they've already received more than they had when we arrived."

"That's how I feel too," says Morris. "I think I'm losing my edge."

He repeated the point about audiences to the American ambassador while they waited for their drivers outside the gala for Amnesty. They had to talk about something.

"You know, if you had real democracy here," said the ambassador, "then you'd have capital punishment. All the polls show that. There's such a thing as trusting the people too much."

"That would be a small price to pay for real democracy," said Matthew, buckling before the temptation of a good line and hating himself immediately. He tried to salvage the scene. "I don't believe that would happen," he said. "Not if there was true democratic debate. Something that went beyond an opinion poll or a mood whipped up. People would listen, they'd weigh consequences, the way a jury does. It's amazing how open and probing people get when they're given genuine responsibility as citizens. They're grateful for it, just having it makes them more careful."

"Now we're in the realm of religious belief," said the ambassador. "I never argue with believers."

Matthew said, "After a real discussion, if they opted for capital punishment, I'd accept it. Either you're serious about democracy or you aren't."

"This is what you're engaged in now," said the ambassador, with a strange combination of query and statement. "What you really care about is the process, the . . . theatre of democracy."

Matthew looked back attentively, on a reverse shot, as it were. He didn't have an answer, but there hadn't really been a question.

"You do think of this as . . . political theatre?" said the ambassador.

"Theatre is public speech," said Matthew. ("O pardon me thou . . .")

"Right. But for what purpose? For explaining to people why what is done must be done. Public speech — democracy, political theatre — it can move things from one point to another. It can change what people are ready to accept. But theatre has a script. The actors know what they're going to say. The audience knows they know what they're going to say."

"Not in all theatre," said Matthew.

"Now you've lost me, I'm afraid," said the ambassador. "But these are real policies you've brought in and they have real consequences. It's not *merely* theatre." His limo arrived. Matthew stood waiting. Security was at a discreet distance. It was embarrassing to be left at the curb in your own country, especially when you were its leader. But it taught you humility, if you needed some.

"There'll be a price to pay for your success," said the ambassador, sliding into velvet darkness through the door.

"I kind of expected there would," said the P.M. The ambassador was already gone. When there is no script, the closing line of a scene is up for grabs. Matthew had spoken last, but from the ambassador's point of view, he too had had the final word.

CHAPTER FIVE

Those who work in improvisation have the chance to see with frightening clarity how rapidly the boundaries of so-called freedom are reached.

— Peter Brook

The international peace action in Colombia began without notice. It was a test case for the joint techniques set up after the peacemaking debacles of the previous decade. Iraq, Bosnia, Rwanda, Haiti, Somalia and elsewhere had taught the world's governments that public support was built at high cost and eroded so fast it wasn't worth the trouble. The bodies responsible for international security were accordingly insulated from public opinion and consultation; instead they followed the models of the new economic and trade agencies. Preliminary air raids were completed and all public and media locations secured before any information was released. It took only four days from the start of the attacks. Dal was inconsolable.

"I've never seen you like this."

"Never?" she says.

Well, not never. There was the time he told her about Ben Johnson and the gold. But that was anger. "Asshole," she said. She was furious Ben hadn't cheated wisely. She was mad at the system that made winning existentially mandatory, because of which cheating was inevitable. So she was angry at herself for soaring when he won and then crashing with him. Anger contained relief; it implied: If this, or if not that — then things could be otherwise. It gave her targets, including her dad — who bore it gladly. If he wasn't outright responsible, except as bearer of the news, he felt so, indirectly: for not preparing her, or not knowing Ben Johnson and stopping him, or not changing the world enough during his time on it to eradicate lapses like Ben's the way polio had been eliminated. If guilt like Matthew's could be liquefied, it would end the energy crisis. Add anger and there'd be a surplus.

Another time was the Gulf War, when the bombing started. By then the series was a national cultural treasure, settled into incomprehensible success, seasons gliding past, he couldn't date things by it the way he could in Ben-and-the-Olympics year, when he was sure they'd receive a swift, deserved cancellation and he could get back to doing work he didn't feel like wearing a disguise for. The day after the first bombs fell on Baghdad, he dropped by the house for . . . something to do with the divorce. Papers, money, regrets. She was there, her mother wasn't. She wouldn't speak, but she was a pillar of sorrow, as Lot's wife was salt. "Let's turn on the TV and watch the war," he said. For him, watching was how to overcome video victimization. He treated TV as a co-combatant. Talk back, toss things, rebut it. Dissect and deconstruct the propaganda — the televised war games, the stand-ups in front of missile launches, long shots of Baghdad in flames, seedy ex-colonels preening before maps and models. The way he used to debunk Watergate over breakfast during rehearsals in the country. They started doing it together when she was twelve. For years after that, they were partners in the news. No more though, she was stone. He tried to get inside with her, give her reasons for this war and thus shift if not lift its weight. But she was stone, just shook her head every few seconds. Her expression was prehistoric. This is human fate, it said, forever; no mitigation, no progress occurs. It shook him, and the limited confidence he'd gained about the transparency of events, along with the possibility of (some) change. She was in a realm where tragedy is eternal and misery unavoidable. He feared for his own equanimity, that precarious sense of the world's improvability which he thought he'd won.

Or, come to think of it, the time she said vaguely she'd like to make people understand "how I feel about the earth." He was reading, or working on a part. "I'm thinking about writing a play," she said.

134

He made an encouraging noise. She went on, still vague, fishing. He looked up. "I just don't know what you're talking about," he said. "It's very abstract but you sound as if I ought to know what you mean. I think you can make theatre out of anything, but you have to tell me what it is and how you're going to do it." She became a mix of sobs and words. He heard "Innu" and "flights." She was bawling now, she couldn't catch her breath. She'd *told* him, this morning, last week, a month ago. He missed it. "Tell me again," he said, "you have to give me another chance." She'd heard an Innu leader on CBC-Radio. He said those NATO jets on training runs in Labrador come up on you at a hundred feet, so fast you don't hear till they're past, they outrun their own sound. He was in a canoe with his nephews, they got so scared they jumped out of the canoe and wouldn't get back in, they towed it to shore, it was lucky they'd been in a shallow part of the river, because of course they couldn't swim, our people don't swim. It broke something in her. She sobbed and wailed, as if she'd met the limits of the human race as it tries to move forward. Sometimes it seems like it's all limits.

But this time was different. "You know why," she said.

He tried looking puzzled but interested. She looked back with disgust. "Because we're in power," he said, like a suspect breaking before his interrogators even start the process.

He tried: "We *aren't* in power. We're merely in government." It was feeble. She didn't bother sneering. He said this system for international conflict resolution was put in place years ago, a natural extension of the economic globalization and free trade deals he'd fought. It was out of the hands of governments, the bankers and generals didn't have to get approval, certainly not his. The machinery clicked into motion. In the old days, small nations like Canada got fucked in the international sphere, but at least they let you do the fucking to yourself.

"Your point?" she said, as she used to say when she was ten. He could have said: "To do what we can with what little is left of power in our hands; how can we know till we at least try?" He tested the line in his mind. He sounded like the Killers of Hope.

The Killers of Hope were the social democrats, especially after they were elected. They'd always had the power to give hope; once they were in government, they could also take it away. He was in a Christmas collective show long ago, based on Canadian poetry for kids; they did it to raise money for their political productions. (This show is political too, he argued at the time, because it's *Canadian*.) The leader of the New Democrats came — the one who wrote children's book reviews to prove he was human — and went backstage afterward. Even the apolitical actors, who'd joined the company temporarily, treated him like Jesus or Olivier or Lorne Greene back in Canada for a visit. Was it the promise of a man in public life who actually cared about normal people, even actors? Was it because they'd never held power, so you could still believe them? Matthew knew about social democrats, in the New Left they were called social fascists. Their job, according to Morris, was to spoil everything they touched. "But I get sucked in. Every damn time," said Morris. Matthew asked why. "Hope," said Morris, "it's about hope. You'd rather lose it again and again than abandon it forever."

They canvassed him in elections. He'd tell them he wouldn't vote for such a half-assed party and get off my porch. They always answered, "What's the alternative?" like it was their party motto. Marx said, "Workers of the world unite!" Mao said, "Power to the people." Social democrats said, "What's the alternative?" Or they'd ask for a special donation. Could they auction him off to do a monologue at some party backer's renovated downtown home? They were different from the communists, who merely stuck you in the cultural part of the evening, when everyone serious left the hall for a smoke or a leak.

After the Berlin Wall came down and the Red Menace departed, no one had big hopes and visions any more. But people still wanted to believe the world could exist differently than it had in the Reagan-Mulroney years; they held modest expectations, not revolutionary ones. Social democracy's hour had struck. For the first time, when they came to canvass, he didn't bait them; he said they had his vote and wished them well up the street. He felt in tune with his countrymen: New Democrats were elected in many provinces — a vessel of those mild ambitions.

But the Killers of Hope explained, once in power, that no real change was possible. They'd come with their fine consciences and carefully examined the possibilities. They were sad to report it, but Reagan and Mulroney were right. You'll have to wake up and smell the coffee, they told the people with modest hopes who put them in power. Their slogan had become "There is no alternative." Come to think of it, that was the wreckage they'd left for Matthew, strewn everywhere. All options had been considered and rejected by those credible witnesses, the Killers of Hope. Then he'd come along and said, Okay, but we'll find another route anyway, we'll *create* it! Now he was telling Dal he couldn't improvise his way out of this. So he stopped and told her how the marriage ended instead.

It was after the wrap party that year. Thirteen more shitty episodes, not a moment of truth in a single one, nor in the seasons that pre-ceded or were ahead. People loved the show, loved me too or my char-acter. She didn't come to the wrap party, I didn't know by then if she wanted me to quit or stay. We used to be so in tune I'd have known without asking. Then after a while, asking seemed like an admission it was too late. She'd accused me of sleeping with Celeste. Celeste played an ironic forensic pathologist who got shoehorned into more and more episodes as the series veered away from normal life and into crime or perversion. You know how Canadian TV always starts off wanting to deal with social issues and ends up trying to be "Dallas." The truth is Celeste and I hadn't slept together, but between scenes we'd been making out like crazy in the trailer. She wanted to sleep with me, I was being true in my fashion and to tell the truth making out — you know, like on your parents' couch, I mean, on my par-ents' couch, I guess — was exciting and satisfying in its way. Maybe it took me back to my teens when sex held such promise because so little had been explored. Or maybe making out just postponed deci-sions. Faced with a hard choice I'll try to take both. It's amazing how often that's possible. So that night at the party she asked me again to sleep with her and I did. Less because I wanted to than because I did-n't want to say no, I was tired of saying no, or afraid of saying no — anyway I did. When I got home it was nearly light. I went down to the basement and fell asleep in the cot at the foot of the stairs. I didn't want to wake your mum or you, if you were there and not sleeping at

*Lyle's or whoever your guy was at the time. I liked Lyle, even though
he said he never watched the show. Maybe that's why I liked him. He
didn't call me Dr. Max. So about 8:30 I heard her in the kitchen
phoning the cops, saying I was missing. I dragged up the stairs and
made an entrance. She asked if I'd slept with Celeste. And I had a
brilliant moment of improv. I confessed. It must have come straight
out of sleep, I must've been working on it those few hours I slept. I
confessed, but not to Celeste. I said it was a woman at the wrap party
I'd never met who kept badgering me and I gave in. So I confirmed
your mum's worst fear and she believed me. But I also denied her very
worst fear, and she wanted to believe that too. So we got by that
night, except after that she wouldn't sleep with me. Or as she put it,
couldn't. She didn't seem angry, more relieved. She forgave me, I
almost felt she was grateful, and I didn't sleep again with Celeste,
and the making out stopped because the shooting was over, and it
didn't start again next season, though she'd become a regular character. But by that time it was finished between us. I'd moved out. We
went to a sex therapist, you know, or maybe you didn't — it was after
that — we thought we could treat it as a technical problem, hand it
to the experts. You could say we both wanted it to work, willed it to
work, we were ready to put in the effort. It just didn't happen. Last
time I saw her — five years ago on my birthday just by accident —
I asked if she was was still angry and she said yes. I asked if she
wanted to take her best shot. She said no. I said it would make me
feel better and she said then she definitely wouldn't. We laughed.
When you laugh like that, you feel something new might be possible.
She said she felt that too, but she didn't want it. I haven't talked to
her since then. You know she won't speak to the press about any of it
and for some reason they've respected that.*

"So could it have been different?" she says. He takes his time on
this. Then he says, "Oh yeah, I think it could've. It just wasn't."
Next night he goes on television to tell the truth, as he puts it, in the
clearest way he can. He says he's disgusted and sickened by the
"international" action against Colombia. He says it's not his idea of
anything associated with that good word, international, and if he
was Lester Pearson at this moment in history, he'd be glad he's

dead. He says bombing and invading a country because it fails to comply with the economic directives of bankers and technocrats makes the excuses for invading Iraq and Vietnam sound noble. He says there's nothing Canada can do because it's locked in by treaties and commitments which remove any elected government from control over what's done with its resources — like troops and money. But there are other places in the international arena where the government isn't so tied up; if he has his way, actions will be taken. All the commentaries which follow wonder aloud about the free trade agreement with the United States, a document that seems as venerable as the British North America Act of 1867, which created Canada, or the Quebec Act a century before. He wouldn't dare, would he?

The Americans acted boldly and acted first. "Everything is in the file," said the ambassador. His aide materialized, file in hand. The ambassador laid it on the desk of Canada's leader, said a few lines, and bowed — bowed out the door, literally. "Les' ride, amigos," muttered the prime minister.

The file was exhaustive. It asked for everything at once. An open door to all foreign — not just U.S. — investment; an end of Canada's right to screen foreign buyers under the few conditions still permitted. Open tenders on procurement at all levels of government, no restrictions of foreign business in any area. Complete integration of Canadian and U.S. defence forces. Full sharing of energy resources with blended pricing and marketing. Culture — ah, culture. Every tabloid and TV network, publishing and pop music, arts funding and subsidy would be subject to the same conditions as procurement: American poets and choreographers would gain the right to apply for Canadian grants. Canadians could do the same, except there were no public granting agencies left in the U.S. One exception: Canada could maintain its major performing arts companies (they'd grown popular with visiting and transferred executives) — *provided* that their employment policies and repertoire did not discriminate against American artists and works. "Little danger there," grumbled Matthew, scanning the list. "They haven't done anything

Canadian in years."

It was a brilliant document. It left no space for negotiation. It was a true artifact of American culture. If it had come with a logo, it would have been *U.S.* — for unconditional surrender.

The ambassador hadn't requested a reply. "In the absence of compliance," he said, "the government of the United States wishes to state its intention to abrogate the free-trade agreement six months from today, according to the pertaining clauses." As he spoke, the same information was being released to the press in Ottawa and in Washington.

"Sons of bitches!" said Morris.

"Brilliant!" said Alex. He saw it happen in the Mideast decades back, when Egypt's Anwar Sadat offered to make peace with Israel. It staggered the Israelis. It gave them what they said they always wanted but were sure they'd never get. Your reality shudders when that happens. You're off balance, the other side can move anywhere on the board while you adjust. The Americans had done it now. They gave Canada — especially those who still believed in their country, like their new leader — just what they'd been demanding: independence from the U.S., release from the odious free-trade agreement that began it all.

For years people like Matthew nursed a belief that they had only one potential weapon in their mismatch with the U.S. They could walk, like a wife threatening to leave a bad marriage. They'd talked about it and fretted over the consequences: what about the kids, what happens to the already-restructured economy? was it too late? was it better to stick it out? Then *he* leaves? How disorienting! While they were still trying to recompose their options, the Americans acted again. This time the president himself, President Stutts who felt he had some personal business with the Canadians after that mid-election gaffe, said: give us access to your water resources. Water — the dread subject — the only thing left off the list of ultimatums. He insisted on immediate, unimpeded access for the stricken southwestern states, plus establishment of a joint authority to dig a great ditch and series of pipelines so that the resource, "which by its nature knows no national boundaries," would be permanently annexed to the continental water grid. Rivers, lakes, cataracts — if it's wet, hand it over. And don't give us any crap about how we plan to use the stuff. If we wanta sprinkle the golf courses of California, that's our business.

It makes no sense, said the Canadian nationalists. We were sure *they'd* never cancel. The agreement gave them everything they wanted, except maybe water, which they were snatching bit by bit anyway. Give us the water, said the Americans, and we'll think about opening discussions on a new trade deal.

Quebec struck next. The coalition government there, following the funeral of former premier Bourassa, declared independence. The issue had lain still since the inconclusive referendum campaigns of the mid-nineties and the stalemated election of 1997, after which the two main parties formed a grand coalition on a nationalist but not independentist basis. Quebec's government now claimed that cancellation of the trade deal created a national crisis for Quebec, since its economy had been drastically rebuilt in the image of free trade. Social and cultural services were dependent on revenues based in the new structures. Quebec, in other words, could not survive *without* free trade. It was a deft reversal of nationalist rhetoric elsewhere in Canada — and anyway it wasn't Quebec's threats and posturing that made the whole mess happen. The "irresponsible" behaviour of the feds, led by some Anglo actor, amounted to dissolving the bonds of trust implicit in Confederation. The government of the new nation had been assured the U.S. would "look favourably" on a request to maintain the status quo ante in the unique case of Quebec. No, the U.S. had not suggested the break, the new president of Quebec said, Quebec had gone to the Americans, inquired about a special arrangement, and received "positive indications." Had the Americans asked Quebec to ask for special status? Laughter, but no answer. Those in Quebec who'd been bitterest about free trade — unions, farmers, artists — were the same people who'd yearned longest for a country of their own. They'd finally adjusted to permanent frustration; now, unexpectedly, after giving up — here it was. They weren't ready to blink and see it vanish. Afterward, sometime down the road, they'd form an opposition and fight to end free trade in their splendid new land. As for the business leaders who'd opposed independence in the past, that was before it was good for business. If free trade followed the flag, so would they.

"Hi. It's me." It's very late. She missed their weekly dinner tonight. No call beforehand, she just didn't show. "I'm fine. Don't worry."

"Okay. What about?"

"I've been — I was arrested."

"Great."

"Great sarcastic or great sincere?" An important choice. Sometimes you don't know till you come to a moment how you're going to say the line. Sometimes it varies, night to night.

"Where?"

"In front of the U.S. Embassy. We went to express our gratitude for liberating us from their control. The cops kept saying, if you hate the U.S., why are you mad at them for letting us go. I don't think they understand my generation's attitude. Actually it was kind of hard to explain."

"Where are you now?"

"I'm not in jail. They arrested us but they didn't keep us."

"Great sincere."

"Really?"

"Somebody has to do something. And it's sure not me at the moment." A touch of self-pity. Self-pity is the least attractive trait in an actor. It's why *Richard II*, with the best poetry Shakespeare wrote, is almost never done. Self-pity is the ultimate theatrical bummer. "I mean I'm grateful to you, and so should everyone be."

"You think this is doing something?" she says. "Were you ever arrested?"

"No," he says. "Not yet. Your mother has. Maybe you should talk to her. I know you've heard about it, but it might sound different now."

"Are you kidding? That's all I've been thinking about since they busted us. In the wagon. In the cell." He winces, she can see him do it over the phone. She goes on, encouraged. "I've been improvising. A performance piece. I think I'm starting to understand her."

"Can we reschedule dinner?" he says. "This I have to hear."

142

"When I was nineteen, I measured myself. I had the same measurements as Miss Universe. That hasn't changed.

"I was born into privilege. My grandfather was attorney general of Ontario; his father was premier. When I was five, my father, who everyone said would go into politics and be a cabinet minister at least, skied to the bottom of the hill at the family chalet, took me in his arms and died. He had something wrong from the time he was a POW after he got shot down during the war. My mother remarried badly, to a salesman. We drifted away from the rest of the family. They offered to send me to private school but I wouldn't take their money. My boyfriend rode a motorcycle.

"I didn't go to my father's university either. Instead I went to a new campus in a small town that called itself the 'Harvard of the North.' By December I was disappointed. I'm always disappointed. The leader of a radical group came and spoke on campus. He said the contradictions in Canadian society were deepening. We were in the late stages of a typical revolutionary process. Quebec would blow first, the cadres there were already in the countryside, rallying the peasantry. He said the privileged few had pillaged their way to the top but others would take back what had been stolen from them. He meant the workers but I thought of myself and what I should have had. I asked if I could come and learn at his feet. He gave me an address in Toronto. I moved into a communal house there in a drab working-class area that depressed me. They said this showed my class roots and told me to criticize myself at meetings. I got a job in a factory. The owner said I spoke well and enrolled me in management training. I had to fight hard to avoid it. My assignment was to organize a union, so we could expose unions as trickery invented to sidetrack workers from their natural revolutionary tendencies. The leader often stayed at our house. He'd call me into his room and tell me to sleep with him as a way of shedding my bourgeois habits. I didn't.

"On May Day, I was arrested outside Old City Hall. A comrade made the adventurist error of taunting a mounted policeman's horse. He grabbed her by the hair and rode down Bay. I caught her feet. We both screamed slogans. I turned down a lawyer, as I'd been trained, and denounced the bourgeois justice system. The judge gave me three weeks. At the Don jail, they put me in solitary for inciting other prisoners and charged me with something else.

"When I went to court on the new charge, my hair had started to fall out and my body had dipped below Miss Universe standards. A well-dressed older man told me my family had sent him. I nodded. I nodded whenever he said anything. He called the Crown attorney Teddy and seemed to know the judge. The case was over quickly. He led me by the arm through the doors, down the marble staircase, across the foyer, and on to the stone steps of Old City Hall, where this hell began. But this time, instead of mounted police — in a black Lincoln, parked illegally, sat my grandmother. 'Get in dear,' she said. We drove to the family mansion in Rosedale. It took me a year to regain my health. I never went back to the communal house. I knew they'd say I'd been a failure as a revolutionary and the truth is they were right.

"I never lost my faith in the explanations I learned from them; I just lost faith in my ability to embody those things. I entered theatre sideways, as a props and costume maker, which needed no training. Then I tried acting. I found I could do it. I was attracted to left-wing and populist companies. There were many in those days, they had a purpose, and they were funded. Even actors who didn't care about politics sometimes pretended to, given the times, the way rock musicians became feminists later because it was a way to get laid. Matthew and I met in the Wagon Train and a year after, we formed our own company. It was him who always seemed unsatisfied with just *showing* political action; he kept wanting to *do* something. For me the whole appeal was that this was 'just' theatre. Yet in the end he left to make films and be a TV star. I was the one who dropped out and began to organize workers. Sooner or later we'd have to leave each other, as we'd both left the company. Or maybe I just couldn't stand the way he drove, or made omelettes. Everyone makes omelettes their own way."

"That's it?" says Matthew. "The way I drove? How I make omelettes? That's the climax?"

"Don't take it personally. I'm still working on it. Anyway that's

144

not the climax. Think of it as a postmodern afterthought."

"Is that the same as a moral?" he says.

"A *moral*?" she asks. "A *moral*?"

"A lesson," he says. "Something we learn from the past that's useful to us in what we're going through now."

She says she has no idea what he means. The past — teaches lessons?

Kristof, who worked with the company often in those years, would help them create a scene on the Riel rebellion or the Winnipeg strike. They'd find a dramatic hook: like, someone's trying to get through with a crucial piece of information. The actors would muck around, try this, try that, get it going — then Kristof would break in and say, "All right, that'll work. But how does it fit with our politics?" Stories were expected to have morals and if they didn't, you'd work them over till they did. Matthew once met a famous historian in the middle of a bloody campus demo: police clubbing students. The historian was dazed. These kids he'd taught — with broken bones and bloody faces. Matthew asked the prof, based on his knowlege of history, what it meant. "I have no idea," said the prof sadly and walked away to his office and his books. "But *we* had a grid," says Matthew. "Marxist, Maoist, Trotskyite. Some people added a Freudian undergrid. Some kind of grid. You were never out there just hearing stories. They illustrated something. You knew that before you began. You just had to crack the code."

"Do you miss it?" she asks. Well, he thought he did. But now that she asks . . .

"What I miss," he says, "is how it armed you. It protected you."

"Against what?" she says.

He thinks about it. "Against everything," he says. "Against criticism."

"Political criticism?" she asks.

"That too," he says. "But even . . . theatre criticism. It may be how I kept going."

"Reviews?" she says, amazed. "In the papers?"

"Yeah," he says sheepishly. "They come and see you pour out your guts. Then they write that you should spend the rest of your

145

life in jail and never open your mouth again because of this piece of shit you produced. That's a big reason people leave theatre. It's inhuman."

"And Marxism helped?" she says.

"Sure it did. I could explain why they didn't like what I did, if they didn't. For example: they were gatekeepers for the status quo and their job was to keep radical ideas from infecting the society. Stuff like that. The worse you got hammered, the more it proved you were on the right track."

"You believed that?"

"That's not the point. It kept you going. Others — better actors than me, writers, directors — took it personally. Being savagely attacked in public. They didn't have a way to explain it as not being a personal failure. They doubted themselves or their art. But if you had a grid to look at the world through, it helped. Maybe you really had done shit, and the critics were right — of course that was possible — but it kept you in the game, so you could learn from the shit you'd done and do something better next time out."

"Whatever gets you through the night?" she says.

He nods. "The night. The show. Your life."

"So it didn't just work on bad reviews."

"No! It worked everywhere."

"What if somebody dumped you?"

He wonders: Are there things she doesn't talk to him about? Has something happened? Is it recent? Is she asking for help?

"You could try it if someone dumped you. For instance, this society makes people value the wrong things. Or, your self-esteem was injured by the insecurity your parents felt because they came from immigrant families and it screwed up your relationships." She's looking dubious. "It doesn't always work," he says. "Are you thinking about yourself?"

"Nope," she says, "I was thinking about you and Mum."

"Do you know what you're going to do?" she says.

"No," he says, he doesn't. "I'm not thinking about it much." She looks querulous. "It's a method that always worked for me," he says. "Give your thoughts a rest when you don't have a solution, and let your unconscious toss up some answers."

"How do you know when that happens?" she says.

"It kind of gives you a call."

"So is that the only part you miss?" she says. She's giving it a rest.

"Of what? Of having a grid that explains everything? To tell the truth, I think so. Because it also can be depressing to know what everything means before it happens. Or know it has a meaning, even if you don't know what that is. It takes away from the story itself, from the plot. It implies a good story isn't good enough. But they are. Good stories are great. Just by themselves."

"Wanta know what I think is wrong with it?" she says. "You could never really learn something from a story, even if you said learning was the whole point. Because you'd already know what everything means. So stories, or experiences, don't really teach. They just . . . illustrate. So it's not very . . . creative."

"Yeah," he says with awe. "That's exactly it."

"The Red Guards are here," said Dal next day from the office.

Uh-oh: flashback.

That's the message the box office sent backstage at the theatre thirty years ago, during *Cultural Revolution for the Hell of It*. It hadn't really been the Red Guards. It was a group called Red Dawn who lived in a communal house on a downtown street that hadn't been occupied yet by renovators. That night they'd been downtown trashing the windows of Simpsons, though not Eaton's. They'd made a Maoist analysis and decided since Eaton's was owned by Canadians, it played a positive role at *this* stage of the Canadian revolution. They'd come direct to the theatre for, as it were, the cultural part of the evening. They stayed after for criticism and self-criticism with the actors, who returned to the stage trembling. "You don't have to be a fucking communist to do a fucking communist play," muttered Michele, who played an old peasant woman. She wasn't intimidated like the rest, but then she'd been a fucking communist herself. Meg, a comrade from Red Dawn, said she liked Michele's character, but thought she should have become a devout revolutionary by the play's end. Matthew knew comrade Meg. She told him she

147

wouldn't sleep with him because he was a careerist, since he had a career. Once he went over to the Red Dawn house to score some dope. Meg looked up from the couch as he came in the door and lowered a slim yellow pamphlet in her hand. "Here I am reading Mao's *On Contradiction*," she said, "and you walk in." Michele handled Meg's criticism. She said, "I'm afraid that's as far as my character can get at her age. She's pretty set in her ways and I think it's impressive she's moved as much as she has in the course of the play." That's when Matthew thought, We should have a kid together. Afterward, he told her it was a perfect dialectical answer. "Don't sound so surprised," she said. "I've been living inside this old girl for three weeks. You know Mao said correct ideas don't fall out of the sky, they come from practice."

These really were called Red Guards. They waited in the outer part of the prime minister's office. He slipped in the private entrance. "I think they mean the name in a kind of retro way," said Dal. He went out and perched on the receptionist's desk. Casual. They started to settle on the floor. One young woman stayed up. "I don't think we should automatically assume a posture of deference to authority when a symbol of patriarchal dominance enters the room." Fair enough. He got on the carpet too.

They were a coalition, they said. But not like coalitions in the anti-free-trade years that he'd been in; those had social respectability; they even had money: unions, farmers, women's organizations, artists' groups — this was different. These people were young and represented no significant economic activity in Canadian society. The jobs were taken or just gone. "I said as much," interjected Matthew, "during the campaign."

Silence and eye rolls. He'd reacted like a politician. "That sounded just like a politician," he said. "Give me another shot." The point is, they went on, ignoring him, they represented constituencies and organizations, but the constituencies were mostly homeless, underemployed, unrepresented, and overeducated. "What we do best," said one, "is critical analysis of society and letters to the editor. We have lots of time and we keep getting better." They'd taken the name because, according to their reading, it symbolized the major political rejection of the twentieth century: the communist revolutionary tradition. This time he didn't say he'd been there. "We feel rejected by the century too," said the woman who spoke first. She stopped. There was a quiet they all seemed comfortable with. He felt he was allowed to speak again. "Sometimes," he said, "I walk past groups of kids on my street in Toronto and feel like they hate me for . . . being the age I am and having what they'll never have." They nodded, more or less collectively. They saw the problem as cultural, they said; they believed in a cultural revolution — since governments can't do anything anyway any more. He glanced at Dal, she was looking at them. If you have money, they went on, you can do something in business. If you don't, you get active in culture. You're right, he thought, You *are* good at analysis. He asked what they wanted from him.

They'd like him to explain, they said, the shit about Canada. Saving the Canadian way, caring about the country. What did it have to do with the pain they saw and felt? Why did he keep connecting it to feeling Canadian? He thought about the hockey series against Russia in 1972 when Paul Henderson scored the winner in Moscow with seconds left and if you'd been in a plane anywhere above Canada, you'd have heard the cheer from below. None of them were alive then. During the free-trade fights, they'd been in grade school. He tried to explain. They were gone again.

"Look," said one, "are you for revolution or against it?" This was progress. Back in the sixties, kids like this used to ask if you were for *the* revolution, as if you could find it in aisle seven, halfway down. Matthew had talked that way. These kids said "revolution" but it was less . . . rhetorical. As if for them it was a necessity. Like: we're running out of air. Are you for breathing or against it? Said it at lower volume too. They just had no alternatives. It was this or revolution. Besides, they didn't remember the Cold War, it probably sounded like the Boer War to them. Nobody was going to accuse them of being Russian spies if they said words like "revolution," so they weren't defensive on terminology. Russia was just another zany free market society where people like them got marginalized and disregarded.

"Thanks for listening," said the woman who hadn't sat. She was like an elder among them. Elders don't have to be old, in the native tradition. "We were starting to wonder," she said, "if you'd become the Pierre Berton of the left." That hit him a hammer blow but he concealed it. He asked how they felt now. She did a kind of look-around canvass. Maybe the jury was still out, maybe the guilty verdict was already in. "Well," she added, "thanks for listening," as if she hadn't just said that. They filed out politely. No bullshit confrontations. He remembered sit-ins and occupations differently. "You got shit in your mouth?" he said to a VP for communications at Dow Chemical's Canadian headquarters during the Vietnam War. "You got shit in your mouth? Zzat how come you talk that way?" It was from an Off-Broadway play, he'd been alert for a chance to use it. These kids though — the New Red Guards — they'd asked their questions. Then they left. "Who the hell is Pierre Berton?" he heard a voice ask, as the last of them dribbled through the oak doors.

Helga Kuznets is back in Canada. Her name is little known beyond theatre professionals, but to them she is legend. "The Empress of Improv": "All acting is improvisation, no less than life itself." She is the only remaining link to both Stanislavsky *and* Brecht. She is in her eighties, maybe ninety by now. When Matthew first heard her name, mere rumours since she never wrote or gave interviews, he didn't know if she was alive or dead. Then, in Paris aeons ago, he attended a workshop. She treated the icons of twentieth-century theatre casually. She dropped their names and butted her Gitanes in them. She gave them no shrift. It should have seemed arrogant — yet it empowered *you*. She got them off your back. She talked tough, like the best of advice columnists in the old days. "Listen, toots — you think those guys would have stuck where they were? They'd have *forgotten* their systems and theories by now. They'd have improvised a new approach every year, maybe every show."

She hasn't been in Canada since the Reagan years, when she was denied entry to a world theatre congress in Rochester because her name was on a list. Maybe it was her remote Russian origins. Or the relationship to Brecht. The demos in Paris she never missed during the Vietnam years. Or just that she lived in Europe. So she came to Canada and addressed the congress by cross-border video.

"To bust their balls," she explained. Matthew threw a party in her honour at his house. The place was blocked with actors, eating mostly, and cursing their agents. When time came to go — she looked frail even then — instead of heading for the door, she drove straight into the heart of the mob and exuberantly said good night to each guest. Most had no idea who she was or why they were there.

She's back for an academic conference on her *oeuvre*, held in Montreal. It's not because an actor has become prime minister, the event was planned long ago. Still, he accepted an invitation to open it, so he can see her again. They meet Sunday morning for Dim Sum. The restaurant is cavernous, it's also empty. The Mounties must have turned everyone away. They know he'd never agree, so they just do it. Dal is there, Morris, who's come for the conference, Alex, and Nataley — who's transcribing his tapes, plus various leftists and artists. They fill a large circular table, mixing French and English though, as usual, most of it ends up English. They talk politics, in deference to the prime minister; then they talk culture. Helga wants to know what's at the movies. Have they seen Tarantino's latest Futura film. Number four in the series, about the hermaphroditic avenger of the year 3000. It hasn't reached France yet. Disgust circles the table: *Oh, Helga, it's racist. Oh, Helga, it's sexist. It's escapist. Technophilia . . . speciesism . . . unbelievably violent* — Helga listens. When they've all spoken, she says, *"Il faut voir ça!"*

That afternoon they make the matinee, just him and her. It wasn't easy to clear the prime minister's schedule, but it wasn't so hard. They sit at the back, security carefully seeded through the place. It's a deal he's worked out with the Mounties. It's a secret that the prime minister is there; though he doesn't think anybody would care. (No one believes that; they think he's feigning modesty, or the common touch.) Matthew and Helga watch the film. It's full of race, sex, violence, deceit, vanity, fine technique, and solid acting. She laughs so hard she tells Matthew she may need an ambulance: does Canada still have medical care? Afterward she wants a brandy and he wants a macchiato. They walk back to the hotel. He keeps her pace, almost.

"Where else," asks Helga, "can you live as you can in film? All the experiences you will never have, even if you get to have a few. Like being the leader of your country." At the hotel, he brews a cup in the little expresso-maker he takes everywhere, including the lake. It's like his slippers: pack them when you travel; you feel stupid putting them in the bag but great when you pull them out and put them on. "I tell you what I think is the mistake," says Helga.

"The mistake in the film?" he says.

"I think you are playing the ending," she says.

He sits. She didn't speak during the discussion about Canadian politics this morning, or ask questions. He assumed she wasn't interested or couldn't follow. He finishes the coffee, fixes another round, and sits again. "How did you catch that?" he says.

She shakes her head. She doesn't know. She says he seems to be playing the part of a person destined for noble defeat. He says that makes sense if it's the only script you can honestly anticipate. "Aha," she says, "but there *is* no script. You are not *acting* a script, you are merely acting *as if* there is one." For the first time he understands how to play Greek tragedy: as if there's a script and you have to say the lines, however much you hate the part. "You know Agamemnon in *Iphigenia in Aulis*?" she says. It doesn't surprise him, she has this capacity. "You are one of the actors who can do either script or improvisation," she says. "I would have been one myself, had I chosen to act. But we both prefer to improvise. And in this case, there is no script. There is only your decision to act as if there is one."

"I don't know what to improvise," says Matthew.

"Neither do I," says Helga. "What do you think you could do?"

She is the director of your dreams. It's so simple. Why are they so rare?

"Could you call an election?" says Helga. It's less suggestion than provocation.

"That's what they want," says Matthew. "That's the script. I might lose, I might win. Nothing would change."

He's up again, pacing. As if they're rehearsing.

"A referendum," he mutters. "Nah." She asks what he just said. He says it was nothing. A bad idea. She persists. "I said I could hold a referendum!" says Matthew. "The Charlottetown referendum was the great political event of my lifetime."

"Perfect!" says Helga. She's certainly never heard of Charlottetown or the referendum known by its name, but her joy in life is to encourage creativity in the moment. "What would your referendum be about?"

"I have no idea," says Matthew. "That's why I dropped it."

"Aha!" she says. "Even better! Now we work."

He's in Toronto to attend the Doras, a link to his theatre past; you do that sometimes, when you're having trouble with the future. When he didn't know what to do with a part, he'd often squander a day reliving roles he knew had worked. Dal is with him, it's become routine, the press expect it, everyone does. When it's over, and the drinks in the lobby, they slip away. They go up to Bloor, to By the Way, formerly Lick'n Chicken and still known by the name, though the sign in the window clearly says, Sorry, No Chicken. It's a warm August night, Toronto at its best, people fill the streets as if they think winter could arrive by morning, and better grab the heat while they can. They stand in line for frozen yogurt. He remembers the first time he tried it here, he thought he'd never go back to ice cream. But ice cream met the challenge, it transformed, even revolutionized itself. What you thought was over, or you couldn't do, doesn't always happen. Now frozen yogurt is a specialty treat, it won't disappear, but it won't fulfil its early promise (and menace) either.

The line advances slowly. They insist on waiting like everyone. Elsewhere in the country it might seem precious: false ordinariness. But people around here know him. When he was a TV star they let him be. Now that he's merely P.M., they're willing to make the same effort. It's a sign of their sophistication. They glance at each other to make sure no one breaks the rule: one look and that's all. If somebody stared, there wouldn't be violence, but deep wordless disapproval. They're closing on the counter. The kids behind it sweat to get cones and cups out. He hears the voices of middle-class Annex residents agonize over their decisions — "There are *so* many flavours" — as if they think the hesitation must be charming to overhear, as if they're milking their best line in a small part. Then, finally, "Well, I think I'll tryyyyy . . . boysenberry?" With that

153

upturn of query tacked on, lest they seem brazen. "Banana," he says curtly.

He finds himself working up an improv. Is it escape? When he feels politically inadequate, does he revert to performance? Representation in place of action. Did their indecisiveness at the counter mirror his? Yet they seem to think they're adorable, these docs and profs and screenwriters who inhabit the streets around. Do they find every move in their lives delightful? Or is there in it, its opposite: "Excuse me, but beneath my complacency I feel a dark stain of bourgeois angst because I know, not far from my smooth surface, that my comfort and privilege are snatched from others, elsewhere in the city or country or world, whom I rarely meet but whose deprivation is required to keep me fitted out this way." The thin voice of middle-class guilt, objectively rooted, since they *don't* deserve what they have; who of us do? He sometimes heard it when they stepped on a bus and asked directions; he knew they wouldn't be shocked if one day the driver swivelled and blasted them: "You lazy snivelling thieves. Who are you that I should ferry you through your lives while you live so much better than me and mine in the bargain? You know it isn't fair, I know it isn't, it's only your luck that I let you get away with it and guess what, I've decided to stop. So step fucking off my bus." And they descend with docility, knowing what they've heard is reasonable; the only wonder is they weren't reamed out that way long ago.

They amble down Bloor with their cones. She took anise, decisively. The strollers are discreet. One look. Kristof used to have a note he made during auditions: "Has access to class." It was the rarest note in his file. Matthew once asked what he based it on. The voice, said Kristof, who'd been a child in England, before his parents completed their trip from Odessa to Montreal, and who had a clearer sense of these matters than those like Matthew who were born here. "The voice of the working class," said Kristof, "goes straight from their mind to your ear. There is no self-involved meandering along its way, as the middle-class voice does." Matthew didn't understand. "It's a timbre," said Kristof, "not an idea." But when they cast for the film version of *Don't Mourn, Organize*, in which the spirit of Joe Hill, labour songster and martyr, returns to inhabit the soul of an unskilled young worker in a factory — they found everything but the voice. Ariel, who they chose — had it all: angry, funny, tender — it seemed. One night Matthew took her to meet Stephania, who the character was based on. They sat in Stephania's parents' kitchen, her mama bringing small cups of Turkish coffee, her father urging on them his homemade grappa. Matthew listened to the two Stephanias — called Marcella in the script. One voice went straight from the mind to the ear; the other dawdled. As they got in his car after, Ariel turned to him bereft. "No way," she said. "I'll never sound like her."

Who are these people, his countrymen? How do you lead if you don't know the led and they don't know each other? Who do you govern for? What do they want? Why should they trust you? How do you figure out what binds them? Why should you assume anything does?

The last time he saw Kristof was in Vancouver. Matthew had performed at the opening of a children's theatre sponsored by a former governor general. He was walking down Granville when he heard the unmistakable sound of forehead hitting lamppost. He didn't even look, he knew it was Kristof. They went into Robsonstrasse and found a mochaccino bar. Kristof was teaching at a community college and workshopping a play by a young playwright, he said he was embarrassed but he couldn't recall the name. It was the first time they'd met since Kristof lost his theatre in Ottawa, the one he started in a working-class area and then moved downtown because none of the workers came and the enlightened middle classes who usually thronged his work were having a hard time finding the place. Then Kristof's board locked him out of his own building, the very board the arts councils had forced him to acquire, or they wouldn't keep funding his attacks on the Canadian state. There'd been a little rally outside the padlocked theatre, Matthew had spoken, so had Kristof, who'd been in his glory.

In Vancouver Kristof was still in rant mode. Matthew did what he always did when Kristof was oblivious. He looked at his watch. Suddenly Kristof was back, talking normally, looking at Matthew, registering his existence. Kristof couldn't stand losing an audience, even an audience of one. It had happened too often. That's why Matthew thought of him now, after the frozen yogurts, and wondering how to frame a referendum. Kristof hadn't so much lost his audiences as dismissed them. The audience he yearned for — the people, the working masses — never came, so he hated them for that. The audience that did come, the "*boo-joisie*," as he put it, in the style of the ghetto blacks he admired — he held in contempt. Their continued support merely magnified his scorn. As though he wouldn't let them humiliate him further by applauding him. All the energy in his shows went into insulting the audience that came, in the name of the one that didn't.

That's why they finally stopped working together. When they did the strike-at-the-tire-factory show, where the union sold out its own members, Kristof brought in an ancient, windup phonograph the day before opening. They still didn't have a last scene. It was the end of twelve long hours, a grind Kristof was famous for putting actors through. They slumped on the set while he wound up the recorder and played "Solidarity Forever," by Pete Seeger and the Almanac Singers, but slowed to half speed and scratchy as hell. Sheer pain on the ear. That's how he wanted to end the show — "because somehow our movement has lost its way." Matthew was furious. He went home and wrote one of his bittersweet — "We may not have won but we haven't lost yet" — endings, which they used after a debate that consumed most of next day and was only settled by a vote of the company minutes before the audience came in. They had the same argument about the ending of the hockey play. Kristof claimed he hated sports because they distract the masses from revolutionary struggle, but Matthew suspected it was because Canadians cared more about hockey than about theatre.

They walked together back to Kristof's Vancouver hotel, an SRO near the train station. Kristof said he wanted Matthew to read the young writer's script. The room smelled, a terrible stench. Kristof couldn't have washed anything in months, including himself. He hadn't opened the windows. He was still smoking cigars, clearly the cheapest brand ever made. Matthew bore it for about a minute, then left. The script had no name on it, it was incoherent, and sentimental where it was coherent. When he called a few days later, they said Kristof had left no forwarding address. He hadn't told Matthew the name of the community college he was teaching at, maybe it didn't exist.

Matthew wishes he knew where Kristof was. He'd like to talk about the relationship between actor and audience, each of whom needs the other in order to exist. The referendum is meant to be where they meet. It's like an improv exercise in reverse. There, the audience throws out the challenge and the actor responds. Here he'll throw the challenge to them. But he still doesn't have the question.

Alex says it's urgent. There is someone Matthew must meet. Alex will bring him to Ottawa.

"It's kind of busy here," says Matthew.

"He's the leader of a national liberation movement," says Alex.

"Which one?" says Matthew, wondering what's left.

"Kurdistan," says Alex. Wow, thinks Matthew.

They make time by extending the day. The Kurdish struggle is ancient and tragic. The Kurds have been fighting so long you forget them but when you look, they're still there battling. As far back as World War I they were promised independence, then sold out. They've been diddled by every force in the region and all the major powers. Somehow they continue. They are as heroic as Cuba, Vietnam, China, and Nicaragua all seemed in their time — yet they've outlasted everyone. Along with the Zapatista rebels of southern Mexico, they recall the hopes of another kind of world, extinguished almost everywhere else. Now, finally, they may be on the verge of success: a Kurdish homeland. Alex has devised this to inspire me, thinks Matthew. And I need it.

They sit late into the night. Their guest is exuberant, his stories are detailed. He's met everyone. He drops names as if he were Kissinger. (Of course he has met Kissinger, who encouraged and then betrayed him.) He spent years in Iraqi, Iranian, and Turkish prisons. Take your pick. He discourses on the culture of his people and their undeniable rights. At 4:00 a.m., when he leaves by government car for his hotel, Matthew turns to Alex.

157

"He's magnificent. Why the hell was I so bored?"

"Me too," says Alex. "You want to prop your eyes open with toothpicks. It's the phenomenon of boring people with interesting lives." Matthew says he used to notice it while interviewing for the collectives. Or just sitting in a bar with other actors. "I've sometimes wondered," says Alex, "if I'm one of those people myself."

"Not yet," says Matthew. "But you have potential. I do too," he yawns. "So why did you bring him?"

"My thesis is: this is the profile of a successful radical in politics," says Alex. Matthew stirs in his drowsiness. "For forty years he's done nothing but work for his people's liberation. He has rarely spent two nights in one bed. Or country. He always has the same conversations and deals with the same internal squabbles. He thinks of only this and seems happy doing it. True radical politics is about saying and doing the same thing, and not wanting anything else in your life. You have to enjoy the repetition or how could you continue? Eventually you might win, if only for a while. Or you might not. What kind of person can do that?"

"Your point?" says Matthew.

"How should I know? You're going into the thick of it, aren't you? In the coming months, it will test you. We'll find out what kind of leader you are. If you have what's needed. I don't know if that's why I brought him but it's a theory."

"Are you trying to make me think the whole thing is pointless?"

"No!" says Alex firmly. "But it is."

Helga's final counsel on how to word the referendum was elliptical. "You know I think well only in terms of theatre," she said over the distorted line from Bali, where she was attending the first All-Asia Improvisational Festival. "But I know that the less you put in stage directions, the more you encourage the creativity of your actors. The more stage directions — the less room they have. Anyway, you've heard the famous story about Brecht." Matthew hadn't. "A director once had rehearsal scripts for a Brecht play typed up with only the dialogue, no stage directions. Brecht of course was famous for the detailed stage directions he included in his scripts. Then they rehearsed. They rehearsed and rehearsed. They tried each scene and each line many ways till it seemed right. Finally they opened. It was a success. Then the director went back to the original text and read over the stage directions that had been omitted. Each one was perfectly fulfilled in the production. To the smallest detail. Because the lines Brecht gave the actors were perfect. From there, everything surrounding them had to follow."

"Were you the director?" asked Matthew.

"Of course I was," said Helga. "But that's not my point. My point is: if you don't have Brecht's flawless ear for dialogue, can you reverse the process? If you can get the surrounding circumstances right, the relationships between players and setting and so forth, then will the lines you need simply follow?"

"Helga," says Matthew, "did you really know Brecht?"

"Know him?" she barks from Bali. "I fucked him!"

CHAPTER SIX

"Face it, we lost."

"No. We just haven't won yet."

— *Scaffold scene from Rebels Ride by Night, about the
failed Canadian revolution of 1837*

A referendum ought to be Gramscian, according to Morris.

"It's about contesting hegemonic control rather than taking direct political action," he said.

"My head hurts," said Matthew, "when you talk that way."

"You know what I mean. It's a fight about the way people think. That's the only fight around."

"So you're not pissed because I haven't seized the means of production yet?"

"You've also been tardy proclaiming the dictatorship of the proletariat."

They were sitting in the window at Bluer. This was impossible, according to security and communications experts. The leader of a country can't sit in a café and definitely not at the counter in the window. At least, he can't do it and expect to hold a normal conversation. It will become a photo op, inevitably. The Mounties were at a cramped table, the one nearest the window, jackets bulging with hardware and software. Mario and his brother Nick were behind the cappuccino machine.

"Another *latte*?" said Mario to Matthew's back.

"I try to avoid that term, it's pretentious," said the prime minister as usual. Mario and Nick mouthed his words.

160

The papers and TV stations had heard. Alert citizens doubtless phoned in the news. Pol-stoppers. Reporters and camera operators lounged across the street, waiting for crowds to form. Small knots did from time to time. Mostly, though, the passersby kept moving. One look. A wink. A thumbs up. A university student did a take when he saw who sat in the window, then pulled a copy of the Yukon land-claims play from his knapsack, the one with Matthew's "Diary of a Collective Creation" as a preface, and waved it like a banner at them.

"I didn't know that was still in print," said Morris.

"It isn't. It's not even remaindered any more," said Matthew. He glanced across the street at the used bookstore down a half-flight of stairs. He shrugged. Such is life, such is art. Citizens of Canada came and went, glancing respectfully, nodding conspiratorially, shaking their heads sadly, once in a while they scowled. They treated the prime minister as they treated their hockey players, rock stars, and internationally successful novelists: not as though they weren't special, but as though they remained human too. Or maybe something else was happening. Had the fascination with celebrity that marked the last half-century begun to wane? Twenty years back, celebrity became — tentatively — an occasional object of ridicule. Were people now weary of it altogether? This prime minister was a good test case for celebrity obsession withdrawal. He was known and recognized long before he came to politics. Any normal need he felt for notice had been slaked. "Thank you, I think I've had enough now," he once told an interviewer who asked how he felt about fame. Maybe that's how the rest of his society had come to feel. "Thank you, we've had enough." Being Canadians, they'd waited for a public figure who wouldn't mind being ignored, with whom they could terminate the procedure in a civil way. What would replace celebrity obsession? Hard to say. In the old old days, when people believed in God, each person was known, at least in the eye of God. Ultimately it didn't matter if others noticed you, because He did. It worked as a motivator too, since He didn't just see you, He judged you. So fame wasn't enough, you had to be good as well. After God died, people lived only in each other's eyes. But to be noticed by others, you had to draw their attention; people struggled for recognition; they fought like hell for centre stage. Then even that ceased to matter. Across the street from Bluer, the camera crews and reporters gradually drifted away.

"There was no point just calling another election," said Matthew, as he surveyed the emptying street. "Or merely having a referendum that amounts to an election between them and us. Whoever they are and whoever we are. What would it decide? All it would decide is who gets to be the next government. We've already established that doesn't make much of a difference."

"You gotta have somebody," said Morris, quoting a politician whose name he'd forgotten. "That's democracy."

"But it wouldn't *touch* anything. It wouldn't really change anything," said Matthew. He raised his hands palms up, the closest to an ethnic gesture in his repertoire. Once the pay movie channel cast him as a Jewish accountant with a social conscience in a pilot for a series on the Mob in Montreal. It was ludicrous. He couldn't say *"Oy vay"*; he couldn't even say *"Oy."* The wedding scene was pathetic. It never went to series.

"That's what Gramsci said," said Morris. "He argued that as long as the terms of discourse were set by the bourgeoisie, no real change could occur in the political or economic spheres." Matthew held his head as if he'd been hit by intellectual shrapnel. Morris maundered on. "It's as though there are no words to describe a really different society, so you can't get to it."

"Even revolution?" said Matthew. He was thinking of the young people who sat in, in the outer office.

"What about revolution? Who uses it any more?" Matthew didn't know if those kids counted in this context or how to describe them. Morris kept maundering. "How long since you used that word without wincing? It exists now within the universe of bourgeois discourse alone, it's bounded by their ways of thinking. There may have been a minute and a half in the sixties when it threatened to escape. But they nabbed it. It sounds like 'corset' if you say it today."

"The computer revolution," said Matthew. "The hair care revolution."

"Power to the people," said Morris. "When the electrical

162

monopolies started using that, you knew the sixties were over. The decade that lasted twenty minutes."

"What about 'bourgeoisie'?"

"What about it?"

"It sounds weirder than revolution." Morris did a kind of shoulder squirm. "Well, it does to me," said Matthew.

Morris liked to think Marx may have been wrong about the future, but he'd been right about the present. Marx's critique of capitalism had survived the demise of communism. It was still the last best word on the current system. He tried the term soundlessly in his mouth. Bourgeois. "Sounds a little . . . *folklorique*, I grant," he said. "But they exist. And if they don't, their worldview does. They dominate us from wherever they are."

"A ghost class?" said Matthew. "Like a phantom limb?"

"Brecht said capitalism had an address," said Morris. "It's not just a theoretical abstraction. It also has a practice. A . . . a routine."

"A shtick," said Matthew. "Gone global. It's drowned out all others. You can't get booked, you can't get an audition, unless you do some version of that shtick. Everyone does it. Former anarchists and terrorists. Islamic fundamentalists. Deep ecologists. Artists. On the bus, in the office, kids in school yards. A lot of them don't even know it's someone else's. They just think it's how you talk. Like Vietnamese musicians singing like Bob Dylan."

Morris nodded. "It's about culture. That's what it's all about. But you have to have a question. You can't just announce a referendum the way you did and then say, 'Try seeing the world differently.' There has to be a question. That's what everybody's waiting for."

Matthew scratched at the window with his fingertips. "It's too bad," he said. "Needing a question narrows things. It cuts off discussion."

"I have a class, if you'll pardon the expression. Let me know if you figure out how to have a referendum without a question."

"The interviews I always liked doing best," said Matthew, "were ones where the interviewer never quite asked a question. They just let you know they were interested in what you wanted to say." Morris was already out the door.

Now the prime minister of the country sat alone in the window of the café. This was the test. Could he pass? Pass as what? A nobody, a man in the window. People went by. Cars did. There's so much to pay attention to here. And it absorbs you so little. On the dock at the lake, you're absorbed, yet by much less, far fewer events (a rustling in the trees as something makes its way to the water; a heron rises through the reeds and flaps ponderously toward the shore; two fishermen and a dog putt-putting along the rock face, veering away when they see you sitting there quietly.)

"You can't have a referendum that gives the answer and asks for the question," said Lars. "It would be like 'Jeopardy.'"

"That's why I thought of it," said Matthew. "I used to watch it in my dressing room, waiting to be called onto the set. The category is Canada. The answer is 'The kind of society you would like it to be.' What is the question?"

Lars laughed — more a yelp. It had something electronic in it. It was a little scary, as if his nervous system had been replaced with circuitry.

"It would be unprecedented," began Tilley, in negative mode. Then she stopped, hearing what she'd just said. "Hm," she mused. "Hmmm . . ."

"They'll laugh you off the stage," said Lars.

"Laughter is okay. I can live with laughter."

"They'll be laughing *at* you." This was life's awfullest prospect for Lars.

"I never bought that distinction," said Matthew.

Tilley said she'd lost track.

"Between laughing at and laughing with," they both said.

"I don't suppose you could lose," said Tilley. "If all you asked for was a question, not an answer."

"It's irresponsible," Lars blurted. "It's a cop-out. It's not leadership."

Matthew hesitated. "What if the question said, 'What do you think the most important question we have to answer is?'"

"Marginally better," said Lars. "But it's not politics, like the kind you have elections and referendums about. If that's the sort of

164

thing you want to do, you shouldn't be in Parliament. You should be in an ashram. Are there still ashrams?"

"Now that has the ring of truth," said Matthew. He sounded relieved, as if he'd eliminated an option.

"Why are you talking to us about this?" said Tilley. She was confused.

"He's working," said Lars. "He's trying stuff out and discarding it. He thinks he still has time before he has to put this sucker in front of an audience."

Just keep improvising. How about: "Would you be willing to consider thinking about governing Canada on a different basis than has been done during the last twenty years (approximately). This difference would extend to the economic, political, social, and cultural realms." Talk about leaden. He tried shortening it: "Are you in favour of new models for government?" Concise but abstract. "Do you believe things could be different?" Terse. He liked it so he tried living with it; it lasted half an hour. What about adding, "Give your reasons." Can you turn a referendum into an essay question? Why not? "For or against: a country is not a business." What about multiple choice? He set himself an improv exercise: have a conversation with Canada, see if you can find out what question it needs to have answered. There was a time he'd have done it easily. Any decent improvisational actor could play Canada. "Look at me. I am a large, sunny house with lots of insulation. I have many levels and rooms . . . But all my windows are closed now and I don't know how to reopen them." You don't know what that kind of thing means or where it might lead but in the past it always took him somewhere. "My question for you is . . . my question is . . . the question I need to know the answer to is . . ." Did the country used to be clearer? Was it possible to conduct a conversation with Canada then but not now? Has national politics become an illusion? Has politics? He had lots of questions but not the one he needed.

In the meantime, improvise a response on Quebec.

It's the twenty-fifth anniversary of the Coupe Stanley d'Improvisation. Since the bitter owner-player confrontations in pro sports began in the mid-1990s, it bills itself as "the only Stanley Cup finals you can be sure will happen." It's held in the same cramped, muggy club off St. Denis where it began. Generations of actors have worked their way through, moving on to stages at the Rideau Vert or the National Arts Centre, the occasional Quebec film, or best of all an enduring role in a *téléroman*. For this celebration, they've invited Matthew Deans, the first Anglo actor who ever appeared at the Coupe, and who's frequently come back as a judge. Of course he won't come, not because he's a politician; more because he's a politician *là bas*, where they're nonplussed by the sudden makeover of Quebec into an independent country. But he shows.

He takes the stage. Not, "Thank you for inviting me . . ." Nor, "Greetings from your former government." Not even, "You're all under arrest, and I brought the army with me." He seizes them with that fabled stillness. He looks them in the eye, collectively (as if he can see through the dazzling lights). So it's clear: he's here as an actor, not a mere prime minister. They're flattered by the choice. He gazes around, beyond them, it seems. "Together in this huge auditorium, this vast arena . . ." he says. And he's conjured it. Suddenly they've shrunk; they huddle in a towering space, it feels chilly and drafty. "Where so many triumphs on the path to independence, and cruel moments, too, have occurred." So it's the Paul Sauvé arena — maybe on that delirious night in '76, when Lévesque said he'd never been so proud to be a Québécois. Or the sad night four years after, when he said if he understood them aright, they meant to say, "Till next time." "The spirit of René Lévesque," he says, "is with us. On the platform. Or maybe over there on the bench. I'd like him to join us." He waits comfortably. He won't take this part himself. On the players' bench, a match flickers, a cigarette glows. Someone steps out as Lévesque. This Lévesque knows how to use silence too. The crowd is worshipful. Lévesque feels the emotion as he comes onstage, he shakes his head and grimaces shyly, palms up. Then he turns to Matthew. He starts in French. He says he never expected to see this moment, *jamais, jamais, jamais,* yet he knew it would come. There are tears in his eyes. Then he stops. Lévesque has always been sensitive to Canadians outside Quebec — not just the need to deal with them — he sympathizes with their anxiety and sense of loss. He switches to English. "If I understand you right," he says to the crowd, "you would like to know what our old friend feels about this change." *À ton tour, mon vieux.* Matthew pauses. Hard to know if he's devising an improvisation or is just absorbed in the moment. "Speaking personally," he says, with a blink of hesitation to let that register, "it's impossible not to be touched when people do something together that others told them couldn't be done. Which even they may have thought was impossible." Are their tears in his eyes too? "But," says Lévesque empathically, "it must be difficult for you?" Matthew shrugs, exactly as Lévesque would. They catch the reference. With ambiguity as context, he moves ahead. "I have no problem with any choice made freely," he says. The figures onstage embrace. The Lévesque character has a moment of inspiration. He's going for it. "Is there something," he says, "that *we* can do for *you*?" The audience gasp. The cameras are there, they take it in.

Others rise from the benches on both sides of the stage. They too play well-known Quebec figures, or social archetypes: the *dépanneur*, the parish priest, the cynical reporter. Some even play themselves, as Matthew has done. Like Lévesque, they embrace the Matthew character. Then they express concern for his problems and a desire to help. They know they'll face similar obstacles once they try to do something with their own independence. The resentments that have comprised the relationship between Quebec and Canada seem to crumble onstage. It's cathartic, a Canadian night of the fourth of August when, in 1789, the French nobility renounced their past and pledged themselves to a new order. In fact the entire improv echoes a scene from Ariane Mnouchkine's famed play about the French Revolution, which they all know. During the scene, the Matthew character withdraws. As it winds toward an end, he returns. He's worked himself to downstage right. The strong position. He draws focus and seems to make the lights come up spontaneously on the audience. They're leaving the land of ambiguity. "I have a request," he tells "Lévesque." "I hope the people of Quebec will participate in the referendum we're about to have. They can do so under the terms of their own referendum law, as they did for the Charlottetown Accord in 1992. I promise the question, when it's announced, will not compromise you." The others on the platform, all these Quebec nationalists, whoever they are at this point, shrug like Lévesque and nod a yes. "It's important for us too," says "Lévesque" in French, to Matthew. "Did you set all this up ahead of time?" shouts a newsman when they leave.

"Where *did* that come from?" says Dal, as they drive away.

He looks at the floor of the car. He breathes in and out like an athlete after the final game of a hard series. His breathing slows. "Sadat, maybe," he says. "Give them what they said they wanted but thought they'd never get. Like the Americans did to us."

"Then what happens?" she says.

After several days of bewildered silence, the new coalition government of Quebec said that in principle they were ready to participate in the referendum. On their own terms.

You could tell the columnists and commentators were perplexed, because they had no common position. Then they announced, in their mysterious collegial way, that round one had gone to the P.M.

The referendum question finally announced read: "Do you believe our human solidarity is the basis for our behaviour toward each other?"

"That's a weird question," said Dal.

"Yeah," he said. "It's the best I can do."

"You told me sometimes the lines you're completely unsure of work best of all," she said.

"Mmhm," he said. "And sometimes they don't."

"It's a weird question," said Alex.

"I was torn," he said.

"What was the alternative?"

"Do you think things can really be different?"

"You're asking me, or that was the alternative question."

"That was it."

"So?"

Matthew wavered, as if he'd forgotten his reason. "It seemed like too much of a stretch."

"I know what you mean," said Alex.

"You do?" said Matthew.

"Who'd have thought," said Alex, "that we'd enter the twenty-first century with capitalism on offer but not socialism? It would have been like starting the nineteenth century with capitalism dead and feudalism thriving."

"So you think it was the right choice?"

Alex shrugged. "If nobody knows how to go forward, you go back. Back to basics. See if you can find the fundamentals. See where you lost them. Then start over. Who knows —"

"I hope you're right," said Matthew. "I mean, I hope I'm right."

The former prime minister led the "Other Side," as it came to be known. They couldn't decide if they were going to vote no, or abstain, or even vote yes but denounce the process and especially the leadership behind it. Some said that of course solidarity was basic, that's why the question was trivial. Others, especially the free market people, said competition, not solidarity, was the basis of human behaviour. Then some of the free market people split off and said competition was the best way to show your solidarity. Matthew said he sympathized with their confusion; it took him a long time to sort out the matter too — and he was still working on it. The pundits said his strategy for dividing the Other Side was effective and wondered who thought it up. The former P.M. said she accepted a leadership role because the debate about solidarity was dividing the country when it needed to be united. Someone had to take charge.

"It's not personal," she said when she phoned to tell him.

He grunted. "Sorry for grunting," he said immediately.

"What was that about?" she asked.

"You reminded me," he said, "of all the talk there used to be about the political and the personal. The personal is political, the political is personal. How we'll never be able to change the world if we can't change ourselves —"

"You were thinking," she said, "that I was making an old facile distinction when I said it isn't personal."

"No," he said. "The truth is I never thought they were the same. I always thought it was easier to change the world than to change yourself."

"I always thought changing yourself would be easier than changing the world," she said.

"That could be right too," he said. "All change is hard."

"Does this mean we'll be friends again when it's over?" she asked.

"I don't know," he said. "What about you? Maybe you won't want to talk to me."

"I have a rule about people I don't talk to," she said. "When I can't remember why I'm not talking to them any more, I start talking to them again. Eventually it happens."

For Matthew it was different from the election. Not because he was now the leader instead of an oddball actor trying out in politics, but because it was a different exercise. Elections were about *you* — the candidate. You could try to focus on issues and tell voters to make up their minds that way. But there was never enough time to talk about all the issues and anyway, after the election, you, the candidate, could change your mind. So what voters really had to decide about was you. That's why his campaign was so autobiographical, he decided. They needed to know. At least that's how he always felt at election time. He wanted to ask candidates: show me something about yourself, even if it's through discussing issues; then I'll make up my mind. It's true the referendum was personal for him, maybe more so than any election including his own, but it wasn't *about* him. They were all centred on something else: that weird question.

Maybe that's why it seemed to have less to do with TV. The nightly reports and national debates felt marginal. This was about meetings in rooms, large and small, where people sat around a topic. Following the meetings, came after-events. He went to many. The topic remained in charge. It was as though it got pried open in the initial sessions. Then it needed more intimate attention. He took this as a sign. *They* didn't find the question weird. It moved something in them.

The first big Toronto meeting of the campaign, held in the auditorium of a vocational high school in the city core, runs late. People want to talk, they're willing to wait, they listen to each other. After, in front of the kids' lockers, the press try to scrum him. *They're* still trying to treat this as an election. He spots a pay phone and fights his way to it. He insists on these gestures, like his own car with his daughter as driver once in a while, or the downtime from security. They finally compromised on *one* Mountie for such occasions: Leon, who looks least like a cop. He calls Bert's private number. There's a message — an address, not far from here. Dal drops him there — a Victorian pointy. Typical Toronto. Looks familiar . . .

Tomorrow Bert will be acclaimed head of Canada's largest union — the Canadian Industrial and General Workers. Tonight he's in the home of Grzegorz, Canada's leading composer of atonal music, and Lydia, editor of the peace/environment magazine, *Still*. Back in the old NDP days, Grzegorz and Lydia regularly sacrificed themselves in ridings the party knew it couldn't win. They're throwing this party in Bert's honour for the remnants of constituencies that used to make up the Canadian left. The door is ajar. There's noise within. He was expecting the old, greying faces from the free-trade fight, the anti-nuke groups, the social contract vets. But they must've left. The older they get, the earlier they go home. Those still here are young, early twenties, he'd say. Grzegorz, one says, has gone to bed. Through the hall in the kitchen, at a counter, he sees Bert with a beer. Bert waves. Down the narrow stairs from the second floor comes Lydia.

She says most of the people still here, these kids, are from the Transient Workers' Union, the one started by high school dropouts who got fired by a McDonald's in Barrie for trying to organize. They're a proud 640 with two and a half staff, plus Lydia who helps with their newsletter. They are the new face of labour in the global marketplace: no steady work, no full-time jobs, no benefits, usually no contracts. They're everything traditional labour has struggled to eliminate. They've worked out a merger agreement with Bert's gargantua. The rest of his executive board were opposed — who the hell needs a few hundred bicycle couriers and telemarketers ten cents above minimum wage? But they let him have his way, a sort of induction present. They've gone back to the Royal York to drink beer in the hospitality suite. Bert alone remains.

Bert introduces Matthew to the kids in the kitchen, as if they wouldn't have any idea who he is. Mauricio, a pastry sous-chef at Pentimento on Cumberland and daytime temp, is dancing barefoot between the beer bottles on the counter. "Matthew Deans," he says. "Matthew Deans, should I know dat name?" "How's Phyllis?" Matthew asks Bert. The three of them met when Matthew narrated a film history the union made for its fiftieth anniversary. Phyllis worked in the communications department. He invited them to the revival of *Marat/Sade* he was doing at the time. It was Bert's first live play ever. Phyllis had seen some musicals. "We split," says Bert. Matthew's face drops. "It's okay," says Bert. "The boys are grown, nobody left at home. I'm living at the Royal York right now. Maybe I'll get a place" — he looks around the tight, warm kitchen — "near here."

Matthew checks the group again. "These kids aren't hard to look at, eh?" says Bert, voice lower. "I won't be taking any of them back to the hotel with me. The girls, I mean. Even if they'd come." Matthew hadn't asked. "That's not why I stayed." Matthew looks Bert in the face and understands. Bert is here for the contact.

Tomorrow he'll become a member of the national elite, as much as that's possible for a labour leader. They still won't invite him to their dinner parties. But the media will call to ask his views on major issues, which they'll sometimes even quote. He'll have the P.M.'s private number — even if the P.M. is no longer Matthew. That's why he stayed with the anarchic dregs of the Transient Workers — kids barely out of their teens, about the ages of Bert's own sons — kind of screwy and familiar with dope, drunk on beer, and banging away at Grzegorz's piano, now Mauricio is doing his dance on the bookshelves that separate the kitchen from Grzegorz's studio. They're mewling and near puking, and they remind Bert of where he's from rather than where he's going. The death of the fishery and his dad. His four sisters and their big families, still down east. Dropping out of grade eight because he hated the courses he was streamed into. Working across the country, gradually understanding what he was: a pair of hands on the market, like everyone he knew. Happening into an electronics assembly plant that had a union that happened into the Steelworkers who merged with the Metalworkers and the auto union around that time. Just luck, mostly.

This youthful band is the stamp with which he'll mark his accession to leadership. His will be a reign not only for the best paid and highly skilled but for the dispossessed and largely unorganized. He believes in it, and anyway, there are few of those great jobs left. If Bert were a manufacturer, he wouldn't linger long in this country either.

Dal arrives. She was at a club, she decided to buzz by and see if anyone needs a lift. Bert is loaded, it's hard to miss. They drive him to the hotel. At the curb she turns and asks Bert if he ever gets intimidated when he has to bargain with all those lawyers and econ-omists and other suits. "You mean if I feel inferior because I just have grade eight?" says Bert. "Nah. We have a very good education program in the union." Up at the union centre on Lake Simcoe, they give month-long courses on how to bargain or lay a grievance, plus labour history and economics from a worker's point of view. It's like Club Med for workers up there. Once he even took a five-day course on acting and improvisation from that guy who had his own series, then ran for Parliament. He winks. (What can you do? thinks Matthew. Some men wink.) He thanks them, shakes hands and gets out. He starts up the stairs of the Royal York, then turns back and leans in the passenger side.

"I don't really know why we're going through this referendum," he says. "Of course I know where I stand." Before Matthew can answer, he adds, "But I didn't really know why I went to that party. Or stayed so long. I trust my gut. Just as well when it's this big." Matthew leans out the window, pats Bert's gut and says, "You're not doing so bad for a guy with grade eight." Bert hangs his head and swings it from side to side, exaggerated. You can't tell if he's really drunk, or just doing an imitation. "At least we're not pissing our lives away," he says, with a beery grin.

"The strangest part of the data," says Tilley in the power corner, "is the people we poll say they don't have a problem with the question. You remember how weird it sounded to us?" Lars asks what the hell it means to them. "That isn't on the questionnaire," she says. "Don't give me that look. I didn't feel we'd get a usable reaction." She's called some of the samples herself though, and asked respondents to explain the question to her. "They can't tell you what solidarity means, but they're comfortable with it."

Lars glowers at his aquavit. "The movement they had in Poland," he says, "the one that started the end of the Soviet Empire. It was called Solidarity."

"But the Poles knew what it meant," she says.

"How do we know?" he says. "Maybe it came out of nowhere there too. They hear this word they never heard before and they jump up and start striking and demonstrating. Ten minutes later, the Russians leave town. Who knows how these things happen? Maybe, maybe, hey maybe —" (Gentlemen, start your engines, thinks Tilley.) "Maybe what happened," mutters Lars, slowing now as he closes in on a theory, "is the son of a bitch ended up with 'Jeopardy' after all. But *negative* 'Jeopardy'! The answer is — solidarity, which is the thing they *don't* have in their lives. Because what they do have is the opposite. Tell me, what are their lives like?"

"Harsh," says Tilley. "Divisive, insecure, atomized, competitive —"

"And no one allowed to give a shit for anybody else," he breaks in. "Because there's not enough money, they get told. Because caring about each other won't work any more. It's naive and obsolete, it's been tried and it failed, you're ignorant and you don't understand, you fucking dummies — which is how they know what it is. Because it's everything they haven't been living with. Then they hear this word and they feel like — *that's* what's missing!"

"Lars," she says, "I don't understand it but it's brilliant." He can't remember her ever calling him by his name. It makes him feel like they're an old married couple. Maybe tonight, he thinks, is the night.

"So why won't they say they're going to vote yes?" she frets. "They're too reluctant. They won't even say they're leaning. If you go very deep and push, they say they're leaning toward leaning. It's completely unstable."

"Ach," he says, full of confidence now, heady with her praise. "It's like my old man. At the end he wouldn't take any tests the doctors told him to take. He wouldn't take any pills. He knew he couldn't have what he wanted so he just went ahead and died."

"What did he want?"

"He wanted to live forever and be healthy in the bargain. What's the point of saying you want something when you're sure you can't have it?"

Matthew took a side trip to Kitimat after the public meeting in Terrace. A poli sci prof from the community college told him there was a collective theatre company making a play about life at the smelter and conflicts between workers, natives, and the company. "We used to do those thirty years ago," said Matthew to the prof. "There haven't been very many since." "This is B.C.," said the prof. "Always faddish, never trendy." He just walked into the union hall while they were rehearsing. They looked at him without surprise. As if the country had grown used to a prime minister who might show up anywhere, anytime. "No cameras?" said an actor. There were none. Only Leon, who slouched to the bar, which wasn't open. Matthew asked if he could watch. The company wanted to talk about the referendum. Sure, he said, afterward. He sat at a table near the back with a retired smelter worker named Nelson, up for some fishing with his buddies. Waiting for the reheasal to end or the bar to open or his pals to get off shift. The actors were doing a "gold watch" scene: worker on the job for twenty-five years is presented with watch, but rejects it. The plant manager and a VP from corporate HQ in Seattle stand on the platform. The worker shambles up. Nelson shifted in his chair beside Matthew.

The worker-actor and the management-actors tussle onstage. They try to force the watch on him; he pushes it away like it has an odour. Then he turns to address his fellow workers and denounce the company. The bosses try to block him. "You all know me," he mumbles. "I'm not much for words but I got something to say after all these years." Nelson snorted. "That's not how it would happen," he said softly. "Wanta take a shot?" said Matthew. Nelson nodded. They waved the rehearsal to a stop.

Nelson takes the actor's place. He steps onto the platform with the suits and mildly accepts their watch. Lesson one: no bullshit confrontations. Then he modestly says he'd like to address "the men." The suits look at each other. Why not? they shrug. Nelson

175

steps downstage and speaks. "Ladies and gentlemen, fellow workers, old friends. As I stand here today I see many faces I know but I'm also reminded of those not with us, friends who left us never to return, victims of those dread diseases that stalk the steps of every man who ever entered the awesome heat of a smelter or went down into the mines: diseases like silicosis." He says the last word with a hiss. It's menacing, a disclosure of power; the management-actors behind him cower. He rumbles on in Churchillian periods, and concludes, "So I have taken your watch. But I'll never put it on."

Another old worker came in during the scene. He nodded to Matthew like they were union brothers. Maybe word had gone round about him being there, maybe the guy wasn't even sure who Matthew was. A face from TV or somewhere. In the silence following Nelson's last line, he whispered to Matthew that Nelson was famous for his speeches. Matthew asked when — when they were voting whether to go on strike? "More like voting whether to *stay* on strike," said Nelson's chum. "That's when you really needed it." Nelson joined them. Matthew asked if he made notes before he spoke. Nelson shook his head. "I talk about what I know."

The actors wanted their turn. What about the arts? What about funding? Matthew asked if they'd play the scene once more, now that they'd seen Nelson do it. Okay, once. Then we talk. They ran it again, with the original actor in the part. Much better. Yet what was missing? Something. The menace. A voice that went from his heart to your ear. *Access to class.*

Closing time. Nelson and his pal, Albie, didn't get the point about menace. You couldn't persuade them; they just didn't feel dangerous. Nelson thought that was damn good acting he'd seen the second time around. He was flattered, doubtless, though he didn't say so, that an actor would play *him.* "I may not know acting," said Nelson. "But you don't know what it's like in there. It's life and death every day. I guess that sounds like just an expression." Matthew said he didn't think it was just an expression. Clichés were rich. When he worked on *Farm Lives,* one of the collectives, he often thought about really making hay while the sun shines or crying over spilt milk. Nelson and Albie looked uncertain; was he patronizing them? Matthew said he'd better turn in. Leon, at the bar, sighed. The end in sight.

"I'll take you there," said Nelson. "Inside. So you can see." Matthew said there wouldn't be time, he'd be gone tomorrow. "Now," said Nelson firmly. Albie squinted. He tried to pull Nelson aside. He said it wasn't possible, there was a new plant manager. Guy from Seattle. He cleared all visitors. "I'll call him," said Matthew. "Right now." The idea of waking up an M.B.A. from the States energized him. Nelson frowned. He'd expended his manhood on that plant. He didn't need permission. "Forget it," said Albie. "Go to the motel," Nelson said to Matthew. "And wait."

At 3:30 there was a knock on the door. Nelson was carrying two hard hats and two lunch boxes. They'd enter with the 4:00 a.m. shift. I go like a spy into the land of the evil ruler, to rescue the fairy princess, thought Matthew, conflating various roles. The trick was getting out of the motel unseen. The plant gate was easy. A guard waved them through. Matthew watched himself on the security monitor, a lowered hard hat carrying a lunch pail, one of hundreds. He played it straight.

Inside was Dantean: vast sooty spaces, eerie huge carts like boxcars tracking across the ceiling. Men in helmets and visors striding around the pots. Pots: pools of molten aluminum bubbling on the floor, like backyard swimming pools which the men circled, as if to clean out leaves that fell in overnight. Should a foot slip in, the way it would to test the temperature, it would come out a stump. It happened. It was life and death.

Everyone knew Nelson. Nelson introduced Matthew. They talked. They knew who he was. But it didn't matter. He wasn't campaigning, he wasn't performing. It wasn't democracy, it wasn't politics. It was Henry V in a rough cloak, on his haunches, leaned up against a tree, down among the troops before battle. He went about in their midst.

"I can see how you got hooked," he said.

Angeline retired into this little house across from the downtown park with the baseball diamond. She and Trev bought it in the 1950s, the worst of times, when they were truly alone together. After

Trev died, she stayed. Retired for her means she only works about sixty hours a week — advising bank workers, native women's rights groups, young organizers. "Yes," she said. "The contact." She knew what it meant because she'd been a middle-class kid too, went to private school, was expected to continue on at university, get married, do volunteer work, instead of joining up with some commie union — in the middle of the depression! In her time, she hadn't had anyone to tell. Not even Trev, who, like Bert, had always had the contact. You only get hooked by it if you came from somewhere else.

"I've been right across the country," he said. "I started this whole thing and I don't really know what's going on."

She pursed her lips and lowered her head. "It's the class struggle," she said with clarity.

He grinned. "Is that the same as when I tell you I know how you got hooked?"

She smiled her killer smile.

"Right," he said. "I've got someone I'd like you to explain that to," and introduced her to Dal.

"Our problem," the ex-prime minister said, "is that he doesn't know what he's doing. He's improvising."

"Then we're in trouble," said her ex-chief of staff. "If he doesn't know what he's doing, how can we figure it out?"

The opposition on the referendum had coalesced organizationally but not tactically. Since Reagan, the right had styled themselves the true revolutionaries. They didn't want to start sounding conservative now. They were also divided between contempt and alarm. You could scorn this referendum as naive but well intentioned, or you could warn it meant the return of communism and totalitarianism. Best of all you could do both. That was their instinct; they just hadn't figured out how. It took time.

At the end of week four, some undecideds began shifting to no. "Why is it happening now?" asked the ex-P.M. "They're thinking something." Next day she issued a challenge. "Ask him," she said through the cameras to the country, "what he'll do if you vote yes." He didn't wait to be asked. "I don't know," he said, as he'd said when he announced the referendum. Is this more brilliant strategy? said the analysts.

"It's the timing, that's all I can think of," said Tilley, the only member of the ex-P.M.'s old team working with the new prime minister. "When the vote was a long way off, they liked the openness and indecision. As it approaches, they get edgy. It's the uncertainty."

"Maybe," said Dal, "they want it both ways."

"They can't have it both ways," Matthew said.

"Yes they can," she said. "They decide they have to go on the way things have been, but they keep thinking about something different."

"If that's so," he said, "then what I'm making is a *geste*, in the Brechtian sense." She had no idea what that meant. "An exaggerated, excessively literal gesture," he said, "which indicates something important to the audience but doesn't try to slide into whatever else is happening in the play. It may look out of place, it may break the flow and seem to have little to do with the rest of the script, the play may continue in spite of it. Yet it says something essential about what's going on."

"Give me an example," she said.

"It can be anything," he said. "When I was young, I saw James Dean in *Rebel Without a Cause*. He wore a red windbreaker over a white T-shirt and kept putting his thumb to his mouth." Matthew stopped, as if he'd been absorbed again in the power of that image. He was doing it.

"Aha," she said. "I saw that at a James Dean festival. But there was nothing in what he did with his thumb that broke context. It was a completely naturalistic film, and so was Dean's performance."

"I guess that's true," said her father. "But it changed my life, and nothing else in the film even touched me. I had to pee just as they went into the planetarium for that great sequence so I rushed up the aisle and found myself doing that motion with my hand. I've seen others of my generation do it ever since, including Bob Dylan. I had no idea what it was about, but I knew it said something about me and the future."

She thought for a while. Then she said, "I don't get it."

"Me neither," he said. "I guess it's not the zinger I was hoping for."

"Makes you human," she said. "I think that's why they like you. You're very appealing when you flounder."

"Anyway," he grunted, "now you know what changed my life."

"Very interesting," said Tilley, doing her Freud imitation. "Rebel without a cause."

"Maybe they're making a *geste* too," said Dal. "Having it both ways. Nothing changes because of it but it matters."

He shook his head. "That's art," he said. "Not politics. They're into art. I'm into art. Who the hell is doing politics any more?"

When I was too young to know much, I got a role in a Canadian film. There weren't many then. I played a suburban kid who rebels, steals the family car, and drives north because that's where he expects to find — it. Right after, I started getting invited to conferences on Canadian film to talk about being a Canadian actor. I could have retired and done nothing else. After one movie. At those events, people come to worship. Whatever you say, they're impressed. It's a seriously delusional environment. So at one conference somebody asked about acting and I said, "Look I don't really give a shit about the Method. I just try to get into the part and let it happen." I could feel approval from the audience wash over me. But there was an old guy on the panel. He'd been an actor since the thirties. He worked a little in the States, then came back here and taught acting. He looked like a Greek statue. He leaned forward, turned his big bald head and beady eyes on me at the other end of the table and said out the side of his mouth, so his words went straight into the mike in front of him, "That is the Method, you twerp." It took guts, remember that was the sixties and everybody was bowing down to youth. I told him after that I'd like to study with him, which I'd never asked anyone. "Nine out of ten teachers do more harm than good anyway," he said. "Like shrinks." He had every book on acting ever written in his apartment. They went floor to ceiling with a double row of books on each shelf, plus more piled on each row. Whenever I had an acting problem, he'd look at the books and say, "You mean, is it up there?" — and wave his hand at the collected wisdom of theatre as if it was a mist the turbulence from his arm could disperse — "Nah, that's all bullshit." Sometimes I'd ask really kindergarten questions. How can I be some-

*body else? If I already know the line I'm going to say, how can it
sound spontaneous? Stuff he'd dealt with a million times. He'd
pause. As though it was the first time he'd thought about it. He never
gave a quick answer like an expert. That's what made me trust him.
You got the idea he thought we didn't live long enough to become
experts. If we lived, say, three or four hundred years, maybe you could
develop expertise and put it in a book where people can look it up. But
when we live seventy, eighty years — which he was approaching?
You had a better shot at nailing the questions.*

Morris shuffled through the cut pieces of drywall to the stove and
poured a cup of coffee. Another shitty victory for individualism, one
more confirmation of the subjectivist, reductionist po-mo worldview.
The trouble with the referendum had dawned on him only slowly. It
ushered people into their heads. That's what seemed appealing at first.
It was about culture. It was like Mao's two-stage theory. Liberate culture, *then* liberate reality. But what if you just liberate your head? How
do you get from in there to out here? It was the state of the house that
brought it home. The point, as Marx said about Feuerbach, isn't just to
have great philosophical visions of the world (and your kitchen); the
point is to change them. The whole thing was a mass exercise in inter-
subjective feeling. In fact, that described him at this very moment:
thinking about thinking. It's what academics do. When he started, in
the sixties, he raged more at the neo-Straussians than about imperialism and class struggle. Those neo-Straussian weasels in the poli sci
departments drove him nuts, slithering around during protests and sit-
ins, passing information to the administration or the cops. Now he
couldn't even remember what bugged him about them. That also happened when you were an intellectual. You lost track of issues you'd
once felt passionate over, and even which side you'd been on in the
debate. All you recalled was that you'd believed something vehement-
ly. He'd made peace with other schools: post-Freudianism, post-
Marxism. But not fucking post-modernism. Not yet, not ever. It cut too
close. We were all sucked in, separate and impotent. He'd never mention these qualms to Matthew though, even if he happened to call; what
was the point? It would just disarm him for the final push and accomplish nothing on the way. The phone rang.

"You have been infected with the po-mo virus!" shrieked Morris into the handset. "I agree it's hard to believe in systems and methodologies the way we once did. I agree it's hard to believe at all. But I draw the line at post-modernism."

"So you've replaced your belief in one system with your disbelief in another!" The prime minister was less accommodating than expected. Being leader of the country made him feisty.

"That is the most undergraduate kind of undergraduate thinking," roared Morris.

Matthew withdrew a strategic distance. As Mao said, "When the enemy advances we retreat; when the enemy retreats, we advance." He didn't think post-modernism was the main problem facing Canada in the twenty-first century, but it bothered him too. Morris was mollified.

"I had decided not to bring it up," he said. "I apologize. What good does it do?"

"Don't mourn," said Matthew. "Organize."

"What?"

"It's what Joe Hill said before he was hung. It was the title of our show. I played Joe."

"I know that. I told you about Joe Hill."

"You told me more than I knew. I'd heard of him. But I meant — don't stand there feeling sorry for me or yourself. Do something. Organize."

"That's the problem," said Morris. "For a hundred years the way to fight for justice was always the same. Organize. They had the power so we had to get the people. In unions or the peace movement or civil rights or the women's movement. What's happened? Nobody is organized. There are no organizations any more. People think being radical is having radical ideas, not getting together with other people and doing radical things."

"That's brilliant, Morris. It's so depressing. You ought to do — ought to organize something."

"Where? In the *weltarein*, as my grandmother would have said? Out in the middle of the cosmos somewhere?"

As though an improv had run dry, and everyone onstage waits for somebody else to risk a move and open a new direction —

Matthew said, "How often does anyone really look out into the cosmos? I know how rarely it happens onstage. You're speaking to another actor and suddenly there are these eyes looking back. Not staring and waiting for a cue. Just looking. It throws you off and turns you on at once. When it happens in the world, over coffee say, it brings time to a stop. The world ceases to be narrative — moving or lurching coherently from point to point — and it becomes . . ."

"Chaos?" said Morris, surprised to hear himself respond to Matthew's move. But he knew this feeling. "Disorganization and chaos?"

"Process," said Matthew. "Sheer process, with no result. It's fantastic. It's happened to me more during this campaign than in all my life as an actor."

Knock knock. It's almost midnight at the motel in Sidney. Knock knock. He must have been sleeping. He flips off the CNN fashion file, slips the latest adventure of Dave Robicheaux, Cajun ex-cop, off his face onto the floor. He goes to the door. She stands there. Blood drips down her front from her mouth and her nostrils. It smears the roomy T-shirt she sleeps in. The shirt says, "Communism collapsed and all I got was this lousy T-shirt." There is an odour of urine and diarrhea. She wears socks but no shoes, no slippers. She collapses in the doorway.

The new and virulent STD had staked its claim across Canada before it became a media story. Total occurrences stabilized; then new cases began trending down mildly. At first it was considered a variant of HIV, but further research made that less clear. Anyway, scientists now said they weren't even sure what they meant by HIV. The reports involving the strain were spread more or less evenly across the country.

"I don't know who I got it from," she said, four days later in Victoria General. She'd been flown from Sidney the day after her collapse. "I was always careful, but how careful is careful? Maybe there's no such thing as safe sex."

"It doesn't matter," he said. He'd been with her since then. Her mother arrived next day and was in the hospital cafeteria now. One of them was always with her. "Maybe you didn't get it from anybody. They don't know how it works. It's . . . new. They say it may even be airborne."

"I could have slipped up without knowing it. You don't always want to think of it as something dangerous." He's looking at the floor. All she can see is the top of his head. "Do you know what I mean?" He pumps his head up and down. "Please talk to me, Dad."

"That's the part of the sixties I wish you hadn't missed," he said.

"Which part?"

"The sex." He swallowed. His head still down.

"Tell me about the sixties."

"There was more rhetoric than politics but that's because nobody knew the difference. Some guy would get up at a university rally and say, I'm sick and tired of bullshit, we gotta *do* something. Everybody would cheer. Then somebody would ask what we were gonna do. Somebody else would say, I move the workers go on a general strike. There'd be a vote. That was doing something."

She laughed, then coughed. "People like you, you're a lot smarter about the world than we were," he said. She laughed some more. He felt useful.

"No matter how left you tried to be someone would out-left you. Once I went to a screening of a big Hollywood movie about a strike. On a Saturday morning. All the left groups were there. But some guerrilla filmmakers thought this was 'tinseltown bullshit.' So they brought a 16-mm projector and a portable generator into the balcony and screened their own strike film on top of the one on the screen."

She laughed and coughed some more. "Tell me about sex in the sixties."

"I can't," he said. "It was kind of . . . it was pleasant. Touch was full of positive possibility. You'd go over to someone's for dinner and sleep with her. Stay the night or go home. Maybe see her again, maybe not. Or, you're occupying the university. You sleep in a prof's office or the student lounge, under a table, with somebody you just met. It's dark, it's exciting, it's forbidden."

"And you don't worry," she said. Between a question and a statement.

"You didn't even think about worrying. The most that could happen was gonorrhea or syphilis. You take a handful of pills and it's gone."

"Like a playground?" she asked.

"I guess," he said.

"Where the worst that can happen is you scrape your knee," she said.

"And somebody's there to clean it up and put on a Band-Aid."

"I like it," she said. "Tell me more."

"No."

"Yes."

"You're backpacking in Europe and you take the overnight train . . . Rome to Paris. It's crowded so you're sitting on your pack in the corridor and you talk to someone." He stopped.

"And?"

"By morning you've moved into a compartment, you're alone, you're feeling wonderful together, the conductor keeps coming in to see what you're up to and pretending he forgot he already checked your ticket. Maybe you get off in Lyon with her, spend a day and go on to Paris next morning."

"Did you see her again?"

"No."

"Do you remember her name?"

"No. I remember her brassiere. There were no cups, just breasts. It was like a prize."

She said nothing. Then she said, "Maybe she remembers your name. Maybe it was different in the sixties for chicks."

He bit his lip hard and tasted some blood. "I need you," he said. "I need you to help me think. I don't think very well without you."

"Okay," she said. "Then listen to me. I didn't say that to make you feel guilty. You have to hang on to what's good. Do it for me. Look what you just gave me. You gave me the sixties. I used to hate them."

"I don't blame you," he said nodding, his jaw quite tight. "It was a trip — in the sixties — but don't let anyone ever tell you it was serious politics."

She laughed, coughed, segued into a chuckle and soon breathed smoothly. Thy deep and dreamless sleep, he thought.

185

"You can stay a minute. She's asleep." They'd been taking turns.

"What if she —"

"Leon's watching."

"The Mountie?"

"He'll call down if she wakes up."

"Isn't he supposed to be watching you?"

"He wants to watch her. Even Mounties get their priorities straight sometimes."

It was the middle of the night and only the vending machines in the cafeteria were working. The hospital said they didn't think he should wander around like an ordinary person. He said he didn't think it would be a problem but mostly he stayed out of the public areas. Michele spent her off time here.

"How are you?" he said.

She nodded. "What does she think about us? About what happened. Do you ever talk to her about it?"

"All the time. She asks. I don't have answers. She's a lot clearer than I am."

Neither are sure they should continue. But they don't want to talk about her, not for a few moments. They're the topic by default. She says, "Once we decided it was over, we got along so well. There didn't seem to be any problems to discuss."

"The last thing you said to me," he says, "I was in the car, you leaned down and said, 'Explain to me again why we're doing this.'"

"I forgot that," she says. "What did you say?"

"Nothing. I wanted to ask you the same thing. We just did it. I drove away."

"I didn't believe it would last," she says. "I never believed we could stay apart. But it wasn't hard, was it? I guess it was right."

He says, "After a while I decided it was because I lost my script somewhere, and you still had yours. The one we both had when we started."

"Politically," she says.

He nods. "I felt so . . . judged," he says. "I couldn't take it. When I came home from doing something — the best I could man-

186

age — it was worse than being alone. No encouragement, no approval —"

"I couldn't," she says. "I didn't —"

"I'd have settled for a cup of tea," he says.

"I knew you were losing the script, as you put it," she says. "You talked about it constantly. I didn't know if I could hang on to it myself with all your doubt around. It was scary. It mattered to me, especially with us mattering less. But I wasn't judging you. I was, but it was really that I was afraid of losing what held me together."

"Wasn't she enough?" he says.

"I didn't want to put that pressure on her. I didn't want her to be all that made sense of my life. We'd aimed for something else. Much more —"

"What about . . . that night? The wrap party," he says.

"There's something I never told you," she says. "I blanked on it myself. In the morning when you told me — we were in the kitchen. We'd just bought a shiny new electric kettle." He nods, for some reason he remembers the kettle. "You turned away," she says, "stricken with guilt or something. And I saw my teeth reflecting in it. I was smiling."

"You were glad?"

"Something in me was. Relieved maybe."

They say nothing for a while. The air grows less thick. "On the other hand," she says, "maybe it was none of that. Maybe it was just because I hated the way you drove the car."

"You really hated it?" he says. "I heard that. You never told me."

"You wouldn't listen," she says. "Anyway I felt petty. But it made me crazy." She's smiling.

Now he's relieved. Maybe it wasn't his politics, it was his fucking driving. At least it wasn't the omelettes. "I'm really sorry," he says, "about the way I drive." She accepts the apology. "Do you wanta take your best shot?" he says.

"No thanks," she says.

"It would make me feel much better," he says.

"Then I definitely won't," she says.

They go back upstairs and sit in the room together till she opens her eyes and sees them. "Now there's a scary sight," she says.

The only daughter of the prime minister, his only child, died four days before the vote on the referendum question. There was a memorial service next morning. She was cremated. He'd stayed with her since her collapse and did not resume campaigning. This made little difference since he hadn't really campaigned throughout the period of debate. It had grown clear — to him and perhaps the country — that he was a bystander and onlooker for this event, unlike the recent election, when he played a central role. There was some restrained media commentary about the occurrence of unexpected deaths prior to both the recent national ballots. "Do they think no one ever dies before a vote?" said the prime minister to his close friends. None of them were sure what he meant.

The political effects were imponderable. Many people said they wouldn't vote. Pollsters said they'd rather not pry into the reasons, but it was their job; they did so reluctantly. Some voters said they were heartsick about the death of the young woman. Others had felt all along the referendum was pointless. The no side, led by the former prime minister, had urged people to vote, as a way to register disagreement with the government's approach; they'd said they would interpret abstentions as a rejection of that approach; they now repositioned on non-voters. It was clear that many people simply doubted, at least for the moment, the point of political activity. The prime minister said he would vote.

"It doesn't fall under capitalism or human nature," said Morris uncomfortably. "It's more like a flood."

"Floods aren't inevitable," said Matthew curtly. "What about flood control? Or global warming. Is that why it flooded? You could have done something about it —"

Morris didn't want this conversation. Matthew had insisted. He set the terms. All right, if it worked for him. Just keep talking. Just keep arguing. "A meteor would be completely inevitable," said Morris.

"STDs are in the flood control and global warming category," said Matthew. "If there had been more research. If it had been a priority —"

"Then," said Morris softly, "she might've died of something else. We don't even know what it was. You aren't going to wipe out disease. I once knew an atheist who said the progress of medicine wouldn't just eliminate disease. Eventually it would eradicate death. Then it might go on and bring back to life everyone who's died. It was the most religious claim I ever heard anyone make."

"Something must have happened," said Matthew. Morris wasn't with him. "To the guy," Matthew explained. "The atheist. I think thoughts like that."

Morris nodded. He thought them too.

"I don't think very clearly," said Matthew. "About anything." They were quiet. "Wanta discuss the results?" he said.

The vote was a clear win for the yes. There was disagreement over whether it should be called overwhelming. The numbers were 62 per cent to 38 per cent, with many spoiled ballots, far more than usual. A number of those were covered by statements written across them and often continuing on the other side. The comments were thoughtful. One publisher applied for permission to collect them in a book: *Mirror of a Nation*. Voting took longer than it did for an election; many polling stations stayed open hours after closing time. People were in there with their ballot, they were composing. They composed themselves, then they composed their views, which they probably knew would nullify the ballot itself. "For the first time in my life, I had no idea what I was going to do," voters confided to each other when they discovered they hadn't been alone. "I stood there tapping my foot, looking at the pencil and the ballot and I thought, I'm not going to be panicked over this. When nothing came clearly, I decided the right thing was to describe how I felt."

Next day, members of the ramshackle cabinet began resigning, saying the time had come to clarify the political situation. The period of improvisation served a purpose, they said, but something practical had to come out of it. Most said they favoured creation of a formal political organization with the prime minister at its head and a clear program; they hoped to run again and serve. Others were equivocal or announced they'd support the former prime minister and join her party. She herself said she felt the country needed a chance to declare itself politically, as it just had philosophically. She heard the sentiment of the voters, she said — a deep and coherent desire for a more humane approach to public policy — and she was ready to lead a government that responded. It was, in other words, time again for politics as usual, but with a difference. The labour movement, the women's movement, and the national farm organizations said they'd support a new party built on the affirmations of the referendum and led, they hoped, by the current prime minister. Other groups — artists, native peoples, social service and anti-poverty groups — added their support. The old popular coalition, which nearly derailed the primeval free-trade agreement of 1988 and then disintegrated, was being reborn. There was a sense of familiar form emerging from the creativity and chaos.

"Yes?" said the prime minister.

They anticipated a statement, brief and dignified. It was an awkward situation. How do you have a press conference at a time like this? "What's your feeling on the referendum result?" asked a reporter.

"I voted yes, and I'm glad many others agreed. It was a good discussion and I appreciate the thought people on both sides put into their choices."

"What happens now?"

"I don't know."

"That's what you've said before. Isn't it time to decide?"

"Yes, I guess it is."

"Then . . . Then what . . . ?"

Hesitation. "I resign," he said calmly.

It's nice to stun an audience. It doesn't happen often.

"Did you just make that decision?"

"Yes."

"Right here? Just now, on the spot."

"Yes."

"Are you sure?"

"Sure what? That I just decided? Yes. That I resign? Yes."

You could hear their thoughts scrambling to a new position. They got there, consolidated, looked around. "Why?"

190

"Sometimes you aren't sure why you do something, but you sense it's right and hope you can eventually explain it. That's how I feel."

He wasn't being obstinate and he wasn't toying with them. The guy was just on another plane. Some of them would have liked to get there with him.

"Is your . . . state of mind after your daughter's . . . death — has it made politics seem pointless?"

He held his hands apart and shook his head. They thought that was what they'd get as an answer and it would have done. But he spoke. "Not, really. If anything it makes it a little more . . . pointful."

"You don't have to resign to run again. You know that."

"I'm not resigning to run again. I won't run again."

"Never?"

"I doubt it."

What else could you ask?

"Thank you," he said, equably. He walked off the stage. They started to pack up. How do you report this? Do you stand in front of the Peace Tower and say, "What the fuck?" Suddenly he was there again, like a vaudeville act backing out from the wings after a false exit to take one more bow. "I thought of something," he said. "It's not really news. Or politics. It's for your interest." They were still. Even sitting down seemed unreachable. He took a seat in the first row, as if the event was over and he'd joined them for a shmooze. He twisted around to take them in. Now they sat. No one turned a camera or tape recorder on.

"It isn't . . . It's not . . . just to be unexpected. But that's it partly. Your reaction when I said it. I felt" — he seemed to go back inside, then — "I felt this was about to be a familiar scene, one I've played often. We lose but we do it well, even beautifully; we survive, we carry on. In my life as an actor, I've often faced what I thought of as the problem of the ending: how to acknowledge the inherently tragic nature of experience — yet not get so discouraged you stop trying. If you're going to depress your audience, better to just cancel the show. Believe me, they've already heard. Should you cheer them up instead and give them hope? But they know the truth, they can't be

191

fooled. That's the problem of the ending. Being honest but not losing hope. I've wrestled with it. I've tried everything I could think of. 'We lost; no we just haven't won yet.' Facing the music in the dirty thirties — and then *dancing* to it. I once ended a play with the line, 'Cheer up, there's no hope!'"

They laughed. The press corps nearly corpsed. He went on.

"I don't think it's about going out a winner. A beautiful winner — who knows that even in winning you also lose, just as in losing you can sort of win. A shitty victory — but the only kind on offer. It's a wash, winning or losing. It's not about that, it's more about changing the script. Maybe if I was an American actor bored with playing winners, I'd turn the opposite way. I don't mean this show is over. I'm just hoping to skip the inevitable conclusion, when you feel the ending moving inexorably toward you.

"Sometimes in improv you have to save yourself from success. You've got a great sketch, terrific premise, everybody cooks with it, you make neat changes from night to night and work it in no matter what the audience tosses to you. There's one problem. It's gone dead. There's no life in it. And that's all that matters in a play or a life. Is it alive or is it dead?"

The press were stirring, starting to squirm. The guy was in trouble. He was rambling. If he cracked, you'd have to report it, but hell, there'd been enough of that stuff.

"Everybody always says you have to be allowed to take risks and fail. Until you fail. You need the guts to ditch the premise. You have to create again from scratch. A new vision. But you don't create the premise. The audience gives you that. Or the world does. We create the vision, but not within the circumstances of our own giving, you might say."

He didn't speak these final words as if they were the end of a set piece. Then he rose and left. He'd lost them by then, though they felt for him: Anyone would get incoherent after what the guy's been through. I hope I never have to find out what it's like. I'd probably be in a lot worse shape than he is. Et cetera.

In that moment, as she slipped away and was gone, something between a growl and a whimper came out of me. I don't know if anyone heard it. Maybe it was only inside. Was I watching, to see my reactions, to store them up and use them? Being an actor is a hateful thing. You don't just watch everyone, you watch yourself, as if you're not fully there even in your own life. It's a shameful confession. What would she say?

"Dad, you're beating yourself up. If you pulled back, it's not because you weren't there or didn't care. It was to protect yourself from . . . disintegrating. It was a shield. I'm glad you did. You have to look after yourself now, because I love you."

This is how I "deal with" it. I don't. She's not dead for me. She sends me messages. I ask her questions and she answers. I never asked her enough. She always asked me to tell her about things. But I can still talk to her, I can make up for it. Because of that I can continue.

CHAPTER SEVEN

*The people you see standing around at mine disasters or similar tragedies
have a stillness and simplicity of movement . . . they are straighter, they don't
make little nervous movements, not when the shock is on them, and I would
guess that they hold eye contacts for longer than normal.*

— Keith Johnstone, Impro

He started to transform, as usual, when he saw the first signs of the
Canadian Shield, those rock outcroppings. It would be a good idea
— a Canadian Shield — as Gandhi said about Western civiliza-
tion. Normally he hit it after Orillia, driving north from Toronto.
This time he was driving west, from Ottawa, along the valley, then
cut through the park. North at Huntsville and almost there. Till he
hit the landing the transformation was internal, like a character or
motive you found in yourself. At the lake, it turned palpable, like
costume and makeup.

The rain sheeted down. Bang, it often happened that way, just
as he reached the lake. He bailed — not much had fallen, the
sponge sufficed — tossed his bag and groceries along with a big jug
of water into the bottom of the boat, threw on his raincoat, yanked
the cord, crouched in the stern of the open fourteen-footer, and
headed onto the lake. Now is when it happened. His other soul.

Halfway over he met Len, in the little boat, even smaller than
his own, that Len used for cottage jobs with water access. Len took
pride in how much he piled into his tiny tub. Enough for a decent
size dock in one trip, plus two workers. This time he only had Brian,

who he introduced: new, young, and probably dumb. Len said you needed someone to send over the side when a hammer fell in the water. They circled a while between slabs of rain, like Saint Thomas and the king in *A Man for All Seasons*, on their horses on the shore, spitting arguments about duty and power. He and Roland played that in Edmonton and again in St. John's. He was the king, then they switched and he took the saint.

Their faces looked like masks in the downpour. Young Brian gaped. "What is it?" he asked. Brian said, "Well, we never met, but I didn't think of you like this." Who did Brian picture? The TV pediatrician? The national politician? There was some lore around him up here. He glanced down. His shirt was open, the zipper on the old yellow raincoat was long gone, it flapped across his chest, his hair was matted, a stubble starting on his chin. "Doesn't take you long to make the change," said Len. Redford as Jeremiah Johnson, mountain man, Matthew thought. Len said they'd been tryna put a couple of coats of Sun Shield on the place as he'd promised to do before winter, but the rain started; no point painting on a stain in the rain, it won't hold. They'd be back once they got a couple of dry days. "Sorry to hear about her," he said as they sputtered off toward the landing.

He made a big fire that night. He hauled the wood in from the pile and, as usual, what was left seemed more than before he took it in. It was cold and he had to turn on the baseboard heaters, in the main room and his bedroom. Then he turned up the thermostat in her room. The heat from the fire shot straight out the chimney. The damper had rusted from rain and snow falling down into it long before he bought the place. The heat from the baseboards rose up the chimney too but what the hell, it kept coming from Niagara Falls (he preferred to think) or the nuclear generators on the Bruce.

Thud. The whole cottage shook with an impact against the bedroom window. Shit. One of the hawks had flown straight into it, going twenty, thirty kliks. It's happened before. He should stick one of those decals of a swooping hawk on that window. They're supposed to scare birds. But would it work on an actual hawk, even a little falcon? The bird had managed to reach to the lower branches of a spruce, clearly concussed, like someone outside a pub after closing time. Matthew went and checked; the bird looked like he'd rather not be seen in that state. At least he could warn other birds about the window. Put a pattern of playing cards with birds and animals on them, there was a drawerful of decks in the dresser, left from earlier owners, along with odds and ends he tossed in himself over the years. Going through the drawer, he came on the baby picture, unexpectedly. As he'd come on the divorce decree not long ago, at the bottom of a chest. Wham. Decree absolute, suitable for framing. He asked Morris if that was a philosophical reference and Morris, who had one of his own, said no, it was the decree absolute as opposed to the decree nisi, which was Latin for unless and meant it was useless "unless" you paid your lawyer whatever you still owed, when they'd send you the decree absolute.

She was generic baby, a few days, at most a week. Eyes shut, puffy face, the rest up to her mouth trussed in pink-and-yellow flannel with chicks or something. She was propped on a pillow that dwarfed her, like the ones up here, maybe that's where it was taken, back when they used to rent it a few weeks at a time, had they brought her here so young? Pinned to the top of the blanket that wrapped her, as if the words on it dripped right out her mouth like drool, was a dark blue button with white letters: THE STRUGGLE CONTINUES. He shuddered.

He remembered. They gave copies of the photo to Morris and others. A 1970s version of the red-diaper babies from the radical families of the thirties. A few years later, when they'd drive a visiting director or playwright around the tonier areas in Toronto, she'd say, "This is where the bosses live." Cute. The phrase on the button was hoary and left but had a freshness at the time because of the bracing news from southern Africa: the uprising in Soweto; the victories of the former Portuguese colonies. That was their slogan: *A luta continuà.*

Come on, Dad. Don't beat yourself up. If I don't feel I was exploited, then you can't feel guilty for doing it to me.

It wasn't the exploitation. It was the cliché. The struggle continues. Who ever said you need slogans? Before every big march of the sixties, organizers spent most of their time deciding the slogans to "raise." Did they think they were in Mao's China? Why not call for an increase in the rice quota? Outlawing slogans at demos would have been a lot more daring than chanting "Two, four, six, eight — organize and smash the state!" in front of the U.S. consulate. No wonder people looked at you oddly as they climbed up from the subway and saw you striding down Yonge. (And heard you before they saw you.) He'd never put a slogan in a play, that's for sure, unless it was to expose the emptiness of slogans.

Then he thought about improv. Ugh. What he always forgot when he rhapsodized over the improvisational process was how it bred cliché. Improv generated cliché as dependably as collectives produced egomania. The actor in Kitimat who said, "You all know me. I'm not much fer words . . ." He was the norm. Peter Brook said the best thing you could say for improv was it confronted actors with their own triteness. When you were out there with no script and no net (ugh, another one), you reached for the sure and reliable, the rusty and familiar. "I'm not much with words . . ." Improv sounded great in theory, like lots of things. Actors loved it. But put it in front of an audience: take care, take care. Exercise judgement. Is that what he subjected the country to? In the name of bravely abandoning all the scripts that failed, dredge up the most predictable formulas strewn around the collective political unconscious? Equivalents of: "Don't put off till tomorrow what you can do today." "That's life." "We lost, no we haven't won yet."

He found the bottle of Crown Royal in the cupboard over the stove. It was invigorating, improv. All it lacked was real creativity. That's why he left it. How could a guy forget?

He only drank Crown Royal up here. Unlike other forms of booze, he left it through the winter. He liked knowing it was in its place. The last Canadian. You don't get the purple sack any more, where you kept your marbles. But it survived in its Canadian way, that is: barely. He wondered if there was dope around but by then he'd drained the Crown Royal and couldn't raise his head off the couch in front of the embers. He slipped into a groggy sleep. The phone woke him next day. It was Mutemba.

He was calling from the U.N. "I thought you were out of politics," said Matthew. "I am," said Mutemba. "I am here solely on a cultural mission, as you were when we failed to meet."

Matthew was a solo Canadian cultural delegation to Mozambique in the late seventies. He thought of it as an extension of his one-man career. They toured him round the country in a Land Rover; in each village people turned out for a "cultural manifestation": poetry, dance, song, sometimes a skit or playlet. The sun beat down on the square, such as it was, with him in a chair at the centre. He felt like the queen. If someone recited a poem on expelling the imperialists, they'd used him, the only white there, as a focus, exactly as he'd have done if he was performing. It was schizzy but exhilarating.

He asked often if he could meet Mutemba. Mutemba no longer wrote, they said, his last play was over a decade ago, though a recent production was mounted in Lisbon. Now he was head of the council on economic planning for the revolutionary government. When Matthew arrived Mutemba was deep in the nationalization of a huge British-owned cashew estate; the Brits had been undermining prices on the international market. When that settled, there was a crisis near the Rhodesian border, as it then still was; followed by a strike threat at the country's two main ports. Matthew had been there all summer, it was time to leave. How could he go and never have met the great playwright/revolutionary?

They told him to make a list of questions; that might persuade Mutemba. Okay. Did Mutemba miss theatre? Did he miss writing? Did he find building a new society a satisfactory creative outlet? Francisco, his guide, brought a harsh answer. "The minister says your questions are personal, but his work is now collective and does not have a personal aspect. He no longer deals in these concerns." "Thank you very much," blurted Matthew, turning and stalking off as he used to in grade school when he didn't get a mark he thought he deserved. He wandered Maputo for hours, down to the beach, above the harbour. He was a fool, a pathetic kid indulging in art while they were remaking the world. He stumbled into the bar at the Polana late that night, where Francisco found him: they'd arranged a trip to the game park at Gorongosa, said Francisco, they were sure

Matthew would find it valuable. Matthew exploded with contempt he felt for himself. He came to see a fucking revolution, not a zoo. Next day he left.

Mutemba said he'd be in Toronto to address the remnants of the old support group for African liberation, and speak with a university publisher about some of his untranslated scripts. He hoped they could meet. "I'm out of politics," said Matthew. "No matter," said Mutemba. "But I always regretted we did not speak years ago when you visited my country." Matthew cringed, as if he was still storming around Maputo ashamed of his shallow life. "They said you wouldn't meet me because I wanted to talk about personal, not political things," he said. It was like yesterday, if he ever needed a fragment to conjure childish humiliation, this would do. "Did they tell you I said that? I couldn't, it would have been untrue," said Mutemba. He sounded hurt. "I wonder if I did," he went on. "I hate being quoted to myself. I hate it more than anything. I'm sorry, whether I said it or not."

"Francisco told me you said it," Matthew went on, unable to let go.

"Francisco," muttered Mutemba, "is now chief liaison to the World Trade Organization, in charge of assisting foreign capital and dismantling the few social and cultural programs that remain. But I may have said it."

"I'll come down on the weekend," said Matthew. "Call me from your hotel and we'll decide where to meet."

"I can tell you where I'd like to go," said Mutemba.

It had to be the falls or the CN Tower. Every revolutionary who ever came through Toronto — Cubans, Vietnamese, Chinese, Grenadians, everyone, after the rally or speech or Q-and-A session with the local support group — they all wanted to go to Niagara Falls and then the top of the tower. Mutemba had seen the falls on a trip to the States before the revolution came undone. But he'd only heard about the revolving restaurant at the top of the tower.

"Maybe I said it," he repeated. He sounded guilty.

"And what do you think now?" asked Matthew. "Do you think it was wrong?"

"I think it was immature," nodded Mutemba. "But I was playing a part I believed in."

"This is a slippery slope," said Matthew, taking some revenge for an old wound. "Ronald Reagan played a part he believed in. So did Hitler." He supposed this was heavy conversation for happy hour. He didn't have much control over what he said lately.

Mutemba seemed disinclined to argue. Below, the SkyDome lay open. A game was on. "Is that the Blue Jays?" he asked. Matthew didn't think so. There were still no women ball players in the American League. "Why do they call it the American League?" said Mutemba, "when it is in Canada?" They signalled the waiter and asked who was playing. The waiter didn't make a fuss about Matthew. Like other people in the bar, like Len and Brian and the rest of the country — they all seemed to have absorbed his desire to put on anonymity. Or did he wear it so well that he really didn't register? The waiter glanced down, as if he could tell at that distance. He said it was the premiers of the provinces against the wives of the Blue Jays. Matthew didn't know what to explain: why the premiers were all in Toronto, or what brought them into competition with the wives of the Blue Jays, or the part about the American League in Canada.

"I thought of myself as a revolutionary artist," said Mutemba. "But there was a lot of slippage" — he savoured this English word — "between the two components. I saw myself mostly as revolutionary, and much less as artist. As you apparently said in your list of questions to me, I wanted to treat the revolution we were attempting to create as my field of art."

"We had a poet named Milton Acorn," said Matthew. "He said he wanted to be a revolutionary poet, then he always added: that's revolutionary in the political, not the artistic, sense."

"Was he really named Milton Acorn?" said Mutemba. "He made it up."

"No," said Matthew. "He was a Milton and he was an Acorn."

"What happened to him?" asked Mutemba.

"He got crazier. And obnoxious. He alienated almost everyone he knew. Then he died," said Matthew. "He was a lousy revolutionary but a great poet. I did a play once, based on his poems." He looked down at the ball game below and thought about Milton's line, "I Shout Love." Once in rehearsal he asked Milton how to do that line. "I shout loooooo . . ." screamed Milton in a rising tone, rushing up the stairs into the lobby and out the door of the theatre. They could hear "oooooovvvveeeee" diminishing down Yonge Street. He looked up at Mutemba and thought about telling the story.

"I think you should go back," said Mutemba.

Matthew laughed. It was abrupt, practically a bark. He sometimes did that. The waiter glanced over.

Mutemba looked injured. Consider that debt paid, thought Matthew. "Why should I go back?" he said.

Mutemba didn't know, but he liked the idea. Speaking actor to actor, the line felt right. Good dialogue justifies itself. Even if you forget the characters, plot, theme — a good line grips an audience on its own. If you have to, you can always find a justification. "Material?" Mutemba said, unleashing his smile.

"What do I tell them when I get there?" said Matthew. "Jorge Dias Mutemba sent me?"

"That depends," said Mutemba, "on who you meet. As you know I have not lived there for five years, by their choice and mine." Well, no actually, Matthew hadn't. "Myself," Mutemba went on, "I now think of myself as a citizen of the theatre. It doesn't matter where I am. Do you know if Havel has managed to write anything since they threw him out as president? Have you ever met Dario Fo? Are there people in theatre here we could speak with?"

"Of course," said Matthew, rising and waving for the bill. "I could, you know," he said with an energy that surprised him. "I have a lot of frequent-flyer points. From before I was in politics."

The phone rang next morning. "What?" he said stupidly.

"It's Mutemba."

"I know. I mean, good morning. What is it?"

"How do you do it?" said Mutemba. "How do they treat you as if you're not there? The waiters, the artists."

"It's not that I'm not there. But they treat me as if I'm not different, not . . . more important. I think it's about being in character."

"Aha!" said Mutemba. "When you are truly in character, the

audience accepts you as an ancient chieftain, or an alien being, or a tree. But that depends on the conventions of the drama."

"That's why I always hated myself for being an actor," said Matthew, eyes still shut. "I could do anything — courage, anger, passion — onstage. I never had the guts to do it except when I was protected by those fucking conventions."

He left for Mozambique from Toronto Island Airport, by way of Newark. You couldn't get regular connections to Africa from Toronto any more. Globalization. The free market had spoken: Canadian routes weren't viable. They banked out over the island homes, then southeast across New York State. He was leaving the country. Signs of guilt? He checked. Nope. The former P.M. had agreed, after coy refusals, to lead an interim government — on condition. The country needed a rest from voting; no new election for at least a year. He had Lonnie Donegan on the Diskman. He first heard Donegan on the headset during his flight home from that earlier African trip, deep in self-loathing. Donegan sang My Old Man's A Dustman with lots of defiance. It helped Matthew out of his pit. They had so little hardware compared to later groups, they built their sound up mainly from adrenaline — like the Mozambicans. What the hell, good for them all. So why was he on his way back? Well, why not? He used the "why not" principle when he couldn't explain the reason he did something in a performance: *It's a nice idea; it's not* in*appropriate. So why not?* He felt his limbs jolting disjointedly, as if shaken by the skiffle riffs. Symptoms of age? Indigestion? No — someone tugging his arm. He lifted his eyelids like a scrim, looked across and back an aisle. A broad face, Slavic and aged. He lowered the scrim, then raised it. Rakovich. "I always use that little airport when I am here. Remember when you first brought me?"

During the 1980s, Rakovich embodied Glasnost to westerners. Gorbachev had plucked him from a TV studio in Sverdlovsk and transported him over many august heads to become chief of a national nightly news hour in Moscow. They operated with great confidence, they attacked everyone. On their first program they *satirized* Gorbachev. Satire was riskier than criticism. Rakovich had seen the Spitting Image puppets while on a studio tour in London.

He swiped one of their Gorbachevs and used it for that first show. Everyone in the Soviet Union knew the drill. Either they'd leave the air immediately, or the mould would set. It set. Rakovich became famous in the West. There were periods he was on "Nightline" more often than Kissinger. His English was fluent and elegant, he had less an accent than a linguistic persona. "Loook, I am wanting to know — ees eet not so?" He also visited Canada to study innovations at the CBC. "The total wisdom of North American video journalism can be summed up in two words," he told Matthew the time they met. "Double-enders." They were in a bar in a laneway off Yonge, and Rakovich had to make a Montreal flight. Matthew wanted more time with this guy. He went to the phone and switched Rakovich's flight from Pearson International to the Island airport. Rakovich kept checking his watch. Twenty minutes to takeoff. Finally they left. Rakovich was twitchy. They drove to the ferry and got on. In fifty-five seconds they were across the harbour and at the gate. Rakovich was enthralled — as if an airport had never before moved him, except once. "It's easy to see," he said to Matthew as the props started whirring, "that in this crazy mixed-up world the problems of two little people don't amount to a hill o' beans." Then he turned and strode across the tarmac behind the businessmen and functionaries boarding for Montreal. He stopped again halfway there and yelled, "Here's lookin' at you kid."

Matthew pulled Donegan off his head and shifted back a row. They leaned toward each other across the aisle. During the failed putsch against Gorbachev, Rakovich had been in Washington, arranging projects with the networks and CNN. He practically took over "Nightline" that week. After Yeltsin beat off the putschists and got rid of Gorbachev too, Rakovich didn't return. They gave him an office at the Kennedy School for International Affairs in Cambridge, plus a retainer on "Nightline." In '95 he went back with rights to a Korean-American computer distributorship. It was all right, he said, and Canada was part of his territory. He always used the Island airport, but how had it survived, he wanted to know. Surely there was pressure to turn it into a big jetport. Canada is funny, Matthew explained. It's susceptible to all the forces of global marketization, there's no real resistance, yet there's a kind of lag element, older ways seem to persist. "You could never get anything very left going there," he said, looking out the window and back in the direction of Ontario, "but you couldn't get anything very right going either." Rakovich said Russia was the opposite. These days you couldn't find a remnant of socialism with the Hubble telescope.

"Does anyone still talk about socialism?" asked Matthew.

"Huu," said Rakovich, "in Russia what don't they talk about? Only talk though. Ever since they all didn't get American cars six months after the fall of communism, they'll consider anything. But right now Marx and Lenin have somewhat less appeal as an option than a czarist restoration."

"Socialism," muttered Matthew, under the hum of the engines. They were descending on Newark. "Marx, Lenin, Mao. The only people on the left who still look credible are Trotsky and Pete Seeger."

"Trotsky," howled Rakovich, drowning out the plane. "If Trotsky had succeeded —" and unfurled a rant about Trotsky's hatred for the ordinary people, his xenophobia toward the peasantry, how Trotsky would have decimated the countryside worse than Stalin because he wouldn't have stopped with the kulaks.

"Okay," said Matthew. "How about Pete Seeger?"

"Who?" burped Rakovich.

"The folksinger."

"*He's* okay!"

Seeger was, improbably, playing in Central Park. On a makeshift stage near the Alice statue and the pond. It held maybe a thousand. Later that night Sting would appear in Sheep Meadow. Matthew read about them in the *Voice*. His flight for Maputo, via Amsterdam, Lagos, and Johannesburg, didn't leave till tomorrow. Improbable things happened when you had no plan, no expectations. In that state, everything is as unlikely as everything else.

Seeger looked part leather, part parchment. The turkey neck, more so than ever, the long face and long fingers. He started with "How do I know my youth is all spent/My getup and go has got up and went . . ." Yes, I'm old. I know it and I want you to know I know it. Everyone relaxed. This concert is for the homeless, he said, looking up at the apartment towers on Fifth Avenue. Then Guthrie's "I Ain't Got No Home." It sounded improvised, like he got the idea from what he just saw. Seeger had been nimble in his politics. He went environmental after the anti-Vietnam years, following civil rights and before that the peace movement, which succeeded anti-fascism in the thirties and forties — as well as the unionism of those times. He sailed his boat up and down the Hudson, rallying people to join the cleanup, an evocative word. "This concert is pure private enterprise," he said, while volunteers from Manhattan Hope for the Homeless passed paper buckets. Then "Guantanamera." Music always survives the vanishing vocabularies of politics. Issues, slogans, leaders, theories — they all slip behind you in the rearview mirror ("If you bend down I can see a little clearer"). Is it because music ventures less? Because it has no theory? But Seeger was more than songs.

You're maybe ten. It's in the late fifties. Yowch, the fifties: still Eisenhower and "Your Hit Parade," charcoal grey sportscoats. Your friend's older brother takes the two of you to see this guy named Pete Seeger play. You both sense this is a grown-up thing to be at. The college guys, like his older brother, talk about it as if they're doing something risky that might not be approved, say, on "Your Hit Parade." It's at Massey Hall, very serious place, a stage but no curtain since it's where the Toronto Symphony plays. You once came on a school trip. Your tickets are on the main floor; the three balconies above are pretty full. There's a few guitars and something else at the back of the stage. You wait for the lights to go down, but they don't. A door opens at the back of the stage and on walks this tall thin guy carrying a banjo with a long neck (the banjo, not the guy). He wears a jacket and tie but the thing your really notice: his shirt under the jacket is coloured, looks orange. Definitely not white. It's the first time you ever saw a man in a jacket and tie but not a white shirt. This is important point number one. He plays something like a lullaby — "Deep blue sea, baby, deep blue sea" — and he's got the whole audience singing with him. This is a concert? When does he start working? "Hey," he says, "wanna learn to yodel?" And he's got them all doing it. He's sweating and puffing a bit, so he puts the banjo down and takes off his jacket. Important point number two: the sleeves of his shirt are rolled up! No cuff links or anything. Remember — it's the fifties. He takes up the banjo again and starts another song. Says it's a work song: "Didn't ol' John/Cross the water/Water on his knees —" He stops and frowns. "This song wasn't made for a banjo," he says and goes to the back of the stage where those guitars (six-string and twelve-string) are propped. But instead he leans down and picks up an axe, an actual axe like you take on overnights at summer camp — and a log! That was a log sitting there. He hauls them down to the mike and starts singing again and, of course, chopping. "Didn't ol' John cross the water on his knees/Let us all rise up/Rise up and face the rising sun/Didn't ol' John . . ." Final point: the world does- n't have to be the way you always thought it did. This is your debt to Seeger.

Three notes now on the banjo, low, high, lower, and he sings, "Way up boys —" The audience is with him: "Wimoweh" in the year 2000. He pulls them together, tenors and sopranos with a breath- less "Wimoweh-uh-wimoweh-uh-wimoweh-uh-wimoweh," and basses just bumping along with "Way up boy." This is how Seeger always worked, less for the audience than with them: chanting, screeching, yowling the high part. It's not quite the way it was at Massey Hall forty years ago but what is? Even "Wimoweh" has lived through a lifetime: a genuine hit in the sixties as "The Lion Sleeps," with actual verses. Seeger doesn't bother with lyrics. You hear the jungle in each note and in your heart too. Next day you take off for Africa.

The stopover was Paris. Luc came in from Lille and met him near Chatelet. Luc finally had tenure in the economics department there. They ordered a Kir for old time's sake: the time when it was still a worker's drink in France, not the *apéritif du jour* it became in Toronto. The barman said he couldn't remember how to make one, but he was kidding.

They'd met in Quebec City during the sixties. Matthew was on a short course at Laval. Luc was a *co-opérant*; in those days French youth could do alternate military service working in a francophone

Third World country. Quebec qualified. Luc would phone and ask how he was; Matthew would say, "Awful." Luc was in awe; how free and spontaneous North Americans were. He introduced Luc to dope; Luc introduced him to Paris and Kir.

They rehashed, as always, the time they saw *1789* out at the Parc du Soleil. They went in the van they'd drive later to Italy, when their friendship came unglued over Nicolina. At *1789* the audience got to wander in the middle of the set; in fact the audience *was* the middle of the set, surrounded by platforms where actors did the tennis court oath, the wavering bourgeoisie, that goof Lafayette, all building, you could tell, to the storming of the Bastille. Agitators darting among you, a kettledrum so low it seemed like your heartbeat but intensifying till you wondered, How the hell will they do the actual battle without it being a letdown? So they skipped it. They went straight to the street festival afterward. The *après-Bastille*. True dramatic genius is knowing what to cut. He wept. Improbable victories over power always made Matthew cry. He wept over thirty years ago when he heard on the radio that the residents of downtown Toronto had stopped the Spadina Expressway from cutting a gash through their city. Poor fools hadn't realized they never stood a chance against the might of developers. He was gazing at his Kir. Luc asked what it was: the child? the position he'd left? "I was thinking that was the first collective creation I ever saw," he said. "And the best. Was it the best because it was the first?"

When Luc caught the late TRV for Lille, he wandered into Le Marais, down from the Bastille, and from the cramped apartment on the rue de Turenne where he and Luc lived the summer they took the acid trip that started by the Seine and shadowed the underground system of canals and locks that draws barges up through Paris to the market. Across the street was a bookstore, still open. It was called *le souris papivore*. Decades ago he read a book on how to pick up girls. Bookstores were good. So was waiting to get on a plane till just before takeoff. He missed a plane once because of that and had to spend a miserable night at Dorval. Inside a slim woman sat by the cash reading. Her hair was grey and soft. She had one of those faces, he thought, you could spend your life across from.

In the sixties, he would go into a bookstore wearing just shorts and a T-shirt and come out with half a dozen paperbacks and at least one hard cover concealed. He got the new translation of Hegel's *Phenomenology of Spirit* that way, after Morris explained that Hegel was the key to Marx, who really was the key. He never read Hegel, but stealing books was considered a revolutionary act.

On a table in the centre of the store was a modest stack of *Cauldron!* in French. He turned and asked the woman if she'd read it? She said yes and came over. Interested. He asked what she'd thought and she said she liked it. Quite a lot. She reread it every once in a while. Had he read it? Yes. As a matter of fact, he'd once both dramatized it and acted in the play based on it. That was long ago. She asked if he'd mind watching the store a moment and disappeared up some stairs. She returned with a man about her age, and as attractive.

In times past, they told him, this bookstore was the intellectual centre of *le mouvement Cauldron*, a radical group which formed during the burnout after the revolutionary events in the streets of Paris in 1968. The group based itself on the book. Had he wandered in here back then, they'd have taken him for a cop. Cops were always dropping by pretending to be sympathizers, though none was ever stupid enough to claim he was an American actor who'd done the book as a show. Canadian, said Matthew. They apologized. Would he join them up the street at the bistro called, also, *le cauldron*, the only other remnant of the movement: a credit union, an employment agency, a crafts co-op, a sports club, and to tell the truth, a street theatre company, were all gone. But some of the comrades might be in the bistro, it was their night of the week to gather, and he was welcome.

Only Marc and Armand had come. They all went upstairs to a private dining room. Now it was for hire, but in those years it was reserved for the comrades. Then the walls were covered with posters, slogans, sign-up sheets — based on tales and lessons contained in *Cauldron!* In fact they were still here, in this drawer; yes of course you may see. Every tortuous moment passed by Fidel and his compañeros, or by the Cuban peasants who experienced revolutionary transformation in its dialectical complexity — had been scanned and used like a field guide by those ex-students and workers, now dwindled to these elderly few. They put each other through rites of criticism and self-criticism in front of the collective — just as Fidel and his band purged themselves before embarking on the course of "exemplary action" which proved to be the match which ignited the potential of the rural masses in Cuba. Those sign-up sheets were for criticism sessions.

Then came their turn, over couscous back downstairs. Had he really done as he claimed, made a *pièce de théâtre* out of their Bible, their blueprint for revolutionary existence? "*Une scène, peut-être*," they said, they could imagine dramatizing an event or two but — *toute une pièce*? Had he really dared? He shrugged; perhaps he'd been lucky, if he'd understood how impossible it was, he wouldn't have gone ahead and done it. They smiled at him as if he was a child from the unspoiled wilderness of North America; they had been *gauchistes* of the French left in its glory; they knew the respect a seminal text deserved.

After a last round of Kirs — they found it cute — he insisted he could make his way back alone. He wanted to find the Deux Magots though he knew for sure Jean-Claude couldn't still be alive and writing orders on the paper tablecloths. He passed the hookers on the rue St. Denis; he used to look at the strawberry tarts in the windows of the patisseries and then at the ones on the street and wonder if he could afford either.

Twice in his hours with the Cauldronistas (they fondly remembered themselves as), he'd alluded to his recent experiences. The first time they nodded yes, they were aware of this, now that they knew who he was. He thought it might be courtesy, that they didn't really follow Canada. But the second time — a wince at the mention of leadership — Armand said they felt they understood, something about the first term of Mitterrand. They pressed him no further. Were they sensing that message he seemed to emit since it ended: treat me as nothing special; I did what I could but my only comfort now is to feel I am not separated from the rest of you? Like . . . Lawrence! Matthew had always wanted to play Lawrence of Arabia. Not Lawrence in the desert or at the calamitous peace conference, but later, when he returned to England and enlisted again under another name, as a lowly soldier, or drove his motor-

bike through the countryside like everyone else, in search of —
anonymity? . . . solidarity? Matthew of Canadia.

No Café des Deux Magots, no waiters. He realized why it had
worked. The audience that celebrated the overthrow of the Bastille
at the Parc du Soleil was in the streets mere years before that fighting the CRS. So were the actors. It wasn't complicated. That's why
1789 was the most powerful evening of theatre he'd ever known.
They had a moment in the world; they lived it again in art. He'd
relived their moment with them in the theatre; had he then gone out
to seek it in the world? The Cauldronistas had aged, but they'd
barely moved; they were still standing on the same path. Was he
retracing his own steps, to see if any were still worth walking in?
There was nothing to look forward to tomorrow except Africa.

They'd scheduled him for the damn game park again. "I didn't ask
for a schedule," he said, "I didn't even tell you I was coming."
Francisco smiled, same shit-eating smile. A former head of state,
and former friend of the nation from the *primeira hora*? He was a
guest of the government, there could be no other way. Note the
smooth switches in terminology: friend of the "nation," not the people; guest of the government, not the party. Francisco made the transitions gracefully. History had absolved him.

They were speaking English, with lapses into Portuguese. This
happened here, only here. He'd read a few phrase books on the long
flight from Europe, and going through the airport already found
himself chatting with the locals. He wasn't good at languages but in
this place he was motivated. Besides, in Mozambique Portuguese
was a second language for everyone; tribal languages came first.
That first trip, Francisco had caught him correcting his official
translator. Resources were stretched in the country, Francisco said,
so would he please act as interpreter for a Western group scheduled
to visit many of his stops anyway. Next night he was seated in a hut
in the bush, hearing a village elder's greeting translated from
Shangan into Portuguese, then him translating to English for the
comrades he'd been forced into company with, then back again with
their questions. "What's the party's position," they wanted to know,
"on gay rights?" The answer, clearly as he could make out, was, "Do

we need to have one?"

That time, when he said no to the game park, he got his way. He was a foreign comrade; they respected his protest. This time he was a mere ex-head of state, and the game park was already laid on. Besides, what's the alternative: a tour of failed revolutionary institutions, socialism's graveyard? Why not a game park? The scripts were down the toilet anyway.

Once they got him there, it was hard to get him to leave. Gorongosa, it turned out, wasn't a big zoo, not even a humane one with the animals roaming beyond a ditch. The people were fenced off, within a compound. The animals surrounded *them*. You could only go out there in a Rover, through the gates — as though the animals let you, on sufferance, into their land without people. Impala bounded across the trail in front of the Rover, which waited like it was at a crosswalk. Dozens leapt in coordination, covering vast ground with each jump, like beautiful young dancers at ballet school. The hippos raised their snouts languidly, transforming from huge waterlogged tree trunks, when the Rover pulled up to water's edge and cut its engine. A rhino ambled down to the shore on the other side. The bearded wildebeest gazed pensively from the trees at the tourists. The animals were at home here, we weren't just outsiders, we were newcomers. Sometimes at the lake back home, as he sat on the dock at night, a sleek black body would slide through the bushes and under the dock. He'd hear the mole or otter chew her catch for her young who squealed as they ate it. He didn't feel he should just leave the dock at those times. He felt he should vanish from the place forever. Or late fall, when he woke in the morning to six inches of snow. Other times you could pretend you belonged, you were part of it, but not then.

The second day, they went out earlier. About mid-afternoon, they entered a copse; above, in the branches, stretched and yawned a dozen lions, lionesses, cubs. The third day, in a glade near a pond, the driver got cute. He cut between an elephant and her calf, then stopped. The elephant mom trumpeted and loped toward the Rover, ears flapping, gathering speed. She was closing at a terrifying rate, plus the flapping and noise. She couldn't have stopped if she'd wanted, and there was nothing Disneyesque about her. The driver

211

laughed so hard he barely got the car in gear. For a while they just maintained their distance. Maybe it happened all the time and was no rarer than standing in the middle of a street with traffic whizzing past on either side while you waited for it to clear. It was his last day there.

That night after dinner, he walked across the compound, under the dimming, luminous African sky. He sat on a bench outside one of the cabins. These were staff quarters. A park official asked if he minded company. They sat silent, then the official pointed above their heads. "Feel there," he said. You had to stretch. There were holes in the wood. They were bullet holes. They'd been left since the war of liberation. This was a favoured vacation spot for the white rulers of South Africa then. It was far south of the liberated zones and battle areas in the north, which Frelimo had infiltrated. The leaders of the movement sent a raid down here to Gorongosa, mainly to let people know they could do it, and rattle the authorities in Maputo and Johannesburg. The raid happened one evening, around this time. Then they withdrew north to Cabo Delgado.

"Was anyone killed?" asked Matthew.

"No," said the administrator. "You can see the bullets are too high to have hit people sitting here, or even standing."

"They missed," said Matthew.

"No, we don't think so. They said they deliberately aimed high. They wanted to show they could easily have killed them but chose not to."

"Why?"

The administrator pulled a packet from his shirt pocket and breathed thoughtfully, as if inviting Matthew to speculate.

"These," said Matthew, "were the most vicious racists in Africa. They were the real rulers of Mozambique. The Portuguese hung on so long only because of the support of the Afrikaners."

"Yes," said the administrator, lighting a Phillip Morris unfiltered. "They said it was a demonstration of revolutionary discipline. I suppose Frelimo thought that might frighten the Boers more than being killed."

Travelling back to Maputo, he felt a play stirring. Its title was

212

Gorongosa. Place matters. Forster was right. Lay too much weight on each other to fulfil our needs, and we all sink, we can't bear it. Other people are frail, they let you down, they die on you. What was in the minds of those Frelimo kids as they crept up to the compound at Gorongosa? Hate, fury, not just their own but the accumulated throw-weight in resentment of their race, including the human race. They crouch inside the fence, snuck past it the way the animals might sometimes want to, after they've been visited and gawked at too often, or humiliated, like the elephant mom. They sight through the scopes on their — probably Czech — weapons. They have a Dutch Afrikaner in the cross hairs: corpulent, contemptuous — and in *their* land. They don't know him personally but the whole point of this war is to vanquish this figure. Everything Fanon said about the cathartic, healing nature of revolutionary violence seems to apply. Yet they lift the barrel a finger's width and fire above him, then leave. What kind of catharsis is that? What do they gain to compensate for the lost pleasure of offing this incarnation of injustice? And now, thirty years later, he's back, in a different suit, as an international banker or World Trade Organization bureaucrat — and was it worthwhile to forgo that satisfaction then and how do they feel about it now? And you, with your own political frustrations of a lifetime and especially the past year, can you measure yours against theirs?

It's a great conflict. (Conflict is the essence of drama, they even know that at the CBC.) But what really excites him as he pictures it onstage is the animals! The impala, adorable and narcissistic. The chimp, shrill and perhaps theoretical. The wildebeest, brooding, experienced, an old Bolshevik, like the one shot down on the steps of the Winter Palace, who died not knowing whether victory was his. The elephant, raging and implacable. For whom nothing will ever remove that rage, so what's the point of change, any change? They are a chorus to the events inside the compound. Do they care? Do they mock?

He was ready to leave. Don't overstay. Last time he hung around and it came to humiliation. Get the plane, go. But they found him in the bar of the Polana. The message said the cabinet would like to meet him. He didn't want to meet them but it had possibilities. A comparative cabinet experience. Did they take down the paintings? He waited in his room. A knock at the door. He hated that sound. They could have called from the lobby. He got his hat and sunglasses and went to the door.

It was Moriah. She looked like a bag lady. "Yes," she said, "you could call me the bag lady of national liberation." They'd always been in tune. "Or the ghost of revolutions past." She specialized in Brit-lit references. She was bony and large framed. She had a broad open face with nothing on it for thoughts or motives to hide behind. He'd always found her sexy. "I heard you'd gone home," he said. She shrugged. "This is home. I am Mozambican. But to tell the truth, I did try those other places I once called home."

That would be Guatemala City, where she was born, or Atlanta, where she went for high school, whence she'd come to Africa as a teenager with a backpack in the mid-sixties. On that trip she was "called" — her term, though an affair with a liberation leader was also involved — to join their struggle. (Ah, the days you used words like "struggle," unembarrassed. "I'd like to know if you have any books on kids in struggle," he once said to the clerk at the Kids' Bookroom. The clerk played it straight, at least till he left the store.) Back in the States, the little support organization Moriah created became the main U.S. base for the movement. She moved here after the victory. When he met her, on his first trip, she was in charge of National Cultural Manifestations. "Whatever the people make of it," she said, when he asked what that meant. The point was to cobble a unified consciousness out of the tribal divisions the Portuguese cultivated ardently. She's a nun, he was told. She's an apparatchik, a Stalinoid. She was virtually central committee, they sent her all the documents for comment. That's why she almost never had time to meet. But they got along, maybe it's that they looked a little alike. Sometimes that happens: you know a person because you see something familiar looking back. They corresponded occasionally, once a year, max. Often her notes just said, "Your turn, Moriah." She burned with the flame of the pure revolutionary fire, but never used that tone with him. The only time she visited Canada, they went to a Blue Jays game. No one believed it was her idea and not his.

"How's the team doing these days?" she said.

"Shitty," he said. There'd been no joy in the game since the '94-'95 strike, at least not for him and the Jays. Maybe it was just the end of the Gillick era. Maybe there'd been a secret protocol in the strike settlement that said Canadian teams weren't allowed to win any more, like the secret terms in the free trade agreement that torpedoed the film distribution bill and forced Canada to maintain a high dollar.

"I'm sorry to hear that," she said.

"Whenever the team is playing badly and it starts to really depress me —" he said. She smiled. It's true, he always tanked when Toronto teams did. Since he was eight and wrote the manager of the Triple A Leafs with a few respectful suggestions for the batting order. "Then I think of you here," he said. "Decades of hunger, dislocation, death. The terrorism backed by the West. The sellouts and traitors. Especially the loss of hope. There was such hope when I was here. I compare that to my ball club losing a few games."

"Doesn't help a bit, does it?" she said.

"Zero," he answered. "Absolutely useless." No one else believed she said things like that. He felt she saved it for him. He also owed her for making him think about career — or stop thinking about it. He once talked to her about how his career was going and she looked at him as if she was an anthropologist. What an odd thing to worry about, in a world like ours.

He wanted to tell her what had happened, though she'd surely heard, but the phone rang. They were here. He asked her to come. On the way she explained she had no government role, though people assumed she still did and often consulted her. They'd ask her to write something up as if she'd always be there for them and they couldn't imagine it otherwise. Even the president. They'd let her keep the same apartment. She had a few contracts from aid groups, bless their little hardship scales. The limo cruised up to the president's mansion, where cabinet meetings were held, he recalled, and drove past. But not far.

There was a small misunderstanding. He had a meeting with the cabinet, but not a cabinet meeting. They were down the road at

Tranquillity Shrine. The place felt like a float at the Rose Bowl parade: a building made from millions of carnations. There were porches, balconies, drooping eaves leaning over the bay below. It was built when the last Frelimo government, under Chissano, converted together — a kind of last gasp for the collective principle which governed their revolution from its days in exile during the 1960s. They joined the Church of the Lordly Aura, under its messianic guru. Once a day they would trundle down the road for a session at the shrine, with the priests. When there was no public business, they'd go anyway. But that was only the beginning, as they used to say when they took over after kicking the Portuguese back to Lisbon.

Successive governments had added on to Tranquillity Shrine, like layers at a dig, or additions in a variorum *Hamlet*. It coincided with democratization, i.e., multi-party elections and alternating governments that all did the same thing. A kind of parallel "democratization" happened at the shrine. It was no longer just transcendental meditation. There were revival halls for born-again Christians, a library of Catholic spiritualism, a padded room for yogic flying, an Islamic mini-mosque, a museum of African animism, and a non-denominational chapel for believers of different faiths to "go their separate ways together." It was like *Tamara*. In the eighties he turned down a show called *Tamara* to shoot a series pilot. All the scenes happened simultaneously in different rooms of a big house; the audience chose which they wanted to see next. The shrine though wasn't open to the public, it was for leadership only: to renew or simply find themselves. Or give them something to do, since the country was now run by bankers far away. In each room, a cabinet minister was introduced. When Matthew asked about policies, they were vague. Maybe they didn't even know what their departments were. They were blissed out.

"What did the little pecker offer that was irresistible?" he said in the limo going back. He'd seen the saviour long ago at Varsity Stadium in Toronto while researching *The Last Messiah*. "The core of his message was three words," she said. "You never know." At first Matthew thought she was commenting on the phenomenon. Then he realized it was the guru's message: "You never know." Like the old men in the sauna say when one of their chums has died. "That's it?" he asked. "It acted like a salve on their wounds," she said. "Maybe it's because they thought for so long that they knew. I've learned not to underestimate clichés."

"Is that because clichés are familiar and comfortable?" he asked, thinking about actors and improv.

"I don't think so," she said. "After many years watching brilliant people analyse complex situations in subtle ways, I'd say the most profound statement I've heard is, Life goes on."

"You never know," he said. "What were they searching for? What did they find?"

"Peace," she said. They sat looking out of the limo. Hordes of people were streaming on foot in every direction. His first time here, on the way from the airport, he asked Francisco where all the people were going. Was there a soccer game or rock concert nearby? Francisco hadn't understood, he didn't know where the people were going. They'd sat as he and Moriah were doing now till Matthew realized they were all walking because they didn't have cars or even bicycles and there were no buses. Everybody walked everywhere. For twenty-five years, she said, these people were at war. With Portugal. The Rhodesians and South Africans. With each other. They tried to win peace in war after war. Generations of life were spent on the premise it might bring peace. Not would, but might. It wasn't death and war that wore them down; it was doubt. It began as suspicion, then it grew. The war would not end. It was endless. He offered peace.

"Peace?" he said. "Shallow self-deluding entirely internalized personal private peace."

""The only kind on offer," she said.

"And what about the other products on offer back there?" he said. "They aren't all about peace."

She had an answer for that too. This generation of Mozambicans believed political action could lead to change. They weren't all fervent, some had more limited expectations. But they shared a disappointment; they'd lived into a time when no change seemed possible. The only change was deterioration: run-down due to entropy. Political power had become an oxymoron. Yet they were still political — like

217

the children of clergy, they had lost their beliefs but still felt attached to the church, through charities, singing in the choir. You can't shake it, politics or the church, it's what you are. But if politics can't make anything happen, then at least it can allow you to feel good as it pointlessly meanders its course. "Does that make sense?" she said.

"Like Reagan," he said. "By his second term, most people in the U.S. had given up on the world being different, no matter who they elected. So you might as well vote for the guy who makes you feel better when you see him on the news every night."

"That's very insightful," she said. He'd never heard her admire a political idea of his, though he knew she esteemed him as a performer.

"I think Chomsky said it," he said. "I once heard him say it." She looked at him differently than he could recall. It was uncomfortable. He searched for something to say. He asked how she knew so much about religion. She seemed surprised. Had she never mentioned her grandfather Ferdinand? He was the Greek Orthodox patriarch of Argentina. He couldn't tell if she was serious. There was also Uncle Marmaduke, who taught comparative ancient mythology at Harvard till he croaked in Scully Square waiting for the MTA. Uncle Marmaduke spent his life cataloguing myths and their cognates. It was pointless really, like collecting statistics in professional sports. But he loved doing it, and he was the happiest person she'd ever known.

At the elevator he started to say goodbye. She got in. Maybe she's weakening, he thought. At his door, she shook hands. He felt like a kid in high school who'd been suckered by a big crush. He shut the door and started toward the mini-bar. There was a knock. She stood there. "Can I come in?" she said. He nodded. "It's about power," she said, "it's about feeling I've made the choice." He'd seen this scene, probably played it. "Ignore me," she said. "I've always been like this." After the sex he felt tired out in a happy way he hardly remembered. He was almost asleep, his head lolling away from her when she moved to him and said, "Hi, darlin'." It was the first time he heard her talk southern. He told her about the last year. Toward the end they slept. He woke, as he often used to, with a haunting melody gliding from his dream into wakefulness. "Beneath thy deep and dreamless sleep . . ." He asked if she'd come to Canada. She scratched the side of her face lightly, thoughtfully. I'm not that kind of girl, it seemed to say. Still, he'd try to think of her when he heard a surprise knock. She'd given him that.

Last trip, when they were still learning to govern, a special unit at the transportation ministry planned his flight home. Francisco gave him the itinerary: Jo'burg, Lisbon, Houston, San Francisco, Toronto. It was the only way to get there, they explained. Matthew erupted. He was raw from Mutemba's rebuff and eager to get back where he had a role in the struggle. "You know where San Francisco is?" he sneered. "Ever seen a map of the world? Know what an airplane looks like?" He managed not to add, "You dumb nig-nogs." Great way to end a trip to the most unracist regime in the world.

This time he was routed back via Mexico. It wasn't bureaucracy, it was the voice on the phone from Tennessee or Sri Lanka or wherever reservations had encamped for the moment, assuring him the flights might be full anyway, or cancelled, that's how the market worked.

In Mexico City the airport was sunk so deep in atmospheric crap, he took a cab to the Zocalo; better to risk a missed flight than suffocate while waiting. He'd wander. Something implausible would happen. If it didn't, that would be implausible too. He knew the Rivera paintings were nearby, but was surprised to find them open to the shitty air (though not the rain). They were like ones he'd seen in Detroit years ago. Except — he found himself searching now for the faces of Lenin and Trotsky the way Dal used to seek out Waldo in her picture books when she was little. She'd rescued a copy from a used bookstore while they were travelling during the referendum. He'd been visiting a high school history class. "This is *my* history," she said later. No lessons in it though, matter of fact she'd decided history wasn't there for what it teaches; but just because it moves us, is us, even if there's no sense or meaning. As she moved him, and in him, wherever he went.

What touched him about Lenin and Trotsky among all those peasants and *federales*? Rivera dropped them into his murals like talismans of faith, like crucifixes or mezuzahs or four-leaf clovers. In the golden days of Matthew's leftism he might have found it embarrassing; unsubtle or over-deferential. Now he happily hunted the faces, not because they had anything to say, but because they were recognizable, had cared as he cared, partners in the struggle, useless as it may have proven. Morris once called Leninism the certainty that there's one and only one solution to every political problem, and if you're smart enough, you'll get it. If not, your revolution will fail. Well, maybe the fucked-over masses of Mexico City couldn't afford to let one of their rare tokens of a better future fade away just because, bright as he was, he got the answer wrong when he took the test.

As he watched, the little Lenins and Trotskys turned frisky. He'd spot a Lenin, glance away, and when he looked back, Lenin was gone! A quick scan of the mural revealed him still there, on the scene as it were — but relocated. And Lenin looked overly stern, as if suppressing the urge to wink. Jetlag. It's like traveller's acid. Pictures vivify under its influence. Music too. After that other flight from Africa years ago, when he discovered Lonnie Donegan, he bought all the albums but never got the feeling again. Now Trotsky moved — switched with Lenin under the brutish gaze of a hacienda overseer. Maybe this is what they mean by magic realism. When you live in Mexico, is it mere naturalism, as everyday as David French's kitchen plays in Canada, with running water in the onstage taps? But these mischievous revolutionaries reminded him of something else Canadian.

Outside the presidential palace, he looked across the piazza toward the cathedral. Hawkers and vendors filled every block of pavement. Doubtless they appeared in the statistics as new cases of small business and the healthy entrepreneurial environment under NAFTA plus, as any donkey with half an acre of hay joined the pact. Milton Acorn — yes! His poem in the sixties on Ché Guevara. Ché had vanished after being second only to Fidel in Cuba following the revolution. Rumour had him underground in Latin America — everywhere in Latin America — leading the revolution (*the* revolution). In Milt's poem, President Johnson is in the White House, about to sign another devilish law; but he pauses, ballpoint suspended (one of hundreds he'll give as souvenirs to his evil backers and beneficiaries), pen poised in midair, while he worries, "Where is Ché Guevara?" Brecht wrote, "There was little I could do/But without me the mighty would have rested less comfortably/At least such was my hope." Do they worry as they shave in the morning, without knowing why? Are any of them right now thinking, Where is that ex-actor? What mischief is he up to?

He wanders. Improbably, he comes on a street theatre company. They are Theatro BarrioStop. At one of the anti-NAFTA conferences held in Canada, he met a Mexican actor called Superbarrio, hero of the slums, who fought poverty, capitalism, imperialism, and NAFTA. The man wore a cape and had a potbelly. There was barely time for a drink at the top of the CN Tower, somebody else took him to the falls. They envied each other. Superbarrio ("Call me Herman") envied Matthew his mass audience. Matthew said, "For what?" He envied Herman's audience — in its intensity. "When there are enough to count," said Super. This troupe is in a dialectical line from Herman (who now writes a column for an opposition newspaper). They say, We have relied too much on heroes, from Zapata to Superbarrio. "We are simply the *barrio*, full stop. From us ourselves must come salvation." Perhaps in the past Matthew would have dismissed them as ultra-leftists, too fearful of leadership, but he is not in a dismissing vein. He doesn't understand what they say in their play, even the rusty Portuguese he dredged back up in Mozambique just leads him astray. So he watches the audience, as always. They feel great. They are alive. They may abhor the lives they live, and sometimes even wish they were dead, but none ever wishes they hadn't been born. Each day they rise in these shacks and gutters, or stream down from the hills (there's a great debate between those who say the population of Mexico City is thirty million and those who say no, just twenty); to survive each day takes such zeal and energy; had they just a fraction left over, they could transform the world with it — easily. He watches them as they watch the show, long into the night. They get to know him, somehow they learn his background as an actor, his travels, his travails — afterward if you asked how such communication was possible with no shared language you'd think you dreamed it, yet it happens, and not rarely. Toward the end of the evening, he starts to doze on his haunches. Someone in the crowd asks when his flight to Canada leaves. He looks at his watch, still on African time, and says, "Yesterday." They all laugh and, together with him, say, *"Mañana!"*

CHAPTER EIGHT

The normal man generally feels once in his life the whole blessedness of love, and once the joy of freedom. Once in his life he hates bitterly. Once with deep grief he buries a loved one, and once, finally, he dies himself. That leaves all too little scope for our innate capacity to love, hate, enjoy and suffer.

— Max Reinhardt

Airport. Arrivals lounge. Lights up on immigrant, battered suitcases in both hands, another wedged under each arm. He staggers toward the sliding glass doors. In the crush beyond he spies a relative, tries to wave without putting bags down. He approaches the doors, which are shut. He lowers his bags to the floor, and steps forward to pry open the doors with his hands. As he moves, they slide apart. He is surprised but pleased. He turns his back, gathers up his bags again, turns around and sees the doors once more shut. He lowers the bags, steps forward, they slide open. He turns again, takes up his burdens, turns, they are shut . . .

It was the only sight gag he ever invented, but new sight gags are notoriously rare. How many actors can claim even one? Invent isn't quite right. Who invents anything in the realm of art? Even the most "creative" artists are basically collators; if you know them and their lives, you'll probably recognize every moment, every character, and each deft phrase. What would it mean to actually "create" something that hadn't already existed somewhere? This one came from *The Immigrant Odyssey*, made many years back to explore — no, celebrate — the true fact that one of every two residents in Toronto was born in another country. Not another city; another country. During research in those days, i.e., while touring the cafés and haunts of little Italy, little Portugal, Chinatown, the Danforth, etc., he heard the same tale. Of course you couldn't do it any more, except as a period piece, which is how he felt as the plane touched down at terminal three and he prepared to re-enter Canada.

Then the offers started. Offers of parts.

The first was from the New York Shakespeare Festival. "*King Lear?*" he said to Elinor. "Lear," she said, reading the proposal. "K. Lear." It included billing and draft publicity along with dates. He asked what she thought. She said they were playing softball. They'd learned Canadians found softball more difficult than hardball. "*Lear* in Central Park?" he marvelled. "You're stalling," she said. "A technique I learned in politics," he said. "Tell them you think I'll be interested but you haven't reached me. Do you think they've got someone else in mind? Do you think I'm the first one they offered it to?"

He found *Lear* in a Yale edition — seemed appropriate for a U.S. offer — and began reading it as he had that day. ("O pardon me thou — ") He played with the lines and words. He let them work into him. He spoke them in that low voice which, as it were, speaks by itself. It was like making his way back to a truth before acting.

Odd how slowly the thinking behind the offer dawned. At first he thought he'd have to explain why he couldn't do it: he'd never make it through act 5, you see, *Re-enter Lear, with Cordelia dead in his arms.* "Thou'lt come no more,/Never, never, never, never, never!—" A wondrous line, he'd always thought. There were other lines he'd long yearned to do, which he could handle: "Absent thee from felicity a while." But he was past Hamlet. "I know thee not, old man. Fall to thy prayers." Far far past that. "It's my daughter," he'd say. "She died." Suddenly he felt more a fool than Lear ever was. That's why they *offered* it. The notoriety, the shock and audacity. Americans like the idea of themselves as ballsy. In the name of art, to be sure. He felt ashamed for not saying no instantly, angrily. What must Elinor think? She'd have known. Anyone with a mind not in storage would know.

would know. The publicity they enclosed didn't mention the connection — because who'd need to? The press would go wild with it on their own. Who wouldn't have seen that except an old, stupid, blind fool? Which made him perfect for the part . . .

Only Americans would have the nerve. Someone like Lebow, Papp's successor in New York. He met Papp once. Papp was in Toronto to open a touring company of some hit. He rented a car and came out to see *Rebels Ride by Night* in Wingham. He came backstage afterward — that is, into the stalls at the auction barn where they performed — and said he'd set up a showcase production in Manhattan, if they wanted. Everyone was dazzled wordless. This was Papp! Matthew had to move fast, before they threw themselves at Papp's feet. "We'd rather go to Thunder Bay," he said. "But we haven't had an offer. We won't take it to the States till it's gone across Canada." Maybe Papp told Lebow and Lebow was getting back for his predecessor. Americans had long memories. Maybe this was a way to finally get him down there.

Elinor said, "I'll tell them you appreciate the offer." He didn't say, "And to get stuffed." She sensed something: he'd been interested.

Other offers came. Stratford-upon-Avon (Stratford-upon-*Avon*!). Would he like to do *Enemy of the People*? "They're just exploiting the fall from power," he said to Elinor. She said nothing. "Okay," he said, "so all casting exploits a connection and this isn't as bad as offering me Lear." She said nothing. "Okay," he went on, "okay, maybe even the Lear offer wasn't totally detestable. Can you find out if they'd still be interested for the summer after next."

Then Canadian offers. Shaw at Niagara-on-the-Lake wanted him for *Arms and the Man*. Stratford — *our* Stratford, the great Satan of Canadian theatre, according to decades of his own rhetoric and experience — had programmed *Tartuffe*. Lorimer, the new artistic director, said she'd always felt Matthew was made for Molière. How did you know? asked Matthew. He always felt right for it too. Something Canadian in that manic undermining of social pretension. Then Encore, the new arts channel, wondered about the Oedipus cycle. No one suggested *Iphigenia in Aulis*, one of the rare classics in which he could say he'd already been onstage.

There'd been Mercutio in a *Romeo and Juliet* for high schools; he adored the swordplay and, besides, he was dead and free to go before intermission, just make it back for the curtain call. Sure, those parts hadn't often been offered, but you could argue he'd ruled himself out beforehand. He'd worked on his one great role so long: the Canadian anti-hero. Could you play Shakespeare that way; well, probably; why not? But they never gave you the chance, and what's the point in sulking? His acting career had a kind of invisible warning wrapper across it: Do Not Cast in Classic Parts. Had the wrapper slipped off? Had he finally played out that Canadian anti-hero in unsurpassable form? How could he top his performance as Canada's failed leader? They'd had it and he'd had it; everyone had had it. Drive on. Those parts made sense to him now. But it was also — hard to admit this — acting seemed to make sense again. Surely just a retreat from the brief sorrows of public life and the inconsolable one in private, and yet — acting felt like a job he hadn't tried before. Having left acting to finally act, had he prepared himself, as if for the first time, to act?

He did *Lear*, but he did it in Newfoundland. Signal Hill, the company at the Arts and Culture in St. John's, wrote asking if he'd be listed as a supporter, then followed up by phone. He said he'd be honoured. He'd done a collective out there — on the sad colonial tale of commission of government in the 1930s. A drunken poet named Reg with a great singing voice used to wake him in the middle of the night and demand by what right he came out here from upalong to teach the locals how to make Newfoundland culture — an argument to which Matthew was sympathetic; he'd made it on the mainland often. But at least when he went home, he left something behind. What were they doing this season? he asked. Start with *Lear*, they said — if we can cast it. Did they know? Was Elinor involved? (She swore not.) He said if he were interested, might they be? Like Mario Lemieux calling the Leafs to say he'd like to play hockey again — if you're interested.

When the run was over — it was successful, reviewers came from everywhere and said so — he had little memory of it. As though it existed entirely in the present in that place, and no residue lingered. He moved from line to line and moment to moment in the play with little anticipation or forethought. When it came, he was there. He'd never been like this onstage. He always counted on anxiety; it held his work together the way elastic bands and chewing gum held old cars together when he was a kid. If anxiety was absent, which it rarely was, he panicked. He took pride in preparation: research, getting to the theatre early, voice exercises, floor exercises. He still did them; but he knew when he came to the moment during the performance, he'd be, as it were, already there. Whatever he had, he'd give; it would suffice. It wasn't the definitive Lear, it was his Lear, as he discovered it each night, he and the play would work it out between them, then offer it to the audience. The arts review on "Newsworld" hooked up to the theatre the day before opening; the interviewer said, "Let's talk about acting." He put his hand to his mouth, an ancient *geste*. "Acting?" he said. "Acting — shmacting."

He felt like Johnny Cash, the man in black. He saw Cash play months before his death, right after he had a quadruple bypass. Cash came on alone with a guitar and sang his grim songs; the voice still deep but feeble. It was as though Cash had stopped performing, as if all his life he'd been playing Johnny Cash, now he was just being him — though as usual there probably wasn't a very big gap between the two. Then, sometimes, someone stops playing the part — that's how he felt as Lear. It was him, as himself, letting Lear be Lear. Like most theory, it sounded silly when you said it.

Nights after the show he'd sit on a stool at the Ship Inn. He knew if he stayed a while, he'd see people he knew and others who knew him. They'd see him back, and let him be. Lawrence of Canadia.

Tonight Evan stopped to chat. Evan was a folklorist at Memorial. He came from the Louisiana bayous and he'd taught a generation of outport youth to play the blues harp. Shut your eyes and you'd swear those kids grew up in cotton fields instead of on wharves. They're planning to deregulate the power grid, Evan said. They've finally given up on privatizing it, after we fought them off for the last six years; they've got another way to accomplish the same thing. Matthew didn't really understand the issue. Does it have something to do with the fishery? he asked. Of course it did. Every little thing in Newfoundland has to do with the fishery. If they deregulate power they can deny service to the outport communities and force those people elsewhere and the battle of wills between governments and fishing villages will finally end. Those fishermen have sat by their boats forever, through endless doom-filled studies issued from Ottawa and St. John's, waiting for the cod to return. But not if you turn out the lights on them. It'll be over. Unless they choose to wait for the cod in the dark, which they might. There was a big rally at the harbour on Saturday. Would he speak? He thought not.

"Uh, Dad. Why . . . ?"

This speech came from some place new. Just before he stepped up, the minister of energy and the leader of the Opposition arrived, breathless. They had just cooked something, you could tell, they were bursting with it. A breakthrough agreement, they said, between the fishing communities and the government. Specifics were vague or undetectable, the rhetoric was florid. The people were wary, but hell, you have to hope; they applauded suspiciously. Evan and the Committee to Do Something were confused. Matthew stepped modestly to the mike, like Nelson in the gold watch scene. "These servants of the people," Matthew said, "may have manipulated us just now into letting our hopes speak for us. They may have manipulated the outports and the government — " He glanced over; they looked spooked; he had their number. He went on, "They may even have manipulated themselves . . ." From there to the end of his speech he couldn't remember a line afterward. They were with him. He felt them as he spoke. This had never happened. He'd read about it. He'd acted it, in Brecht's play on the rise of Hitler. But he'd never done it, though actually it felt more like something done to him. As he finished each thought with no idea of what came next, he felt carried ahead by their cheers or their stillness. He wasn't opening his life to them, as during the election. He wasn't letting them take over and find their own thoughts, as during the referendum. It was closer to the moment when someone in the cast goes for it. But when you do that onstage, others stand back and wish you the best; you fly alone while they watch. Here they were in flight together.

Neither script nor improv, it was beyond improv. It was, possibly, leadership. You let them use you — is that what it's about?

"You were mad."

"I get mad. You know that. I have access to anger. Specially onstage."

"But this was different."

"How?"

"You were . . . loose. You . . . enjoyed it!

He stopped at the liquor store on Yonge. He was low on Irish, which he'd been drinking; it was less depressive than scotch and he saved the rye for the island. The lot was full so he parked in the spaces for the chi-chi stores nearby. Roland was unlocking his car door, looking wry and robust, a bag of groceries in the other hand. He smiled at Roland, who blanked for a moment. "You grew a beard!" he bellowed.

"I've been spotted," said Matthew.

Roland and Matthew were alters. Everything Matthew did, Roland strove to emulate; everything Roland was, Matthew wished to be. They spent their careers admiring each other. When Matthew created a part, Roland sought a chance to play it. They rarely worked together; but they talked about doing it all the time. When Matthew quit his series, Roland left his own, and they conspired to revive the legendary Voyageurs, the company Roland's dad, Patrick, had toured the Canadian North with in the 1950s. They had exhilarating talks about it; they raised money, though it didn't happen. Roland had the ability to attract work; there was always a film or series, usually shot in exotic places: New Zealand, Prague. Not necessarily work to be proud of, but Roland's secret was: that didn't bother him, or if it did he beat it back. He was one of those people who never spend more than ten seconds on regret. He did voice-overs too — promos, narrations, sports films. He lacked the arrogance that in Matthew engendered righteous self-denunciations for mere underachievement; it's what Matthew envied him most. They'd seen each other rarely since the politics began, and ended. There was a warm inarticulate note after she died. Now Roland nearly choked him with a hug. "It's okay," said Matthew, "I'm okay." Roland hugged him again. "No, it's not only that. I've wanted for so long to say yes to something in this country," said Roland. "I got exhaused with the no's. No to free trade. No to Meech Lake. I did a promo for the Charlottetown Accord, if you recall." Matthew did; because of it they hadn't spoken for a long time afterward. "Not because I was in love with it, I just yearned to say a yes, though I wound up voting no. Then while you were up there you gave me that. With all the fighting back and fighting against you had to do, you still found a way to offer us something to be for. It was brilliant. I don't think you know how great that felt."

He hadn't. Sometimes you do your best work without meaning to. "We even won," he said.

"No," said Roland on cue. "We just haven't lost yet. Come to the house for lunch. Right now. You know where we are."

"Will anyone else be there?"

"Just the two of us and you. Will that do?"

"I'll come. I mean, thanks, love to. Let me bring something. I know it's not necessary but I'll feel better. I'll stop in one of these stores and be right over."

"Sure," said Roland, but a shadow slipped across his face as he watched Matthew cross the lot and walk into grocery hell.

It comes on him slowly, idling among the specialized produce and containers of dressing. At the soup counter he asks for a litre of butternut squash and one of gazpacho. Maybe Roland and Ally will serve it for lunch, maybe they'll store it like an emblem of his affection. "Would you like it frozen?" says the young woman doling soup behind the counter. "We have it frozen if you'd like." He asks if it costs the same. "Twenty-nine, ninety-nine both ways," she says. A twitch of discomfort as he wanders to the arugula on a whim, three little bags full. The kind of detail Roland and Ally like in their meals. Others waft down the aisles, their little carts on silent wheels, the new kind that corner gracefully; an electronic whir at the cash, the hushed helpfulness of the clerks. Ahead of him someone rings up two small items and lays down a fifty. The fire starts to rise in him, begins to consume the place as well, though in no hurry.

Sixty bucks for two containers of soup. Nineteen for *lettuce*. The faces surrounding him seem masked. The villainy of history in a mini-mart. They all are here to spend nineteen dollars on lettuce.

Something is taking over. "Nineteen . . ." he breathes. "Nineteen dollars." The clerk at the cash smiles. "That's right," she says. To her it seems normal. The other shoppers raise and lower items, they drop some in their carts, languidly return others to the shelves. His disgust slithers as if on its own up and down the discreet aisles. A few customers glance over. Can they see what he's feeling? If so, the staff will handle it. The checkout kid is on the phone. Is she calling the police? Does this grocery pay off the local division the way booze-cans and bars do? Do cops line up at the cash on payday so that a call to 911 always brings a swift response? Is there a private security firm on contract? Do freakouts happen often? He deep-breathes, that should calm him down. It does, but the rage rises higher. Damping it makes him madder. He breathes again, cools, then feels the heat rushing from his feet to his forehead, like it might split his brow and pour into the aisles, then ooze onto Yonge like lava. He's afraid to breathe again, to turn or even fidget, he could explode and splatter on the produce. His eyes dart, the rest of him is still. "Matty." He starts, it felt like he leapt to the ceiling but he hasn't moved. Roland is at his side. "I thought I should come back," says Roland. "Sometimes this happens in here."

He skipped lunch. "You're still angry," Roland said when they got outside. "Of course I'm still mad," he said. "I'm sorry I'm not on schedule for the phases of mourning. Does that make the obscenity in there okay?" Roland settled for the promise of a phone call, soon, and drove away. Matthew stood there in the lot looking at his car like it was a lifelong enemy. A standoff between him and the car. Fuck it. He got in and drove south. He was at the other lake, Ontario, in ten minutes. But Harbourfront had the tall ships and people there tended to gawk. They hadn't got the memo about ignoring him that the rest of the country seemed to have. He drove to the Leslie Spit and walked. Birders, joggers. Couples. He didn't want people. He headed for High Park. It would be filled with families, maybe even strolling players. Where can you go in this society to be alone? Your car. That's where we spend time with our thoughts. That's why the traffic torture called rush hour every morning and night hasn't caused a revolution — yet. He drove to the Exhibition grounds and parked outside the Pure Foods Building. Good place to ponder shopping hell. Dads were teaching their teenagers to drive.

The Evil People's Grocery Boutique wasn't about food, it was about contempt, like a feudal tower where the lords exercise *droit de seigneur* over the peasant women on their wedding nights (Charlton Heston in the best acting he ever did). The place had the outline of Auschwitz for him. He once played the first Canadian soldier who stumbled into Dachau unprepared — same damn feeling. Could a mini-mart be a link on the road (back) to Auschwitz? He didn't want to hear the connection was absurd, he felt it, passionately. That's our human fate: we *suffer* our passions, we don't choose them. It's what drove Spinoza crazy — Morris explained it to him when he got a role as Spinoza in a series for educational TV. Spinoza embraced abstract thought not because he was an intellectual snob, but because he yearned for something in his life which didn't just happen to him, the way emotions do, but over which he had control, about which he felt some choice. Yet sometimes even your ideas just come to you. You suffer *them*, it's as if *they* think *you*. That's how he felt about the images in his head. Were they even ideas, or just emotions in costume? Is that another distinction that's been lost since all the moorings began to slip? He felt morally, politically, artistically adrift. It was a year to the day since she died.

"Tell me about class."

"Who knows? Everybody used to talk about class as if they knew what they meant. Now nobody mentions it. It dropped from sight like 'the revolution' and 'the deepening contradictions of capitalism.' It's the last taboo. Name me one other thing you never hear talked about. It would be like farting in public — not done. I always thought being middle class meant you felt surrounded by people you rarely saw but who were deployed to look after your needs, like what you ate and wore and where you lived. They were the workers, and they never expected you to look after what they needed, even if you did some-

thing for them once in a while, like get them a divorce or make a movie they went to. Why do you ask?"

He went back to the liquor store for the Irish he hadn't got earlier but he fell asleep without opening it. He slept defiantly through a series of invasions and attempted break-ins: local kids, cats, ninja warriors, women he knew and didn't know. "I could be bounded by a nutshell and count myself a king of space," he proclaimed as he boarded the doors of the house in which he slept, "were it not that I have bad dreams." He recalled none of it when he woke, except those lines. "Hamlet had the blues," he muttered, as he clambered toward day. Hamlet had friends, lovers, even fans; it didn't help. Hamlet looked down at his succulent, simmering breakfast plate and he shuddered. It was the blues. You have to face them, you have to deal with them. Just before noon the phone rang. Cheryl said she'd be by in an hour, in her car. They were driving to Niagara-on-the-Lake for a party. It was a costume party, she'd bring costumes. He said he didn't wear costumes or go to parties. He could sit outside in the car, she said. But they were going, no argument. See you in an hour. Cheryl, he thought, knows Roland and Ally.

Cheryl wrote about men and women in books with flowers on the covers and sappy titles. She wasn't very successful at relationships herself, which is probably where she got her insights. The books sold wildly. Men called from all over the world when they read them and begged her to marry them. He met her in the 1980s at an opening after she was appointed to the arts council; she was unfamiliar with theatre and said she'd been told to avoid two people in the field; he was one, so she sought him out. She never told him the other, maybe she made it up so he wouldn't be hurt. She had a huge heart, even if she always reduced politics to emotions. She was the only person he talked to about Dal.

The "summer house" in Niagara-on-the-Lake was the size of SkyDome. The theme of the party was *"Bloomsbury People,"* based on a British series they'd all been watching on the death star. The hosts were former exec producers in TV news who now did co-productions. He sat outside with Cheryl watching the guests enter in their costumes. "It should be bombed," he said. "It should be razed. It's contemptible — " She looked worried. "It's evil — " he tried to crank it tighter but he just sputtered. "Can you explain to me why?" she said evenly. Fair question, she was willing to understand, but he couldn't explain. Those people — the straw boaters, the parasols — many had followed and supported his work for decades. When you called them elitists they took it as a compliment. So what if they dressed up as avant-garde Londoners from a century ago — though can you imagine a garden party in Hampstead at which Londoners dress as Canadians? Look at them — coming, going, kissing — they didn't watch television, even those who worked in it. They watched CBC or PBS. Now they watched the BBC and Channel Four on the death star. Boobs watched TV. What can you say? They had no consciousness of being evil. Back in the New Left, you learned to judge not by what people said, but whether they'd still be there beside you when the cops spurred their horses into the crowd. He couldn't explain; it was just more passion, another rent into the dimension of rage, a breach through which it poured. She smiled and reached for the door. He didn't hesitate. They went together.

"Tell me about costumes."

"When Morris got arrested — I know that's hard to picture. It was before you were born. We went up to the picket line at that appliance factory your mother organized after she left the theatre company. Morris went kind of nuts when one of the cops got him in a thumb-lock. The workers on the line all went to help him, maybe because he looked so out of place. They charged him with 'obstruct police,' 'assault police with intent to resist arrest,' they made him sound like Rambo. His lawyer, Lloyd — we called him 'Lloyd the lawyer' — said they wanted to make an example because smart people like Morris should stay out of these things. Lloyd said he found a precedent from Queensland, Australia, in 1890-something. The night before the trial Morris phoned and said, 'That Queensland thing sounds really feeble.' He was worried. I couldn't think of much but I took him down to costume at the CBC — it was over in the east end, before they centralized it all on Front Street. We found this three-piece wool suit from a lawyer show that fit him. 'So what?' he said. 'Trust me,' I said. I mean you know how he always looks — like an exploded

*laundry bag. But not in this suit. Next morning I went to his place
and we called a cab. We're on the front steps of his apartment, it's a
bright fall morning. The cab pulls up, we get in, the driver turns and
says to Morris, 'Where to, sir?' He completely ignores me while Morris
is looking around for who this cabbie's talking to. At the courthouse
we go in the cafeteria for donuts and the cashier says to Morris,
'Eighty cents, sir.' The commissionaire in the hallway says, 'That elevator, sir.' By then he was doing it just to see it happen. When we
walked into court, the Crown glanced up and his face went pale. He
knew what we were up to. So did the cops. Morris got an absolute dis-
charge, whatever that means. He said he learned more about class
that day than in all the books he ever read about it — or would write
on it for that matter."*

"So costumes are about class. Or class is about costumes — "

*"I used to think costumes were cheating. Because the real effect
had to come from inside."*

"I can feel your pain," said the American director for the fourth or
fifth time, laying a soft hand on Matthew's arm.

"Here," he said, swiping with his arm and flicking his wrist.
"Feel some of your own."

"I'd have preferred if you'd stayed in the car and smouldered,"
said Cheryl, guiding him out the door and back to the Jag. She said
the American director had a lot of caps and bridgework on his front
teeth where Matthew's deft flick had connected — Cheryl knew
these things, or maybe she just assumed all Americans in showbiz
had dental work; anyway they might hear from his lawyer. Matthew
didn't think so. "They let you get away with this stuff a lot when
you're an artist," he said. "They say, 'Oh well, he's an artist, you
know.' They sort of count on you to blow up in ways they can't themselves." He was talking as if he'd never been prime minister. "It's
not that the guy was trying to be sympathetic," he went on. "It's that
fucking imperial attitude that they know everything anyone in the
world could think or feel, because after all they're the centre of it.
If he'd said, 'It's impossible for me to imagine what you must be
feeling,' I don't think I'd have hit him."

On the drive back he told Cheryl he once wanted to make a play called *The Hidden Injuries of Class,* based on a book. She asked what the book was like. He said he didn't know, it was very academic and he didn't get far into it. "Sometimes all you need to read is a title," she said. They drove a while. "He looked so vulnerable as we left," she said. "You'd think Hitler looked vulnerable," he said. "Well, you know," she said breezily, "he had a very unhappy childhood." He thought about that a while and then he told her that once during the free trade fight he'd actually found himself understanding Mulroney, knowing what the son of a bitch was feeling. "That sounds like a confession," she said. "It is," he said. "I've never told anyone. It was scary." She looked hard with concern at him as he stepped from the car. If you have people in your life who care about you that much, you probably shouldn't complain.

He sat at the counter in the kitchen and glared at the mountain of unread magazines. How do you untangle the injuries and their effects?

I had a windbreaker when I was a kid, a black-and-white striped thing. I never thought of it as shabby. But sometimes I was late for school and I'd run down this walk to the student's entrance and kids inside where attendance was already being taken would look at me through the windows from the different floors of the school. I never thought about it at the time. But then why do I still remember it, and that crummy jacket — that I feel like they were looking down their noses at and snickering . . .

What if they hadn't moved when he was nine from downtown, where deprivation was normal, north to the burbs where everyone else lived in a house with a backyard and a rec room, while they alone rented; the kids all went to summer camps while he delivered for the pharmacy. So he wasn't asked to parties or to join frats, which he, in a brilliant countermove, chose to interpret as a sign of his own moral superiority. What if there'd been someone to talk to: an uncle, a teacher, someone like Morris, just to say: this exclusion you feel

— it's not your fault. Would it have come to the same passion and rage — for the poor, the workers, the Third World? But they *were* oppressed. Just because he came to outrage through his own injury, that didn't nullify the world's. What if he became less furious? The world wouldn't be less outrageous.

He failed with Michele because she was too good, that was axiomatic. He didn't deserve a life spent across from that face, that voice. The comfort of her presence. It was beyond his reach, except in character. He knew it from the start, it had to be temporary. The good things that came to him worked for him onstage and sometimes they worked briefly out in the world. What was the difference? Either place you're building fictions. You do it one way by acting in a drama, the other by acting in politics. But underneath you hope those parts you create will somehow become you too, alongside the other things you are. You're trying to become human. It's hard and you have to be creative. That's all.

"Tell me something that's creative."

"Burying a man alive. Onstage."

"You buried somebody alive onstage?"

"That's what the Cuban overseers did to peasants if they withheld part of their rent, or even some of their own excrement for fertilizer. 'Let's try it,' I said. The other actors laid the peasant on the ground and mimed shovelling dirt on him, like they were playing at the beach. So I told them how it was done. You dig a narrow pit chin high, set the man in it, pile earth in till the pressure forces blood from his mouth, nose and ears, and makes his eyes pop out. Then hammer him straight into the ground with a mallet till his head is level with it. Then we did it. No props. No hole."

"And it worked?"

"I think so. Nobody in the audience laughed. Never."

"Who played the peasant?"

"I did. I played pure hate. What I want, I thought each night during that scene, is with my final spasms to hate and curse these animals."

"Was it satisfying?"

"Completely. Like anger has always been for me. But — won't it ever end?"

236

"Anger isn't just something to be got over."
When she said that (in his head) he smiled and relaxed.

The disintegration of the global status quo was clear only in retrospect. At the time it seemed not to be happening; then only fitfully and with no apparent pattern. The case of the former Yugoslavia was dismissed as a matter of inattention till too late. The dismemberment of the old Soviet Union was troubling. But the names were unfamiliar — Kazakhstan, Uzbekistan, Nagorno-Karabakh — chaos and pointless bloodshed seemed always to have been their nature. Russia itself was more sinister; it fell apart into principalities ruled by Mafia bosses and warlords. This was seen in the West as a matter of police breakdown more than political failure. Spain's collapse could still be assigned to the shadow of the Third World. Italy was different. Its partition into three nations was unsettling. But Italy had been the last of the European nations to coalesce into a country, and its chaotic system of parties and parliaments could not be sustained. As for Britain, there was nothing new about Ireland. And the state of siege in the urban centres, especially in the north, was about social unrest, not political crisis, since there was no disagreement among the main parties over it. In contrast, tensions in France and Germany, though unimaginable a decade before, seemed minor. The uproar in Mexico, Indonesia, and most of Africa was almost normal. Yet there were centrifugal tendencies even in the United States. The Hispanic near-majority in southern California favoured a separate state or secession. The state comptroller had been "detained" briefly to "make a point in the public mind." In Texas a "gang war" looked eerily like an insurrection bent on restoring the territory to its Mexican origins. The government in Washington had ceased to play a role in the daily lives of citizens, making its appeals to national unity ring hollow. The country was scarcely a democracy; less than a third now voted. This justified the movement to postpone the coming presidential election. It all happened gradually. Only when you took a swift cutaway rather than a leisurely overview, did an awesome deterioration appear to have happened. Besides, who really wanted to know? Maybe acknowledgement of the catastrophe was awaiting a solution, even the mild hint of one, before facing what had become unbearable.

In the Canadian form of the malaise, people began to disobey the law. Not in the sense of street crime. This was ordinary people ignoring ordinary laws. It started when employers failed to honour contracts they'd signed with unions or their obligations under labour codes. When unions grieved or employees complained, their protests went to the bottom of unmanageable lists. It didn't start as a conscious strategy; companies were just cutting corners, as they must under the pressures of global competition. But managers soon realized enforcement mechanisms were overloaded; many had simply vanished in the wake of budget cuts. At that point disregarding the law became sensible business practice. Governments meantime concluded that the good intentions behind certain genres of legislation — like non-discrimination and employment equity — meant little without funding to enforce them. This liberated the politicians: they passed new laws responding to the demands of disparate groups, knowing they wouldn't be blamed when nothing happened since, as everyone knew, there was no money.

In Quebec, the weary negotiations over limited sovereignty that began following the second referendum had grown ornate and incomprehensible. Even the negotiators admitted they were unsure what their goal was. On many global agencies, Canada and Quebec each had seats, leading the agencies to suspend credentials from either until the situation clarified. People in Quebec began choosing which authorities to recognize and to whom they'd pay taxes; often they didn't pay at all. Canadians in other regions were envious.

The native populations took to behaving as if their right to self-government had already been granted. Like everyone else, they found that if they acted as though something were their right, no enforcement process got in the way. Since there was little national coordination and few resources at their disposal, band fiefdoms proliferated, ruled by what many natives themselves called tin-pot dictators or warlords without armies. This is why we voted against the self-government clause back in '91 — said those who remembered.

School attendance had declined, though no one knew how much since truancy offices were decimated. Those who could afford to sent their children to private schools or hired tutors who were paid often in kind. Even traffic laws were widely ignored. During the past decade, when corporate taxation effectively disappeared and individual taxes were stripped down, speeding, parking, and other traffic fines had become part of government revenue strategies. This worked briefly and revenues rose. But public resentment led to the need for increased police to protect parking patrols, tow-truck operators, and the traffic courts themselves, where small riots occurred, though they were never described that way. Inevitably drivers discovered what business had already learned: you could ignore the law and the odds were on your side. This became easier when the police were largely privatized; trading of favours, straight bribery, or exchanges in kind effectively replaced fines while previous fines went unpaid. It was Canada's way of going down the toilet.

"Did you ever feel when you were prime minister that you were turning into a ghost? You're fading but somewhere else another person might be materializing in your place. Like the transporter beam in 'Star Trek.' " He slips the fingertips of his right hand against the small of her back and presses in a circular, downward motion, pushing her around his crotch, hoping to stimulate something. She chuckles. She slides the tips of her fingers under the shaft of his penis, tapping and pressing. "Too hard?" she says. "Uh-uh," he said. "Harder." He sighs. "I think it's pretty simple," she says. "People should do to others what they like having done to themselves." She says it louder than the thought about becoming a ghost. That was a whisper.

Now she's swiping at his nipple with her lips. He does something between a sigh and a moan, definitely positive: *Harder.* Or: *More please.* "You have bigger nipples than I do," she says. She tries it with her teeth. It hardens. Men like their nipples done, she thinks, they let you know. A nipple job. Once she was at the family cottage on her way to the dock. Her dad and a few of his buds didn't notice her pass near them. They were absorbed. One said, "Do you like your nipples bitten as you come?" They all said yes. Maybe it was something new that came in around then, she sensed it was a historic change. It wouldn't have happened a little earlier:

probably not the act, definitely not the conversation between guys like her dad. Is this a sign of progress in human history? You could chalk it up to feminism. It's a qualitative change in human interaction and she can't think of many. It's true that she, a woman, is now prime minister — for the second time. But she knows how much that does and doesn't mean, and it seems less momentous, more compromised. She slides her teeth off his nipple. If this is as good as it gets for progress in the human race, it wouldn't bother her, she's never been a believer. But he has, it would exasperate him. She slides further down, pushing him higher inside her and touching his penis with her fingertips again.

He moves his hand onto her clitoris and lightly over it. "You can do that harder," she says. "There. Press down, now up." This too may be progress. When she was young, her girlfriends marvelled at her. "You really tell them what to do?" they'd say. She moves counter to his motions. "Like that," she says. "Don't stop." After a while she relaxes and then takes hold of him again. "Come," she says. He moves. She slides her hand up and down. "Keep doing it when I come," he says. "Mmhm," she says. He starts with a roar that rises to a scream, she hears it run from his crotch up his body; it sounds like it's going to blow out the top of his head. She's laughing as he subsides.

"Do you always do that?" she says.

"Nope," he says. "That was the first time ever."

"Right," she says.

"I once was in a show," he says later. "We called it *The Earth Moved*. It was a collection of sex scenes. They changed from night to night, more than any show I ever did. It's the one thing where you feel something new might always happen. Or — maybe it's that the feelings can always surprise you, even if nothing new is really there. It's so fresh you imagine — this must never have happened to me before. It's . . . totally renewable."

"So will you join the government?" she says. "You could have any role you want." Politics *über alles*. But there's something else in her voice and it sounds like fear. She feels what others are feeling. That it's coming unstuck. Everything is adrift. We could crash, we could sink — people with power are usually the last to know. She's among the first of the last to know. When she's scared, it's scary. Not because she's a strong person — which she is — but because those like her are protected from fear by their egos and their position. "Can't do that," he says. A moment of panic ripples her face. "You can't stay out," she says.

He strokes his recent beard. He hasn't worn one since the sixties. For stage purposes he used a stage beard. He supposes you could use a stage beard for life purposes too, why not? "I won't stay out," he says. "I couldn't do that either." She expected no less, now there's only mild concern in her face. So he'll fight her in Parliament. She can handle that. "I won't be back there either," he says, and tries to explain.

He often thought about the old Bolshevik who died just before the storming of the Winter Palace in 1917 in St. Petersburg. It was no one he knew, or knew of; it was a person he imagined, the one he planned to use as the model for the character of the wildebeest. Maybe the guy died in his sleep the night before the battle, maybe he was gunned down on the steps in the middle of it. Did he feel it was all a waste? Did he die confident? Or in despair? It was the best and most sincere who fell before victory was sure; they made success possible; he knew that, he'd been told it by every revolutionary who ever went to the top of the CN Tower with him. The opportunists and careerists, the less committed, survived to guide their societies after liberation; sometimes they stayed true, often they went over to the marketplace or whatever eventually triumphed.

"What about him?" she asked.

"He died confident," he said. "He died happy. I have no doubt. Even if the attack on the Winter Palace failed, he knew it would finally succeed. The main thing was, he believed when they did overthrow the palace or the barracks, it would mean something. Though not the end, of course."

"Like winning an election," she said.

"Okay," he said. "Like an election."

"Is it that now you feel nothing will make a difference?" she asked.

He answered surprisingly quickly. "No. That would be arrogant." He sounded relieved to hear himself say it.

"So you don't know what difference it will make," she said. "Though you're not convinced it's pointless." He grunted. It must mean yes. "Then why do anything at all?" she said.

"It's on another level," he said. "I think it's on another level."

"All in all, I'd rather have done the mini-series."

"Why didn't you?"

"You need the grid. If you have it, you can project your plot and characters, toss them onto it like the icons in a board game. The first toss sets your story in motion, the grid defines basic moves and outcomes. Left-wing leader from working-class background becomes P.M. of U.K., tries to pull out of NATO; CIA works with Brit elite against him, he fights back, calls snap election — You tilt the grid this way or that for different results. It's not predictable but it happens on known terrain. Then wham — no grid. Like someone pulled the carpet out and there isn't a floor underneath, just a rough shifting surface. I mean, if Kristof turned to me now, as he used to, and said, 'Okay, that works. Now does it fit with our politics' — but no one would even ask. Because our politics was part of the grid, the one that's not there any more. You felt there were possible solutions, ways forward."

"Like running in an election."

"Elections were part of the grid. Even when you knew how superficial they were. It was the same with the socialist countries, so-called; sure, they were rotten, but they were real places that talked about a different kind of society. Even hope betrayed was a version of hope. Now there's nowhere on the map you can jab and say: 'Here, though it went wrong — '"

"What about Seeger?"

"Seeger?"

"We played his songs. We went to see him. Remember? You always said Seeger . . ."

When he was a kid, about ten, his dad took him down to Bentley's bicycle and TV store and bought him a CCM two-wheeler. Then his dad showed him how to ride it. From the way he taught, Matthew wasn't sure his dad had ever ridden a bike himself. He told Matthew to balance one foot on the pedal and glide along kind of sidesaddle. Then when he felt comfortable, he could swing his leg over and try really riding. He was certain other dads put their kids on the seat straightaway and walked or jogged alongside till the kids got the hang of it, ready to catch and steady them if they started to fall. He was on his own.

By next day after school, he was riding, on the sidewalk only. He turned off their street and up another. The sidewalk ran between the lawns of the houses and a little boulevard strip that edged the road. He'd push along, hike his leg over, ride a while, hike it back. Feeling okay. But then, coming toward him, walking — a woman. It wasn't much of a decision. He hauled his leg over the frame and stepped onto the ground to walk it past her. She looked at him and said, "There's lots of room." He smiled back and said, "I'm just a beginner." She laughed and went by. She understood. They'd communicated! She, a stranger; he, a boy acquiring competence. He'd never seen her before and never would again of course, but they had an exchange. He acted on his own as part of a world bigger than his family, but to which he belonged — now. It was on that level.

Or on the level of making plays at home when he was a kid. As young Stanislavsky and the other kids made plays at the country estate: rehearse, promote and perform them. Or the play Jane Austen had the kids work up in *Mansfield Park*, but which never got shown because Papa came home from the plantation in the West Indies and restored decorum to the manor. Matthew gave his first performance as a puppeteer in the dining room. He rigged a big carton that the new fridge came in. He cut a rectangle above his head and used the hand puppets he made with his mum's help from an activity book he saved for the days he stayed home from school sick. The puppet show had a musical theme; he may have heard it from some kids at recess. It had just one word, "Tumba," repeated. "Hey, tumba tumba tumba. Hey, tumba tumba tumba." He didn't know what it meant, it was a song word, it was sheer rhythm and effect. He crouched down there manipulating the puppets and doing the

Tumba song. Looking through from the living room were his parents. Yet he didn't feel this was a mere family event. It seemed less personal, more generalized than that — because they couldn't see him, and he wasn't speaking in his own voice anyway, he was a soundtrack. It transcended family. He was the voice of a world beyond immediacy. It was about publicness, that was the level it was on.

Publicness was what the people of his country granted him by letting him simply be in their midst, without separation, and it was his greatest comfort. Not merely as if they all were having Warhol's fifteen minutes together, preening collectively in the light of fame; more as if they'd already had their fame, so it was no longer an issue, some lives didn't count more than others any more; everyone existed finally in a comparable human way, owing each other no envy and a similar amazement. That was what true publicness would be like some day but he'd had a foretaste, they gave it to him. It made him yearn for the future.

It was also on the level of the growl that escaped his throat when Dal, age three, headed toward an open spot on the railing as the ferry crossed Toronto harbour, and he lunged like the elephant mom toward her calf, aware even as he moved, like Talma, of his own primitive responses as he had them. Or the cry which left him as she slipped from life, just like that. And the whimper that remained, following the cries he screamed moments ago here in bed. They weren't public utterances, like speeches in Parliament; they were pre-public, primal and animal. They subtended everything constructed upon them. The publicness he felt he would return to now, because he had no choice, was not about ideology or mission; it was about what you simply are and cannot be other than. It was on that level.

EPILOGUE

Let's put the social back in socialism.

— *A slogan for the future*

<u>Playing God: Notes for a Soliloquy</u>

Starry night. POV from far above. Below, seen through vast reaches of space, the darkened, starlit surface of a plain. A lone human figure in a cowboy hat sits astride a horse. The voice of the figure rises thinly but feelingly through the night sky. It sings,

> How often at night, in the pale moonlight,
> Under the glittering stars,
> Have I stood there amazed, and asked as I gazed,
> If their glory exceeds that of ours.

> Home, home on the range . . . (et cetera)

GOD
In my view, one place they went seriously astray, was when they began thinking I had created them. Not just that, but also that I made a special job of them. That I did everything else first and left them for last, like the cherry on a sundae — after the animals and all other beings. Breathed life into them, gave them a special relationship to me . . .

Voice rising from below, now a rocky hillside, with sheep scattered upon it. A young shepherd gazes up. It is his voice:

When I behold thy heavens, the work of thy fingers,
The moon and stars which thou hast established,
What is man that thou art mindful of him . . .
Yet thou hast made him but little lower than the angels,
And crowned him with glory and honour . . .
Thou hast put all things under his feet.
Sheep and oxen . . . the beasts of the field . . . the fowl of the air . . .

GOD
They're gripped by their sense of self-importance. Their notion of the "sanctity" of human life, whatever that means. It became the justification for slaughtering and demeaning each other — because they believed their lives were of such inestimable value, even to the gods.

Far below now, still starlit, a rocky coastline, water rushing against it. Large wooden boats anchored nearby. Agamemnon, king of the Greeks, stands at the altar, a knife in hand. His daughter, Iphigenia, is bound to the altar. He raises the knife above her and gazes heavenward.

GOD
They're always so flabbergasted when they behave badly . . .

The field below is now green and hilly. Around it are scattered human limbs and torsos, as well as the remnants of tents and huts. The dead people are all black. A camera operator moves silently through the carnage, camera pointed downward. Standing still in the centre is a white journalist, who is speaking notes into a recorder. The reporter says:

I know this tangle of corpses and limbs ought to be an affront to my modern sensibilities about the dignity of the individual, but there is something about the "massness" of these sites that prevents me from seeing the uniqueness of the individuals lying here in a jumble, even though I believe with all my heart in that uniqueness . . .

GOD

What are they so surprised about? The shock is not that they behave brutally toward each other but that sometimes they don't.

This is the essence of their art and drama too: it's all built on their immense sense of importance about what happens to individual human characters on the stage or the screen.

Yet there is little uniqueness among them. They are all types. They may yearn to distinguish themselves from others of their type, but every casting director is aware that those within a type have far more in common than separates them. Know them by their callbacks. And even the types have much more in common than what sets them apart. Looking from a distance [*POV: heaven*] they are immensely more alike than they are different. It is one of the few facts in their makeup which could lead to a harmonious outcome for their history, but it is unlikely to matter. It conflicts too severely with their precious conceits about uniqueness.

When they try to change their lot, they exhibit the same sense of amazed outrage. "Workers of the world unite," they say, "you have nothing to lose but your chains." Or, "Man is born free, but he is everywhere in chains." As if a state of dignity for humans is normal and ordained. (By me.) And the absence of dignity is not. They thunder about it in my name. No wonder so many spend their lives in grief and anger.

In my view [*POV: God, Looking Down on Earth*] it is a vale of woe through which they all will pass. Some traverse it in a coach or a limo. Others crawl. But it's a vale of woe for every one of them. That does not make me a conservative. Those who say attempts to change social reality do more harm than good are usually those with reasonably good seats for the journey. I don't see why they shouldn't enjoy themselves as much as possible while passing through. If they are going to be miserable, they might as well have a good time doing it. Why should they put up with unnecessary or avoidable death and degradation, slavery, demeaned lives, or wasted childhoods? It would be foolish to not act, even if acting is doomed. They are doomed anyway. So act and know you have acted. Just don't whine and don't delude yourselves. They are at best a mixed lot from whom it would be wrong to expect too much. Still, they ought to be able to do better than they've done, for the most part, up to now.

If you ask me, they are in flight from their normality. From their unspecialness. Their accidental and contingent existence. They could as well not exist as exist. It makes no difference to me, but they cringe at the thought.

They have potential. They are capable of being creative. They were creative enough to invent me. But I don't exist. And they are not gods. They're on their own. They have only each other. If they realize that, who knows . . .